*I AM PUTTING THIS FLYER DOWN AND
THEN I'M GONNA FRY YOUR EYES RIGHT
OUT OF YOUR HEAD!*

As if in answer to Coyote's thought, the flyer
headed down into an open field, controlled by
something or someone other than Coyote.
Helplessly, he sat and stared out the
window—and that was when he saw it! It was
completely impossible—it was a mule flying
right along beside his craft! Its teeth were bared,
its ears were laid back, and it flew without
wings, without so much as moving its legs. But it
was alive, a mule, and ninety feet up in the air!

Coyote looked at it, and it looked at him, and the
lights went out; so far as he could tell he was at
a dead stop in a box of black glue. He was almost
grateful for the change until he realized that for
all he knew this was IT, and he was just too
dumb to realize that he was dead. . . .

YONDER COMES THE OTHER END OF TIME

Suzette Haden Elgin

DAW Books, Inc.
Donald A. Wollheim, Publisher
1633 Broadway, New York, NY 10019

Cover art by Richard Courtney.

DAW Collectors Book No. 663

First Printing, February 1986

1 2 3 4 5 6 7 8 9

Printed in the U.S.A.

CHAPTER ONE

"Ah, hell's mindmildew, Fish! I *did* that already."

"I beg your pardon?" The Fish peered at him coldly, from behind an antique desk with legs on it that looked absurd surrounded by the grubby off-white plastic walls and floor. "You did what already?"

"I fetched you a rogue telepath already," said Coyote Jones. "Three years ago, I did that. It turned out to be a little tiny baby that time—and I told you then not to send me on anything like that ever again. You want your mind refreshed?"

Because his respect for Coyote's ability to rearrange his head's interior was sizable, the Fish raised a delaying hand. "I remember the incident," he said hastily. "Don't excite yourself."

"Look, Fish," Coyote went on, "if you government goons have let another Factor Q kid through your net, you can just hand the job of rounding it up to somebody else. Let Tzana Kai have a turn. She's better at that stuff than I am. And besides, I *did* mine."

"It isn't a baby this time."

"Oh, sure. It's a full-grown adult that you've just happened to overlook its whole life long." Coyote made a rude noise. "I don't believe it."

"It isn't a baby. It isn't even a small child. I give you my solemn word."

Coyote was not impressed.

"You didn't expect the last one to be a baby, either," he reminded his chief.

"Mister Jones," the Fish declared, "it *isn't* a baby. Babies, however awesome their psibilities, do not project telepathic twentieth-century formulations of generative transformational grammar."

That shut Coyote right up, and the Fish filed the fact away for future reference. Few things could silence Coyote Jones; the Fish could use some examples of such things.

"*Further*more," he began, but the shock had worn off; Coyote interrupted him.

"What the diddle," he demanded, "is generative informational grammar?"

"Generative *trans*formational grammar."

"That, then. What is it?"

"An ancient method of analyzing the grammars of languages and fooling about with them. Associated with Noam Chomsky."

"Nah. Chomsky was a political radical."

"*Mister* Jones. . . ." The Fish laid one hand on his chest and looked smug. "Just because you have acquired a certain minimal expertise in twentieth-century history as part of your cover, do *not* assume that you are an authority on the subject. You know all there is to know about twentieth-century ballads—generative grammar was part of twentieth-century *sci*ence. And I assure you that Noam Chomsky *was* the major figure in generative transformational grammar. The computers say so, and the computers know everything there is to know about *every*thing. And babies . . . if we may get back to our subject . . . do not *do* generative transformational grammar."

"Well. . . ." Coyote leaned back in the uncomfortable chair, also afflicted with legs, that was all the Fish allowed other people to sit in when in his office. He scratched his beard ferociously, and pursed his lips in his most judicious manner, and said, "All right. I guess it's not a kid. But I still don't want to go."

"Mister Jones," the Fish said, "allow me to remind you that you *never* want to go on assignment. Not ever. Not once." His white teeth flashed in what was almost a smile. "Not even the very first time. Not in all the years that you have, after a fashion, served the Tri-Galactic Intelligence Service. Why should this be any different? Picky, picky, picky, Mister Jones!"

Coyote sighed. It was true. If it wasn't this effing assignment it would be some other, perhaps even more effing assignment.

"I'll talk about it," he said grudgingly.

"Thank you *so* much."

"How'd it go again?"

"One of the Communipaths, transferring a routine commercial message out toward the Middle Galaxy, found herself receiving this rather elegant form of telepathic static. She didn't understand it, of course, but she recorded it, and the computers ran it down immediately. Something like a mathematical equation, but with grammatical terminology in among the squiggles. As the Communipath described it, 'it was just hanging there in the air, going around and around.' "

"What does *that* mean?"

The Fish shrugged his narrow shoulders. "I have no idea," he said. "But that's how she put it. You know how the Communipaths talk."

Coyote did know, and it fascinated him. When you

were almost totally mind-deaf, as he was, unable to see or hear or feel or in any way sense telepathic projections, everything about the normal telepathic communication of normal human beings was fascinating. And the Communipaths, with their magnificent psibilities that carried communications across the Three Galaxies in a matter of seconds, were more than fascinating. They were enchanting. They had a hard time making the languages of the Federation fit what their heads did, and Coyote loved to hear the things they said. They were like found poems; he supposed poets had a similar problem.

Coyote knew a few mathematical equations, memorized laboriously from the mass-ed computers. Just to get the feel of it, he projected the image of one he remembered, and he made it hang in the air between him and the Fish, going around and around.

"Stop that!" snapped the Fish.

"Why?"

"Because you're wasting my time, damn it! Get that thing out from under my nose!"

"It isn't really there, you know," Coyote said gravely. "It's an illusion. Why don't you just ignore it?"

"Because, if you choose for me to perceive anything whatsoever, no matter how childish or stupid, I *will* perceive it! You know that perfectly well. If I had wanted a child to come to my office and play little games, Mister Jones, I would have sent for a child—I would not have sent for you. Now will you please remove that string of vulgar symbols, so that we can continue our discussion?"

Vulgar? Coyote stared at the Fish, surprised. He couldn't see the output of his own projections, of course, and that meant he could only know his intentions, never what he actually delivered. But he'd thought that it was an ordinary boring abstract sort of equation. Why vulgar?

"Because," the Fish told him, "you have made each of

the symbols a different gaudy shade of the rainbow. And you have managed to fix it so that as it goes around it *twinkles.* Trashy, Mister Jones! And it's wrong."

"Wrong?"

"Yes. Wrong. It has an error in it. Will you get rid of it? Please?"

Oh, well. Coyote had never pretended to be a scientist. He chuckled and let it go, and the Fish drew a long breath.

"*Thank* you," he said. "Now, if you're ready to be a great big man again, we'll go on."

"Pray do let's," said the great big man. "Pray continue."

"There's not a great deal more to tell you. Whoever was projecting that quaint old formalism, they're not on the Federal Register of Telepaths—or on our confidential register, either. That means a rogue. We can't have that, and you know it."

"So send some fedrobots to get this person. Why do I have to go?"

"Because there's a funny wrinkle here."

"What funny wrinkle?"

"We established the coordinates of the message, Mister Jones, and we ran the information through the data banks. And we alerted a Coast Guard spacecruiser to go take a look at the planet in question."

"And?"

"And, all the instruments indicated that it—the planet— was there, that it was a very Earth-like planet, its atmosphere such and such, all the usual. Sentient beings on it. Planets. Minerals. *You* know. But the Coast Guard couldn't see anything."

"I don't follow you."

"Where the planet was, and is, according to the computers and the scientific instruments, the men on board the spacecruiser could see nothing but empty space."

Coyote thought about that. "Hmmm," he said, after a while. "It's interesting."

"Only interesting?"

"Sure. Why? Am I missing something?"

"Well," said the Fish, "could *you* do that?"

"Certainly," said Coyote. "You'd need an alarm system that went off any time something containing a sentient creature entered your airspace. You'd need good projective telepaths monitoring the alarm system—maybe wearing perpetual beepers, whatever. And whenever the alarm went off, they'd just project something along the lines of 'THERE IS NOTHING HERE TO SEE BUT EMPTY SPACE . . . A PERSON MIGHT JUST AS WELL TURN AROUND AND GO SOMEWHERE ELSE.' At considerable strength, and with frills, maybe, but that's the general idea."

"That would do it?"

Coyote gave his chief a close look, puzzled. "Why not?" he asked. "It's not especially complicated. What did you *think* it would take?"

The Fish looked down at his desk, and licked his lips, and the note of relief in his voice when he answered was unmistakable.

"I had assumed it would require a telepathic illusion of a planet-sized chunk of empty space," he said. "Convincing enough to blank out an entire world to any eye looking in that direction."

"No," said Coyote firmly, shaking his head. "You mean an illusion to actually make a whole planet invisible? You wouldn't need anything like that, Fish. Even if it were possible—and it's not—it would be ridiculous. Nobody would go to all that trouble and waste all that energy."

"So we're not dealing with anything spectacular."

"Nah," said Coyote. He liked to say "Nah," because the

Fish found it so totally inappropriate for a TGIS man. "Nah, just ordinary garden variety telepathy."

"You're sure?"

"I'm absolutely sure."

"Could just one rogue be handling an operation like that?"

"Maybe. Is there a lot of traffic around this place?"

"No. It's way off the regular routes."

"Well, then. Alarm system. Beeper. The occasional nothing-here-go-away-it's-boring message. Nothing to it."

"Well, I'm pleased to hear it," said the Fish. "It would be most inconvenient to lose you to some psimonster with antiquarian tendencies." He folded his hands, looking satisfied, and said, "Good. This will be a routine mission after all, then."

"If it's routine," Coyote complained, "it won't be any fun."

"Your assignments are not required to be fun, Mister Jones. Only useful, and necessary. You are the only agent we have who is immune to telepathic projection, and you are therefore elected to go find out what's going on."

"How come we haven't noticed this before? This pseudo-invisible planet, I mean?"

"It's a big galaxy, Mister Jones. A big *three* galaxies. There are many hundreds of thousands of planets we've never even looked at. This is simply one of those hundreds of thousands."

"What if I won't go?"

"You always ask that."

"Come, on, Fish—what if I won't go?"

"Then we'll fire a drone rocket into the 'empty space' and see what happens."

"With sentient creatures registering on the sensors?" Coyote was outraged. "You wouldn't do that."

"Oh yes we would," the Fish said. "If somebody care-

fully sets up the illusion that there's nothing there, they
can't say much when somebody does a routine test through
their middle. And we can't have rogue telepaths messing
up the telepathic network for the Communipaths. You
know that. It's got to be stopped."

Coyote groaned. "Aah, BEMdung," he said. "I guess I
have to go see to it."

"I guess you do."

"I don't like it, Fish," Coyote declared. "Why would a
whole planet be hiding out like that? I don't like the sound
of it, I don't like the smell of it, I don't like anything about
it."

"Try to set aside your natural distaste," intoned the Fish
solemnly, with a straight face. "The peoples of the Tri-
Galactic Federation will be eternally in your debt. O
Mighty TGIS Man."

"Where *is* this thrill-stuffed nothing?"

"Just at the edge of the First Galaxy." The Fish pressed
a stud and activated the map that took up all of one wall of
his office. There were a lot of dots on the map marked
"Vast Area of Empty Space," as a way of keeping the map
small enough to go on a single wall. And there was a small
blinking dot, where the funny wrinkle was located.

"That close!" said Coyote.

"That close. Speak to my secretary on the way out. It
will give you the coordinates, the briefing microfiche,
whatever else you need."

"What I need is—"

"Spare me, Mister Jones. There isn't any *time* to play
games this morning. We really have to get right at this
task, find out who is responsible, and determine what
measures are necessary to deal with the problem. Before
there's any serious interference with intergalactic communication."

"Do I need to know about this generating whatsis grammar?"

"It's in your briefing fiche, man. Naturally."

"Okay. Phooey."

Coyote hauled himself out of the chair reluctantly, and went out the door without saying anything more to his chief. On the way, he projected a deafening SLAM, something that an irising door can't provide of its self. He didn't go back and look to see if the Fish had been suitably startled by the noise. His projections might be vulgar, they might lack elegance antiquarian or contemporary, they might TWINKLE in a low-class and inaccurate fashion, but they by damn always *worked*.

Tzana Kai read it out to him, and he copied it down with scrupulous care, and then he looked it over, tugging at the end of his beard and muttering happily to himself, until she lost patience.

"Well, Coyote," she asked, "do you intend to let me in on this, or are you satisfied just talking to yourself? If that's it, I've got work piled to the roof in there that I could be doing while you indulge in your own witticisms."

Coyote only beamed at her, and she made a soft frustrated noise.

"You sound like a chicken," he said.

"Thank you. *You* sound like a drunken teenager. And an expression to match on your silly face."

"Tzana," he sighed, "I understand it. I truly do understand it, bless you for your wondrous brain and your wondrous power of explanation. It's just *fine*, this stuff! What a way to make an imp disappear!"

Tzana looked at the ceiling, and he reached over to stroke her hair. "Peace," he said. "Harmony. Here, I'll show you." And he began singing, to the tune of "The Asteroid that Shimmied Like a Lady," at the top of his lungs. "Boundary symbol," he warbled, "there's the IMP, oh gimme a nice variable, then a you and a verb, you simp, because there's another variable comin' along, and a boundary symbol to end my song, and that's IMP disappearing, it's IMP disappearing, oh, yeah, yeah, yeah. . . ."

He snapped his fingers and twitched his butt smartly, not all that easy when you're sitting on the floor, and was just opening his mouth to start again when Tzana clapped her hand over it.

"No!" she said decisively. "Once is enough."

"Tzana, people got paid for playing with this stuff," he marveled, mumbling through her hand and nibbling at her palm. "You realize that?"

"They surely did. They got to be big fancy professors at big fancy universities."

"Well, I like it," he announced. And added, "Now that I've got it figured out."

It hadn't been simple. Or quick. He had looked at the formidable gibberish on his briefing fiche, given up at once, and headed straight for Tzana Kai, yelling for help. And she'd whacked the comset for a hard copy of a historical piece or two and read them over, shaking her head, and whacked it for a couple more, while he paced.

"Do you think you really have to know about this?" she'd asked him.

"Don't you think I should?"

"Well . . . if the rogue had been transmitting labor pains would you feel obliged to get pregnant?"

"That's ridiculous."

"You'd look ridiculous pregnant, I can't argue with that. But I don't see the need for this. It's the kind of stuff that takes a very long time to learn, Coyote."

"I don't have to learn it. I just want a rough idea what it's about."

"Why?"

"Because I might need it!"

"How could you need it?"

"We don't know what's doing this," he told her. "We don't know anything about it. For all I know this creature doesn't talk anything else *but* generative transformational grammar."

"Oh, Light's beard," Tzana objected. "Coyote, that transmission used the Roman alphabet!"

"You can't tell," he had insisted. "You never know."

Tzana had glared at him and he had concentrated on glaring right back, crossing his eyes at her from time to time.

"You're just curious," she said disgustedly. "You just can't stand it, having something in your very own briefing fiche, *and* in the Roman alphabet, that you can't understand. That's all that's the matter with you. And for the sake of your curiosity, you are keeping me away from work that I really need to do."

He didn't deny it.

"Shame on you," she fussed. "How do you expect me to keep this place going, not to mention cavorting about on the side for the TGIS, and still waste time on your nonsense?"

Coyote touched her cheek with one gentle finger; he doted on Tzana Kai, and on all her works. "Try me once more," he coaxed. "One more time. And if that doesn't do it, I'll give it up. Try me on one of the baby ones, love."

"Hmmmph." She had stared at the stack of papers, and then she had gone through it just once more. Grudgingly. *Fast*.

"You take an ordinary command," she said flatly. "You call that part of it that *means* 'command' *IMP*. For *imperative*."

"Command," he said. "Got it."

"Then you write it down like this. First term, that squiggle that means beginning of the sentence, plus that X . . . the variable. Second term, the IMP. Third term, the word 'you.' The *Panglish* word 'you,' please notice! Fourth term, any old verb, I guess. Fifth term, one more variable and the squiggle for the end of the sentence. One, two, three, four, five. Like that. And then you dump the third term, and you've got a command. All right?"

He looked at the sheet of paper she laid in front of him on the floor, which said:

$$\# \ X \ \text{IMP} \ \text{you} \ \text{Verb} \ Y \ \#$$
$$1 \quad 2 \quad 3 \quad 4 \quad 5$$

"Goes to," he said carefully. "Goes to one, two, nothing at all, four, five." He took the marker and wrote it down for her. "1, 2, 0, 4, 5."

"Right. You delete the 'you.' Leaving stuff like 'eat your peas.' Okay?"

"Why in the world," he asked wonderingly, "would anybody have gone to all that trouble when they already knew *how* to speak Panglish? Much less, pay somebody to do it?"

"I don't know, Coyote. It was a long long time ago. It was a crazy century—just consider the kind of *songs* it produced."

"I don't like making 'you' disappear anyway," he said. "I want to make the IMP disappear. And I know how, too."

He leaned over, wrote a rule that deleted IMP, and showed her.

"See? Isn't that better?"

"No, it's not better," she said crossly, "and it's not worse, either. But I don't understand this stuff well enough to explain why not, so don't ask me."

"Try. Indulge me, Tzana. *Try.*"

She had tried awhile, and he had tried awhile, and he had encouraged her with bright sayings in the silences.

And now, finally, he did understand. He wasn't ready to tackle anything else in the way of squiggles, but he did understand this one.

"Four possible things you can do, right?" he asked her, checking. "Deletion. Insertion. Movement. Substitution."

"Right. Much good may it do you."

"I may go into it *deeply*, Tzana! I may have found my true calling."

"Coyote . . . singing twentieth-century horrible songs is bad enough. Do not add the unspeakable to the unbearable. One noxious hobby is all that you are allowed."

"Nevertheless. When I meet this being now, I'll know what to say. 'Good morning,' I'll say, 'Delete *you*, fella!' And that will get us started on the right foot."

Tzana gave up and lay down flat on her back on the floor and laughed until she was gasping.

"What an image," she moaned. "Oh, beards and butter, what an image! This tentacled thing about sixty feet high—"

"On an Earth-gravity planet?"

"Ah, never mind accuracy, you're spoiling it! This tentacled thing about sixty feet high, with flames coming out of its ears, and more psibility than all the Communipaths put together, and you walk up to it and say 'Delete *you*, fella!' Oh, Coyote, you are such a comfort to me!"

"Allow me to comfort you some more," he suggested. "In a more concrete fashion."

"I'm too tired," she sighed. "I don't have enough strength left to do more than just breathe."

"Good enough," said Coyote, and he gathered her to him, settling her comfortably against his chest. "In that case, we'll just lie here in the rays of the setting sun and breathe in and out together. And from time to time I'll sing you that IMP song." He made the gesture that activated her computer; and the tasteful sign that read "Translation Bureau—Tzana Kai, Certified Federal Translator" blinked out in her window, and it went opaque.

"Coyote," she said, muffled against him, "it doesn't make the IMP disappear. For the ten thousandth time, it makes the '*you*' disappear!"

"If the you disappeared," he assured her, "I would die of grief. Let's keep you and dump the IMP."

And he held her tenderly and sang "Cement Mixer, Putty, Putty," and "I'd Love to Get You on a Slow Boat to China" until she begged him to stop.

CHAPTER TWO

Later, Coyote would agree without argument that he'd been both reckless and stupid. You don't take an unarmed personal flyer and land it on a planet about which you know only that it's got a rogue telepath on it somewhere, and from which you're getting signals not only of an objection to your landing but of unmistakable outright hostility. You don't *do* that. You go back to Mars Central and you report, and then somebody else decides whether to send out the Fedrobots with suitable enforcement devices or what.

It wasn't that Coyote didn't know all that; he'd been a TGIS man a long time, and it wasn't his habit to go charging into obvious trouble. But he was so damn *mad* at the time that he didn't care what else happened, just so long as he got a chance to show the bastards they couldn't push him around.

He'd had no trouble seeing Planet X in the spot where the Coast Guard had seen only empty space. It flickered from time to time, and it had the kind of blurred shimmer to it that things get when you look at them ahead of you down a road in hot weather, but he could see it. If he'd been *totally* mind-deaf, there wouldn't have been even that much interference with his perceptions; but the fact that there was any interference at all made him nervous. Considering the size of the object to be perceived, it told him something about the projective power of the rogue. It had to be phenomenal, and it inspired respect—until he'd started getting mad, he'd been a very wary agent.

He'd been in a landing pattern, just holding and thinking, when turbulence hit him out of nowhere. And he found himself regretting, for once, that he'd ripped out the autopilot items meant to keep him steady through unexpected bad weather. He was socked so hard, and from so many directions at once, that it was only the combined contradictions that kept the flyer from flipping over and going into a spin. And he was thrown against his safety harness and slammed back into the seat until he felt like a Ping-Pong ball in a world class volley. He'd have been doing frantic evasive maneuvers if he'd been able to get his hands on the controls, but he wasn't even sure where the controls *were*. And only after he'd bellowed uselessly into the communicator for many minutes did he remember that there was probably nothing on the other end of the line, leaving him bellowing to his elbow.

He switched then, hanging at a spine-cracking angle in his harness, and projected full strength: IN SERIOUS DIFFICULTY. PERMISSION TO MAKE IMMEDIATE EMERGENCY LANDING REQUESTED.

The turbulence stopped abruptly, and he groped for the stick; but before he could reach it the flyer went into a new kind of dance that was worse than the previous one. This time it wasn't violent, and he didn't have to worry about crashing. This time it was the Ultimate Motion Sickness Inducer . . . a sudden drop, maybe five or six feet, then a slow rise with a steady roll from side to side, then the drop again. Over and over and over. Gentle. Safe. And unspeakably stomach-turning.

"You will not vomit," Coyote announced to himself sternly, out loud. And then he had just barely time to grab the plastic sicktube with its clever vomit-composting chemicals and surrender his breakfast before the flyer dropped out from under him again.

It was somewhere along in there, between dry heaves, that he started getting really mad. Not just everyday mad, but the absolutely calm eye-of-a-tornado kind of mad. The "I don't care if I get killed, if I can just take you with me" kind of mad.

Because this was beyond any question something being done *to* him, on purpose. The violent stuff had been different—it was freaky, but he was willing to believe it had been natural. *This* was something else; this had a pattern that belonged to no natural phenomenon. This was SOMEBODY, doing him dirt.

He took a deep breath, between retching and choking, and he laid it out mind to mind: I AM PUTTING THIS FLYER DOWN, YOU DEMENTED SONOFABITCH, AND THEN I'M GONNA FRY YOUR EYES RIGHT OUT OF YOUR EFFING HEAD.

He didn't like to think about how it had gone from then on. He'd fight his way down maybe twenty feet, and whatever-it-was would fling him back up thirty and hand him another dose of the sick stuff. He'd do his best to dive for the planet surface, gagging and spitting and seeing blurrily through the rivulets of cold sweat running down his face . . . and it would let him hang there a minute, nose down, and then put him through a couple of figure eights before going back to the other routine. It was dueling *heads*, no mistake, and he would have lost the flyer along with the contents of his stomach, he was certain, if it hadn't just suddenly stopped and let him be.

That was of course the most ominous thing that had happened to him yet. It scared him sweatless and turned what was left of him limp, waiting for the axe to fall. When somebody has demonstrated to you elaborately that they can whip you nine ways to Tuesday, and they just let you go like that, it generally means they've decided it would be less trouble to deal with you simply and directly. Coyote had been pretty sure he was going to his death as the flyer went down through the now placid skies, and the only comfort he'd had was that death was preferable to the way he felt at that point.

The flyer headed down into an open field, controlled by something or somebody other than Coyote, and he was staring out the window at what looked like maybe a nice stand of corn, when the last straw fell. It was no big thing, and it caused him no physical discomfort, but there was something about it that made his various internal indicators all flip to "TOO MUCH already." He looked numbly at the mule that was flying along beside him. It had a long tail looped up in a braid, but it was most definitely a mule. Its teeth were bared, and its ears we laid back, and it flew without wings and without so much as moving its legs, and if it hadn't been for the way it was flaring its nostrils he might have taken it for an alien species' idea of a hot air balloon. But the nostrils told him it was a living creature. A living mule. About ninety feet up in the air.

Coyote looked at it, and it looked at him, and the lights went out; so far as he could tell he was at a dead stop in a box of black glue. It was grim, but it didn't involve any more frills for his stomach, and he was giving grateful thanks for that until he realized that for all he knew this was IT, and he was just too dumb to realize that he was dead. If that was so, he knew he wasn't going to like it. His last thought was that he could handle heavenly choirs or platoons of devils with pitchforks but he could *not* handle eternal boredom. And then consciousness went the way of his breakfast and the lights.

When he woke up he was more comfortable, but he wasn't pleased; it was just a hair or two short of waking in a cave surrounded by Neanderthals. He stared at the wooden footboard of the narrow bed where he lay, and he patted the white cotton sheets and the plump white pillows in their neat pillowcases with the embroidered rosebuds, and he gave the patchwork quilt spread neatly over him and turned down under his arms the sort of glance he'd have given something that *ticked*. The room had stone walls, and a wooden door, and one tiny window set high up and letting in sunshine and birdsong. And beside him, rocking gently in a wooden rocking chair, working away at some esoteric needlework involving a little lavender aluminum gadget with a hook at one end was a skinny young woman with a placid look and little else to recommend her. She was humming softly, and fiddling with the little gadget and a basket of yarn, and keeping her eyes to herself.

"Well, what's this," he asked as politely as suited him, which wasn't particularly, "the Intergalactic Historical Museum for Stranded Travelers?"

She turned and looked at him, and raised her eyebrows, and said, "No, it's not. Is that where you were headed?"

Coyote was amazed some more . . . he'd never heard Panglish exactly like that she was speaking, but it was definitely some variety from the very late twentieth century, or very early twenty-first, of Old Earth.

"If you'll speak slowly," he said carefully, doing his best to shift to the period needed, "I believe I will be able to understand you."

"Count your blessings," she said smartly, but she slowed

down as requested, and Coyote abandoned his attempts at wit for the good old standards.

"Where am I?" he asked.

"In a bed, in a room, in a castle, on a world," she said. "Does that help?"

"Not very much."

"You're on Planet Ozark, my friend," she said then. "In Brightwater Kingdom, and a guest at the castle. An unin*vited* guest, mind you, but guest you be all the same. And if you're not comfortable, I'd suggest you speak up and let your needs be known."

"Planet Ozark. Brightwater Kingdom. The castle."

"Echo in here," she said, and clipped off her yarn with her teeth.

"Well," he objected, "you've got to admit it's not probable."

"What's not probable?"

"Planet Whatsis. Brightwater Kingdom. Et cetera. Where's the king this morning?"

"We've no king, Mister Jones. Nor, praise be, any other such claptrap."

"Fresh out?"

She sniffed, and tightened her lips, indicating how funny she found him, and repeated herself.

"I don't intend to sit here admiring you all the day long," she said firmly, "and if you've *got* any needs you'd best state them."

"All right," Coyote said. "I need to get up, get my clothes on, take a good look around, check out my flyer, and then—the Light being merciful—go home."

"My goodness Mercy Maud," she said, and gave him a smile so sweet it almost fooled him into smiling back. "That's quite a list, isn't it? And such a shame none of it's possible, Mister Jones. That crash you decided to have instead of a landing disarranged you more than somewhat—you'll not be leaving that bed for a week at least."

The pillows he was propped on were *very* comfortable. He scooted them back so that he could sit up straighter, and he looked her right in the eye. And he spoke to her cautiously, because he hadn't any idea how much he wanted her to know.

"I did *not* 'decide,' as you put it, to crash rather than to land. I had a little help. And I don't *feel* injured, which come to think of it is pretty astonishing. Are you a doctor, Citizen?"

Up went her eyebrows again, and she gave him the stare that comes to "Whaddaya mean, *'Citizen'*?" and he shifted registers and tried again. Wherever this was, it was sure as hell not modern, and he should have known from the quilt and the quaint that "Citizen" would not be the local term of address for young ladies. He had a feeling that the Fish might have really liked it here. So far.

"I beg your pardon," he said, carefully. "Are you a doctor, *Madam*?"

"Dozens," she said crossly. "Turn twenty-four and they're ready to bury you without so much as a check-you-over!"

"I beg your pardon *again*. What *should* I call you?"

"Miss," she said. "It's *Miss*. Miss Responsible of Brightwater, at your service. Reluctantly, but competently. And no, I'm not a doctor, nor do I have any need of one. Magician's been and gone, and he's mended the worst of it, but he says you're to stay put. Now give me no sass, please; I'm in no mood for it. I just stopped by to see if you had any reasonable requests, and that's my third offer and my last. Now speak up, Mister Jones. Are you hungry? Thirsty? Anything hurt you? Bowels, bladder, or beard need tending? Anything at all?"

"Miss," he said. "Miss Responsible?"

"Twelve points for accuracy," she said back. "And two off for lack of either dispatch or originality."

"What I would like most of all," he went on doggedly, "is to know where I am and why I am here—how I got here, for instance—and then to get on with my business. If I've offended you in some way, please blame it on my ignorance of your local customs, and not on ill will. Miss Responsible, I have had a *very* hard day."

She stared at him, her lower lip tucked under her upper teeth, and sighed a long and weary sigh, while he waited. She did swift things with the needlework gadget and put it and the yarn all away in a bag she had hanging over the back of the rocker. And then she folded her hands in her lap and spoke to him as she would have spoken to a child.

"My dear Mister Jones," it went, "I do believe that the amazing lack of speed with which your mind functions should be a *clue* . . . the state of your head ought to worry you a sight more than the state of your bitsy feelings. I have told you in some detail just where you are; as to how you got here, you ought to be able to figure out that somebody had to go to the bother of carrying you here and cleaning up the mess you left behind. Your business, whatever it might be, will have to wait until you are less peaked and less puny, not to mention waiting until you are through whining."

That did it. He might be peaked, and he might be puny, but he did not whine.

"I was not whining!" he bellowed, and he shook his fist at her to punctuate the sentiment.

The maddening female raised her eyes eloquently to the ceiling, that it might bear witness to what she had to endure, and said, "And a temper fit on top of it, Mister Jones! And you a man full grown, so far as I can tell through the shrubbery."

What came next was all bellow and no words, and it

helped not at all. She simply stood up, set her arms akimbo and watched him until the roar died away.

"If you think," she said then, "that I've nothing better to do with my time than sit here and listen to a half-tamed offworlder pule and puke and carry on like a he-goat in rut, you'd best think again. You've had three chances, Mister Jones; you'll not get a fourth. Now you *lie* there, and if you're uncomfortable you've surely got it coming, and there'll be somebody along later to try common courtesy on you again and find out if a few hours' silent contemplation have done your manners any good. I must say, I am purely *dis*gusted with the spectacle you present!"

And off she went, leaving him sputtering, her skirts swishing smartly about her ankles and her needlework bag flung over her shoulder, and the door slammed behind her. A real honest-to-god slam. None of your illusions.

Coyote was out of the bed and at that door in one leap, while the slam was still reverberating in his ears. Secret Agent Makes Mighty Bound! he advised himself as he landed. Makes It Belatedly! he tacked on, reaching for the knob to fling the door wide and chase Miss Responsible Whoozis to her lair, or wherever it was she kept her nasty self.

He was not pleased when the knob refused to turn.

He stood there, fanny flapping in the wind, and gave the door a careful look. Perfectly ordinary door, if you happened to live in the twentieth century. Perfectly ordinary doorknob. Perfectly ordinary lock, in which no doubt a perfectly ordinary key had been turned as her ladyship sailed out. And on that doorknob hung a wreath of dried and dusty-looking stuff that proved on closer examination to be lilac, wound all around with cloves of reeking garlic.

"Sheeeeesh," said Coyote, long and slow and tonal. Somewhere in his mind, which he was now willing to grant had been scrambled in the crash, he finally pro-

cessed something she'd said a long way back. No need for
doctors, she'd said, and she'd pronounced the word "doctor" about the same way he'd have pronounced "axe murderer." And then she'd noted that the Magician had been
and gone and had seen to the worst of it. And there was
garlic round the doorknob.

Where, in the name of the Light and all its blistering
rays, *was* he?

He went back to the bed and lay down, pulling the quilt
up to his chin for consolation, and he thought about it
awhile. That thing hanging on the doorknob . . . that had
to be something meant for magic. Nobody would use
garlic, stinking like that garlic, and old dried up flowers,
just for decoration. He was, according to the female, in a
castle, in a kingdom, on a planet he knew she'd named but
could not remember through the fog that was leaking out
his ears. Planet Hobart? Something like that. And although few things were more improbable, he would have
unhesitatingly wagered his arm and his legs that the woman
was not just humanoid but *human*. Earth-stock human.

It was time, and past time, to get out of this room and
do some superspy stuff. If he'd known he was going to be
facing a twentieth-century door and a twentieth-century
lock he'd have brought along something suitable for getting them open, but he'd had no such expectations, and he
was equipped with nothing but his person. The room had
the bed and the rocker and an empty peg or two on the
wall and an inspirational homily in a small wooden frame,
and. . . . A thought struck him, and he looked under the
bed, and marveled at what he saw there. Add to the list
one chamberpot. Could he open the door with a chamberpot,
be it ever so splendidly blue enameled and adorned with
white speckles? He doubted it. Let us, he thought, just do
something very basic and uncomplicated. And he lay back

on the wonderful pillows, making a mental note that when he got home he had to get some just like that if he had to burglarize a museum to do it, and projected gently:

THERE IS SOMEONE IN THIS ROOM WHO NEEDS HELP, PLEASE.

He didn't want crowds of people rushing in, supposing there *were* crowds of people. Just one or two citizens who knew how to open doors or knew whom to tell if they couldn't do it themselves.

THERE IS SOMEONE IN THIS ROOM . . . WHO NEEDS HELP. PLEASE.

He kept it up a while, longer than he'd expected, and was wondering if he was going to have to take a chance on the crowds, when he finally heard a kind of scurrying noise outside the door, and little high-pitched whispers. Elves? he wondered. To go with the Magician and the garlic. Goblins? Trolls? Helga Diks?

No. It was children, he decided. Just children, and it sounded like a little boy and a little girl. Whispering pretty frantically. One of them going on at some length about "we are not *sposed* to go in there, you *know* we're not sposed to go in there" and what would happen if they got caught; and the other whimpering a little but insisting that even so they *had* to go in there, because they just *had* to, that was why. That would be the little girl, he thought, from the sound of the voice.

CHILDREN. . . . He was very gentle and careful. THERE IS SOMEONE IN HERE WHO NEEDS HELP, PLEASE. PLEASE COME IN.

"Well, *I* won't go in there, Marydell! I don't care *what* you say!"

"I have to." Miserable little voice. Coyote felt guilty.

"You do, and you know what'll happen to *you*, Missy!"

There was a whimper, and then the little voice said, "*I* know! I can *look*! Nobody said not to *look*."

Snort of disgust. Clearly a boy-type snort.

"Huh! As if anybody *needed* to be told not go looking through keyholes stead of mindin' their own business! Huh!"

"I'm going to."

"Don't you dare!"

"I *am*!"

It was a fierce little voice, and a determined one, and there was a rustle and a bit of a scrabble, presumably the process of putting eye to keyhole.

And then a long silence, until the boy said, "Well? *Well?*"

"Oh, John *Ben*jamin!" wailed the smaller voice, not fierce now but absolutely awestruck, "there is a great big old ugly *toad* sitting in there on top of a stack of three pillows, just as sassy as you please! A *toad*, John Benjamin!"

The boy's moral scruples were not enough to sustain him against a bait like that, and Coyote heard the scratch and shuffle of two determined youngsters each aiming to occupy the same spot; and then the boy, having won due no doubt to being larger and stronger, said, "*Dozens*, Marydell! It *is* a toad!"

"Well, I said it was, didn't I?" Outraged.

Coyote thought fast. He didn't understand any of this. But he was certain that the next sound he heard was going to be running feet, if he didn't do something in a hell of a hurry, and the chances that the kids would feel obligated to report the presence of a toad—and risk getting in trouble for a toad—were too slim to suit him. He had to heat things up a little, and he did, right off the top of his head. And was rewarded with a piercing scream that nearly ripped his ears out. The little girl must have been taking another look.

"Marydell, what's the *matter* with you? It's nothin' but a

ol' toad . . . Here, let me take a look, Marydell. Move over, *will you?*"

It happened so fast Coyote didn't have time to make any changes, and he got the running feet all the same, with one or both children screaming bloody blue murder as they pounded away down what must be a pretty long hall.

"I wonder," Coyote said slowly, in the general direction of the doorknob. "I wonder what happens now."

He was uneasy, now that he had time to think. The snake's body had been bad enough. The three heads, all from different monsters, might have been a little excessive. It was just possible that he was going to wish he'd been somewhat more conservative in his projections. It might have been just a little *much*.

Responsible of Brightwater, standing at the foot of his bed fairly breathing flames and smoke, with a terrified and tearful child clinging to each of her hands and staring at him with enormous eyes, clearly agreed with him. There was no question about it, and Coyote braced himself. She did not disappoint him, but she took care of a bit of domestic business first.

"Marydell of Guthrie?" she demanded. "John Benjamin? You two wicked little sprats, not an obedient bone in either one of your bodies? *You*, Marydell, John Benjamin! You take a good long look there, and you tell me what it is that you see! *Right* quick!"

The little girl tried to run and hide behind her skirts, but Responsible whipped her back out front and center and shook her like a rug, and ordered her to speak up and state what she saw there.

"A . . . an old lady, Miss Responsible!" gasped the child.

"And you, John Benjamin Brightwater the 14th?"

"An old lady, Miss Responsible! Just an old lady!"

"Not a *toad*, then?"

"No, Miss!" came the terrified chorus.

"Not a *monster*, then? With three heads . . . one of them a lion, one of them a dragon, and one of them unspeakable?"

"No, Miss!"

"You do under*stand* why you saw nasty things?" she demanded. And she shook them both this time, one with each arm, not hard enough to do any damage but enough to impress Coyote. More muscle there than he would have expected from the look of her.

"Yes, *Ma'am*, Miss Responsible!"

"Well, spit it out!"

"We-saw-awful-stuff-cause-we-went-and-looked-through-a-keyhole-into-a-room-that-wasn't-ours-and-wasn't-our-business-and-it-was-warded-besides!"

"And it served you right, what you saw, didn't it? *Didn't* it?"

"Yes, *Ma'am*, Miss Responsible!"

"And?"

"And-we'll-never-ever-do-any-such-a-wicked-thing-again, Miss Responsible!"

"I should sincerely and forevermore hope *not!*"

She gave them a last shake, and they stood there clinging to each other and shivering while she made them apologize nicely to the "old lady" for disturbing her; and then she threw them both out and Coyote heard them run hell bent for the highroads down the hall; and with all his heart he wished he was running with them. He slid down as far under the quilt as he dared, and tried not to notice the way that Responsible of Brightwater was spitting sparks.

"*Well!*" she had at him. "I hope you are *sat*isfied!"

"Yes, *Ma'am*, Miss Responsible," said Coyote.

"I don't know how things are done in whatever misbegotten hole of a world you hail from, Mister Highandmighty

Pitiful Jones, but on *this* planet a Magician with powers like yours would no more stoop to use them to scare little children than he'd eat warts for breakfast! Whatever in the wide and weary world were you *think*ing of, doing that?"

Coyote cleared his throat, long and elaborate, and scooted down just a bit more under the covers.

"You're right," he managed.

"That was never in question. And don't mumble at me!"

"You're right," he said again. "You're right—I shouldn't have done that."

"Do tell and declare!"

"That too."

"If you were so desperate for diversion that you couldn't make do with the perfectly respectable toad I left you being, Mister Jones, you could just of made a tad *bigg*er toad, you know! That would have scared the tadlings sufficiently to send them running for somebody! There was no *need* for a spangled snake as big around as I am, trailing itself all over the bed. And there was no *need* for three heads on the thing; and there was no *need* for three separate colors of blood, one to each head, and. . . . Oh! You despicable excuse for a whatever-you-are, if you had to show off, couldn't you have settled for a double-sized *toad*?"

It was all true. It went on a long, long time, and she did not lack for variety of expression, and it was all deserved. The part about how those children would never get over it, and the nightmares they'd have. The part about using hatchets to slice bread with. The part about warped people that pull wings off flies and lust to torment innocent children. All the other parts.

"You—perverted exhibitionist *sadist!*" she flung at him, to finish it off. She stood there not even out of breath; and he gave up completely and pulled the patchwork quilt right up over his head. He had never felt smaller or more contemptible or more worthless or more just plain *stupid* in his entire life.

From under the safe blackness of the bedding, he asked her what was going to happen next, and waited to be told he'd be shot at sunrise, but she had other ideas.

"*Now*," she said, "I am going to try yet one more time to do some of the work that needs doing around here. I am on my way to Castle Airy, and I'll be gone all this day and maybe—because of *you*, Mister Jones, and the way you've kept me here hour after hour—maybe part of to-morrow. And while I am gone you will lie there in that bed, and people will bring you food and come for your slops and see to you in general, and you will cause *no* trouble! And when I get back I will come up here and decide what must be done next."

"And what will people see when they come in here to do my slops and so on?" he hazarded, mumbling through the sheets and the quilt.

"You come out of there, you coward!" she ordered, and out he came, and asked her again.

"They will see a nice old lady with soft white curls and soft rosy cheeks and lovely blue veins to her hands, smiling and polite and grateful for their company! If you know what is good for you."

"Not a toad."

"No. Not a toad. And not a three-headed giant serpent created by a twisted mind, either."

"You're sure of that?"

"Clear to my toenails."

"All the way from that other castle?"

"My word on it, you nasty bully of a male!"

"Clear till tomorrow? All the rest of today and till tomorrow?"

She whirled on her heel without a word and was gone, leaving him still staring and babbling.

He lay there and he thought about it. There was a good deal that required thinking about. He was Coyote *Jones*, after all. Most powerful projective telepath in the Three Galaxies, which constituted the entire known universe. Long time valuable and respected agent of the Tri-Galactic Intelligence Service. Able to stop whole armies of demented fanatics dead in their tracks . . . well, not dead, but *stopped* in their tracks . . . at a distance of several miles. Able to both stop and start riots. Able to convince entire crowds of people that they saw whatever he chose that they should see. A man of *power*. Mind-deaf, of course, but nobody's perfect—a man of power, all the same.

And here he lay. And this scarecrow of a young female person, dressed up like a milkmaid in a period play, and a primitive period at that, this *Miss* Responsible of Brightwater with her improbable name and her improbable getup and her improbable environment, proposed that she could:

(1) cause him to be perceived as a sweet little old lady, him and his six feet plus of muscle and his bright red beard and all the rest of it;
(2) cause him to be so perceived while she was herself far enough away that it would take awhile to get there and awhile to get back again;
(3) keep that up all the rest of this day and through the night and well into tomorrow, if need be;
(4) all of the above in spite of whatever feelings he might have about it.

A number of possibilities presented themselves. She could be bluffing, for example—probably, almost certainly, was bluffing. And counting on him to be like the children, so scared by her bluster that he'd lie there docile and do as he was told. On the other hand, those children looking through the keyhole *had* seen him as a toad until he'd

done something to change that; and when she'd brought
them back, they *had* seen him as a sweet little old lady,
just as advertised.

It brought interesting ideas to mind. She hadn't mentioned telepathic projection, or any other kind of psibility—
she'd been talking Magic. But she obviously hadn't turned
him into either a toad *or* a sweet little old lady; she'd just
managed to cause him to be *perceived* as one or the other.
And when you thought about it, in those ancient molder-
ing wonderful stories about princes turned into frogs, they
hadn't really been "turned into" frogs, either. If they had
been, they would have been satisfied to be frogs, and their
frog brains would never in the world have sent them
wandering the face of the earth in search of princesses to
kiss them and change them back. That led somewhere
very interesting, when he could get time to follow it
along. . . . Like, which senses were affected? The children *saw* him as a toad, but would they have heard him
talk as a man? If they'd touched him, would they have felt
toad or man? Could they have put him in a box? Down a
hole? Just because they perceived a toad, and toads will fit
in boxes and holes? Or was it just the eyes that were
fooled by this "magic"? Later, he'd think about all of that.
Right now there were more urgent questions.

For instance, this young woman had never said that she
was herself the one responsible. Her name was Responsible,
no way to avoid the puns, but she'd never once claimed to
be personally doing any of the special effects. She'd said
she'd see to it, or she'd give her word on it, or she'd
decide what was to be done. But never had she said
specifically that she was the one *doing* anything. Which
meant that maybe she was the rogue telepath, capable of
causing an entire planet to be perceived as a void, and
maybe she was just someone who had the rogue's ear. The
idea that it might be her turned Coyote's blood cold. But

it didn't seem likely. She was skinny and homely and freckled and nervous and gawky, and her hair was jerked up on top of her head in a knot, and she'd said she was only twenty-four years old. She was not your stereotypical image of a rogue telepath. Only the fact that the last one he'd encountered had been a "helpless" infant made him even consider the possibility. And either way, he didn't know. Not yet.

If she was *not* the rogue, the claims she was making were on the rogue's behalf. And if he could do the things she claimed for him (or if she could do them), then this was power of a kind not known in the Three Galaxies. Coyote could, as he'd already reminded himself, create wondrous telepathic illusions that made crowds of people helpless against him. But he had to *be* there. He couldn't just put the illusion in place and go off about his business and leave it operating, like turning a light on and going away and leaving it burning. He had to actively keep that illusion going, and he could only keep one going at a time, and he got tired in a hurry. Half an hour, maybe, he could have kept something elaborate going. But all of an afternoon and a night and into the next morning? While he went on a jaunt to the neighboring castle and carried on business?

Nope. That was beyond even wishing for, let alone doing.

Which brought up the horrible possibility that it wasn't just one rogue telepath doing all this stuff, assuming it was no bluff. What if it was a whole platoon of them, spelling each other, taking turns? What if it was everybody, the Light help and spare us from such a catastrophe, what if it was the whole population of Planet Hobart? *Then* what, O Mighty Tri-Galactic Federation, with your registered telepaths and your rules about their behavior?

And how was he, Coyote Jones, going to find out any of

this without putting some foot into it so far that it could
not without disaster be withdrawn?

"Oh, boy," said Coyote softly and with deep feeling,
into the silence of the little room. "Oh, boy!"

CHAPTER THREE

They sat there in the smallest of Castle Airy's Meetingrooms and the most private—only one tall window here looking out over the sea and hung with the inevitable burgundy draperies. Six worried women with much on their minds. There was Responsible of Brightwater, looking frazzled; and Charity of Airy, looking concerned; and Teacher Josepha of Farson, looking grave; and Grannys Forthright, Flyswift, and Heatherknit, all looking cross well beyond the usual. Even Granny Heatherknit, growing a bit frail now at 116, looked mean.

"Well," demanded Granny Flyswift belligerently, "we just going to sit here like this the livelong day and stare at each other?"

"No," said Charity of Airy. "No, of course not. We don't have time for that. But the question is, what are we going to *do*?"

She looked at Responsible, and all the Grannys looked at Responsible; even the Teacher glanced at her once before returning her eyes to her folded hands. And Responsible stared round the table at the grim-faced rigid waiting women, and she moaned. Soft and low and short, but a moan all the same. She looked at them, and she looked up at the ceiling to see what might be written there, and then she put her face in her hands and announced that she had not the least idea what they were going to do.

"Well, if that's the best you've got to offer us," snapped Granny Flyswift, "I don't wonder you go mumbling it through the back of your hand! Why don't you slide down there underneath the table and tell it to the carpet, Responsible, while you're at it?"

"Granny," Responsible pleaded, raising her head to look at the old lady, and clasping her hands tightly together to keep them out of mischief, "I really and truly do *not* know what to do, nor even where to begin. If I did, I'd have done it already, instead of hauling all of you in here to talk it over with me. You're always faulting me for pride, you Grannys—well, I'm not proud now, I'm downright humble. I do not have even a *notion* what to do, and that's a fact."

"Well, you are *supposed* to know what to do!" declared the Granny, and the sounds of agreement went round the table without a single objection. The Grannys were forever telling Responsible things like that—she was supposed to know, she was supposed to remember, she was supposed to understand, she was supposed to *be able*. She only wished she had their faith in her competence, however misplaced; she might have felt less frightened now.

Responsible moaned again, and was rewarded by a series of snorts and sniffs from the Grannys, and an exchange of significant glances between Charity of Airy and the Teacher.

"You'd best de*cide* what to do, Missy," warned Granny Forthright, "and that with more than considerable dispatch, 'cause time's a-wasting!"

"It was bound to happen sometime," said Responsible. Tentatively. Testing the waters.

"No, it wasn't," stated the Granny. "It might could of been that Earth blew its foul self clear to hell and back afore anybody else but us ever got *off* it. I suppose I'm obliged to be glad it didn't happen that way."

"Granny Forthright!" said Charity of Airy, shocked. "Think what you are saying!"

"I *am* thinking," retorted the Granny. "Can't you hear me, Charity? For sure, Responsible, if the folks we left behind on Earth are out tootling round the skies like they were no more than cow pastures, the day *was* bound to come when they'd find us. I agree with you on that. What's amazing is that it took 'em so long, unless that's just an indication that they're all as shiftless and wrong-headed and bound and determined on lunacy as they were when we left. Might could be they found out how to travel in space and then they set theirselves up a government department to work out the *details—that* would of kept 'em Earthbound a thousand years easy! I can just hear it now. '*Oh*, Mister *Pres*ident, do you suppose the spaceliners ought to have *pink* windows, or *blue* ones? Or maybe they had ought to be *green*, Mister President? Or do you reckon we'd best appoint a blue-ribbon *panel* . . . no, a blue-ribbon com*miss*ion, to decide that, Mister President, sir, your majesty? Oh, Mister *Pres*ident—' "

"Granny!" said Responsible, and she clapped both hands over her ears. "Please don't go on like that. It's awful."

"Bunch of administrative cowflop," the Granny told her, sailing right along, "and you know it as well as *I* do! We'd all of *drowned* in cowflop, and not just the administrative variety, either, if we'd of sat around on Earth waiting for the government to get us off the ground!"

"Well, somebody has gotten them off now, Granny," said Responsible sadly, "and *that* is the problem."

"You're sure, Missy?"

"That they're off the ground?"

"No, that they're from off *Earth!* You're certain sure?"

"Well," said Responsible, "the man's garments were more than somewhat curious, what there was of them. A kind of nicely tailored diaper arrangement in navy blue, he had on, *with* a narrow pinstripe, and over that a sort of long shirt with no sleeves, and it no more than halfway to his knees. And no proper shoes, just *soles* of shoes stuck on his feet somehow. But you put him in decent garb and walk him down the main street of Capital City, nobody'd even turn their head except to suggest that with hair that color a full beard is a tad more than is decent. He's Earthborn stock, Granny, I'm sure he is. And Earth stubborn. And Earth arrogant."

"Foof," said Granny Heatherknit. "I say turn him back into a toad and leave him that way. Down in the basement in a commodious bucket, and a tadling assigned to him round the clock to catch him flies."

"Now there's a kind heart," observed Charity of Airy. "Why not just turn the poor man in*to* a bucket, and save the tadling's trouble? How you talk, Granny Heatherknit!"

"Didn't none of us invite him," said the Granny stubbornly, her annoyance making the tremble of her head more emphatic. "And it was made most clear he wasn't wanted down here, from what Responsible tells us. I see *no* reason to concern myself with his welfare!"

"It would do no good to mistreat him," said Teacher Josepha then, and they all paid attention. Senior of the Teaching Order on Airy, and high-placed in the Order beyond Airy's boundaries, she had the skills of speech in great abundance; Teacher Josepha could read a shopping list aloud and make it sound important. "It would be useless, even if we were cruel enough to take the Granny's suggestions seriously. And just keeping the man here, in his own natural form, would do no good either. Because you know, all of you, that he will surely be missed—whether he just happened onto Ozark by accident or was sent here by something we're ignorant of as yet, when he does not come promptly back there will be others seeking him. That craft Responsible describes was never meant for long voyages."

"Oh, she's right," Responsible agreed. "The gadget he was flying couldn't hold more than food and supplies for a week at best, and it's got OFFICIAL and FEDERAL and GOVERNMENT EQUIPMENT BOUGHT AND IF NOT PAID FOR AT LEAST ON GOVERNMENT LIEN written all over it. There'd be more such out looking for him if he lingers here, just as the Teacher says, and then we'd have multiplied our problems. To put a dot on it, I'm a tad surprised nobody's turned up before this to see what's become of him."

"There's no procedure in the old books and records for dealing with this, if it were ever to happen?" asked the Teacher.

"No," said Responsible wearily. "There's no guidelines for this. Law, ladies—I don't even know why he's here. I was afraid to ask him."

"Run it by us again, girl," said Granny Flyswift. "One more time. Just so as I'm sure I've got it all straight in my head."

Responsible repeated it all, patiently. She'd been called on the comset and told that there was some kind of flying craft coming in fast; she'd run for the Magician of Rank and had some fancy and very localized nasty weather trotted out to discourage whoever it was; the man had announced himself with mindspeech and threatened to fry somebody's eyes right out of their head, instead of getting discouraged; and when it had become obvious that he wasn't going to give up and go away, she'd had him brought on in. And he lay now at Castle Brightwater, under a Spell of Deception that made him look like a sweet little old thing of ninety or so, pondering.

"Pondering?"

"That's what he was doing when I left him, Granny," said Responsible. "He'd near turned the air curdled with his pondering. Lying there trying to puzzle it out, and making little progress . . . and trying to decide what he dares do, I fancy."

"Cautious, is he?"

"Cautious enough, except when his temper gets the best of him. And then he's just like a skunked cat—you never saw the like. If I'd known what I was dealing with, I'd have seen to it that he wasn't made to lose that temper . . . there should have been something done to just distract him, something to make him want to move along to the next thing, instead of trying to scare him off. But I didn't know, you see. I thought he'd be scared, whatever he was, and leave with his tail smoking. I never once guessed he'd behave as he did."

There was a long silence, no sound but the soft fall of a steady rain on the roof and against the window, all of them thinking hard; and then at last the Teacher spoke again.

"Might could do," she said slowly, "might could be this would be a time for asking advice of the other peoples of this world. It's possible the Gentles would know what to do, or that the Skerrys would. And it's *more* than possible they don't care to see more Earthers on their planet, any more than we do; chances are they think there are far too many of us already."

"The Skerrys did help us the one time before, Responsible," said Charity of Airy slowly. "When those giant crystals were hanging over our cities and we were in danger from the Out-Cabal of the Garnet Ring, it was the Skerrys that helped us. Might could be, as she says, they'd help us again. Them, or the Gentles."

Responsible shook her head. "We won't bother the Gentles," she said flatly. "We've bothered them enough and a whole lot left over. They have our word—we leave them to themselves, and we don't involve them in our problems *nor* our solutions."

"I should hope *not*," said Granny Heatherknit. "Bad enough us running them underground and messing their planet like we did. All in accordance with the treaties, grant us that, but not what they'd of chosen if they'd had their druthers. As for the Skerrys . . ." She stopped and looked at Teacher Josepha. "You ever try to find a Skerry, girl?"

"No, Ma'am, I never have."

"Well, it's just as well, 'cause a more fool activity than that I couldn't specify. Lessen it was looking for one of the Wise Ones, them in the deeps of the oceans and not seen one time lo these many many hundreds of years. The Skerrys would tell us we got our own selves into this and we could get our own selves out. *If* we could find one, which I doubt. No. . . . We've got to handle this all on our own—as, I might point out, is only proper. It appears to be Earth *troub*le, and we're the only Earth stock around."

"Responsible," said Granny Forthright, nodding agreement, "I'll tell you what *I* think—and then you others, you-all can put your oars in if you've a mind to."

"You do that, Granny," Responsible said. "I'd appreciate it."

"I think the only thing you *can* do, seeing as how things are as they are, and seeing as how the man is after all *kin* of a kind . . . I think the only thing you can do is go back and just tell him how it is. Honest and forthright and all in the open. Saying as little of any significance as possible, naturally—no need for him to know any more than what he *has* to know."

"But what do I say to him, Granny?"

"Why, you say the same thing you'd say to one of your relations as came along and stayed at your place with invitation or by-your-leave. You say you've shown him courtesy, you've fed him and given him a bed and seen to his hurts, and you say he's had all the courtesy he's entitled to and you'll thank him to go on home now. And then you tell him it'd be *much* appreciated if he'd just kindly not mention to the rest of the family where it is he found us. Wouldn't hurt to just hint as how if he won't go along with that you might could make him pass the rest of his days as a doorstop at Castle Brightwater, don't you know."

"You think that would work? You think we could trust him, even if he agreed to that?"

The Granny wrinkled up her face. "Responsible," she snapped, "I said I'd give you the benefit of my opinion, and I've done that! Now you're the one as is supposed to know whether what I've said is sense or flumdiddle, and I know you to be Properly Named. What's got into you anyway, girl? All this backing and filling and carry-on!"

"What *do* you think, Responsible?" put in Charity of Airy.

"I think," said Responsible slowly, "it could be Granny's suggestion is less likely to bring down on us whatever has become of the United States Air Force than anything else we might try doing. And I also think that if I'm wrong there's going to be a long hard row to hoe, up ahead."

"Humph," snorted Granny Heatherknit. "And that being so, you thought you'd set things up so as we'd be partly to blame for what you did, eh, Missy?"

"I expect so, Granny," sighed Responsible. "I believe I'm getting old."

"Them as is old," the Granny noted, "they have confidence enough in theirselves not to go looking for skirts to hide behind. It's because you're *young* that you're behaving like one foot was in the coals and the other hanging out the window! Young, and pretty near a virgin. You're not getting old, Responsible, you're barely weaned. And I'll thank you not to try tricking your elders. It's not becoming."

"And it doesn't work."

"There's that."

"Well . . . maybe I ought to go back to Spells and such," said Responsible. "Maybe I might ought to have him put under a Binding Spell, so that he couldn't talk of us even if he chose to. Maybe—"

"Responsible," the Teacher said gently, shaking her head, "you know that's no use. It wouldn't work once he was off Ozark, I'll wager, and I'll wager the Grannys back me in that, don't you?" She waited, and saw them nod, and went on. "I think you'd best try talking to him, as the Granny said. It's been a thousand years, after all. Might could be that Earth has changed. Might could be there are now Terrans that listen to reason, and have come to be a bit above the ravening beasts."

"I don't believe it," said Responsible angrily. "I'll wager my *self* that they're just like they always were! Bent on death and destruction and hurry hurry HURRY let's get all there is and use it up so we'll need more! *I* don't believe there was ever any hope they'd change, and I wasn't even there to *see* them!"

"Child," said Granny Flyswift sensibly, "we'll be no worse off after you talk to him. He'll still be here. We can try something else—not that I see anything else to try, far as that goes. But we'll be no *worse* off. Law, it's not as if he couldn't see for himself how the land lies! And it's something to do, for starters."

"It's a beginning," Responsible admitted.

"Well, then."

"We've seen hard times before," said Charity of Airy. "We'll come through—we always do."

"Thank you, Charity," said Responsible. "We can use the sunshine. But I don't want to go talk to him by myself. To start with, I am nervous about this entire business—I am no diplomat, nor ever was or will be. To go on with, I want a witness there. Somebody I can trust. Somebody that will have gumption enough to report just what happened, when the rumors start to fly. Teacher Josepha, will you go back to Brightwater with me and stand at my side?"

The Teacher steepled her fingers against her lips, and she looked long and hard at Responsible, and then at the others to see how they felt about it.

"That safe for the Teacher, Responsible?" Granny Flyswift interrupted. "You're accustomed to dealing with fancy magic, but she is *not*. And Airy needs her whole and hearty, not damaged by this off-worlder's tricks."

"If he knew any dangerous magic," Responsible said, "don't you reckon he would have fried our eyes as advertised? The temper he's got, Granny, he'd never in this world have been able to resist doing his worst, if he had any worst at his disposal. I don't think there's one thing he could do that the Magician of Rank can't handle easily, or I'd never have asked for the Teacher in the first place."

"One of us Grannys best go, all the same," said Granny Heatherknit. "No sense taking chances, to my mind."

"Granny, I'll go with her," Josepha put in. "Truly, I see no reason she should go alone, and I'm not afraid of any Earth male, be he ever so outlandish and bad-tempered. I'll go be your witness, Responsible, and that most willingly."

"I'm beholden to you, Teacher Josepha."

The older woman stood up smiling, the long sleeves of

her blue habit falling into graceful points as she hid her clasped hands inside them. "I'm more than willing, if you want me there. And I think we'd best get to it. I don't have all that much faith in a Spell of Deception; it may quiet the flesh, but it won't quiet the mind."

The others were not given to dawdling. Now that there was a decision made, they moved as one to bring the meeting to a close and go on about the business of their day. A mannerly scrape of the chair legs on the floor, a rustle of skirts, and they were on their way, wishing Responsible and the Teacher whatever portion of luck they might have coming. Only Charity of Airy stopped to put her arm round Responsible, while the Teacher stood waiting.

"Do the best you can, child," Charity said. "That's all anyone can ask of you—just do your best."

"Not at all, Charity of Airy," Josepha corrected her. "Be *perfect*, the Teaching Stories say. Not 'be as perfect as you can.' "

"Well, *I* can't be perfect!" fussed Responsible. "That's ridiculous."

"Let's go try," said the Teacher calmly. "You never know what you can do until you try. And I will watch, and see that it's all fairly reported, whatever may happen."

"Law," muttered Responsible. "I'd rather do as the Granny first proposed, and have the man turned into a toad after all."

"Now, now," said Teacher Josepha. "Let's maintain our standards, so long as we're able."

The man at Castle Brightwater, released from the spell and clothed in a manner fit for Ozark eyes to view, sat before the two women in a straight-backed chair and listened to what Responsible had to say, nodding every once in a while.

When she'd finished, he considered a moment. And then he said, "Let me just review this, all right? You people—you Ozarkers—claim that you came here from Earth a thousand years ago, more or less. You came here because your ancestors thought Earth was a disgusting mess and wanted nothing more to do with it. And now you'd like me to go back where I came from, knowing what I know now, and not even mention you're here. Despite the fact that this is a major item of news, to say the very least. Despite the way you've treated me. Do I have that straight, Miss Responsible?"

"Mostly," she said.

"What's the 'mostly' for? Did I leave something out?"

"You've not been badly treated, Mister Jones. You've been treated as a guest of this Castle and of this world, and you don't appear to me to have suffered any serious damage."

"Throwing me all over the place in my flyer and making me crash," Coyote observed.

"Really, Mister Jones," answered Responsible, dropping her lashes in a most maidenly way. "I can't be held to account for the weather."

"Turning me into a toad," he went on, firmly.

"Nor can I be held to account for the delusions of little children, as will imagine things, no matter how they're taught."

"Turning me into an old *lady*, and leaving me shut up here for almost two days!"

"While you ate fried fowl and our good cornbread and my mother's best chocolate layer cake and put away enough strong ale to supply a very respectable wedding reception!" she scoffed. "*And* lay here with not a lick to do but think up things to complain about, which is a far cry in a long tunnel from the way a lady of *any* age spends her days and night, Mister Jones! I don't call that bad treatment. I could do with some of that treatment myself, and I'd have better sense than to complain."

She waited, and the Teacher waited, watching him warily, and at last he nodded.

"All right," he said. "I'll go home—provided you'll let me leave without any more of your 'weather.' "

"Done," said Responsible briskly. "Weather like that, it comes along *most* rarely."

"My flyer's repaired, and fit to fly?"

"We aren't vandals, Mister Jones. Certainly it is—anything that broke has been fixed."

"Good enough. And when I get home . . . well, I'll see what I can do. I'll tell my chief that I got lost, and he'll believe that. He doesn't have a high opinion of my competence. But he'll want to know where I got lost *to*, Miss Responsible. And he knows I couldn't have been all this time in the air without refueling. I'll have to tell him something."

"In other words," said Responsible coldly, "you plan to gossip."

"I didn't say that."

"I believe you did."

"You have to understand," said Coyote patient, "I am not anybody in particular—I'm an *employee*. I am obligated to turn in a report. I was on business when your 'weather' brought me down, and I'm not a tourist. I'm required to provide reasonable explanations. Given all that, I'll see what I can do, and that's all that I can say. I'm afraid my hands are pretty thoroughly tied."

"Oh, misery!" Responsible said, tugging at a strand of unruly hair above her left eyebrow. "The man will be back here in a week with an army, and a navy, and a spacefleet, and whatever hellishness the bombs have grown into over these ten centuries! I just know it!"

Something moved over Coyote's face, some expression

that meant something, but it was too fleeting for her to read. And all he said was, "I'll try. I don't think you realize what you're asking, but I'll try. That's all."

"And hearing that," demanded Responsible, "you think we should just say good-bye without further ado?"

He shrugged his shoulders. "That's up to you, isn't it?"

"What is Earth like now, Mister Jones?" the Teacher broke in suddenly. "What has become of it? Before you leave us. . . ."

"It's a giant farm and orchard," he answered. "It was, like you said, pretty much of a mess, almost unfit for any sort of use; but that's over long ago. Now it's an agricultural planet. Nobody lives there except the few human beings it takes to supervise the agrirobots. It's just used to grow things for the rest of the inhabited worlds."

"Dozens," sighed Responsible, "that'd be handy."

"It is."

"And where *is* everybody now? That was on Earth, before?"

"Everybody," Coyote told her solemnly, "is everywhere. All over. All over three galaxies."

"It's mighty hard to believe," said the Teacher, "considering what's in our history archives."

"So are flying mules," Coyote pointed out.

"*Those*," said Responsible "you saw with your own eyes. We've seen nothing of your three galaxies. For all we know, you lie, and Earth remains the pesthole it was, like the pit under a privy badly kept, and you're only the point man for the filth to follow."

"True enough," he said. "I don't have any way to prove anything I say—I don't pretend to. It's up to you to decide."

"And live with the consequences." Responsible's voice was bitter; she stood up, and the Teacher stood up with her. "Go home, then, man," she told him. "Go back where you came from, in your little toy plane. And if you have any decency, say *only* that you've been lost, and keep the rest of what you know to yourself. Claim to have lost your memory, claim you've been bewitched—I don't care. But don't bring the poxes of Earth down on us Ozarkers again, after all we went through to escape them!"

When they were gone, Coyote sat thinking, his mind running through the possibilities. So far, he had accomplished nothing at all. He hadn't found the rogue. He hadn't yet found himself in a situation where he felt it was safe even to *mention* the rogue. He had no idea how much the Ozarkers knew . . . maybe every thought he'd had since contact had been as open to them as if he'd spoken aloud, and they were playing as elaborate a game with him as he was with them. On the other hand, maybe they knew nothing more than what they appeared to know—he had no way of telling.

He longed for Tzana Kai, who had normal telepathic skills, both sending and receiving, as well as being one of the finest agents the TGIS had ever had. She would have been able to get him some real information, some reliable facts . . . but she wasn't here. And he'd been told to take his toys and go home.

He could not possibly leave. He'd barely begun. But he was damned if he knew what to do next. Maybe the ancient wheezing, "Gee, I'm sure sorry, but my flyer won't start" routine? Maybe. He sure as hell had to find *some* way to delay his departure.

CHAPTER FOUR

They were a noble family, and they lay nobly strung; the chfal lapped gently round them, warmed to precisely the body temperature of the eldest in their octave. It should have been a pleasant afternoon, a time for watching the rays of light from the sunslits above them spangle the surface of the chfal, a time for sounding triads at their ease and perhaps sharing the thoughts of the other octaves who were their closest friends and relatives. It was the season of the year when the afternoons were long and lazy, a time traditionally given over to friendship and contemplation and the trying out of new and perhaps audacious harmonies.

But there was little serenity among the octaves now, and little contemplation; the problem of the planet called Ozark made the air thick with the fretting of every citizen old enough to understand the situation. It was discordant. It jangled their nerves, made them uneasy in the pools, and it made them miserable.

DO-323 had been trying for the past two hours just to ignore it, he and his octave together. He had suggested that they do slow scales as a means for achieving a more settled and appropriate state of mind, and they had done them obediently, dozens of them, each member of the octave sounding his or her own note in sequence from DO to DO-prime and back down again. But it hadn't helped at all, and it was DO-323's place to acknowledge the futility of it.

THAT'S ENOUGH, he told them sorrowfully, his mindspeech unpleasantly heavy with minor tones and dragging tempos. WE MIGHT AS WELL GIVE IT UP AND DISCUSS WHAT IS REALLY ON OUR MINDS.

At his side, RE-323 rippled her agreement, and that was signal enough for them all; the vigor with which they joined the discussion set small waves dancing across the chfal pool.

WHAT ARE WE GOING TO DO ABOUT IT?

WHAT *CAN* WE DO ABOUT IT? NOTHING AT ALL, IT SEEMS TO ME!

THERE MUST BE SOMETHING WE CAN DO!

DO-323 understood their distress; but he could not permit the sort of jangled cacophony that they were producing, not in his own pool. He sounded a sharp note of reproof, bringing them to startled order, and the chfal began to settle into stillness around them again.

WHEN THE MAN GOES BACK TO MARS CENTRAL AND REPORTS PLANET OZARK, said RE-323, welcoming the quiet, THE NEXT STEP WILL BE A DELEGATION INVITING OZARK TO JOIN THE TRI-GALACTIC FEDERATION. YOU KNOW THAT, MY DEARS . . . AND WHEN THAT HAPPENS, OZARK WILL BE LOST TO US FOREVER. AND I CANNOT BEAR IT. *SURELY*, HUSBAND, THERE IS SOMETHING THAT WE CAN DO!

The response was strong, and fully concordant; it was everyone's feeling. Their world was crowded even beyond the tolerance of a people accustomed to spending their entire lives lying side by side. So closely were they strung in the square pools, so thickly layered the pools themselves, that not half a dozen families on all Phona had space now for more than a single octave. There had been a time when the family that ran to less than two full octaves was considered odd or unfortunate, and the family that ran to three had not been rare, but no more. They were too many, and Phona too small; they needed room, and there were no directions left to go. The pools could not be built one above the other forever, because of the weight of the chfal; the time came when the last possible layer had been added, and another would have brought the whole structure crashing down upon its inhabitants. The pools could not be built smaller, not if a decent resonance was to be maintained, not if the members of the family were to be properly strung to the frames of the pools. There were limits, and very precise limits, beyond which no further economy was possible.

And there had been hints, lately, from the government, of grotesque measures. Limiting all future families to only seven notes—even limiting them to six! Such ideas were not just unseemly, they approached blasphemy; for most Phonans they were a violation of everything they held sacred. For had they not been put here in this universe for the single purpose of creating ever more extended and elaborate harmonies? If that was not their purpose, then what was life *for*? A repellent philosophy, and an even more repellent theology, were beginning to put out almost imperceptible tendrils. . . .

WE HAVE TO HAVE MORE ROOM!

The units of meaning rode the tones of a great minor chord, and there was no hint of dissenting timbre.

But how was this to be accomplished? Where was the space to be found? For so long as Ozark had gone unnoticed, unaware even of the existence of the Tri-Galactic

Federation, and the Federation equally unaware of Ozark, there had been at least the *possibility* that Phona might take it as a colony world. It was a glorious planet, its population kept absurdly and artificially small, with a wealth of wilderness into which the Phonans could have expanded. There was timber in abundance for building the frames of the pools; there was water in abundance, to which the catalyst that formed chfal could be added to fill the pools. Ozark was an Eden, and the Phonans wanted it desperately, had been trying desperately to find a way out of the ethical barriers to simply grabbing it for their own.

By their law, they could appropriate Ozark under only two conditions: if the planet was in so desperate a state, due to some natural catastrophe such as plague or famine or earthquake, that the move could plausibly be looked upon as an act of mercy; or if the planet was in that state of total discord called anarchy, without government, in which case it would again be only mercy to put an end to the misery. The Ozarkers were so stubbornly competent that the first condition seemed unlikely ever to be met, but they had a hatred of government—any sort of government— that had made the second seem almost inevitable. And only a decade ago there had been a collapse in the primitive government they did allow that had nearly brought Ozark within Phona's grasp. It had been possible to go so far as to set energy crystals humming above each of their major towns and cities and to begin charging them for the final act of conquest. . . .

And then, heartbreaking, it had fallen through at the last minute. That had been a bitter, bitter time—to come so close, and then to fail. In the legislature there had been ingenious pleas for some trivial revisions of the law—perhaps a definition of anarchy was less than such and such a number of governing elements rather than total absence, something of that kind, some way to reshape the taking over of Ozark so that it could be viewed as *for its own good*. It was a matter of considerable pride to the citizens of Phona that these devious attempts to get *around* the law had been confined to only a few radicals and had met with a resounding defeat when put to the vote. But the failure was no less bitter. All that empty land! All that water, left to flow wild! All that *emptiness*, unused!

AND NOW . . . It was SOL-323, the eldest son, who mindspoke. NOW EVEN THE SLIM CHANCE WE HAD BEFORE WILL BE GONE. ONCE OZARK IS WITHIN THE FEDERATION, IT WILL BE BEYOND OUR GRASP FOREVER. ITS GOVERNMENT MAY DISAPPEAR COMPLETELY, ITS POPULATION BE DECIMATED BY ANY SORT OF CATASTROPHE—IT WILL MAKE NO DIFFERENCE.

IT WOULD HAVE BEEN ONE THING, agreed DO-323, TO HAVE PRESENTED THE FEDERATION WITH AN ACCOMPLISHED FACT. OZARK JOINED TO PHONA WITHIN THE GARNET RING, AND THE THING DONE SOMETIME, SOMEHOW, VAGUELY PAST. IT WILL BE QUITE ANOTHER—IT WILL BE IMPOSSIBLE—TO TAKE OVER A PLANET MEMBER OF THE TRI-GALACTIC FEDERATION, WITH ITS OWN DELEGATE TO THE COUNCIL AND ITS OWN STATUS ALREADY REGISTERED ON THE CENTRAL COMPUTERS.

THEN WE MUST SEIZE THE PLANET *BEFORE* IT JOINS THE FEDERATION, put in DO-prime-323, the youngest and thus perhaps not to blame for the nonsense he proposed.

IT'S TOO LATE, SON, said DO-323 gravely. FAR TOO LATE. THE MAN HAS ALREADY SEEN THE PLANET. HE ALREADY KNOWS THAT IT IS NOT PART OF THE GARNET RING, BUT AN INDEPENDENT ENTITY. THE OPPORTUNITY IS LOST TO US.

WELL, THEN, said DO-prime-323, WE MUST CAP-TURE THIS MAN BEFORE HE CAN MAKE A REPORT.

There were bubbles of amusement in the chfal pool, then; the child was outrageous, but he was also endearing.

YOU THINK, asked his father indulgently, THAT THE TRI-GALACTIC FEDERATION WOULD NOT NOTICE IF AN AGENT OF ITS INTELLIGENCE SERVICE JUST DISAPPEARED? AND PERHAPS YOU THINK THE TGF WOULD NOT IMMEDIATELY SEND OUT OTHER AGENTS TO INVESTIGATE?

AND HERE WE'D BE, said RE-323, completing the figure, HOLDING THE MAN HOSTAGE FOR ALL THE WORLDS TO SEE. FLATTED SECONDS, SON! WE WOULD HAVE A SQUADRON OF FEDROBOTS HERE ON PHONA WITH FULL BATTLE GEAR BEFORE WE COULD RUN A SCALE!

OH, said the child plaintively. I DIDN'T THINK OF ALL THAT.

NEVER MIND, put in FA-323; she loved her little brother dearly and hated to see him distressed. THERE WERE GROWN MALES IN THE LEGISLATURE NOT SO AWFULLY LONG AGO WHO HAD IDEAS NO BETTER THAN THAT ONE. DO-PRIME! YOU ARE TOO YOUNG TO REMEMBER, BUT *I* REMEMBER.

A thought, a mere rage of a thought, floated through the pool. . . . It was some other octave, one strange to them, exquisitely polite in its attempt to join this discussion sending nothing but a semantic marker, empty of all other content, easily rejected if the 323's did not wish to communicate further.

WELCOME, AND MAY YOU BE ALWAYS IN PER-FECT TEMPER, said DO-323 graciously. He was in a good humor at his youngest son's charming innocence, and willing for the moment to be a bit liberal.

THANK YOU, came the thought, formed now. IT IS
THE DOUBLE OCTAVE 43 THAT SPEAKS.

There was a stunned silence, while everyone adjusted
to this news. A double octave! And 43—one of the oldest
and most distinguished of all Phonana families. Joining in
the idle talk of the 323's!

UH. . . . DO-323 struggled to regain his equilibrium.
PLEASE CONTINUE, he managed.

WE HAVE GIVEN THIS A GOOD DEAL OF
THOUGHT, came the message, bracketed now with the
pansensory mindsignature of DO-43 himself. AND IT
SEEMS TO US THAT IT MIGHT BE WORTH OUR
WHILE TO ATTEMPT TO AT LEAST GAIN A LITTLE
TIME. IF, SAY, SOME OZARKER WERE TO DETAIN
THE TGIS MAN, WHILE WE ON PHONA CONSIDER
THE MATTER TOGETHER. PERHAPS IN THIS MO-
MENT OF URGENT CRISIS, IF WE SET ALL ELSE
ASIDE AND LEND ALL OUR MINDS TO THE PROB-
LEM, AN IDEA WILL OCCUR TO US FOR SALVAG-
ING THIS TERRIBLE SITUATION. AND THERE IS,'
AFTER ALL, NOTHING TO *LOSE*.

No one said anything; no one dared. And the double
octave 43 knew that, and moved at once to fill the embar-
rassing silence.

WE HAVE A PLAN, said DO-43. IF WE MIGHT
HAVE THE FULL ATTENTION OF ALL THE OC-
TAVES . . .

The Phonans were too desperate to stand on ceremony
now; every octave dropped its privacy brackets instantly
and without any demand for the usual preliminary courte-
sies, and lay tight strung and waiting for the proposal of
the double octave 43. If only it could be something permissible within Phonan ethics, and not some barbarism
that would have to be immediately rejected! (The rejec-

tion to come from one of the other double octaves, of course, and at the uppermost levels of society.)

And if only it could be clear-cut, and not an impossible ethical tangle! Every adult Phonan remembered only too well the wrangling that had gone on when Ozark had faced famine and devastation ten years ago. There had been one group passionately given over to the hypothesis that now Ozark *did* meet the law's criteria for legal annexation as a colony. There had been another, equally passionate, to declare that Phona had *no* rights in the matter, because it had been Phona's intrusion into Ozark's internal affairs that had aggravated an already difficult situation and caused it to escalate to disaster. There had been those who actually insisted that it was Phona's duty to report Ozark's existence and its plight to the Tri-Galactic Federation so that assistance could be given by a neutral party.

And there had been endless and bitter debate, division even *within* octaves, until agreement had at last been reached: justice demanded that the Ozarkers be given a reasonable period of time to recover, and only when it became clear that they could *not* recover would Phona be legally justified in taking over. And then the cursed Ozarkers had defied all logic by managing perfectly well, setting their affairs and their planet to rights in an impossibly short time! In some ways, that had been an even more bitter pill to swallow than the first one.

They listened, hoping against hope, to the double octave 43.

On Ozark, the yellow cat minced across the floor of the stable at Castle Brightwater, leaped onto the door of the Mule's stall, and settled itself there with its tail lashing softly against the wood. Inside the stall, Sterling snorted her disgust—the *Mule's* disgust—and turned her rump smartly to the little animal, muscles flickering, ready for the swift kick. Instantly, the cat blurred and changed. A pretty little red snake with blue jewel eyes took its place and flowed up the square post of the stall gate, winding round it.

YOU ARE BAD-TEMPERED, MULE! It observed.

BETTER THAT THAN A TRESPASSER SUCH AS YOU, Sterling answered with contempt.

HAH! BETTER A TRESPASSER THAN A BEAST OF BURDEN FOR HUMANS!

THE MULE IS A SCIENTIST, came the steady answer, AND THE MULE CHOOSES TO OBSERVE.

WHAT CAN YOU LEARN, LIVING AS YOU DO? CARRYING HUMANS ON YOUR BACK! CARRYING THEIR BUNDLES, LIVING IN A BARN . . . HAVING YOUR TAIL BRAIDED AND YOUR EARS DECORATED. . . . IT MAKES ME SICK! WHAT CAN YOU LEARN, LIVING LIKE THAT?

MORE THAN *YOU* CAN LEARN, DEPENDING ON THE PICKLES.

PICKLES? The small snake's emerald tongue quivered in the air. WHAT IS A PICKLE?

The Mule made a rumbling noise deep in her throat.

YOU SEE, she gloated. YOU DO NOT EVEN KNOW THAT THE OZARKERS CALL YOUR SPY SENSORS 'PICKLES'! AND YOU PRESUME TO CRITICIZE THE MULE!

WHAT DOES IT MEAN. . . . 'PICKLE'?

The minutes went by, and the snake turned an ugly brown with the humiliation of it, but the Mule would not give in, and at last the snake could bear it no longer.

PLEASE. It mindspoke almost in a whisper, squirming at the shame of the word. WHAT DOES THE WORD 'PICKLE' MEAN? BE MAGNANIMOUS, MULE! YOU ARE NEARER TO US BY FAR THAN YOU ARE TO THE HUMANS!

IT MEANS, said Sterling, NOW THAT YOU'VE ASKED PROPERLY. . . .

WELL? urged the snake, and Sterling grinned the Mule's terrible toothy grin.

ANCIENTLY, IT MEANT A FOOD PRESERVED IN BRINE. BUT THE OZARKERS HAVE FORGOTTEN THAT. THEY THINK IT IS THE NAME OF A LITTLE PEST OF A CREATURE LIKE ANY OTHER SUCH PEST. LIKE A FLEA, FOR EXAMPLE.

I SEE.

YOU MIGHT THANK THE MULE, Sterling noted. IT IS A BIT UNUSUAL NOT TO KNOW EVEN WHAT YOU ARE CALLED BY THOSE YOU SPY UPON.

SPY UPON! The snake spat venom, not caring that the Mule was immune. WHEN *YOU* GATHER INFORMATION, IT IS CALLED *SCIENCE*—WHEN *WE* DO THE SAME, IT IS CALLED *SPYING*! A CURIOUS SYSTEM, MULE!

AH, BUT THE TWO ARE QUITE DIFFERENT, Sterling said serenely. THE MULE HAS BEEN *INVITED*. YOU, ON THE OTHER HAND, MUST SNEAK ABOUT, BEING A CAT ONE MINUTE, A SNAKE THE NEXT, A FISH FIVE MINUTES LATER. *YOU* ARE AN INTRUDER. THE MULE IS AN HONORED COMPANION.

There was nothing to be said to this, and the snake, well aware of it, simply sulked.

SOMETHING IS HAPPENING IN THE GARNET RING, it said firmly.

SOMETHING IS ALWAYS HAPPENING IN THE GARNET RING; IF NOTHING IS HAPPENING OF ITSELF, SOMETHING IS INVENTED.

SOON IT MAY BE NECESSARY TO CALL THE RESPONSIBLE AND GIVE HER ANOTHER MESSAGE

GIVE IT YOURSELF, said Sterling. DO NOT BOTHER THE MULE. THE MULE IS BUSY.

YOU KNOW PERFECTLY WELL, CURSE YOU, THAT THE HUMANS CANNOT UNDERSTAND OUR MINDSPEECH!

The Mule whuffled, vastly amused.

PERHAPS THE MULE WILL CONSIDER DELIVERING YOUR MESSAGE, she said, AND THEN AGAIN PERHAPS THE MULE WILL *NOT*.

The snake went back to its sulking.

CHAPTER FIVE

"I can only tell you that the man must have lost his senses," said the Magician uncomfortably. He was accustomed to dealing with the citizens of his own town of Blue Ear, and always managed to maintain in those dealings the air of dignity proper to his calling. But he had never before had to try to maintain it against the icy sustained distaste of a Magician of Rank, such as sat before him now. Veritas Truebreed Motley the 4th was no housewife with a complaint about the way her vegetables were slow to come up or a need for a spell to turn a lump in her breast back to hale and hearty flesh. Magician Stewart Sheridan Brightwater the 9th quailed before him, in spite of his determination not to do so, and a good hour spent describing to his wife the manner in which he intended not to do so.

"Well, how," demanded Veritas, "have things come to such a pass in your town that a man there can go mad and you never so much as suspect it till he's berserk and has wreaked bloody havoc about the countryside?"

"It was just *one thing*," muttered Stewart Sheridan,

staring at his shoes. "It wasn't bloody havoc about the countryside."

Veritas fixed the other man with an iron glance, and said, "When 'just one thing' is smashing in the skull of the first off-worlder to appear on Ozark in a thousand years, Stewart Sheridan Brightwater, it is a very *large* 'just one thing'!"

"I am truly sorry," said the Magician doggedly. "I am sorrier than I can even begin to tell you. This isn't pleasant for me either. But there it is. It's been done, Veritas Truebreed, and it can't be undone."

Veritas grabbed his chin with his hand and twisted his mouth around in a way that Stewart Sheridan could hardly bear to look at; it meant he was thinking, no doubt, but it wasn't a nice sight.

"Tell me again," he said abruptly. "Everything that happened."

"I've told you—"

"Tell me again!"

"Well. . . . right after breakfast this morning, maybe a little after that, this off-worlder came down to my barn, where Miss Responsible had his flyin' machine stored. Like I told you already, Veritas. And he had me give him a hand pulling it out to look it over and be certain it was fit to fly. And while we were doin' that, along came Lucas McDaniels Brightwater the 23rd, that I've known since he was no bigger than a minute, and all his kin as well, and every one of 'em as sane as you or me, and blessed if he didn't just up and take a rock the size of a bucket and smack this Jones person over the head with it and knock him clean out. And I had Jones brought up here to the Castle and turned over to you, and that is all I know. Except of course for Lucas McDaniels, who is this minute sitting in my front room under a Binding Spell, and is not going anywhere atall, you have my word on it."

"And you didn't try to treat Jones' injuries?"

"I should say I did not! What do I know about the way an off-worlder is put together?" The Magician was almost angry enough to have his dignity back.

"He's of Earth," said Veritas sharply, "the same as you are!"

"So you say. But it's been many and many a century since he and I were of the same ecosystem, and no way to know what changes may have come about inside Terrans in all this time! Tampering with Mister Jones is a task for a Magician of Rank, as well you know, and if I'd tried it myself you'd be putting a Binding Spell on me this minute, Veritas. I may be only a Magician, but I am not stupid."

"That's open to dispute," snapped the Magician of Rank.

"If you've nothing in mind but abusing me, Veritas, I'll be on my way." The Magician of Blue Ear clasped his hands behind his back and straightened his shoulders. "I've seen bad manners before. No need for you to give me new examples."

"You talk a good line, Magician," said Veritas.

"I know my place," said Stewart Sheridan calmly. "And I know my worth. Blue Ear is run quiet and decent and efficient—nobody has any complaints that I can't clear up in a minute or two. And you may come at me with all the hifalutin' airs you choose to put on, but you don't change that. And it is *not* my place to deal with this, however much you insult me."

Veritas glared at him awhile, but Stewart Sheridan stood his ground, and finally the Magician of Rank nodded.

"Quite right, of course," he said coldly. "And you'd best be getting back to the tasks you do so well, and let me get on with this."

"Happy to," said Stewart Sheridan, and he turned his back on the Magician of Rank without another word. He'd

have a few things to say at the hotel that night, when the
mugs of ale went round, about Magicians of Rank who
thought they were *divine*, for all that they were of woman
born like any other man whether they remembered it or
not.

He'd gone no more than ten paces when the Magician
of Rank said, "Just a minute, please," however. Stewart
Sheridan stopped and turned around, taking his time about
it, his resentment sustaining him.

"What is it?"

"What I want you to do, Stewart Sheridan, is go back
and get our demented friend out of your front room and
bring him up here to the Castle. As quickly as possible,
please. I want to hear what he has to say for himself."

"Oh, fine," said the Magician. "*I've* got nothing else to
do today but traipse up and down the roads hauling people."

"Good. Then it won't take you long."

The Magician threw up his hands to indicate his anger,
shrugged his shoulders to indicate his helplessness, and
headed straight for home and Lucas McDaniels Brightwater
the 23rd.

An hour later, plus five minutes, they were all in the
small bedroom where Coyote had once again taken up
residence in the bed with the wonderful pillows. And he
was staring, and listening, in total astonishment, as Lucas
McDaniels told a tale that he unquestionably believed to
be the truth.

It seemed that Coyote Jones had gone into the man's
garden . . .

"—that is all I have pretty near, to feed me and my wife
and our child through this season, what with the way
there's no market this year for anything I know how to
sell. And this—this *off*-worlder—he destroyed my garden!
I tell you he destroyed it utterly! Up one row and down

the other, rampaging through the potatoes and the corn, ripping through the tomatoes and the bellpeppers, charging through the jebroot and the squash . . . I tell you, you have never *seen* such complete devastation! Why, it looks like . . . it looks like . . ." He stopped and swallowed hard and shook himself a little, as if he'd been lost in the contemplation of the awful spectacle. "I can't *tell* you what it looks like," he said, more quietly. "Words fail me— you'd have to see it for yourself to appreciate it. But I can tell you this—there is *nothing* left of my garden. Nothing! Nothing even in good enough shape after this offworlder's rampage so as it might be put *by*. It's gone. All of it. Gone! And no reason, no reason atall—I've never harmed the man! I've never laid eyes on him before this day, that he'd want to destroy my garden and take the food from my child's mouth as *he has done*."

"And when you saw this—" Veritas began.

"Devastation!"

"—when you saw this devastation, you lost your temper."

"Veritas Truebreed, that doesn't even begin to describe it! What I lost was my *mind*, as isn't all that strong these days anyway, what with the sales in my store as near no sales at all. I lost my entire *mind*."

"And you picked up a rock and went down to Stewart Sheridan's here and smashed Mister Jones over the head with it, rendering him unconscious," Veritas summed up.

"Knocked him cold. I sure did," agreed Lucas. "And I'm sorry for it. It was an unbecoming way to behave. But for a minute there, I tell you I was not myself atall. All I could think of was all the work put in, and all the vegetables that were doing *so* fine, and that—person—tearing it all to hell in five minutes flat. For *no* reason!"

"Well, well, well," Veritas intoned. He made a solemn long-drawn-out invocation of it, and he stared fiercely at the Magician of Blue Ear. "That puts a slightly different

light on the matter. Why didn't you tell me this, Stewart
Sheridan Brightwater?"

"He didn't bother to tell *me*, that's why!" said the
Magician, tight-lipped and furious, and itching to get Lucas alone and tell him precisely how he felt about idiots
that had no more decency and no more sense than to
make their Magician look like a damn fool.

As for Coyote, he lay there and marveled. He'd done
nothing of the kind, gone nowhere near anybody's garden—
much less destroyed it. He'd gone straight from his session with Responsible of Brightwater and the Teacher to
the place where his flyer was being kept for him. But
Lucas was unquestionably telling the truth as he knew the
truth. He had *seen* Coyote tear up his food supply, with
his own eyes, and he was only telling them the FACTS.

Which could only mean one thing: somebody had stepped
in and stirred the pot a little. But who? That Responsible
female? It was possible; maybe she'd decided she didn't
care to trust him to decide for himself about keeping the
Ozarkers a secret from the Federation, which would have
been very good sense on her part. But surely she was
smart enough to realize that if he didn't come back fairly
promptly there'd be others sent to find out what had
happened to him. She'd impressed him as far too smart for
a shenanigan like this . . . On the other hand, if the
telepathic illusion that had so upset Lucas had not been
ordered up by Responsible of Brightwater, then who *had*
arranged it? And for what purpose?

"I don't condone this," Veritas was saying sternly. "I
want you to know that. We do *not* settle our differences
by violence in *this* kingdom, Lucas!"

"Yes, sir. I know that."

"I'm shocked. I don't mind saying that I am *shocked*."

"Yes, sir," said the man again. "I expect you are. I'm
pretty shocked myself."

"But this is a new and unique situation," the Magician of Rank went on, "and I can understand that you might not have known precisely what to do about it."

"That I didn't. For sure I didn't."

Veritas rubbed his chin, and looked over at Coyote, who looked blandly back at him. "Mister Jones," he asked, "do you have anything to say for yourself?"

Coyote thought fast. He didn't think this planet was likely to be one of those places that chopped off your arm at the wrist for minor offenses. And he was curious.

"I don't remember a thing," he said firmly. "Not a thing. It may be that I'll remember later, after the effects of that rock on my skull have worn off. But right now? I do not remember."

"Could you have done what he says you did?"

"*Somebody* did," put in the Magician of Blue Ear. "I went and made sure of that, before I brought him up here. Just as soon as he'd told me all this, that he ought to have told me in the *first* place. Devastation *is* the proper word for his garden."

Coyote put a hand to the back of his head, wincing elaborately as he touched the wound, and said, "Perhaps I could have. I've been under a great deal of strain lately, what with the decidedly unorthodox welcome I got at the hands of you people. Perhaps my mind snapped, temporarily. Perhaps it was too much sun. I just can't remember."

He was alert, and he was fully prepared to remember beyond any question that he had done nothing at all, in case things began to get rocky. But he needn't have worried. Veritas Truebreed Motley pursed his lips and rubbed his hands together, looked at each one of them in turn as if he couldn't stand the sight of them, and made his announcement.

"One week house arrest for the off-worlder," he declared, "Here at the Castle. And restitution—the full value of the foodstuffs destroyed. And that will be sufficient." And to Lucas McDaniels, "As for you, you'll go talk to the Reverend about your temper, and I rather expect that when he turns you loose you will feel suitably chastised. *This* time! If anything like this happens again, you won't get off so easily, I promise you."

"Anything like this ever happen before?" demanded Lucas belligerently. "*Ever* before?"

"No," said Veritas, "you've been a sane and a sober man, of even temper. I have taken that into consideration in deciding the penalty."

"And that's *it*?" Coyote asked, amazed. . . . it was, after all, the year 3021, not some year back in the Old West of Old Earth! This episode lacked only a noose in the Magician of Rank's hand and a silver star on his chest.

Veritas's eyebrows rose.

"You want something more?"

"Well . . . No trial? No jury? No judge, no lawyers? Isn't this a little abrupt?"

Veritas looked at him with disgust. "You may have all those things if you like," he replied evenly. "You certainly may. That is your right. And it will take about three months to carry it all out, while you wait. Is that your preference, Mister Jones?"

Hastily, Coyote shook his head. "No speedy justice on Planet Ozark, eh?" he said.

"I have *offered* you speedy justice," said Veritas, "and am fully empowered to do so. And you have complained, and have suggested a procedure that would be twelve times less speedy. I am not impressed with your rational processes, Mister Jones of Earth."

"Sorry," Coyote corrected him. "*Not* of Earth. Nobody at all is 'of Earth' anymore—nobody has been for centuries."

"Ah, yes," Veritas said. "My apologies. Mister Jones of

Wherever You Come From, then. You are Earth *stock*, certainly."

"Right. I am."

"Well? Which would you rather have? A week shut up here at the Castle, with the ladies for company wearing your ears off, or a three-month folderol with judges and lawyers and juries and all suitable pomp and circumstances?"

And Coyote realized that this was perfect. There'd be no need for the "my flyer won't start" scene after all, no need to come up with ever more new and devious alleged mechanical failures to stand up against Ozark's inevitable "magic" repair efforts. He was going to be handed his spying time on a platter here, if he didn't ruin it all by malignant stupidity.

"I'll take the week," he said promptly. He could learn a lot in a week.

"And the fine," Veritas reminded him.

"Of course. Happy to take care of it. Don't know what could have come over me, tearing up a garden like that . . . if I did tear up a garden."

"Are you *sure* you don't want the trial and the jury and so on?" Veritas demanded, with a fierce eye, and a finger pointed rudely right in his face.

"Absolutely," Coyote assured him. "I was just surprised there for a minute."

"Last chance, now!"

"Absolutely! I'll take it. The week and the fine. Thank you very much."

"And you, Lucas McDaniels?" asked Veritas, turning to look at the damaged party. "You're satisfied with the arrangements? Stewart Sheridan, you're satisfied?"

They nodded, and he nodded, and Coyote nodded. Nods all round.

The Magician of Blue Ear cleared his throat politely, a small gap in the proceedings having at last presented itself, and assumed a look of significance. He was about to speak as well, but Veritas stopped him, whipping out a sheet of pliofilm and a stylus and making a series of rapid expansive flourishes over the pliofilm's surface.

"There you are," he said. "All set down, dates and times and amounts, whatnot. Sign here . . . You, Lucas McDaniels, sign here . . . You, Stewart Sheridan, as official Magician, sign here . . . Good enough, all done, excuse me, gentlemen!" And he rolled up the pliofilm, tucked it away again in his pouch, and was gone.

The others looked after him, and at each other, and felt a little awkward. To put an end to it, Coyote asked for some basic items of explanation. Such as the terms of the house arrest. And how much, exactly, fifty dollars—the sum specified—came to in Federation credits. And how fast he had to produce the money.

The house arrest part was easy enough; he just wasn't to go out of the doors of the Castle for one week, and then he was free. And during the week he could go anywhere he liked inside the Castle, so long as he bothered nobody and respected the decencies. But the penalty sum was not so simply settled.

"What good would it do me," demanded Lucas McDaniels plaintively after they'd worked out the arithmetic involved, "to have your fourteen and a half 'credits'? I can't buy anything on this world with 'credits,' and I don't fancy crossing space to fetch my groceries."

Coyote and the Magician could see his point, and Coyote offered to give the man some of his personal possessions instead of credits—and was turned down again, since that wouldn't buy groceries either—and at last the Magician went in search of Veritas Truebreed once again. He brought him back promptly, but he wasn't a happy Magician of Rank.

"This is turning into a _serious_ inconvenience!" Veritas

was protesting as he came through the door. "I do not appreciate it, and I shall keep in mind precisely who is responsible. Can't you people do anything for yourselves?"

Coyote was just opening his mouth to explain the problem when the Magician of Rank raised his two hands before him, made a half dozen swift gestures in the air—producing a double-shafted golden arrow that stretched from palm to palm—and there was a soft hiss as the arrow disappeared. And there on the table beside Coyote, where he'd counted them out during the previous discussion, were the Federation credits. Except that now they were crisp new dollars. Fifty of them.

"Well, I'll be stir-fried!" breathed Coyote. "Now how did you *do* that, Veritas Truebreed?" *This*, if it was not just very expert sleight-of-hand, was something the Federation needed to know a lot more about.

The Magician of Rank raised his eyebrows again, and sniffed sharply. "I did it by the exercise of Hifalutin Magic, of course," he snapped. "Which is my profession—as should be more than obvious, Mister Jones. And now I am leaving; do *not* trouble me further with this nonsense."

Coyote reached for the dollars, but Lucas McDaniels Brightwater the 23rd was faster than he was; he had them swooped up and into his shirt pocket before Coyote could even explain that all he'd wanted to do was *look* at them.

"That'll be all now, Lucas McDaniels," said the Magician. "You go on back home, and clean yourself up till you're fit for the church, and then you get on over and talk to the Reverend and let's see the end of all this."

"I'm ready," said Lucas. "I surely am ready."

"Well, go on, then; what's keeping you?"

The man bobbed his head at them politely, and left, with Coyote thinking mournfully that there went his chance to examine the dollars. And that was a shame, because how was he, on house arrest at the Castle, going to get

Lucas McDaniels to bring them back and let him have a
chance at them?

"Mister Jones?"

Coyote jumped, and came guiltily out of his fog of
concentration. "Mmm?" he mumbled.

"If you're through lollygagging there, Mister Jones, I'd
like to see you down to the first floor and explain all this to
the women so as I can go on home my*self*. I've lost half a
day to this benighted mess, and I'll be three days catching
up, and if *that's* not a mystery I'll turn you in my belly
button. How is it that being gone half a day always and
forever means you're three days behind, I ask you?"

Coyote admitted that he didn't know.

"No, I'm sure you don't, and nobody does. Now come
along, and bring your stuff . . . whatever you've got left,
after paying fifty dollars for ten dollars' worth of sorry
vegetables, if you ask *me*, but then you had plenty of
chance to speak up for yourself if you were a mind to, and
you said nary a word . . . and let's *do* this! Time's a-wasting,
Mister Jones!"

Coyote grabbed at his satchel, that being all he'd had
with him when he woke up here in this mad place again,
and he stood up to follow the Magician.

"Lead on," he said solemnly. "Whither thou goest, and
all that."

"What?" The other man stopped short and stared at
him.

"Just babbling," Coyote said reassuringly. "Just part of a
bit from the old King James Bible, Twentieth century of
Old Earth. That period is a kind of hobby of mine." And a
very good thing, too, he thought, because otherwise he'd
have had the devil's own time understanding Ozark
Panglish.

The Magician stood there, dead still as if poleaxed, and
Coyote's heart sank. No doubt "the Bible" was a taboo

phrase here or some such thing. He was wondering how many weeks of house arrest he'd do now when Stewart Sheridan reached over and took hold of him with both hands, just above the elbows, and he realized that the man was shaking.

"The Bible!" he said, and Coyote recognized the intonation. It wasn't anger; it was awe.

"Yes," said Coyote carefully. "The Bible."

"Mister Jones, do you *have* a Bible?"

"Well, not *with* me. But I could get one. Would you like to have one?"

The Magician was pale with emotion, and there were beads of sweat on his upper lip. "Oh, yes," he said, nearly whispering the words. "Oh, yes!"

"I'll get one to you," Coyote said. It seemed safe to move now, and he backed away gently, disengaging his arms as unobtrusively as possible.

"You could really *do that*?"

"I'll find a way," said Coyote expansively, although he had not the faintest notion how he would keep his promise. Planet Ozark was definitely not on anybody's mail route. But he was surprised; he could have sworn that the Ozark mountain people of Old Earth had been staunch Christians. Why didn't they have the Bible?

"Say, Lucas," he hazarded. "You *do* have a Bible of your own, don't you? Or access to one, at least? I mean . . . not the King James, probably, after all this time . . . but an Ozark Bible?"

"No. No, I don't. We don't. We lost it."

"Lost it? Lost the whole Bible? But—"

The Magician of Blue Ear mopped his brow with the back of his hand and sighed; he was a sorry sight, and twitching all over.

"Mister Jones," he interrupted, "I'm sorry, I can't explain it to you now. I really can't. I don't even know if it would be allowed. And I really do have to get on back and do my work. But I want you to know that if you could actually lay your hands on a Bible for me . . . well! Now that would be a wonder, Mister Jones! I surely would be grateful to you."

"All right," said Coyote. "Consider it done."

"And one more thing."

"What's that?"

"I'd consider it a favor if you'd let this be our secret. Yours and mine."

"Sure," Coyote said, watching the man carefully. "Why not?"

Stewart Sheridan grabbed his hand and began pumping it vigorously, and Coyote, who had come across the hand-shaking custom before, did his best to return the gesture with equal enthusiasm.

"Your word on it?" asked the Magician, double-checking.

"Well, sure," said Coyote. "You have my word."

"Fine!" said the man, beaming now, and opened the door to usher Coyote out. And all the way down the stairs he gave little hops and bounces of delight, and from time to time poked Coyote conspiratorially in the ribs, and generally behaved like an idiot.

Coyote was fascinated. He wouldn't have missed all this for anything.

CHAPTER SIX

The Fish was outraged. He told his gloomy agent about it from various points of view and in various tempos, while Coyote sat back and let him exhaust himself. First principle for dealing with furious administrators, on any planet whatsoever: let them exhaust themselves. And eventually it wound down, ending with a flat declaration that the Fish was *shocked*.

"*Shocked*, Mister Jones!"

"Well," Coyote said comfortingly, "you're old and mean—you'll live through it."

"How *could* you just take it upon yourself . . . entirely without authorization . . . how, on your own authority and without even an advisory directive . . . how could . . ."

Coyote sat up straight and paid attention. It hadn't been his intention to actually drive the poor old thing into babbling dementia.

"Hold on!" he said. "I think that's enough, now."

"How *could*—"

"I SAID, HOLD ON!"

Coyote said it at the top of his lungs, and he projected it

at the top of his mind, simultaneously, and it achieved silence. A *pregnant* silence, but silence nevertheless.

"Now," said Coyote, in the humming quiet. "Now, *I* would like to say a few words." He waited, ready to add more juice if necessary, but the Fish only sat there making funny mouths at him, and he decided it was safe to continue.

"I understand," he said, "that I was sent out to that planet to do a job, and that I haven't done it. I understand that it still has to be done, and that I've managed to double the cost of the mission. I understand that that's an intolerable burden on the taxpayers of the Federation and an inexcusable piece of work on my part. And once all that's understood, we can go on to the fact that there was nothing else that I could do and that's why I did what I did."

"I don't see it," said the Fish, watching Coyote warily.

"What's not to see?"

"You found the planet, you landed on it, you found the rogue telepath—who turns out to be a rather unimpressive and bad-tempered woman in her twenties, if I hear you correctly—and you just turned around and came back without her. I don't *see* it, Mister Jones!"

"That's partly right," Coyote told him. "All but the part about the rogue, Fish. All but the *important* part."

"If you'd come back when you ran into that turbulence as you were trying to land, I would have understood—that would have been entirely correct. You had no business landing under those circumstances. But once you'd done it, and once you'd seen what the situation was . . . What's the matter, Jones, did you simply lose your nerve?"

Coyote sighed, and leaned back again in the miserable chair. He was going to be here awhile yet. As was often the case, the Fish had not heard a single word he'd said; he'd heard something else, concocted in his own mind and filtered through his own preconceptions. Coyote got up from the chair and sat down on the edge of the Fish's desk, ignoring the way it creaked beneath him on its silly skinny legs, and he leaned over toward his chief and told him one more time.

"Fish," he said, "listen to me. I'm *talk*ing. This is a planet that's been sitting there all by itself, undetected, for many thousands of years. This is a planet settled by a dozen or so families out of the Ozark Mountains of Old Earth, if its inhabitants are to be believed. This is a planet managed by old ladies called 'Grannys' and a handful of men that call themselves Magicians. This is a planet that was settled at the tail end of the twentieth century, give or take a decade or so, but it is the most ridiculous amalgamation of advanced technology and primitive claptrap that you ever saw in your life. This is a planet with as advanced a system of communication as anyone could ask for— whatever else they left behind, they sure as hell took their *comsets* along—and this is at the same time a planet with flying *mules*. It's got *king*doms, Fish, and it's got castles— but it's got no royalty and damn near no government. The whole planet runs, they tell me, on *magic*. And Fish, I have never been so bewildered by anything as I am by Planet Ozark. Not ever."

The Fish glared at him, and Coyote resisted the urge to give him a brisk shaking. He settled for more brisk talk.

"I didn't dare make another move, of *any* kind," he said, "without checking it with the TGIS first. And Fish— Planet Ozark is not on the Communipath Network, remember? I could have gone somewhere else, and had a Communipath contact you for me, sure—but there wasn't any place enough closer than Mars Central to make it worth doing that way. You couldn't have done it any more cheaply if you'd been there yourself."

"All right!" The Fish put both hands flat on the desk in front of him and stuck his chin out belligerently. "All right! You needed instructions; I can see that. But why didn't you bring back the rogue?"

Coyote stared at him. The man was even more bewildered than *he* was.

"Fish," he said, "you aren't hearing me. I'm handicapped. Remember? I'm *mind-deaf*. How would I *know* if she was the rogue? I asked some discreet questions, sure. And according to the people of Planet Ozark, no woman *has* mindspeech. Furthermore, there's no such thing as psience. No telekinesis. No precognition. No clairvoyance. Damn little telepathy. Only the top dog Magicians, the ones they call Magicians of Rank, have any telepathy at all, according to the Ozarkers, and I'm not sure they really approve of even that. There is *magic*—period. The reason you chose me for this junket was because I'm mind-deaf, meaning I can't check any of that for accuracy. If Responsible of Brightwater is the lady doing the telepathic jim-jams on the Communipath Network, hell, *I* can't hear her!"

Toward the end of this speech, the Fish had begun nodding a little, slowly; with any luck, that meant Coyote had finally gotten through to him.

"Could it be the Magicians of Rank, then?" he asked. "The ones the Ozarkers claim *do* have mindspeech?"

"Not as it's described to me," Coyote answered patiently. "If the Ozarkers were telling me the truth, the Magicians of Rank could only have very primitive and undeveloped psibilities—nothing like what alerted the Communipaths. But I had no way—*no* way, Fish—to check any of that out. I can report what they said to me, that's all."

"Is it possible that you just misunderstood a lot of the details because their speech is so different from ours?"

"I don't think so," Coyote said. "They're so determined to maintain their ancient culture, Fish—they resist change *very* systematically. The kids get vast quantities of their language input, from birth, watching copies of videotapes from the late twentieth century and very early twenty-first. Especially some little old lady they call First Granny, telling stories in Old Earth English. Naturally that hasn't stopped language change completely, but it's held it back to an amazing degree. Enough that the twentieth century English that *I* know is not really all that different."

The Fish muttered something unintelligible, but Coyote knew what he had to be saying, and he agreed with it. "I know," he said. "I know it's improbable. But they *work* at maintaining their old speech forms. The kids have to recite the stories and stuff *along with* the old ladies on the tapes, matching them sound for sound and breath for breath. It isn't left to chance. I admit that a major communication gap exists, you bet—but it's not due to the language itself."

The Fish muttered some more about strained coincidences, and Coyote shrugged and agreed some more.

"Blind luck," he said. "I could just as well have had twenty-*eighth*-century ballads as my cover all these years instead of twentieth-century ones. Or crop rotation. And I wouldn't have understood a word they said. I would have had to come back for a historical linguist. But there it is, Fish . . . I just have to talk slowly and listen hard, and they do the same. We get by."

"And they claim that everything is done by magic."

"That's what they say."

"But that's ridiculous, too."

"Maybe."

"Oh, nonsense. You're a social disaster, but you are a man of considerable sophistication! Don't put on your bumpkin act with me, Mister Jones; it won't work."

"For my money," Coyote told him, "their so-called

magic is nothing but fancy psibilities wrapped up in unnecessary rituals."

"Generative transformational grammar and garlic."

"Right. Generative transformational grammar and primitive 'magic' out of the mountains. But my friend—it cures cancer. It does surgery. It makes rain fall if and only if needed and wanted. It by heaven flew a *space* ship from Old Earth to Planet Ozark, with magic alone for *fuel*."

"That's not possible." The Fish was adamant. Two and two are four, he was saying.

Coyote threw up his hands and closed his eyes elaborately.

"All right," he said, "then how did they get there? They *are* there, you know. Would you like to speculate on the probability that in the year 2012 a dozen Old Earth hill families had the materials and the skills necessary to build and equip a working spaceship—in total secrecy, mind you, because there's no record anywhere of *any* of this happening—and fly it right off the Earth? And land it on an Earth-type planet out at the edge of the First Galaxy? Come *on*, Fish!"

"It's more likely than that they did it by magic," the Fish insisted.

"How can you *say* that?" Coyote demanded. "I'm talking about the year twenty-effing-twelve! I can't imagine either possibility, and that doesn't make me happy. But I have seen their technology, Fish, and it runs to solar cells and competent old-style computers. And I have seen their magic, and *it* runs to miracles and wonders."

"It defies belief," moaned the Fish. "It simply defies belief."

"It works. Has worked for ten centuries. It is *there*."

There was a silence, while they both stared glumly at nothing at all. And then the Fish said, "By the way. There was one mention of the place, after all. One of those little piddly pompous scholarly journals from the back of nowhere, from the late 2800's. A scientist ran across the same problem we did—the planet showed up on scientific instruments, but could not be seen by the human eye. He proposed that there was a very simple explanation; he hypothesized that the atmosphere of the planet was of a color outside the spectrum of colors visible to human beings."

"And that was supposed to make it look like empty space?"

"Not exactly. His idea was that the human eye, faced with this particular set of unprocessable data, automatically reinterpreted it as Piece of Empty Space. Something like the way literate people interpret pictures of optical illusions. It was strained, I'll admit, but it had a certain ingenuity."

"Lame," said Coyote with contempt. "Lame!"

The Fish wiggled the fingers of one hand and pursed his lips, signifying maybe.

"Lame," said Coyote again. "We've got instruments that will check that one out, if you care to take it seriously."

"We did that, while you were gone," said the Fish. "On the off chance. Just as soon as the computers ran down the reference. But there was nothing to it, of course."

Coyote was restless and cross; he didn't like being stumped. He especially didn't like being stumped by primitive mumbojumbo. He walked over to the wall behind the Fish's desk and pushed the button that made it transparent, and he stared down gloomily through it at the blur of green one hundred and thirteen stories below. That would be trees, and he was grateful that Mars Central now *had* trees. But they didn't do much to lessen the impact of block after block after block of identical two-hundred-story office buildings. Ugly. Necessary, of course—but ugly. Something like the hard cold reality—necessary, but *ugly*— that had caused him to come right back to Mars Central and tell the Fish every single thing the women of Ozark had begged him to keep silent about. True, he'd warned them that he couldn't promise silence, and he had explained why. But it was still ugly.

"Mister Jones, *what* are you doing?"

"Looking out your window." Thinking ugly thoughts.

"Would you please come back here and sit down so that we can continue our discussion?"

Coyote went back and folded himself into the chair again, "Sorry," he said, not feeling sorry at all. "I'm just in a bad mood, Fish. I'm discouraged."

"And you expect to see something encouraging out that window?"

Coyote didn't answer, and the Fish coughed once and went on.

"Well, it's done," he declared. "I'm not happy about it, I don't understand even a tenth of it, and I'm going to have a difficult time explaining all this to Budgets. But it's done. Let's move on."

"Good enough. Move on to where?"

"You just sit there. And try not to spend any of the taxpayers' money while you do it."

The Fish punched a stud, and the voice of his Amanuensis IV—the very latest model—came on sweet and cloying with "Good morning, sir! What may I do for you?"

"Get me the Department of Planets & Asteroids," ordered the Fish. "One of the liaison people . . . somebody in Booking. Cheltharp, if he's there."

"Yes, sir," warbled the Amanuensis IV, and Coyote opened his mouth to make some observations about people who criticize other people for spending taxpayers' money, and then waste that same money on machines to do for them things they could perfectly well do for themselves. But the Fish cut him off abruptly.

"Just keep that to yourself, Mister Jones," he said grimly.

"I've heard it before. We've discussed it at length. I'm not interested in your opinions on the subject."

Coyote shut his mouth and sat there until the comlight glowed red and the Fish said, "Hello? Who am I speaking to?"

"It's Phil, Fish."

"Oh, Cheltharp! Glad you were there. Listen, we need a honeymoon team put together."

"Again?"

"Ever forward, ever onward, et cetera, et cetera. We've got a nice little Earth-type planet out on the edge of the First Galaxy, calls itself Ozark, and we need the usual. A couple of mid-rank diplomats to issue the formal invitation and accept the response. A fedrobot for escort and to serve as legal personnel."

"You need a linguist? What kind of language are we dealing with? You need interpreters? Translators?"

The Fish cleared his throat.

"This is a little strange, Cheltharp," he said.

"It always is."

"This is even stranger than usual. What you need to do is put a couple of diplomats on a crash-intensive in Old Earth Early Panglish/Late English—say the last decade of the twentieth century and the first decade of the twenty-first."

There was a silence on the other end of the line, and the Fish cleared his throat again and moved his head a little like a turkey gobbler. Coyote grinned, his annoyance at his predicament somewhat tempered by his pleasure in seeing Old Fishface sharing it with him.

"I know what you're thinking, Cheltharp," said the Fish. "But I assure you—that's what we need. It's a different dialect, naturally, but it's comprehensible. Have your people watch threedys, give them hypnotapes; do what you'd do if it were any other language we have materials on. You must have some appropriate stuff in your archives."

"Okay, Fish," said the voice. "If you say so. But in my experience, languages—"

"These people don't change," the Fish stated flatly. "They refuse to. Trust me, Cheltharp, and quit quibbling."

"Light's Beard," Coyote protested, "they signal social status by their speech mode, Fish! I told you that. And they teach it from copies of ancient tapes to keep it artificially stable! That's not—"

The Fish glared at him, and signed, "They don't need to know any of that at DPA," in Ameslan-Extended.

"How fast can you get a team ready?" he asked Cheltharp.

"How fast do you need it?"

"Tomorrow. Today. Yesterday, if you can do it."

"Tomorrow, Fish. That's the best I can do, even if you're willing to take just anybody."

"Well, I'm not," said the Fish sternly. "I need some people who know how to be tactful. And at least one of them has to have a fairly high telepathy rating—better than just high normal, Cheltharp."

"Tomorrow, then. By noon, approximately. Okay?"

"If that's the best you can do."

There was another silence on the line, and the Fish ignored Coyote, who was signing "He already said that" with both hands, the basics tricked out with elaborate flourishes and obscene variations.

"Send them over here as early as possible," said the Fish into the silence, "and I'll do the final briefing here. And we have an agent going along . . . you'll need about a five-place flyer, Cheltharp."

"Any special instructions? Tentacle-pencils, anything like that?"

"No . . . These aren't just humanoids, my friend. These are Old Earthers. That's confidential, of course."

"You're joking!" Cheltharp's voice was deadly serious, as befitted the solemnity of the occasion. The Fish *did not* joke. Ever. On the other hand, there were no Old Earthers sitting around undiscovered in space. Anybody knew that. Every smallest trip off Earth had been a matter of official record since before the Soviet Union's first Sputnik. Therefore, this had to be the Fish's first joke. Cheltharp was suitably impressed. His voice almost had a quaver.

"No," said the Fish, "it's not a joke. It's bizarre, but it's no joke."

"Seriously?"

"Seriously."

"Well, then. I'm coming along, too. I want to hear this briefing for myself."

"As you like. It's routine, I warn you. Nothing exciting."

"Oh, sure. Just your average timewarp/spacewarp combined, and the most gigantic coverup in recorded history thrown in. Just routine. I'll see you tomorrow, Fish." And the comlight went out, followed by the lyrical sounds of the Amanuensis IV wanting to know if there was any little thing else it could do.

"No, thank you," said the Fish. "That will be all."

"Very good, sir," went the voice, and Coyote rubbed his index fingers briskly together in front of his nose.

"Why not 'prithee, milord,' while you're at it?" he jeered. And did "shame, shame" some more with his fingers.

The Fish paid no attention. Their violently opposed ideas about the antiquated manner in which he ran his office were an overworked subject, as was his insistence on archaic forms of address. On Mars Central, nobody but the Fish (and the Amanuensis IV, programmed not to know better) had called anyone, male or female, anything much but "Citizen" for at least a hundred years . . . that didn't bother the Fish a bit. He went right on mistering and madaming. And he *loved* machines that would treat him with total reverence.

"You'll go along with the honeymoon team, Jones," he said placidly, instead of retorting.

"Thinkest thou that—"

"Shut up, Jones!" barked the chief; his reserve of serenity was not large. "You're tiresome."

And because Coyote was a good-natured man, and fond of the Fish in spite of it all, he agreed. "All right," he said. "I'll stop. But explain to me why I have to go back out there."

"One," said the Fish, counting it out on his palm, "you know these people, you know your way around, and you had a whole week—on government time—to learn the basics about the culture. Sending you will save most of the time of a formal briefing. You can handle the questions yourself."

"I can tell them everything I know right here. Before they go."

"Two," the Fish continued, "there's no crash-intensive language course that's going to give the team the kind of expertise with the Ozark dialect that you already have. They'll need you to help with the language, Mister Jones."

"All P and A's flunkies have to do is say *rituals*, for the Light's sake! Do invitations. Read stuff out loud. Understand yes and no and thank you and hello/good-bye. They don't need me for that."

"Three," said the Fish, unperturbed. "We don't have that rogue yet."

"Once the Ozarkers are Citizens of the Federation," Coyote observed, "they'll have to turn in the rogue, under Federation law."

"Oh, *well*!" said the Fish, sarcastically. "Naturally that solves the problem! Once they know it's the *law*, they'll just rush to correct the situation!"

"Well." Coyote tugged at his beard with one hand, and waved the other vaguely, and smiled his emptiest smile.

"You sound like an agent on his first solo mission," said the Fish disgustedly. "Federation law, indeed. Please do not insult me with such a performance."

"I can always try," said Coyote.

"No. Don't try. I want you to go, Mister Jones, and go you will. I want you there to decide if the proper way to handle this *is* just to inform them of the law and demand that the rogue be turned over, or if something more covert is required. You don't even know whether those people are aware that they *have* a rogue, do you?"

"Nope. Haven't the remotest idea."

"Really, Mister Jones!"

Coyote gave him his very best melodramatic secret agent face. Eyes narrowed and squinty and intense. Nostrils flared. Lips tight and pinched and grim. Cheek muscles rigid—one twitching.

The Fish looked right through him and down at the file on the desktop. "Now I'll need the name of the head of state. . . . No, sorry. Primitive planet, no planetary government. I'll need the names of the heads of state, *plural*."

"No such animals," Coyote told him. "Sorry."

"No heads of state?" The Fish flicked the file with one elegantly manicured fingernail. "Six continents, it says here. Twelve separate political divisions."

"That's the kingdoms."

"Well? Who runs the kingdoms, then?"

"Nobody, so far as I could tell. Each one has a family that is a kind of in-house Civil Service . . . lives in the castle and breeds many little Civil Servants for administrative work, while everybody else gets limited to two or three kids *max*imum. But nobody *runs* the kingdoms."

"Mister Jones. Please. There has to be some sort of structure for this society."

"Each castle has a couple that they call 'Master' and 'Missus' of the thing."

"They will do."

"The Master has no authority to do anything at all except within his own household, where he has whatever authority any man has in such a situation. The Missus runs nothing but the house itself."

"Patriarchal culture?"

"All the way. Except—"

"Except what?"

Coyote thought about the Grannys. And he thought about Responsible of Brightwater. And then he thought about how bewildered he was, and how much less he'd have to retract later on if he said little now.

"Nothing," he said aloud. "Patriarchal."

"All right, then. I need the names of the twelve 'Masters,' however limited their authority may be."

"It's in the file," Coyote told him. "Third or fourth microfiche down. Have your mechanical slave out there print it up for the briefing and get it on the documents."

"Hmmmm." The Fish looked up at him, frowning now. "Is this going to mean that the team has to do twelve separate ceremonies? Twelve separate invitations? Twelve separate signings? The whole works, a dozen times over?"

"I don't know. They have the technology to do it all by comset; or they can call a meeting and bring everybody in to one of the castles . . . but that would take forever. Transportation is all ground and water. A kind of groundcar they call tinlizzies, and your standard average variety of boats and ships. No air transport."

"Except flying mules," said the Fish icily. "With no wings."

"I tell you, I *saw* one," Coyote said. "But they can't carry crowds of people."

The Fish was tiring; he raised his eyebrows and let it pass.

"Do what you can," he said, "to get this done by comset. If it's not possible, it's not possible—you and the team will have to trot round the planet and do it all over twelve times. But *try*. This is costing a horrendous amount of money, Mister Jones."

"I'll do what I can, sure," Coyote said. "But I had a week there, remember, not a year. And a week shut up in a castle, at that. I just know bits and pieces off the top. For all I know, even suggesting that all this be done by comset is a gross insult."

"Well, we'll warn the Department team. That's *their* job . . . they'll watch for the signals, and take it slowly."

"Good enough," said Coyote. "Is that it?"

"Is what it?"

"Are we through? I can go now?"

"I suppose. Unless you have something useful to report to me. Like how, precisely, a wingless mule can be made to fly."

"Nope. Nothing to report."

"That's all, then. But *this* time—try to remember, Mister Jones, that you are a public servant. Try to keep that in mind."

Coyote made a disrespectful gesture behind his back, smiled cheerfully to the old man's face, and left whistling. He didn't really mind going back out to Ozark; he was in fact anxious to do so. He hadn't learned one one-hundredth of what he wanted to know about the elaborate psi-illusions that the Ozarkers insisted were "magic." But it was bad form not to object to his assignment—the Fish would have had his whole day ruined if Coyote had admitted that he was *eager* to go.

And there was Coyote's image as a difficult and cantankerous and uncooperative agent. He had an obligation to maintain that. He might need it sometime.

CHAPTER SEVEN

On Phona, DO-323 and the rest of the octave lay sullen and depressed in their pool. It had been an ugly and discordant day. The message from the Communipath Network had been humiliating . . . almost degrading. And there had been nothing that they could have said in their own defense.

YOU ARE GUILTY OF A SERIOUS VIOLATION OF FEDERATION LAW, PEOPLE OF PHONA, the Communipath manning the nearest station on the Bucket had said. Addressing the adepts in the legislature, of course, but allowing all of Phona to hear.

FIRST: YOU HAVE KNOWN OF THE EXISTENCE OF A PLANET HAVING SENTIENT BEINGS, ELIGIBLE FOR MEMBERSHIP IN THE TRI-GALACTIC FEDERATION, AND YOU HAVE KEPT THIS INFORMATION SECRET INSTEAD OF REPORTING IT AS YOUR CITIZENLY DUTY REQUIRED. AND THIS HAS BEEN GOVERNMENT *POLICY*, NOT SIMPLY INDIVIDUAL WRONGDOING! THIS IS A SHOCKING DISPLAY OF BAD CITIZENSHIP, AND OF DECEIT.

All that was true; it could not be denied.

SECOND: YOU HAVE SOMEHOW MANAGED TO INTERFERE WITH AN AGENT OF THE TRI-GALAC-TIC INTELLIGENCE SERVICE, CAUSING HIM TO BE DELAYED ON PLANET OZARK FOR AN ENTIRE WEEK, UNDER HOUSE ARREST, COSTING THE FEDERATION A CONSIDERABLE SUM, AND SERI-OUSLY MEDDLING IN THE BUSINESS OF OTHERS—CRIMINALLY MEDDLING.

They might have tried to deny that, perhaps, but they hadn't been sure whether they could bring it off. During the week that Coyote Jones had spent on Ozark, he was sure to have seen at least one of their spy-sensors. On a staircase, perhaps. Behind a piece of furniture. Hidden away in a corner of a corridor. There were so many of them scattered about Planet Ozark, and the Ozarkers were so accustomed to their being there. The chances were more than excellent that Coyote Jones had identified Phona as the source of his problems. He would have recognized the devices, certainly.

THIRD: ACCORDING TO A NUMBER OF THE OZARKERS, AS REPORTED BY THE GOVERNMENT AGENT, A DECADE AGO PLANET PHONA LITER-ALLY ATTEMPTED TO *TAKE OVER* PLANET OZARK, INSTALLING ENERGY CRYSTALS ABOVE ITS CIT-IES AND INTIMIDATING ITS POPULATION. THIS, CITIZENS OF PHONA, IS AN OFFENSE THAT—HAD IT SUCCEEDED—WOULD MEAN MARTIAL LAW FOR YOU FOR A VERY LONG TIME. YOU ARE FOR-TUNATE THAT IT FAILED.

Aha. Whether the agent had seen the sensors or not, he'd been told the story of their abortive attempt to com-mit the crime of conquest. They had offered no denials of the third charge, either, and had been grateful they'd let the second pass without objection.

FOURTH: IT APPEARS ALL TOO OBVIOUS THAT PHONA IS *STILL* IN THE MOOD FOR CONQUEST OF PLANET OZARK, AND HAS BEEN KEEPING THAT PLANET UNDER ILLEGAL OBSERVATION WITH A VIEW TO USURPING ITS RIGHTS AND ITS TERRITORIES.

Uhuh. The agent had seen the spy-sensors.

PAY CLOSE ATTENTION, CITIZENS OF PHONA, the Communipath had continued. YOU ARE HEREBY ADVISED THAT THE FEDERATION DOES NOT WISH TO WASTE ITS TIME OR ITS RESOURCES IN PROSECUTION OF THESE PAST OFFENSES. NO CHARGES WILL BE BROUGHT AGAINST YOU ON POINTS ONE THROUGH THREE ABOVE.

A note of relief had rippled from pool to pool. This much at least they could be grateful for.

WITH REGARD TO THE FOURTH ITEM, BE ADVISED THAT STEPS WILL BE TAKEN TO DEACTIVATE THE ILLEGAL SENSOR DEVICES YOU HAVE PLACED ON PLANET OZARK. THEY WILL NOT BE RETURNED TO YOU. BE FURTHER ADVISED THAT SHOULD ANY SUCH DEVICE, OR ANY SIMILAR DEVICE, APPEAR ON OZARK IN THE FUTURE AND BE TRACEABLE TO PHONA, PROSECUTION WILL BE INITIATED IMMEDIATELY.

Another point to be grateful for—the government apparently did not know of the existence of the *other* spies Phona had on Ozark. That was a relief. Unless it was a trick.

CITIZENS OF PHONA, THIS IS THE FEDERATION GOVERNMENT SPEAKING, THROUGH THE DEPARTMENT OF JUSTICE. GIVE US YOUR TOTAL ATTENTION.

A pause, for effect. Then. . . .

ANY FURTHER INDICATION, HOWEVER TRIVIAL,

THAT YOU HAVE TERRITORIAL DESIGNS UPON
THE PLANET OZARK WILL BE MET WITH SWIFT
ACTION. IT WILL *NOT* BE TOLERATED. IT IS UN-
CIVILIZED BEHAVIOR, AND WILL BE PUT DOWN
WITH THE STERNEST AND SWIFTEST MEASURES
AVAILABLE TO THE DEPARTMENT OF JUSTICE,
WITH FULL CONSIDERATION GIVEN TO THE FACT
THAT IT WOULD BE *REPETITION* OF EARLIER
CRIMINAL BEHAVIOR. AND ANY FURTHER INDI-
CATION, HOWEVER TRIVIAL, THAT PHONA CON-
SIDERS ITSELF ENTITLED TO INTERFERE WITH
THE ACTIONS OF THE TRI-GALACTIC INTELLI-
GENCE SERVICE, OR ANY OTHER DEPARTMENT
OR AGENT OF THE GOVERNMENT, WILL NOT BE
TOLERATED. THERE WILL BE A SQUAD OF FED-
ROBOTS WITH FULL ENFORCEMENT POWERS ON
YOUR WORLD WITHIN HOURS OF ANY SIGN—
HOWEVER TRIVIAL—THAT YOUR PREVIOUS OF-
FENSES ARE ABOUT TO BE COMMITTED AGAIN.
LET THAT BE FULLY AND CLEARLY UNDERSTOOD.
END OF MESSAGE.

The shame. The humiliation. The Phonans had writhed
in their pools. The discord had been agonizing, shrilling
and roaring through the chfla and resonating in the chambers. But they had had no defense. It *was* against the law
to attempt to conquer another people's world, its territories, its possessions. But uncivilized? *Uncivilized* was the
behavior of the Ozarkers, who let their uncountable abundance lie fallow, unused, running wild, while others were
strangled for lack of space and resources. *That*, whatever
the law, was uncivilized; that was barbarism.

But you could not say so. Not under the present circumstances. Not from a sounding board of disgrace.

Not when you had been caught in the act, as they had been.

And it had all been for nothing! A waste! The whole purpose of delaying the TGIS agent had been to gain them time, and in that sense it had succeeded; they had had more than a week for discussion and debate before the man had been able to get back to Mars Central to make his report. But they might as well have had no time at all. In spite of marathon scheming sessions, they had been unable to devise any plan with even a minimal chance of working. There was of course the small satisfaction that went with having once again demonstrated to Mars Central that the Phonans were not *serfs* of the Federation, but could take vigorous independent action on their own behalf. Still, it was a *very* small satisfaction, dependent on petty emotions in many ways unworthy of a Phonan; it was not enough. It was not enough to offset the nuisance of having drawn to Phona this new constant scrutiny by the government. Especially when they had not even a plan to show for all their trouble.

Now they lay side by side in despair, and worried, each in his or her own fashion. What was Phona going to do? They knew what the government of the Federation would say to that question: "Limit your population, as does any overcrowded world. Or go out into space, out to the colony worlds that are still eager for new citizens. And *leave your neighbors alone.*"

The Phonans could not contemplate either of those proposed solutions. To limit their population was blasphemous, a betrayal of their religious faith. And to go out to the Third Galaxy, to become colonists . . . horrible, it was horrible! They were a people of harmony and classical order; they needed certain comforts if they were to be that people. To travel through space curled tightly in sealed pods with life-support systems to maintain them for the journey . . . To spend years in miserable primitive conditions on some hellish undeveloped planet at the end of nowhere, *beyond* the end of nowhere, doing brutal psi-labor to build something resembling a decent environment, an environment that they themselves would die before completing and that would benefit only the octaves of later generations . . . To give up the pools of chfla, to lie in pools of *raw water*!

No. Those were not options. It did not bear thinking of. They were the *Octaves*! They were a cut above . . . several cuts above . . . most of the people of the Federation. They would not be driven to either of the obscene extremes that the government would no doubt have gloried in seeing them adopt.

But for a while they were going to have to be painfully careful. Because the people of Phona were very fond of the comforts that came to them as citizens of the TGF. Losing those comforts, falling under martial law—or becoming a prison planet, as had happened to Gilos-6 only two years ago—did not appeal to them any more than expeditions out to the far reaches of the galaxies did.

They lay in their pools, and they fretted, and the minor chords sounded one after another in dirge-like succession all through that day and night and the next day and night and the one after that as well. Phona was a sorrowful place . . . and what were they going to do?

For once, Responsible of Brightwater was totally in agreement with Coyote and the Fish. She was shocked by the very idea of the expense in time, funds, and energy required to set up twelve separate negotiation meetings between the team from Planets and Asteroids and the Castle Masters.

"We can do this by comset in nothing flat," she said briskly, "and that's how we *will* do it. You just give me an hour to set up the conference . . . might could be somebody you're inviting isn't right to hand on such short notice. And then we'll get all this hooha out of the way."

All this hooha? Hallden Fru and Stefano Ariatto, the two diplomats from P and A, looked at each other from out of the corners of their eyes, diplomatically. The young woman certainly didn't seem impressed. As for the rest of the family scattered around the big room, they weren't even listening.

The diplomats sat and waited, with the fedrobot and a much amused—though wary—Coyote Jones, while Responsible went off to arrange for the comset conference. They tried not to fidget; they were *trained* not to fidget, after all. But they were uncomfortable. They'd had extensive experience with bizarre alien lifeforms and almost unimaginable environments, and they could have dealt with yet another of those, casually. But this—this society of people who looked just like themselves, who'd somehow escaped Old Earth right before things got worse there and had hidden out here under the very nose of the Federation for all these centuries, who lived and dressed and spoke and behaved in a manner out of the Middle Histories—this was somehow more unnerving than any number of tentacled extraterrestrials could have been.

They were made aware of how obvious their discomfort was when Thorn of Guthrie laid down her diary, closing it with a snap, and sent one of the collection of nieces present to fetch "refreshments," as she put it. "Something reasonably strong," she told the child. "You tell Sally of Lewis to put together an assortment that will go a considerable distance toward re-starching the limp, and to be prompt about it."

The two old women sitting at either side of the fireplace in rocking chairs, both knitting away at blinding speed, looked at the men from Mars Central over the tops of their eyeglasses and snickered; and the diplomats felt their faces redden.

"Air too thin for you, young man?" demanded the one called Granny Hazelbide. According to Jones of TGIS, she was ninety-nine years old; according to Jones, that was little more than decent maturity for an Ozark Granny, with a Granny of one hundred and twenty and up not even considered unusual. It was, Jones had said solemnly, their meanness—they were pickled in it. Funny fellow, that Jones.

"No, ma'am," replied Hallden Fru, speaking slowly and carefully in the unfamiliar dialect. "No, ma'am, it's fine."

"He's just tired," said the other crone, the one improbably called Granny Gableframe. "No doubt he had a hard day, flying through the air with no company but his peaked associate there, and Coyote Jones—as has no manners atall, and is given to gossip—and that giant coffeepot. Enough to wear anybody out, you ask me."

"Granny," Coyote chided. "You know what a robot is. Cut it out."

"Looks like a giant coffeepot to me," said the old lady staunchly. "All it needs is a handle on one side."

"It's a fedrobot, ma'am," said Steffano Ariatto. "It has the same legal status as a Federation agent, or a frontier marshal."

"No more than that?" Granny Gableframe grabbed her glasses with one hand, moved them clear to the end of her nose, tipped up her head, and peered squinty-eyed at the robot. "Poor old dented beatup thing!" she said. "It tears at the heartstrings, doesn't it, Hazelbide?"

"Indeed it does," Granny Hazelbide answered. "And before it leaves here, I intend to see that it gets a decent polish to it."

Both diplomats turned their heads to look at the fedrobot, which was completely indifferent to this exchange. It was a reliable model, one they'd taken out countless times on diplomatic expeditions, and they'd gotten accustomed to the way it looked. Now, under the piercing eyes of the Grannys, they realized that the fedrobot *did* look shabby. Its metal was dull and scruffy-looking, and Hallden Fru had the horrified feeling that there was something particularly nasty crusted around the base of its pedestal.

"The fedrobot doesn't need to be fancy, ma'am," he said stiffly. "It's only required to be efficient in the performance of its duties."

"That's all we require of *our* coffeepots, too," the Granny snapped, "but we don't consider that an excuse to let them get filthy! Especially if we can plan to sashay round the universe showing them off to strangers."

Granny Gableframe got up and came over to the group, and both Fru and Ariatto held their ground as she bore down on them, knitting needles first and the points glittering. She took her index finger and ran it around the fedrobot's cylindrical shoulders, leaving a trail behind. And she proceeded to write in the thick dust the words "Government Agent," clucking her tongue all the time like a Geiger counter.

"Mercy!" she said, when she'd crossed the final *t*. "Where *is* that child, anyway?" And she gave a sharp fierce high whistle that made both diplomats duck, training or no training, and brought the little girl running.

"Yes, Granny?" she asked breathlessly.

"You gave Sally of Lewis the message, did you?"

"Yes, ma'am, Granny."

"All right, Beatrice of Airy, you get ready and go give her another one, you hear? You go tell her I want a servingmaid in here quick as spit to do some cleaning, and you tell her to send somebody as is *sturdy!* This nasty old coffeepot here's not fit to be in the stables, much less in the front room. Hurry now!"

"Yes, *ma'am*, Granny!" said the child, and left as fast as she'd come, pigtails and apron strings flying.

Coyote was having a wonderful time watching the Grannys torment Fru and Ariatto. He was having so much fun that it nearly took his mind off the worrisome question of why Responsible of Brightwater hadn't so much as given him a cross look, much less subjected him to the tongue-lashing and psi-effects that he'd been expecting. He'd tried to warn the diplomats what to expect here, and had been told for his trouble that they were "fully accustomed to dealing with cross-cultural conflicts, thank you," and needed no help from him, thank you twice. Now they were suffering the consequences of their over-confidence, and that pleased him. It spoke to his sense of the fitness of things.

"Hazelbide," observed Granny Gableframe, "I see the federal government's as worthless as it ever was, and as filthy of habit. Wouldn't you think they'd of changed a tad?"

"Law, Gableframe, it's only been a thousand years," said Granny Hazelbide. "That's not half long enough for a change in the federal government. Be patient. Just *be* patient! Come another thousand years or two, come a millennium, might could be, they'll learn how to *dust*."

Hallden Fru considered making a point of the fact that it was not the "federal" government but the Federation government, and that the difference was not insignificant, but he thought better of it. And was rewarded by a young woman pushing a cart loaded with enough food and drink for any embassy reception and a picnic left over.

"Young man," said the Granny standing by the robot, "I recommend the ale, it's strengthening. Justina of Farson, you pour the young man a large glass of that ale, and one for his friend as well, would you? And have some sandwiches so as the ale doesn't go to yourall's heads. Justina, you hand each of these youngsters a couple of those squawker sandwiches."

Ariatto had found himself forced to eat some very curious things during his years of government service; nevertheless, he looked a bit apprehensive, and Coyote felt good enough about the way things were going to spend a few words reassuring him.

"Squawker," said Coyote. "It's about the same as chicken, as I recall."

"I see," said Ariatto. "Well. Glad to know that." And his colleague nodded relieved agreement.

The servingmaid passed the mugs of strong ale around, along with the sandwiches, to the human members of the honeymoon team; and then she pushed the teacart over into the middle of the room where the members of the Family could help themselves.

"Will that do it, Missus?" she asked Thorn of Guthrie.

"That's fine, Justina of Farson," said Thorn. "You tell Sally of Lewis that the selection was proper, and remind her that there'll be three extra for supper."

"Yes, Missus."

"*And*," put in Granny Hazelbide, "you tell her we're still waiting for that cleaning crew."

"Oh!" said Justina of Farson. "I forgot! Sally of Lewis said I was to say that anything dirty enough to set the Grannys off like that is too dirty to be cleaned anyplace but the workroom. She said I was to bring whatever it was along with me after I left you all the refreshments."

Hallden Fru could not quite place the strange sound that came from his throat at the idea of the fedrobot being trundled off to the "workroom" and scoured by the servants of Castle Brightwater, except that it appeared to be the same sound that came from Stefano Ariatto's throat. And Coyote, just delighted, hid his chin in his hand and stared at the floor in a desperate effort not to roar with laughter. After all, this fedrobot might very well have to arrest somebody before the day was over. Read them their rights, pronounce the charges, all with due pomp and a big rich bass voice, administer a tranquilizing injection, lead the culprit off to the ship—all this after having been scoured and polished to a faretheewell by an assortment of Ozark females. It was priceless. He was sorry the fedrobot had no cognitive facilities adequate for appreciating it. The diplomats were looking at him frantically for help . . . WHADDA WE DO NOW, SUPERSPY? Coyote concentrated on counting the leaves in the pattern of flowering vines that bordered the front room rug under his feet.

"Hazelbide," said Granny Gableframe in the elaborate silence, "might could be that coffeepot's dirtied up our clean floor, too."

"Oh? How so?"

"Well . . . Coyote Jones for sure sees something there that fascinates him! You suppose they trekked in here by way of the stable yards, Hazelbide?" And with infinite delicacy, the Granny sniffed the air.

It was too much for Coyote. He gave up and just sat there and laughed, the effort of doing it quietly making his whole body shake and tears roll down his cheeks and into his beard.

"I do not see anything to laugh about," muttered Hallden Fru through clenched teeth. "It isn't funny."

"Oh, certainly not," Coyote said weakly. "The dignity of the whole damn Tri-Galactic Federation is at stake here . . ." And he collapsed again, laughing out loud now, while Fru and Ariatto grew redder and more rigid and more tight-lipped with every passing moment.

"Granny?" asked the servingmaid, who'd been watching them all with a look of resignation. "Shall I take this along now?"

Coyote did know his duty, and in a crisis he prided

himself on being a man you could count on. Now that they were actually backed to the wall, actually going down for the third time, actually at their last gasp and their last inch of rope, he pulled himself together and stepped in.

"Granny Hazelbide," he said firmly, "and you, Granny Gableframe, you both *know* better! Where are your much-touted good manners, ladies?"

"Hmmmph," said Granny Hazelbide, "will you only listen to who presumes to talk on *others'* manners!" But her lips were twitching and her eyes dancing. And when she spoke to the servingmaid she said, "Child, you leave it be. I'll see to it myself in a bit."

"But, Granny—"

"Never *mind*, now!" the Granny said. "I said I'll see to it. You need me to repeat that for you a few more times?"

The bewildered young woman left with a resigned "No, Granny," and the rest of the company sat demurely sipping and chewing until Responsible came back to tell them she had it all arranged, with Coyote steadfastly ignoring the glares of outrage from the diplomats. From time to time he'd look sadly at the fedrobot and give it an ostentatious sympathetic pat, whenever Fru and Ariatto showed signs of getting over their discomfort. Coyote liked to keep a good thing going.

He'd been prepared for the Grannys to tease the diplomats, and for Responsible of Brightwater to be tart as a persimmon before the first frost, and he'd been anticipating an interesting interlude or two. He had *not* been prepared for what happened after the senior of the two diplomats, with proper solemnity, read off to the participants of the comset conference the list of privileges and responsibilities of the TGF citizen and issued the formal official invitation to Planet Ozark to join up.

It was an imposing list, and Hallden Fru read it with pride, adjusting it to the Ozark dialect as he went along with a skill that Coyote found worth noticing—when he got back, he intended to make special mention of it in his report.

"To every citizen of the Tri-Galactic Federation, *from birth*," it began, "the following rights and privileges are guaranteed:

"Full and complete medical care, at no cost to the Citizen.

"An ample and nutritious diet, together with those liquids associated with said diet, at no cost to the Citizen.

"Housing of decent comfort and no less than four hundred square feet per person, except that a single family under one roof shall be provided a maximum of two thousand square feet of such housing, no matter how numerous its members. (NOTE: For special exceptions due to religious laws, the citizen may apply to the Bureau of Housing on Mars Central.)

"An allowance of thirty Federation credits per person for furnishings and clothing and miscellaneous household items, the sum to be annually adjusted for inflation.

"An adequate supply of those environmental substances necessary to the citizen's survival, such as water and minerals, in a quantity and quality appropriate to health and well-being. (For the list of approved substances, quantities, and standards, contact the Bureau of Environmental Affairs on Mars Central.)

"Full and equal access to every facility and agency of the Federation government, such as law enforcement, urban and rural safety. . . ."

It went on like that, through a transportation allowance and a guarantee of an adequate transportation *system*, through guaranteed full employment at no less than minimum wage, through guaranteed freedom of speech and of religion, through guaranteed free education, through full and free access to all information facilities, to the free right of travel throughout the Federation's boundaries; and it ended with a guarantee of decent provision at the time of the Citizen's death in accordance with the laws and customs of his or her culture. There were stipulations and disclaimers and conditions of various kinds, to be sure, but essentially the document guaranteed to every Citizen of the TGF everything that was basic to a decent life, from birth to death, as well as a variety of mechanisms for obtaining more than just the basics. All this in return for only four obligations: obedience to the law, the paying of taxes, the providing of a delegate or delegates to the legislative body of the Federation, and the unconditional surrendering of Factor Q infants to become the legal wards of the Communipath Crèche. It struck Coyote, as it had struck countless millions, as a truly exceptional bargain.

Coyote listened to the reading, and turned to look at the comset screens where the faces of the Masters of the Castles were somewhat blurrily in evidence, and waited for the answer. When it came, however, it stunned him; one at a time, and without the slightest hesitation, each one said simply, "No, thank you, we're not interested." Without so much as a word of discussion. Only Donovan Elihu Purdy the 40th, Master of Castle Purdy, seemed to have even a passing curiosity about the matter.

"Would you just go over that Factor Q business for me one more time?" he asked, when his turn came.

Stefano Ariatto explained it to him courteously. Every infant born into the Tri-Galactic Federation had a blood sample taken at birth, which was checked for a number of things, among them the substance known as Factor Q that signaled an unusually high potential for possibilities. And any baby in which Factor Q appeared was taken from its parents immediately—to avoid unnecessary pain for both parents and child, Ariatto told Donovan Elihu Purdy carefully—and brought up in the Communipath Crèche on Mars Central. Where its possibilities could be trained and honed and brought to their fullest flower under expert supervision.

The Master of Castle Purdy cleared his throat.

"That's disgusting," he said flatly.

"I beg your pardon?"

"I *say*, that's disgusting! Taking a baby away from its own folks like that! I never heard of such a thing. *No*, thanks!" And to make sure they understood him, he said it again. "No, thanks. Purdy Kingdom is not interested."

The two diplomats exchanged glances. It was not the first time they had encountered heads of state who chose to be coy, thinking that exceptions might be made or special privileges granted. And their briefing had warned them that Ozarkers were always famous for being canny bargainers.

"I'm sorry," said Fru firmly, "but that list is applied to every Federation Citizen, without exception. As is just and right. You can of course request Novice Planet status for a period of one hundred years, if you like, during which time no one will be allowed to visit Planet Ozark without your express invitation—that is quite usual. But you don't appear to have any reason to do that, really; that is, you are of Earth, as are we. There is no reason to assume that human tourists or other visitors, with the occasional alien always accompanied by a human tourist, would be any sort of shock to your culture."

Responsible of Brightwater, who'd been leaning against a far wall with her arms crossed over her chest, watching the proceedings, spoke up before anything else could be said. "Three minutes, gentlemen," she said, "by the clock. And then we'll go round once more, for your final answer." She raised her wrist and stared at her timepiece, clearly marking the minutes, while the team tried to think of something sensible to say. And then she said, "Here we go again, youall. Your votes, please, on joining this Federation."

And back came the answers, eleven from the other Masters and one from Donald Patrick Brightwater the 133rd, Responsible's uncle, who served in the Master's role at Brightwater.

"No, thanks," it was. Unanimously.

The team from Mars Central was flabbergasted.

This didn't happen. Hadn't *ever* happened. There were worlds that had to wait quite a long time to be asked to join, and there were worlds that had to meet a number of complex conditions before they were asked, but there was no such thing as a world that turned the Tri-Galactic Federation *down*.

Coyote would have argued; and in fact he did open his mouth to break out his opening thesis. But the diplomats hushed him efficiently. They might not be good at fencing with old ladies, but they did know a thing or two about normal diplomacy. This was not the time, nor the place, for a discussion of this thunderbolt. *Privately*, back on Mars Central, with officials present to give orders and to take responsibility, they would discuss it.

Except, thought Coyote . . .

"Wait a minute!" he said, thinking fast, ignoring the two tugging discreetly at him. "Miss Responsible, I thought you people prided yourself on being democratic on this planet."

"We do," she said.

"Well, how can just twelve of you speak for the whole population? It might be that if your people *knew* what you were throwing away on their behalf they wouldn't appreciate it much!"

Responsible nodded, and folded her arms again. "That's so," she said. "We have as many damn fools as any other world, I'll grant you that."

"Well, then?" Coyote demanded. "That's not democratic, that's. . . .*fascist* or something! It's not right, and I'm disappointed in you!"

"Well, we can't have that, can we?" said Responsible, giving him a flat look that made him uneasy in spite of his feeling that he was on the winning track for once. "I'll tell you what we'll do, Mister Jones. We'll poll them all. Everybody over the age of twelve years, as is our custom. Unless you insist on polling the tadlings and the babes in their cradles, Mister Jones?"

"But that would take—" Coyote began, his uneasiness growing on toward early panic.

"About fifteen minutes," snapped Responsible of Brightwater, cutting him off. "One thing we are set up for here, it's the casting of votes. There's comsets everywhere, including out in the fields and the woods . . . might could be you'll get ten, maybe fifteen percent that aren't close enough to one to join in, but that won't affect the total. According to our histories, the United States of America considered itself lucky when it could get *half* its qualified population to bother to vote—we can do a sight better than that. Here we go, ladies and gentlemen!"

The team had no time to decide if they thought this was a good idea or not; before they could open their mouths, she had issued the call to vote, read off the list of privileges and responsibilities from the copy in her hand, and was directing their attention to the wide board above the comset screens.

"Voting display," said Responsible. "It'll come in, one district at a time, one Kingdom at a time, in alphabetical order, till they're all done. Purple for yes, gentlemen. White for no."

And they watched as the display ran, and the lights flashed, and the tally flickered faster than they could read it at the right side of the board. Fifteen minutes and eleven seconds later, as promised, they had it. On all of Ozark, with eighty-two per cent of the population over twelve voting, there were only seventeen votes for Federation citizenship.

"Like I told you," Responsible observed. "Seventeen damn fools."

"Light's Beard," breathed Coyote. Hallden Fru and Stefano Ariatto were pointedly avoiding his eyes; they looked sick, and he *felt* sick. He'd really put his foot in it this time.

He *could* have gone back with the report of a rejection of Federation citizenship from twelve people with no valid political authority. There'd have been a chance, then, to put together some kind of plan, worked out by experts in such matters, and to try to come back with the goal of making the Ozarkers see what was obviously in their own best interests. But that wasn't possible now. He had sewn it up tight. This was democracy with a vengeance. . . .

And Planet Ozark, as with a single voice, had told the Tri-Galactic Federation that it could take its gewgaws and its silly toys and go play by itself. Ozark wasn't interested.

CHAPTER EIGHT

"I can't *believe* this!" the Fish announced, and the expression on his face backed up his words.

"You can't believe my total destruction of the diplomatic mission? Or you can't believe that Ozark turned down Federation membership?"

"Your personal failure does not surprise me in any way," said the Fish coldly. "I am accustomed to your miserable failures. If it were not for the unique characteristic that makes you so valuable to the TGIS, Mister Jones, your record of extraordinary—I might say awesome—blundering would have had you booted out of the Service long ago. Never mind that part of this. It's *typical* of your method of operation that you would take over control of something about which you know nothing at all, despite the presence of two highly trained experts in the act in question. But for this picayune primitive pimple of a planet to say 'No, thank you, we don't *choose* to join your Federation.' Now *that* goes beyond my capacity for either understanding *or* belief!"

"Mine, too," said Coyote mournfully. "But it's true."

"But how *can* they? How can they possibly prefer to live in . . . in *squalor* . . . when the populations of the Federation worlds live in leisure and luxury undreamed of even by the wealthy for most of recorded history? When the populations of hundreds of colony worlds are breaking their backs in the attempt to reach a status that allows the Federation to provide them with that same leisure and luxury? How *can* they?"

"Damned if I know," said Coyote flatly. "I don't pretend to understand it. But they are *very* firm about it, and here I am back again, no farther along than I was to begin with."

"You'll have to go back," declared the Fish. "You know that."

"To do what? If you think I am going to participate in a kidnap—especially when I'm not certain whom *to* kidnap— you'd better think again. I truly, truly will not do that, Fish."

"I wasn't going to suggest any such thing!"

"I am grateful to hear that," said Coyote. "Because I *won't.*"

The Fish was beating his fingers in a frantic rhythm on the edge of the desk, and chewing on his lower lip, and behaving in a generally un-Fishlike manner. Coyote had never seen him so unhinged; he found that it made *him* unhinged, too. It was unnerving.

"I don't believe it," the Fish was muttering, and he punched the stud for the Amanuensis IV and told it, "I want you to do a total computer search for me . . . you get Justice, and any other division you need, and you find me the law that forbids a planet to refuse an invitation to become a member of the Federation. And get the information back to me *fast*, because I need it yesterday!" And then he was muttering again.

"Fish . . . I don't think—"

"Correct. You don't think. I *do* think. And I think there must be some provision in the law for a situation like this."

"Aw, Fish, nobody ever *imagined* a situation like this!"

"Never is a long time, Mister Jones. Just because *we* never imagined it—that doesn't mean that the founders, in earlier and less sophisticated times, didn't imagine it. Perhaps it would have seemed no more unlikely to them than . . . oh, winning one's mate by batting her over the head with a club and dragging her home by the hair. Perhaps it is only from our present historical perspective that it seems incomprehensible. I'll wager there's provision for it in the law. Somewhere."

Coyote made a grudging mouth, and stared at the ceiling.

"Maybe so," he said. "I hadn't thought about it exactly that way. How long will the search take?"

"Not long. It never takes long."

They sat there for precisely four and one half minutes, with the Fish issuing time bulletins every thirty seconds or so, and both of them fidgeting. But when the report came, it was no help. As Coyote had expected, there was plenty on what to do about a world that wanted to join the TGF but didn't meet the standards for membership, but there was not one word about dealing with a world that just plain wasn't interested.

"There has *got* to be a way to make them join!" the Fish shrieked, bringing Coyote half out of his chair with astonishment at such behavior from a man normally almost without emotions. "There has *got* to be! We can't have a telepath—or telepaths—of that strength and range running loose, totally uncontrolled! It can't be *allowed!*"

Coyote went to the old man, took him firmly by the arm, and led him over to the narrow couch against the wall—never used before, to Coyote's knowledge, and even more fearsomely uncomfortable than the chairs—and gently laid him down.

"You lie there," he said firmly. "And I mean that. You try to get up, I'll project a five-hundred-pound rock onto your chest. It will be an illusion, of course, but it will keep you flat."

The Fish lay there, breathing rapidly, much too flushed for Coyote's comfort, and blinking his eyes wildly, but he did stay put. And Coyote rang up the Amanuensis to send for a calming concoction of some kind, wishing he had a Granny handy to specify the contents.

"Now," he said, "while we're waiting for that, and while you are putting yourself back together, maybe I could make a suggestion."

The Fish opened his mouth, but Coyote laid one hand over it.

"Just listen," he said. "Don't talk. Okay?"

When the Fish nodded, he removed the hand and went on.

"When I was on Ozark for that week's house arrest, I spent as much time as I could learning everything I could cram into my head about the planet, the culture, the works. And there were a couple of things of particular interest, Fish. One: the Phonan spy-sensor gadgets, which are lying all over Planet Ozark and which the Ozarkers believe to be little noxious creatures. They call them 'Pickles.' Remember? Second: the attempt Phona made about ten years ago to take over the planet. Clearly, Phona wants Ozark and is willing to risk a lot to get it; clearly, although their first attempt failed abysmally, they haven't given up."

"We have—" the Fish began, and then he saw Coyote's hand coming at him and dodged it. "*Let me talk*! We have already sent a message to Phona by Communipath that will put a stop to that, Mister Jones. They may not have known they were through trying to conquer Ozark, but they know it *now*. And they are through interfering with government agents as well."

"*You* know that," said Coyote patiently, "and *I* know that. But the Ozarkers don't know it, and they aren't in a very good position to find out about it. They've never even heard of Phona. They talk about 'the Garnet Ring.' And a mysterious group of alien whizbangs called 'the Out-Cabal'—pronounced to rhyme with 'Shout, Mabel!' by the way. The Phonans have really done a con job on those people."

"So?"

"So what if I go back out there and tell them the part about the takeover attempt is still going on? What if I talk up the Garnet Ring as a really fearsome group of heavies instead of the piddly little planet plus three asteroids and a couple of shabby moons that it actually is? And I don't tell them that Phona already belongs to the Federation and that its behavior violates Federation law and that it's already been muzzled and tied down. What if I convince them they're in terrible danger . . . using a little judicious telepathy to help that along . . . and then offer them total protection as a benefit of Federation membership?"

"But they must know that's included in membership," the Fish protested, taking the drink that Coyote handed him and drinking it straight down. "They had the list read to them, as always. One of the benefits on the list is guaranteed law enforcement service, and all attendant et ceteras. It didn't impress them then; why should it impress them now?"

Coyote took the glass away from him and set it down on the floor. "They weren't aware that they needed any protection when we read them the list," he explained. "I will *make* them aware, and I'll see to it that they feel thoroughly frightened of the Garnet Ring. Wait till I give them my best BEM description of the Phonans, Fish."

"Light's groin, man," the Fish objected, "the Phonans don't look anything like Bug-Eyed Monsters. The only thing they resemble in any coherent way is giant red licorice sticks."

"Like I said. You know that. I know that. But the Ozarkers are pretty well one hundred per cent ignorant of anything beyond the boundaries of their own planet. In fact, considering the way the place is littered with those spy-sensors, they're substantially ignorant of things *within* the boundaries of their own planet. I can make giant red licorice sticks, whose lives are devoted to humming, sound like The-End-of-the-World right on their doorstep, I promise you. Making them scared, Fish—that's baby stuff."

"You'd find a way to mess it up."

"Possibly," said Coyote. "Send somebody else, then, to do the same thing. One of the other agents."

"We do not have anybody else who would be immune to the rogue's projections, and you know it."

"Do what*ever*," Coyote said. "But let's try it, one way or another. If they really feel that they're in danger, and that the Federation would keep them safe, maybe it will get around this lunatic idea they have that government is next to ungodliness. Unless you have a better plan."

"How about sending forty divisions of fedrobots, fully armed and empowered, to bring them to their senses? How does that strike you?"

"As very like the behavior of the Phonans," Coyote answered.

"Thank you *so* much!"

"Well? How is it different? Phona wants to take over Ozark for its purposes, you want to take over Ozark for your purposes—it's conquest either way. And *that*, my friend, you'll have no trouble finding laws against."

"There are times when the law is meant to be broken."

"Tsk," went Coyote. "That's not what you told the Phonans."

"It's not the same."

"Fish," said Coyote patiently, pushing him back down on the couch, "I have bent a law or two in my time. Who hasn't? But you do that after everything else has been tried. We're not there yet."

"Mister Jones," blustered the Fish, "any moment, any *second*, that rogue telepath could seriously disrupt the affairs of the entire Federation with another wild projection! This is an emergency!"

"*Come on*, Fish."

"What? *What?*"

"Has it happened again? I mean, since that first time?"

"No."

"All right. And it hadn't happened before. It does *not* seem to be any kind of constant threat . . . it was just some kind of stray noise wandering around. Inversion in the projection layers or something. A freak."

"Nevertheless—"

"Nevertheless, we need the rogue, because we need the rogue's *skills*. I agree with you. What we really want is the handy-dandy instructions for making mules fly and controlling the weather without so much as leaving your chair and setting up telepathic illusions that run themselves. Me, too, Fish. I want *all* of that. We *need* all of that, and I'm willing to do my best to get it for us. But I do not agree that it's any kind of emergency, and the Council wouldn't agree with you either. It just won't wash, Fish."

"Ah, the hell with it," said the Fish mournfully, startling Coyote again; the Fish never used profanity. "Do you have to be right this time, Mister Jones? You are so addicted to being wrong—no, don't push me down, I'm all right now and I am going back to my desk—why can't you be wrong *this* time, in your customary fashion?"

"Because I am *right*. This time."

"Do you know what it's costing, this regular milk run of yours between Mars Central and Planet Ozark?"

"I can imagine."

"I doubt that!" The Fish pulled back his chair and sat down at his desk with a petulant thump.

"Do you know what it would cost to send the army you were suggesting?"

"Down to the last centicredit, I know what that would cost! I also know it would *work!* Sending you out there three times a week, and twice on Sundays, may go on for the rest of my life without ever getting me anything but stupid *reports*."

"I don't think so. If this doesn't work, I don't have any other ideas to try. I think this should just about wind it up."

The Fish blew air through puckered lips. "All right," he said. "All right. Go on, I'll authorize it. You think they'll let you land?"

Coyote shrugged. "I don't know . . . they let me last time, and they had very good reason not to. I suppose they don't think I'm worth the trouble involved in stopping me."

"Well. Go on, then. But make it good. And make it quick. And make it *work*, Mister Jones!"

"I will do the very best I can," Coyote assured him. "And that is all that I can do. And then if you want to send in troops, and you can get approval to do that—okay. But I'll give this my best efforts first."

The Fish nodded. "Get on with it," he said. "And no side trips to visit Miss Tzana Kai on the way, Jones. Go straight there."

"Yessir," Coyote said, tugging his forelock and doing a little shuffle. "On my way, sir. Right now, sir."

"Go, curse you!" hissed the Fish. "Get out of here!"

Coyote went. Dancing all the way.

"Now," Coyote began, "I have asked you to hold this conference—realizing that you're very busy people and that I've been imposing on your courtesy a good deal lately—because I feel that the information I am about to pass along to you is crucial to your survival. I won't apologize for asking for this meeting, under the circumstances; it was, and it is, a necessity."

"You have our attention," said Thorn of Guthrie crisply. "Now if you'd move along to the crucial *details*, we'd all be grateful."

"The Tri-Galactic Federation feels that you must know that Planet Ozark is in serious danger," said Coyote sternly. "You are under a serious, and dangerous, threat to your security. You will remember that just about ten years ago you had an unpleasant experience with the citizens of the Garnet Ring, who attempted to take over this planet—as I understand it, it was a near thing."

"Near enough," said Thorn. "But long past now."

"Well," said Coyote, "I'd like to tell you a little bit about this Garnet Ring, and what it means to you."

He had their interest now as well as their attention; he could see it in their faces. He went on quickly.

"The population of the Garnet Ring," he told them, "where the Out-Cabal is located, is made up entirely of a people called Phonans. They represent the most extreme example of divergent evolution known in the Three Galaxies."

"Which means, when you've strained out the claptrap?"

That was Granny Hazelbide. And Granny Gableframe glaring at him to indicate her agreement.

"Which means that, if we did not have solid physiological evidence that sometime in the dim reaches of prehistory the Phonans and the Terrans had a common ancestor, we would find it hard to believe. Even *with* the evidence, it's hard to believe, because the similarities are mostly internal. On the outside, you'd never know. An adult Phonan male is about eight feet long, is shaped exactly like a hose or a tube except for two prehensile appendages at each end, is about twenty inches around, and is a deep red color. Females, and offspring, are the same except for being smaller in size. And of course there are sexual gender differences, but they aren't obvious to the eye. The Phonans look like exactly what you would get if you had a giant scarlet snake and you cut out the middle, before the taper at each end. We have no idea how one Phonan identifies another Phonan, but we know for certain that it's not because of *visual* characteristics. They have nothing we can identify as faces, for instance, although there are vestigial dimples at one end that are the external markers of their eyes, noses, ears, and mouths. They take in nourishment through an opening at that end of the tube, but in addition they absorb much of what keeps them alive, through their flesh. They spend their lives in pools of liquid, side by side, attached at either end by the appendages to a wooden frame. A family of Phonans looks like nothing so much as an ancient *harp*, with the Phonans for strings, and the frame they're 'strung' to straight at one end and tapered at the other to accommodate the smaller members. And their entire culture—everything, from education to politics to religion to you name it—is based upon and revolves around music."

Coyote heard his voice in the silence, going on and on and on; he stopped to take a breath, hoping for a helpful question, and took a look at the faces around him. It was not an encouraging prospect. None of the Brightwater

family actually present in the room, and none of the
eleven images in the windows of the comset screen, offered him any encouragement whatsoever.

"It is *true!*" he declared. "However improbable it may
sound, my friends, it is true. Every word."

"Speak your piece," said Responsible of Brightwater
grimly. No helpful questions from her.

"I wanted first to acquaint you—"

"Mister Jones," she snapped, "we are Ozarkers. We've
seen strange critters aplenty. We have strange critters *on
this planet*. If what you're after is a lot of agitation over
your red snakestrings, you're wasting your time and ours.
We believe you; and some other time we'd much enjoy
hearing you tell us all about the Phonans, and what it's
like to run your whole life around music. We're not so
backward we don't find that interesting. But it is for sure
not something you'd ordinarily call a planetwide comset
conference for, and I suppose you must have something
more in mind." She glanced at the clock, and went "tsk"
at the sight of it. "I do *hope* you do, because you're tying
up every spare channel of the comsystem, plus a sizable
portion of the ones we ordinarily use for the tadlings'
schooling, and you're costing us precisely two hundred
and seventy-three dollars a minute. By my reckoning you've
spent two thousand seven hundred and thirty dollars of
our money on this Weird Critters Fable already, and
precious little to show for it."

"Well, if you'd shut up, Responsible," put in James
John Guthrie the 17th, Master of Castle Guthrie, "he
might could get to his point here. I'd say it's *you* that's
holding us up, not the offworlder."

Responsible considered that a second, and agreed. "You're
right," she said. "And I apologize. You might do us the
favor of continuing, then, Mister Jones."

"Thank you," said Coyote. "I appreciate that. Now, you

might think that because of their unusual physical characteristics, and the fact that music is their life, the Phonans wouldn't represent any kind of threat to more human-like peoples. But you would be wrong, as you Ozarkers discovered. The Phonans have one of the most highly developed psientific systems—" He caught himself, realizing what they would have heard, and went back. "That's 'psience,' with a *p. p-s-i-e-n-c-e*, 'psience.' The scientific theory and application of psibilities such as telepathy, telekinesis, precognition, and the like."

"Magic," said Responsible.

"No! *Psience*."

"Go right on, Mister Jones," said Thorn of Guthrie. "Never mind her."

"The Phonans," Coyote struggled on, "have one of the most highly developed such systems in the Federation. They don't have to get up and go haul their rocks—or their weapons—they do everything by psi-power. For most peoples, it's a lot more trouble to use telekinesis to wash dishes than it is to just go wash them—for the Phonans that's not true. They're essentially immobile creatures. They're not even any use as Communipaths, because their telepathic skills are so over-developed that their projections are actually physically harmful to everybody else, and if you don't let them stay with other Phonans they just use their powers to make themselves sick. For the Phonans, psibilities are their arms and their legs and their tools and their machines—and they are *incredibly* powerful."

He paused, and then he spoke with what he hoped was an impressively emphatic delivery. "And the Phonans are determined, in spite of the years that have gone by without any further open acts on their part, to conquer Planet Ozark and own it absolutely."

"Why?" asked the Master of Castle Brightwater. "What

the devil do a horde of animated harp strings want with Planet Ozark?"

"The key word there," Coyote answered, "is 'horde.' That's exactly the point, and I'm glad you made it. The Phonans' ideal family unit is an *octave*, a musical octave, with each family member being the representative of one of the eight notes. To be really important on Phona, you have to expand your family to a double octave, with fifteen notes, or even a triple one. Furthermore, their religion is one of those 'be fruitful and multiply' creeds, with the problem that they have to multiply by sevens and eights to feel that they are fulfilling their purpose in the universe. And they have used up all their space. It's just that simple. They need more room, and they don't have any left on their own planet."

"Planets, isn't it?" asked Thorn of Guthrie.

Coyote thought about that, and decided to be creative. "Phona is the *major* planet of the Garnet Ring," he said, hedging it as heavily as he dared. "There's no room on any of the smaller bodies either. They are crammed in together without an inch to spare. And you Ozarkers, from the Phonan point of view, have uncounted billions of inches just going to waste."

"The Wilderness Lands!"

"Those in particular, yes. Especially on your continents of Kintucky and Tinaseeh. The Phonans want them, since you don't seem to be using them."

"Can they live here?" asked Responsible. "In this atmosphere? This gravity?"

"Their primary need is for water . . . they add something to it, but the basic ingredient is water. You've got lots of water."

"And you think they are a genuine threat to us?"

"I do," said Coyote solemnly. "Indeed I do. And the

government of the Tri-Galactic Federation feels that they are."

Carefully, not wanting to overdo it, he projected a set of nicely vague accompaniments along the lines of PHONANS ARE TERRIFYING . . . THE PHONANS ARE OUT TO DESTROY US . . . WE NEED HELP OR WE WILL LOSE OZARK TO THE PHONANS . . . THE PHONANS ARE CREEPY MONSTERS . . .

And found himself sitting on the floor, knocked right off his chair by the psi-equivalent of a right-handed wallop to the side of the head. YOU DO THAT AGAIN, YOU'LL GO *THROUGH* THE FLOOR! was the obvious message that went with the wallop, and Coyote sat there blinking and shuddering, until Thorn of Guthrie suggested to him that he might be more comfortable in his chair. The tone of her suggestion included a whole collection of unstated comments about off-worlders who arrive drunk or demented to transact business.

Which one of them had it been?

Which one, he wondered, through the echoes sounding through his skull and down his spine. He was torn between gratitude for the mind-deafness that had probably protected him from most of the message—giving him nothing but the intonation and other "body language" that went with it—and frustration because that same handicap kept him from being able to identify the source. Every face within his vision was as bland as a blank sheet of paper, except for an understandable polite distaste over his falling off his chair. It could have been any one of them. Or all of them. Or somebody not even present. Or somebodies.

Coyote gathered himself together, stood up, dusted off his tunic, bowed slightly, sat down carefully, and lied some more.

"I'm sorry," he said. "I have a neurological disorder that

does strange things to me from time to time. I don't think it will happen again."

They made polite noises, all of them wearing faces of complete innocence. Ruth of Motley, Responsible's grandmother, even managed a look of sympathy and concern. But there was no question about it in Coyote's mind—it would *not* happen again. He was going to have to carry this one on the strength of his eloquence and charm alone; he wasn't about to risk having his brain frizzled in his head for the offense of telepathic projection.

"The Tri-Galactic Federation," he said slowly, "is both willing and able to protect Planet Ozark against this threat. We feel that it would be prudent and sensible for you to avail yourselves of the Federation's resources in this matter. As citizens of the Federation you could be absolutely sure that Phona would never be able to use its massive resources for psi-violence against you."

"*Aha!*" said Thorn of Guthrie. "There we are!"

"Yes, indeed," said Responsible. "You're back with your join-us-and-live-in-bliss routine, Mister Jones."

"And live in *safety!*" Coyote protested. "Your people, your lands, your world—all are in danger. We offer you safety!"

"Oh, law," said Responsible, and drew a long sighing breath. "You already had our answer on that!"

"But that was before you knew of the danger! That was—"

"Cowflop," said Responsible. "It's neighborly of you to let us know there's a kind of telepathic orchestra after our land. Thank you. It cost us a fortune, and you could just as well have put it in a brief note and dropped it off, instead of this circus of extravagance you tricked us into. I reckon we ought to be grateful, strictly speaking. But it doesn't change our position."

"Miss Re—"

"Gentlemen?" asked Responsible. "Masters of the Castles? You want to vote, here?"

"First let me tell you what the Phonans can—"

They drowned him out, inexorably. They were not going to let him describe the potential horrors of the Great Phonan Psi-Invasion, at two hundred seventy-three dollars a minute. They were not going to do anything but transmit their emphatic NO votes and sign off. Which they did, each of the windows flickering abruptly and going dead gray on the screen.

And Coyote sat there, insulted and frustrated and enraged beyond the limits of his endurance.

"*Now see here!*" he bellowed. "*And don't you interrupt me again!* You seem to feel that the Federation is wasting your time, and your money, and your energies, on a lot of nonsense. I want you to know that it costs *us*, too! You have no idea how much money it's costing to keep sending me back here to try to deal with you pig-headed people! You think a flyer goes from Mars Central to Ozark and ·back for free? You think a TGIS agent doesn't get paid?" He stared at them with his fists clenched and weaving in front of him, and they stared right back without a word.

"*Well?* Haven't you got anything to say at all, damn you?"

Responsible leaned over and turned off the comset, saying, "You might recall, Mister Jones, that you ordered us not to interrupt you again."

"I didn't order you to go catatonic!"

They kept staring, eyebrows raised and an expression of uniform genteel revulsion on their faces, until he was ready to go punch a hole right through their Castle wall. And he knew, miserably, that he'd done it again—as a diplomatic envoy he could be replaced by a chimpanzee. The chimpanzee would probably have been better at it.

"I'm sorry," he said finally, hopelessly. "I lost my temper."

"Well," said Responsible, "we've seen men carry on before, Mister Jones. You want to throw a fit, you go right ahead and throw it. Just try not to tie up our whole comset network for the occasion, in future."

"I'm sorry."

"You said that," Thorn of Guthrie told him. "We *heard* you."

"You really don't want the protection of the Federation?" he asked them desperately. "You really don't care if there's no line of defense between you and the Garnet Ring? After what they tried to do to you last time?"

"We really don't," Responsible told him. "Really and truly and forevermore. We have taken care of ourselves now for a thousand years, and we can no doubt take care of ourselves a little longer."

"But the government of the Federation worlds has resources at its disposal, mechanisms for maintaining order, that you cannot even imagine!"

Responsible gave him a look that stopped him flat, and made him swallow hard.

"In the histories," she said, "there's a right smart quantity of information about the kinds of resources and mechanisms that human governments fancy. There's torture, for example. That's a real good way of maintaining order, and the governments of Earth had an amazing skill at it. There's chemical warfare. There's nuclear bombs, and hydrogen bombs, and neutron bombs, and laser bombs. There's FILTH WITHOUT END OR BOUNDARY, Mister Jones. We do not want any of it."

"It's not like that," Coyote protested. "Not anymore!"

"When the Ozarkers lived on Earth," said Responsible, "it was the position of most governments that it 'wasn't like that' *then*. But there *was* torture. And there *was* killing. And there was rape. And there was destruction of the water and the air and the earth and the plants and the animals. . . . But if you had asked Earth's governments, Mister Jones, they would have said 'Oh, it's not like that. Not anymore!' "

It was true. Coyote knew that.

"And now," she went on, "you are prepared to swear to me that no government, of twenty thousand and more member worlds, uses violence and corruption as a 'mechanism for maintaining order'?"

He wasn't. As a member of the Tri-Galactic Intelligence Service, he knew far more about violence and corruption than he cared to remember.

"All in all," he said cautiously, "we have very little of the sort of thing that made your people leave Earth. *Very* little."

"All in all," said Responsible gravely, "we have *none* of it. And want none. And want none of its representatives, either."

"Dozens, Responsible!" said Thorn of Guthrie. *"That's* polite!"

"Mother, polite is not involved here. Mister Jones, I want you to understand that we don't want you back. We've indulged you, we've let you just come dropping in and out of here whenever you had a fancy to do so, never mind the nuisance, we've tried to be neighborly, we've listened to everything you had to say, and we've gone along with all this truck—and now *that's enough*. Don't you come knocking on our door again, Mister Jones. And you tell your government that we don't want anyone else here on its behalf, demonstrating 'mechanisms for maintaining order' or anything else, ever again. Is that clear, Mister Jones?"

And she finished it off by explaining that she was downright positive—she had a feeling in her bones—that any future visitors come to call on Ozark were going to be met by truly nasty turbulence in the airspace. She regretted

this, but she felt entirely helpless about it; and she thought
it only fair that Coyote Jones should be explicitly warned
so that no one would be taken by surprise.

It made Coyote so blind furious raving mad that he
marched out of the room with his blood boiling and his
stomach churning and his heart pounding away in his
chest, without ever remembering to tell them about the
little Phonan spy-sensors lying everywhere like dustmice.
He remembered eventually, perhaps ten feet from the
Castle gates, but there weren't enough credits left on
Mars Central to make him go back and deliver the message. The hell with them. He, Coyote Jones, was *through*
being nice. Let them find out for themselves, or let them
rot. He didn't care.

Still fuming, he was just about to step into his flyer when
he heard a soft voice beside him and turned to see a man
pretending elaborate interest in the little craft.

"Yes?" he said, trying not to take out on this innocent
stranger the way he felt about Ozarkers.

"Mister Jones," the fellow said, "I'd appreciate it if
you'd just make out like we were talking about this little
ship of yours."

And he patted the flyer, and made admiring faces, and
went on, "But what I am really here for is to tell you that
Smith Kingdom *does* want to join the Tri-Galactic Federation."

It took Coyote a minute to understand, and then he
finally heard the words and got a little bit of his attention
off his fury.

"You voted against it," he said, watching. "I heard you."

"Well . . . you wouldn't be in a position to understand
our ways, Mister Jones. But there are a lot of us as don't
feel that Responsible of Brightwater needs to know our
business, if you take my meaning. And we at Smith are

prepared to secede from the Confederation of Continents of Ozark and join up with the Tri-Galactic Federation, if you'll have us. We'd be proud to. We've run the vote ourselves, Mister Jones, and it's near eighty percent for joining."

Coyote was taken aback. This was a proposition completely outside his experience.

"I don't know what to say," he said, and that was the truth. "I'll have to go back and talk with my government. This wasn't part of my briefing."

"I understand. But I'll ask you to respect our confidence. That is, I wouldn't want the word to get out about this on Ozark."

"Of course not. And we'll contact you. At once."

"How?"

Coyote thought about that. He thought about the reaction he would get to the idea of yet another trip out here. He thought about the nicely laid out little problem of "turbulence" in Ozark's airspace. And he put them both aside for the moment and said, "I'll meet you here at this same time, as near one week from today as is possible, to discuss formal arrangements. Will that be suitable?"

They shook hands on it, and Coyote flew back to tell Fish the awful results of his day's work. As predicted, he had found a way to mess it up. He thought.

Could a single nation secede from one world and join another?

Coyote had no idea.

CHAPTER NINE

"All I can tell you is that we can't find anything specifically forbidding it," said the man from Justice.

"The search was thorough?"

The man shrugged. "You tell a computer to search, it searches. Computers aren't programmed to do superficial searches, Citizen."

"But nothing specifically permits it? There's no authorized procedure for an instance like this?"

"Look, there's no section of the legislative code that says anything like 'Taking Portions of Worlds Into the Federation After Secession, Procedures For.' Nothing remotely like that. But as I said, there's nothing that says you *can't* do it, either. And there are precedents. Of a very strained sort, but precedents."

"For example?" The Fish was eager; he was as sick of all the delays as Coyote was.

"For example, there've been a number of instances where a planet was inhabited mostly by indigenous non-humanoid beings who had no desire to join the Federation . . . at least, so far as we could *tell*, they had none, if you

133

know what I mean. I mean, how can you be sure whether or not a thinking gas cloud would enjoy being a member of your group? But so far as we could tell, they didn't cáre to join, and there was a small population of humanoids who *did* care to. We have, in those instances, accepted the population into citizenship despite the fact that they were only a minority of the world's inhabitants."

"This isn't much like that," Coyote pointed out. "This is a situation where we *know* that most of the inhabitants don't want anything to do with us, and there's no question about it. And it's not because they aren't suited for membership, it's because they just plain don't *want* it."

"I understand that," said the man from Justice.

"If we do this," Coyote said to the Fish, "the Council will introduce legislation to keep it from happening again."

"Probably. Locking the barn door after the horse is out—just barely out. But we can, presumably, do it this once."

"There'll be considerable outrage over it," the man warned them. "The member worlds are not going to care much for the idea that some eccentric segment of their population might decide on its own to deal unilaterally with the Federation government—that has an ugly ring to it, you know. You can count on legislative safeguards going into place in a hurry."

"Good enough," said the Fish briskly. "That means we have to move fast before something leaks and gives them a chance to get a law in place that would stop us. Coyote will have to go right back out."

The man from Justice cleared his throat and started gathering up his microfiches. "You'd better haul ass," he said bluntly, "if you'll pardon a quaint old figure of speech. Because I have to report this little effort of yours. Today."

"Today?" The Fish struck the desk with the heel of his

hand. "Look here—you can give us a little more time than that."

"No, I can't give you a little time. I gave you a *lot* of time when I came over here and reported to you without already ringing the bell on you, Citizen Wythllewyn. I could get away with that. Because I can take the position that I fully expected you to say—after you heard my remarks on the situation—that of course you wouldn't go ahead with this. That, I can manage. But no more."

"How long do we have?" The Fish didn't try to argue; the correctness of the man's position was obvious.

"I can stretch this until mid-afternoon. . . . I've got a stack of other stuff to do, calls to make, computer conferences to oversee . . . that kind of thing. But by sixteen hundred hours there'll be a full report in. That's the best I can offer you."

"Four o'clock," said the Fish, frowning. "That's it?"

"That's it. I can't do better."

The Fish nodded slowly, and went through the briefest ritual of thank you and good-bye consistent with civilized behavior, and then he started hitting the studs and the buttons. Coyote didn't bother telling him that it wasn't going to work out exactly right, because even allowing for the time coming and going he wasn't going to arrive back on Planet Ozark at the specified one-week-later-at-this-same-time that he'd agreed on. He'd just have to manage when he got there, and that was all there was to it. He was beginning to feel like a driver for the Greyhound Rockets, and it was deadly. How they stood it, doing the same thing over and over and over as they did, he couldn't begin to imagine.

"What are you up to?" he asked the Fish, the first time he saw him come up for air. "Fill me in! I'm the one that has to *do* this, you know."

"The problem," said the Fish, crisp and clean and humming right along, "is how to get this done fast, in view of the unreasonable attitude the Ozarkers have taken."

"Unreasonable doesn't cover it, Fish. Hostile. Barbaric. Violent. Deranged. *Those* might do it."

"I know that."

"*Any*body shows up in their airspace," Coyote went on doggedly, "anybody at all, they get that 'turbulence' I got the first time, and it keeps on until they give up and go home. Unless you think you can arrange to send in troops, and that doesn't seem likely to me."

"I understand all that."

"What are you doing, then? You've pushed everything there is to push, and some of it twice."

"I'm arranging to get a Communipath to help us out, Mister Jones."

Coyote's eyebrows went up, and he gave a low admiring whistle. You didn't just go calling up a Communipath and asking for a favor. That was something that required months of patient filling out of forms. Even then, it wasn't easy. The Communipaths were too important, and too busy, and too few.

"You must be good at what you do, Fish," he said generously.

"It warms my heart to hear you say so. Now I will be able to go on with my work with renewed confidence, et cetera, et cetera."

"You're welcome, I'm sure."

"The Communipath has the coordinates for this rogue— and will get the young woman you call Responsible when she uses them, I suppose."

"I think so," Coyote said. "Not that that tells us anything more than that Responsible is the one participating at that particular moment. But I'm pretty sure that's who you'll get."

"I don't understand the function of that young woman."

Coyote shrugged. "Neither do I," he said. "And the Ozarkers don't seem to understand it either. She's got no title, no power that I can see, no trappings—but they're mighty quick to move when Responsible *says* move. And it was Responsible who told me what would happen if we tried coming back again. Either she just knows, or she's in charge; certainly, she's authorized to hand out the messages."

"We could use some more information," said the Fish. "But we don't have time to try to get it, and we're going ahead as we are. I've got a Communipath right now, clearing her message decks so that she can go after the rogue's coordinates. Whoever or whatever she gets at that end, she's going to ask for permission for you to come back for one more visit."

"She won't get it," said Coyote, with total conviction.

The Fish smiled at him, and rubbed his hands together, palm to long white palm. "You don't know that," he said. "Remember the man that you promised a copy of the King James Bible to, Mister Jones? You *promised*."

"So I did. That doesn't make it possible."

"Given the rigid morality of these Ozarkers," the Fish went on, "I don't consider it at all unlikely that if we tell Responsible . . . or whomever . . . that you made a solemn *promise* while you were there and need time to carry it out, they'll let you do it. A promise is a promise. A man's word is his bond, and so on. All those primitive stipulations—Ozark seems to take them seriously. Not to mention the fact that even Ozark will realize that if a promise is important enough to be given the attention of a Federation Communipath it's not a trivial matter. It's not as if *you* were the one asking."

"Huh," said Coyote.

"Well?"

"It's possible," he admitted, grudgingly. "But I also promised to keep the promise a secret."

"Mister Jones . . ." The Fish's white teeth flashed. "You can *count* on that! If we told them the promise was only a book, they'd just tell us to pitch it over the side of the flyer, or some such nonsense. We'll tell them that you made a promise, but were booted off so abruptly that you couldn't fulfill it—and this troubles your conscience deeply— and that the promise is so significant that you also gave your word you would keep it a secret. Unless I have misjudged the Ozarkers by a very wide margin, that will push all the right buttons, and they'll let you do your duty."

"I don't know," said Coyote wearily. "Maybe you're right. What's going on at this particular moment?"

"Right now we're just waiting for the 'Path to get back to us. And with any luck, right now we're almost ready for you to head out there again. For the last time."

"Oh, please," Coyote said reverently. "Please let it be the last time."

"Mister Jones?"

"Mmmmm?"

"Do you have any idea why the man wanted a Bible so badly?"

"Well," said Coyote, rubbing fretfully at his beard, "they don't have even one copy on the planet, according to him—that would make it pretty spectacular in the 'rare book' line. And over ten centuries I suppose it's become fabled as well as sacred. I can see why he'd want it—it would be worth a fortune."

"Reasonable," said the Fish. "Yes, that's reasonable. See what you can get him to trade for it. I fancy rare books, and fortunes, my*self*."

"How about one of their manuals of nasty potions? You could have a potion-tasting party for the holidays."

The Fish snickered, and then they sat there. There was no small talk made in that office. There was business, and there was waiting for business, but that was absolutely all there was. Coyote tried to amuse himself by reviewing old song lyrics in his head, and he broke the tedium occasionally by going to the window and staring down at the tiny dots that were living beings far below. As for the Fish, he just sat. Quietly. Hands folded, and face placid.

When the answer came in from the Communipath, it made them both jump. They'd been expecting it to be on the Fish's scrambled line, of course, but they hadn't expected it to come in on Topsecret, purple lights flashing along with the red one to alert them.

The Fish punched the necessary studs and motioned to Coyote to pick up an ear contact—this didn't look like something he'd want on general broadcast even in *his* office. Coyote grabbed the ear and heard the end of the opening obligatories. Including the Fish—the Fish!—calling the woman "Citizen"!

"Yes; thank you," the old man was saying. "Now if you'd tell us what happened. Quickly, please—we have a lot to do. Did you get through?"

"I did," came the reply. "That was no problem. The young woman said, and I quote, 'it's a blessed lot easier than having to go through the mules.' Whatever that may mean. I didn't want to take time to explore the question."

"Quite right," said the Fish. "You got Responsible of Brightwater, then?"

"Not exactly."

Coyote and the Fish looked at each other, and they both said, "What do you mean, not exactly?" as if they'd rehearsed it.

"It's a little complicated."

"Try!"

"Well . . . let me see how I can put this. Citizen Wythllewyn, there is a whole group of 'Responsibles.' There is the current one, from this time period. And then there are the others, from other time periods—I could not be sure, in that brief contact, whether they are all from earlier times or perhaps from future times as well. But I counted a dozen at least, trying to be quick."

That silenced even the Fish; he sat chewing his lower lip, and if it had not been a Communipath on the line there might have been some query as to whether he was still there. Since it *was* a Communipath, nothing happened until he asked her to hold on for a moment and she agreed.

"Mister Jones?" asked the Fish slowly. "Do you know anything about this?"

Coyote shook his head. "Not one thing."

"All this stuff about a dozen Responsibles? Past and future time periods?"

"Fish—it makes no sense to me at all. *None.*"

"You never heard anything about this on Ozark? Not even a hint?"

"Nothing. Period. But I tell you, it settles the question of whether Responsible of Brightwater is herself a telepath— I'd say she is at *least* that."

The Fish nodded, and then he spoke to the Communipath again, his words coming with uncharacteristic hesitation. He said, "Citizen, we will want to discuss this at *length*, very soon—and you did the proper thing in putting it on this line. Thank you. But there's no time to explore it right now. Right now, I'm just going to pretend that it all seems perfectly normal to me. Please tell me, as quickly as you can, what happened. I won't ask questions."

"I put out a call on the coordinates we had," said the Communipath. "I got not one, but at least thirteen Responsibles, perhaps more. The one present in this time

period is not aware that the others are . . . participating?
. . . I don't know how to put it."

"You're doing fine," the Fish assured her. "Please go
on."

"Roughly, the other Responsibles know of one another,
and are in contact with one another. They also are in
contact with the current Responsible, if I did not misunderstand. They are *all* in contact, Citizen Wythllewyn.
But the current one doesn't know it. Apparently there is
some sort of mental guard against that, for her."

"You spoke to them all, then?"

"It's not possible to do anything else. To speak to one is
to speak to all, despite the current young woman's ignorance of that fact. I mindspoke *all* the Responsibles. I told
them that Citizen Jones had made a promise, that it was
both solemn and confidential, and that he was distressed
at not being able to keep his word. I asked for one exception to the ban on travel to Ozark, so that he could be
relieved of this obligation."

"And?"

"And they weren't especially pleasant," came the answer. "But they did agree. After some rather sarcastic
remarks about waste and frivolousness and bad manners,
and so on."

"All of them agreed?"

"All of them. With the current one believing that she
acts independently, of course. Citizen Jones has been
granted one hour on Ozark—sixty minutes, Old Earth
time, almost precisely."

"It can't be done!" the Fish protested. "Not in one
hour!"

"They were very specific," said the Communipath. "One
hour or not at all. And they were reluctant to do *that*, I
assure you. I suggest you take it and be glad you have it,

Citizen. It is all that you are going to be allowed. Without the use of force of some sort, that is."

"One hour . . ." The Fish was concentrating so hard that there was almost normal color in his face. "One hour *when*, Citizen?"

"Nothing specified," said the Communipath. "Whenever he arrives, they'll give him one hour from instant of landing to instant of departure, without any interference. So long as he does not abuse their courtesy, they said—and that is a quote."

"Citizen," said the Fish slowly, "you have done very well. The Bureau appreciates it. But I wonder . . . did you get any sort of idea what these—these Responsibles—do? What they are *for*, in other words? Obviously they are all telepaths, but what *else* are they?"

"I'm sorry. I had no instructions to seek that information."

The Fish sighed. "No," he agreed. "Of course you didn't. My apologies."

"And I was somewhat startled, you understand. This was not what I had been told to expect. I was afraid of creating some sort of problem; I made every effort to be discreet."

"I understand," said the Fish. "Congratulations, on a job well done."

"Thank you. I do try. Is that everything, then?"

"Almost," said the Fish. "One more thing. This information is not to go any farther. You understand that."

"Of course. But it will have to be reported to my Chief—in confidence—at tomorrow's briefing. It's not exactly a routine episode."

"I know. No problem. Just don't mention it prior to that time, not to anyone. My authority is sufficient to make that stipulation, Citizen."

"Certainly," she answered. "That's quite clear."

"And then, subsequent to that briefing, we'll want to set up a special meeting to explore this development. But right now, I am going to dismiss you with the grateful thanks of your government, Citizen. Because we obviously do not have much time."

Talk of understatements, Coyote thought. The only thing that might make this possible was the ludicrous slow turning of the bureaucratic wheels. The Justice man's report would go in today, sure; but the chances that it would be examined before late tomorrow were slim, even if he flagged it for prompt attention. *Everything* that happened at Justice was flagged for prompt attention. The Communipath would pass on what she'd learned, tomorrow morning, to her superior; and there'd be a report turned in on *that* sometime soon after the briefing—but again, it might be a whole day, even longer, before anyone took a serious look at it. Everything had to go through channels; and even with the computers, the channels for managing the affairs of more than twenty thousand worlds were not set up for breakneck speed. Which was just as well. If there was one thing that had been learned as the peoples of the Three Galaxies struggled to make things work, it was that the ancient "Don't just sit there, *do* something!" imperative was not suitable for their purposes. In the long run, the stately deliberate pace of government was the only possible pace. And in this very peculiar instance, chances were good that it would give Coyote time to get in and get out before anything could be done to clock the mission.

If, he realized, snapping to attention, *if he moved!* Right this instant!

"I've got to get going," he told his chief, coming out of the chair in a single motion that nearly turned it over. "There's not a second to spare here. Don't give me a long list of stuff, don't give me a briefing—I don't need it. Just

let me get out of here before I get my tail caught in some
door, Fish. This one is going to be cut close."

"How are you—"

"BEMdung!" Coyote roared. "How do *I* know? How
am I going to find the representative from Castle Smith?
How am I going to get the treaties out and explained and
signed and the ceremonies all over and all that garbage?
How am I going to do all that, and get back out, and do it
in one hour? I don't *know* how I'm going to do it, Fish,
but I do know that if I don't head out of here *right* now
there isn't a prayer. I've still got copies of all the cursed
documents, the Light be praised!"

"All right," the Fish said. "You're right. Go, Mister
Jones. We'll tie up the loose ends when you get back. Cut
all the corners you need to cut on the ceremonial parts—
I'll back you up."

"Just one thing."

"Name it."

"I want a Communipath checking for messages at those
coordinates on Ozark, *and* the coordinates for Smith Kingdom, Fish. You can get those by extrapolating from the
Brightwater ones. I want a Communipath checking *both*
places for messages every thirty minutes. I don't care how
many strings you have to pull—pull the one you pulled to
get that message out this morning—and I don't care what
the policy is about agents on assignment being on their
own. I do this if and only if I know there's some way for
me to yell for help if I need it. This situation is *strange!*"

"Agreed," said the Fish.

"I have no intention of being swallowed up by some
mysterious 'Circle of Responsibles' from out of the future
and the past! Light's Testicles, Fish! I—"

"I said, *agreed.*"

"Every thirty minutes?"

"Every thirty minutes. Both places. You've got it. I

don't think it's unreasonable at all, which is a first for you, Mister Jones."

"Okay," said Coyote. "Here I go."

And he went.

CHAPTER TEN

They must have had somebody watching for him, Coyote thought. His arrival was nowhere near the "one week from today" that had been specified, but there was a Smith waiting and ready as he touched down, sitting on the back of a Mule and raring to go.

He'd come in gingerly, braced for fancy turbulence and damn grateful when he didn't encounter any, the little Bible tucked in an outside pocket where he could get to it fast. It had been expensive, getting it in book form instead of on fiche, but he'd been sure that a *book*, be it ever so tiny, was what the Magician of Blue Ear had had in mind. Even on Mars Central, people still had to labor to view a microfiche as sacred.

Coyote had turned off the flyer, set foot on Ozark, and been told to climb up behind the Smith, in about three minutes flat.

"But—"

"No buts," said the fellow on the Mule, who was wearing the fancy costume that Coyote had seen on Veritas

Truebreed Motley at Castle Brightwater. A Magician of Rank, then. "Climb on up here! There's no time to waste!"

Coyote planted his feet and folded his arms over his chest.

"I have one errand to do," he said stubbornly. "And I don't move till I do it."

"What is it?"

Coyote pulled the packet, innocuous to the eye, from his tunic. "This," he said. "It's got to go to the Magician at Blue Ear. I gave him my word."

"What's in it?" the Magician of Rank demanded, but Coyote shook his head and smiled a kind of sanctimonious reproof.

"None of your business," he said, knowing quite well how to handle this. "Don't you have any concern at all for privacy?"

The Magician of Rank flushed and responded just as Coyote had thought he would. It was of *course* not his business, and he was indeed sorry to have pried into another's affairs . . . Coyote was proud. He felt like a diplomat at last. And he stood his ground while the Magician whistled up a youngster of maybe thirteen and charged him with taking the packet to the Magician of Blue Ear. That took perhaps two more minutes.

"Now," said the man from Smith Kingdom, "that's done! And I'd be pleased to see you climb up, Mister Jones, and that right smartly."

"I'm not much for—" Coyote began, but the Magician lifted a hand to hush him.

"The Mule will stand, however much you fumble it," he said. "I am Joseph Everholt Purdy the 46th, Magician of Rank to Castle Smith and Smith Kingdom, brother to Marygold of Purdy, Missus of Castle Smith, at your service; the Mule is called Willow. And we have things to do. Up, Mister Jones!"

The getting up wasn't much of a chore; Coyote congratulated himself on having done it rather well, considering. But he had a surprise coming. His tail end was applied to the Mule's back, there in the field beside his flyer in the heart of Brightwater Kingdom; and then he was somewhere else entirely, in the courtyard of a castle that was certainly not Castle Brightwater. With nothing at all in between, so far as he could determine.

In front of him, Joseph Everholt said, "You can get down now, Mister Jones. We're here."

Coyote swallowed twice before he found his voice.

"*Oh* no," he said, then. "*Oh*, no!"

"I beg your pardon?"

"I said *no*."

"No?" The Magician of Rank turned his head and stared at his fellow passenger. "You want to transact your business from the back of the Mule?" He was clearly taken aback. "That's a curious custom, Mister Jones, but if it's what the Tri-Galactic Federation ordinarily does, I suppose we'll have to abide by it. You'd be a great deal more comfortable, however, if you'd go inside the Castle with me and do this in their Meetingroom instead."

Coyote thought it over.

"Where are we?" he asked, clinging to the Mule. "And how did we get here?"

The Magician of Rank's eyebrows went up, and he vaulted smartly to the ground and reached a hand to help the tremulous off-worlder. "We're at Castle Smith," he said, "where we ought to be. As to how we got here, I SNAPPED us here. It's abrupt, but it's efficient. A great saving of time."

"It's instantaneous?"

"As near as makes no difference."

"And the Mule does it?"

Joseph Everholt drew himself stiffly up to his full height

and glared. "Of course not!" he snapped. "The Magicians of Rank do it."

"Can you do it without a Mule? Can you do it if you're in a boat? Or in one of your tinlizzies?"

The expression of disdain on the man's face intensified. And curious as he was, Coyote was forced to agree with the impatience he saw there. There in fact *wasn't* time for this. Later. Later, along with everything else. A dozen or more Responsibles, some from the past, some maybe from the future. Travel across time and space, with no middle. Flying beasts of burden, with no wings. Telepathic illusions that functioned on automatic. It was *too much,* and it would all have to wait.

"Sorry, friend," he said. "I'm getting down right now. Willow, you hold still, please."

The Mule whuffled, and her ears went back, but she held, and Coyote was grateful again. He brushed himself off, not that there was so much as a fleck of dust on him to show he'd been anywhere, and he followed the Magician of Rank into the castle with as much dignity as the wobble of his legs would allow.

He was certain, exactly seventeen minutes later, that there had never in the history of the Federation been any such truncated set of treaty ceremonies as those with Smith Kingdom. There'd been people ready at tables with pens poised, pens in the ancient mode and suitable for use on real paper; there'd been styluses to hand, in case that was what was needed; there'd been a bottle of something powerful, to be opened as the last squiggle was added, and toasts poured and drunk all round. And each time Coyote had tried to go through some of the usual diplomatic ritual they'd said the same thing.

"Never mind," they'd said. "Sign here."

But didn't they want him to read once again the responsibilities of the TGF citizen? Never mind, they said. Didn't they want him to read once again the list of privileges and benefits of the TGF citizen? Never mind. Didn't they want him to go over the terms of the treaty, the provision for one hundred years of Novice Planet status, the details? Never mind. Sign here. Sign there. It was done at top speed, start to finish; and when Smith Kingdom, formerly of Planet Ozark's Confederation of Continents, had become the two thousand three hundred ninety-fourth member world of the Tri-Galactic Federation, Coyote had been on the planet a sum total of twenty-four minutes. As the Ozarkers would have said, he had never seen the like. He had never even *imagined* the like.

Responsible of Brightwater had put out the word of his visit and its terms by comset, they'd told him in passing. "She says you have one hour, and one hour only, not one second more. And we'll have you back at your flyer with ten minutes to spare, and all our business done, you see if we don't."

Looking around him at his new fellow Citizens, Coyote believed it.

"Well!" he said. "Welcome to the Tri-Galactic Federation!"

"Thank you kindly," said Delldon Mallard Smith the 2nd, the Master of the Castle, and his lady Missus echoed it and it ran round the room.

"How long," asked Delldon Mallard, "will it take for . . . uh . . . the system to begin working?"

How long before the goodies arrive, Coyote thought. All perfectly normal.

"I can't tell you that," he said frankly. "This is a new experience for us—we've never had anyone join us in this way. Ordinarily it would be only the amount of time required to send in various teams to equip the planet for transmission of services, and so on, and it wouldn't have been much with a planet so nearly like Old Earth to work on. But we can't do it that way here, and I am not sure exactly how we *will* do it. I can promise you it will be done as rapidly as it's possible to do it."

"That's fair," said Delldon Mallard. "It . . . uh . . . makes sense."

"I'd say the first step would be to notify the rest of Ozark that you're no longer part of them, politically speaking," Coyote said. And he was just opening his mouth to add that it would be wise to let him get *off* Ozark before they did that when they told him it had already been taken care of.

"Message went out by comset while we were drinking to the occasion," said one of the various Smith brothers standing near him.

"You mean they already know?" Coyote was horrified.

"They surely do," chuckled Delldon Mallard. "They surely do. And I'd give a good deal to see the faces on Responsible of Brightwater and all her crew right this minute . . . happy they won't be, Mister . . . uh . . . Jones!"

"Don't you think you should have waited until after you'd seen me safely away from here?" Coyote demanded furiously.

"You afraid of that scrawny female?"

"Damn right, I'm afraid of her!" Coyote said. "If she's the one that turns flyers into whirligigs in the air, I'm scared *blue* of that woman! And I don't appreciate your turning me over to her tender mercies!"

"No problem, Mister Jones," said the Magician of Rank soothingly. "You have one hour's safe conduct. I'll SNAP you right back to your vehicle—right now, Mister Jones— and you'll be gone well within the time you were given. She wouldn't lay a finger on you while you're an invited guest."

"Are you sure of that?"

"Absolutely sure. You have it wrong anyway—it's not Responsible you should worry about, it's the Magicians of Rank. Of which she's got only one, and I assure you I am a match for him."

"Then let's get out of here! I want to be well out of your airspace when my sixty minutes run out!"

"Are we all through here?"

"Signed, sealed, and delivered," Coyote told them. "I've got the treaties in my pocket, you've got your copies—it's *done*. Now get me out of here." He started for the door, and then he paused for one second. "What did they *say?*" he asked. "When you told them the news."

"We don't know," said Joseph Everholt.

"How can you not know? You told them, they said something."

"We told them, they turned off the comsets," observed the Magician of Rank.

"I don't understand."

"All comset transmission originates from or is forwarded by Brightwater," said Joseph Everholt. "When we told them we'd seceded from Ozark and joined the Federation, Brightwater just cut us off. There was no time for anybody to say anything."

Coyote looked around him. Nobody seemed upset . . . everyone looked as if nothing could be more normal than to find yourself suddenly without communications and reduced to . . . what? Sending people SNAPPING off to Brightwater, he guessed, to negotiate to have them turned back on. Not his problem, anyway.

"All right," he said. "Let's go, then, and hope for the best. We're cutting it awfully close."

He thought, as he and the Magician of Rank hurried toward the courtyard and the astonishing Mule that waited for them there, that this was one noisy kingdom. He'd had no chance, in the rush, to look around the city that surrounded the castle; but it had to be a big and a bustling one. It reminded him of Jerdany, on Antus, where the constant roar of people and traffic was like a mighty surf all day and all night long. And he expected, as they went out the door, to see a crowd going about its daily business in and around the castle.

He did *not* expect what he actually saw, nor, it was obvious, had the Magician of Rank expected it. They both stopped short in the wide double doorway and stared in amazement. And Coyote winced a little—he was deeply weary of surprises and amazements.

"What the Dozens is going *on* out here?" his companion demanded.

As well he might. There were terrified screams, there was muffled shouting of the sort that goes with civil emergencies, there was pounding of running feet, there was what Coyote was reasonably sure was hysterical weeping, and it came from every direction, pouring over them in a flood of noise that was like a physical blow.

Coyote looked at the Magician of Rank for an explanation, and saw only confusion and the beginnings of serious alarm; apparently this was not just a normal business day in Red Arches.

"Something's wrong, I guess," he said, aware that it was superfluous, but anxious to bring Joseph Everholt out of his state of shock and get away from here before his hour had expired. The meter was ticking, as Coyote was well aware.

"Yes. Something. Is. Wrong."

"Well? Do you know what it is?"

"Look there," said the man, in a voice that shook slightly, and he raised his arm to direct Coyote's eyes. "Look there, Mister Jones!"

Coyote looked where he was pointing, and looked long

and hard, but he had no idea what he was supposed to be seeing. He had to shout over the growing clamor from all around them. "What is it? I don't see anything to cause all this commotion!"

The Magician of Rank let his arm fall and stood there with his chin in his hand; he was as pale as his robes. "It's that wall, Mister Jones," he said. "That quite *new* wall."

"Wall?" Coyote looked again, and there was indeed a wall, perhaps ten feet high, running all around as far as he could see. "I see it . . . is there something wrong with it?"

"I don't know," declared the Magician of Rank. "But I do know it wasn't there when we went into the Castle. It's gone up in the last few minutes, while we were inside."

"That's not possible," Coyote scoffed.

"It's there. You see it."

"If it wasn't there half an hour ago, it's an illusion," said Coyote firmly. "And if it's frightening your people, I'm sorry about that. But it's something you'll have to see to later, Joseph Everholt, because we've got about ten minutes to get me off this planet. The stuff your government dishes up for those not allowed in its airspace is not anything I care to experience again, thank you, wall or no wall!"

The Magician of Rank gave him a blank look, as if he couldn't remember exactly who he was or what he was doing there, and then something inside him made a necessary adjustment and his face cleared.

"You're right," he said. "I don't know what I'm thinking of! We could have gone and been back while I'm standing here like a fool servingmaid. Come along, and we'll get this done."

They ran for the Mule and climbed to its back, and Coyote grabbed the Magician and waited for the same nothing that he'd experienced when they'd come here. And that was what he got, except that they *went* nowhere, so far as he could tell. At least, if they'd been somewhere it had been no use, because they were still right there in the courtyard.

The Magician of Rank came up with a curse that had an ingenuity even Coyote felt free to marvel at, and told him to hold on while they tried again.

Nothing. There they sat.

Coyote sighed. He'd known, from the first minute, that this was all going far too easily. The man from Smith being there the instant he landed. The neat trip to Smith Kingdom, with its instantaneous mode of travel. Everything ready to go and all done without the least hitch. The beautiful orchestration of it all, to take not one second over the sixty minutes allotted. It had been beautiful, but it had made him nervous, as did any too perfect series of events. It wasn't natural for things to go like that, and he had known somewhere inside that it couldn't keep *on* like that.

"It isn't working," he said mournfully.

"What isn't working?"

"This SNAPPING business. It's—broken. Out of order. Whatever."

"No," said the Magician of Rank. "It's working, all right."

"Aw, Joseph Overholt. . . . we're still right here!"

"But this 'here' is not exactly the same 'here,' Mister Jones. We'll try it one more time, but first you take a good long look around you. Notice where Willow's feet are set—take good note of what's by them. Mind that stone there by her left rear hoof? Now . . . here we go!"

Nothing.

"Now look again, Mister Jones! Look well—what do you see?"

Ah, yes. Coyote saw it now. They *had* been moving. The stone that had been beside the Mule's hoof was now a good six inches away from it—they were not in exactly the same place they had been. Somebody had put a short tether—a very short tether—on the range of the SNAP. And he only had five minutes left in his safe passage.

Coyote didn't hesitate. He shouted for the Magician of Rank to follow him and bring his damn Mule, and he ran for the gate he saw at the end of the street leading out of the courtyard. Perhaps if they could get ouside the mysterious wall the "magic" would work again, not that he believed it could work in any case, but this was no time for metaphysical quibbles. He and the Magician of Rank pounded down the street, the Mule following somewhat more sedately, the Magician's hand light on her bridle, and they raced out the gate with about two minutes' grace.

And were, as they went out, right back inside again.

"Ah, BEMdung," said Coyote, feeling sick.

He tested it again, just to be sure, but he knew already what was going to happen. You could walk right out through the gate, no impediment to your progress whatsoever. You could run through it, you could jump through it, you could go through at any point. It made no difference. When you got out, you were back inside. And when you tried, as they eventually did try, to go *over* the wall, the same thing happened. Nothing hindered you, you could climb right up your ladder and down the ladder on the other side to the ground—but when you set foot on that ground you were once again inside the wall. And Coyote's hour was long past.

"Well, well, well," said Coyote. Secret Agent Makes Profound Comment. "Well, well, *well! Now* what?"

"Now, wait a minute!" said the Magician of Rank, very cross. "Just hold on a minute." And he called an assortment of the men near them who seemed to have themselves approximately under control, and gave a few quick orders.

"I want you to spread out," he said. "Get everybody you can to help you. I want you to take ladders and try going over the wall *everywhere* along its length. . . . I suppose it runs right round the kingdom, curse it twelve times twelve times! I'll go in and send out a message to the rest—"

He stopped short, remembering. The comset wasn't working anymore.

"Never mind," he said. "We'll have to just spread the word by each one telling those nearest him. I want not one inch of the wall missed, you understand? It might be there's a break somewhere along it, some scrap of space that's not properly warded, where we could get through."

"Huh," said a man at his side, all scorn. "Not likely, Joseph Everholt. Not likely *a*tall, and well you know it!"

"Do you have a better suggestion?" asked the Magician of Rank. "Would you like to spend the next month trapped in here and then find out that the tangle only held just here and there along the wall, and if we'd had the gumption to check we could have left any time? Does that strike your fancy, man?"

The men looked at him, grumbling, and then they shrugged and went off to start the process of checking the wall for quality control, and Coyote said, "What's next?"

"Wait again," said the Magician of Rank.

He stepped skillfully to the back of the Mule, raised both his hands into the air in front of him, made a few motions that Coyote wasn't quick enough to follow, and then spoke as a golden arrow flickered into being between his palms. And Coyote was much impressed; as the man talked, his words appeared beside his head as a line of gold and went sailing off, presumably to carry the message all over Smith Kingdom. Coyote suppressed the impulse to applaud, not so astonished that he couldn't see it wouldn't be appropriate, and watched the words go winging away.

They said, approximately, that there was nothing to be afraid of. That the wall was only magic. That no doubt Brightwater Kingdom, jealous of the wonderful life about to begin for the citizens of Smith as members of the Tri-Galactic Federation, was at the bottom of this. That the Magician of Rank was working on the problem and expected to have it solved momentarily. That everyone should calm down and go about their business. That as they could easily see, if they'd stop their caterwauling and carrying on, there was no *dan*ger. And that he hoped they had too much pride to be panicked by a shabby Brightwater mean-spirited petty trick.

It must have been the right set of messages. The roaring of crowds in and out of sight slowly subsided to a murmur, punctuated now and then by the cries of children. It was reasonable that the children would find it harder to be calm about all this, since it would not have been the wall itself that frightened them, but the behavior of their elders.

"There now," said the Magician finally. "That should hold them for a while."

"Well done!" said Coyote, and he meant it sincerely. He fancied himself a connoisseur of crowd control, and he judged the other man from an expert's point of view, and found no fault with him. "Very impressive."

The Magician of Rank gave him a quick look and nodded acknowledgment. One professional to another. And then he came down from Willow's back, and Coyote tried again.

"*Now* what?"

"Your hour's long since gone," said the Magician of Rank.

"I am painfully aware of that."

"And your flyer's far away from here."

"That too."

"I'm afraid that for the moment you are stuck here,

Mister Jones. Until I can figure out what to do about this—or until it pleases them to take it away."

"Who 'them'?"

He made a vague gesture. "This will be the work of the Magician of Rank at Brightwater," he said, "and at least two or three more Magicians of Rank from other Kingdoms. It's an expensive sort of spell . . . hard to imagine one man doing it on his own."

"You're sure that's who's doing it?"

"There's nobody else on this planet that has the skill, Mister Jones."

"And you understand how it's done?"

"Certainly. Don't you?"

Coyote admitted that he didn't understand it at all, and got an odd look for his candor. But as the two of them made their way back to Castle Smith, with Willow leading this time, the Magician of Rank explained it to him.

"It would be an Insertion Transformation," he said, as casually as Coyote would have discussed the workings of his flyer. "No different, except in scale, from causing a flower to appear where there wasn't one before, or some such baby trick. But a wall like this! It's very simple in theory, but in practice it would take a tremendous amount of power."

"You think it goes all the way around the kingdom? All those hundreds of miles?" Coyote asked. "Is that possible?"

"Well, it's far more likely than that it just goes a short distance."

"I don't see that."

"To do a *piece* of a wall," said the Magician of Rank, "you'd probably use a Substitution Transformation. You'd find something already going along the edge of the kingdom, such as a path or a hedge, and you'd Substitute a wall for it for as far as it went. But there's nothing that runs even as far as what we can see from right here, not that I know of. Not unbroken in its length and regular like this. And it's far easier to do a *whole* wall—that's a closed set, don't you see?—than it would be to set up some irregular figure with open ends. This way, it just goes round and round."

Coyote was reminded of what the Communipath had said about the first contact with the Ozark rogue. It had been a formal notation of some kind, "just hanging there going round and round."

"I still don't follow you," he said slowly.

"You don't?"

"No. I don't."

"We were given to understand that you were a pretty skillful Magician yourself, Mister Jones," said the Magician of Rank. "I should think you would understand something as elementary as . . . as elegance. And economy. And the path of least resistance."

Coyote raised his hands to stop the flow of accusing speech.

"I never claimed to be a magician," he said. "If that claim is going around, I'm not its source."

"Didn't you cause two Brightwater children to see you as a many-headed snake?" demanded the Magician of Rank. They had come to a stop in the courtyard; he handed the Mule over to a stableman and went on talking. "That's the tale I was told of you, and with considerable confidence!"

"Yes, I did that," Coyote admitted. "But I didn't do it with magic. I did it with psience. *P-s-i-e-n-c-e*."

"Meaning?"

"Meaning it was just a projected telepathic illusion. No charms. No spells. No transformations. Just your everyday garden variety telepathic illusion."

"No magic," said the Magician of Rank dubiously.

"Not a scrap. I don't know how to do magic. I don't even *believe* in magic."

The man cleared his throat, and motioned courteously for Coyote to precede him into the castle. Ahead of them a servingmaid came hurrying with an ample tray of food and drink, leading them into the front room to take refreshment once again.

"How, precisely," asked Joseph Everholt Purdy the 46th, helping himself to a glass of ale and a sandwich, "do you explain the way you got here to Smith? If you don't believe in magic, that is. Do you assume that this entire kingdom, with all its beings and artifacts, is a giant telepathic illusion?"

Coyote resented being asked that question. He wasn't about to answer it. He didn't even intend to think it to himself in privacy. He ignored it, loftily, maintaining what he hoped was an expression of amused and supercilious superiority. Secret Agent Tolerates Primitive Native, he was doing. Secret Agent Knows All but Will Not Tell for Fear of Upsetting Equilibrium of Primitive Culture. That sort of thing.

And then, in the silence, with the Magician of Rank smirking at him and the two of them fortifying their bellies, he risked being knocked flat again for mental insolence and sent out a message at full strength. In four parts.

ONE: SMITH KINGDOM NOW A PART OF THE FEDERATION AND ENTITLED TO FULL PRIVILEGES STARTING IMMEDIATELY—BUT IS UNDER SOME SORT OF SIEGE I DO NOT AT   THIS POINT UNDERSTAND.

TWO: SOMEBODY PLEASE CONTACT RESPONSIBLE OF BRIGHTWATER AND ASK HER TO CALL UP THE MAGICIANS OF RANK AND HAVE THEM COME TO SMITH KINGDOM FOR A PARLEY.

THREE: UNTIL I TELL YOU OTHERWISE, SEND NOBODY AND NOTHING TO SMITH KINGDOM.

YOU CAN GET IN, BUT YOU CAN'T GET BACK OUT. I AM WORKING ON THAT.
FOUR: UNTIL I TELL YOU OTHERWISE, SEND NOBODY—PERIOD. THE MAGIC WEATHER FAIRY IS STILL ON DUTY.

Nothing happened. Nobody knocked him down with a blast of psiforce. He made so bold as to repeat the part about ringing up Brightwater on the Communipath Network and asking that somebody be sent along to negotiate. And he checked the time; he would repeat this every ten minutes for so long as he was able to get away with it, for at least an hour, and then switch to hourly projection until something happened.

At Mars Central, the Fish was grateful that Coyote was not capable of receiving the response to his request for a parley. Responsible of Brightwater had once again been the agent for the message, and she had not bothered to be subtle. She had said, the Communipath told the Fish: LET THE MIGHTY COYOTE USE HIS *OWN* MAGIC TO BRING DOWN THE WALL!

Short. Acerbic. Right to the point. It was just as well Coyote didn't have that message to think about. And the Fish, much embroiled in a series of intricate explanations to outraged bureaus and personnel about this latest Ozark expedition, wished that he had been fortunate enough not to know about it either.

CHAPTER ELEVEN

Coyote was not a happy man. He was well fed and well housed and well treated; nobody seemed to blame him for the mess that they were in, as yet, and he had everything he could have wanted for his comfort, within reason. There was a fascinating culture to examine, ample leisure for the process, people by the dozens to talk to as a means of satisfying his curiosity . . . and everyone seemingly perfectly happy to indulge him so long as he kept his questions general and impersonal.

And he understood the inaction of his own government; that wasn't worrying him. There was the rule that an agent in place is on his own and has no reason to expect himself to be rescued—that went with being an agent. There was the fact that he himself had sent out a message, and repeated it often enough to be certain that it had gotten through, and that message had said specifically *not* to send anything or anyone to Ozark until he advised differently. There was the fact that the Fish knew about the "turbulence" that would greet anyone sent to Planet Ozark with prior clearance from the Ozarkers. Coyote understood and approved of the waiting game that was being played. If he had been on Mars Central to give orders, he would have advised them to do exactly what he assumed they were doing, i.e., putting the whole thing On Hold.

But he was miserable, in spite of all his advantages and in spite of his logical grasp of the situation. Because *he* was On Hold, too. Entirely stumped. Unable to do one smallest thing. Surrounded by the polite contempt of these people, who had been promised wonders, who had given up citizenship in their world in anticipation of those wonders, and who now saw him stopped dead by a little ten-foot wall. They had believed him, and had believed in his government, and now look at them—prisoners in their own country, with the Great Off-world Representative mooning about and as helpless as they were.

It was intolerable, and Coyote writhed under the burden of it. He was no elitist, never had been. But this planet, for all its quaint and folksy charm, was a *primitive* world! It was stuck back in the twenty-first century at best, nine hundred years and more behind the times. It lacked even the most rudimentary elements of the science and technology that Coyote was accustomed to taking for granted. It was only just barely civilized. Its people were superstitious and ignorant, they hadn't the sophistication of even the child of nine or ten in the member worlds of the Federation. They believed in *magic*, for the love of Light!

Coyote didn't believe in magic for one moment. How the Ozarkers did what they did, he wasn't prepared to say. But that it wasn't "magic," he would have defended to his last breath. There was, he knew quite well, no such *thing* as magic. So why, something inside him mocked, are you still here? Still looking at that unmagic wall over there? Still unable to get out and go about your business? And are you still *sure* that the difficulty of seeing Planet Ozark

comes from telepaths on duty projecting NOTHING
THERE, GO AWAY messages, and not from a Spell of
Invisibility, as the Grannys have told you it does? The
something inside him kept saying rudely, Oh *yeah*? And
he kept telling it to shut up, and growing more and more
frustrated and infuriated.

They gave him a kind of babysitter, a young woman
from the local staff of Teachers, to wander around with
him and answer questions and explain things. He suspected that her main function was to put up with his bad
humor and spare the rest of the population, but he wasn't
too proud to accept her services. He would have gone
mad with boredom if he hadn't had her there, like a living
encyclopedia, to pass some of the time while he fretted
and fumed inside his head and worried away at the impossible conundrum of his imprisonment.

On a pleasant day four days after the wall had appeared
and three days past the limit of his tolerance of the wall,
he and the Teacher were walking along the bank of a
lovely little river that ran along the outside of the town.
The wall had obligingly moved itself back to accommodate
them as it always did; it was very cooperative. Wherever
you were, inside the borders of Smith Kingdom, the wall
ran around the area where you found yourself. Your town.
Your farm. Whatever. And if you moved beyond that area,
so did the wall, out to the edge of the kingdom, where it
moved no farther. Always, the wall was your near horizon;
as the Magician of Rank had said, it was elegant.

Coyote was sullen. He could only think, over and over:
that wall is a telepathic illusion; I am immune to telepathic
illusions; therefore, for me, that wall is not there. And
then he would look up, and there it would be. His heart
was black and his soul was slimy and he hated himself and
the Ozarkers and all the universe beyond with a lusty
hatred which he felt there was no reason not to share,

perhaps by peeing in the lovely little river. He hated *it*, too.

"I hate this," he said to the woman; she was called "Teacher Philomena," and she was dressed almost like a nun of Old Earth in full habit, except for the color. She wore a deep violet blue instead of black.

"As does everyone," she answered.

"Not the way I do."

"Oh? What is it about the way you hate it that is so different?" She looked at him courteously enough, and her voice was smooth, but he saw the twitch at the corner of her lips and knew she thought he was funny.

"I can't stand it," he said dramatically, and added a large two-armed dramatic gesture to support the words. "That's the difference!"

"Can't you? You *are* standing it."

"Well, I can't go on any longer." Secret Agent Delivers Ultimatum.

"That's absurd," she said, chiding him. Gently, but she was bygod *chiding* him.

"I don't care if it's absurd or not," he complained. "I can't stand it. I can't stand being trapped. I can't stand being cooped up."

"Mister Jones!" She was laughing at him openly now. "You are 'cooped up' in a space a thousand miles square! It's hardly the sort of thing that causes claustrophobia!"

"That makes no difference!" he insisted. "I'm used to having all of three galaxies to move around in. I'm not like you people, I never had just one world to call my own. I'm not used to being kept to a single area like this. And it's the principle of the thing anyway—it's not how big the prison is, it's that it *is* a prison!"

"Well, mercy," observed the woman, "that's downright unpleasant, isn't it? But I don't know what can be done to fix it, Mister Jones. It seems to be pretty solidly in place, that wall . . . Might could be you ought to try to calm yourself."

Coyote knew he was being melodramatic. He knew all the things Tzana Kai would have said to him if she could have seen how he was acting. He didn't care. It passed the time. He said, "If it goes on, I swear I'll kill myself." And he waited for her to laugh again, which would give him a chance for a speech on her hardness of heart.

The Teacher didn't laugh, only looked at him as if he had said something particularly stupid. He stood facing her, come to a full stop now, and waited defiantly, beard jutting, until finally she spoke to him.

"Perhaps you would," she said. He could hear the distaste in her voice, and something else he couldn't quite identify. Pity? "But no Ozarker would."

"I don't believe it!" he said, and spat deliberately, that being the most disgustingly primitive thing he could think of to do in front of a lady who made him think of a cloistered nun. "Every culture, no matter how placid, has people who can't bear their life and choose to take it themselves."

"Not here," she said calmly. "Suicide is almost unknown here. It happens in the hopelessly insane, those beyond even the healing skills of the Magicians of Rank. It might happen in an ordinary person in some extraordinary situation that I cannot even imagine; but almost never, Mister Jones. Ozark does not have more than one suicide in the course of a hundred years. And never—not *ever*—over a piece of foolishness such as *this*, Mister Jones!"

Coyote laughed, a laugh he knew to be ugly, and an ugliness he gloried in. He wished he could have made it uglier.

"Why? Are Ozarkers so stupid they can't manage it?"

The Teacher looked at him awhile, and he glared fiercely

back at her, and then he saw a look of decision on her face.

"I see no reason why you should have to stay ignorant," she said, then, not the least disturbed when her words turned him purple with indignation. "Every Ozark child knows—it's certainly no secret."

He was too furious to speak, but she ignored him and went right on, taking a small object from a pocket in her habit and giving it a quick snap of the wrist that unfolded it into a traditional teacher's pointer. She set its tip in the wet sand between them and said, "Please pay attention, Mister Jones." And she drew a large circle in the wet sand.

"This," she told him, "is the timeline of Ozark. It is eternity, you notice; it has no beginning and no end. To us it seems that one thing happens and then another thing, but that is an illusion—everything that happens, whenever it happens, is here within this circle. Past, present, future, they are all here simultaneously. All right?"

She glanced at him, at him staring rudely at her, and set the pointer to the sand again; now she drew smaller circles within the large one, a ring of circles around the inner rim of the large one, each separate but touching all the others.

"These," she said, "are the timelines of the Responsibles. There would be thirteen if I tried to reflect our recorded history. How many there are in truth I do not know, of course, but Responsible of Brightwater is the thirteenth since we arrived on this planet. And each of *these*, you see, is also without beginning or end."

Coyote said nothing. He was busy fighting the urge to take his foot and rub out her stupid circles in the stupid sand.

"Inside each of these," she continued, "though I couldn't draw them, are the many many timelines that belong to

each of the human beings living during the larger timelines—
again with no beginning and no end. Every one of these,
every life, is *eternal*. The symbols are awkward, but they
are the clearest that I know. Do you understand?"

"Sure," he muttered. Next it would be squawker en-
trails and burnt feathers. "I don't see what it has to do
with anything."

"Oh, but you do see," she said, folding her pointer and
slipping it away out of sight again. "To commit suicide,
Mister Jones, is as fool a thing as there is to do in all this
universe. Because you just begin again, you know. You
don't escape the life you found so awful, you just start it
over again, with all its problems to be dealt with *over*
again. We Ozarkers don't fancy that as a solution. Bad
enough to have it all to do over when the Almighty sees fit
to *say* it's time to do that!"

Coyote's stare lost some of its rudeness; he looked at
her, and at the crude diagram in the sand, and for a
moment he forgot about his black foul mood. This was
very interesting stuff.

"You believe that?" he asked her, fascinated at the
prospect. "Really believe it?"

"With all my heart," she said sturdily. "As does *every*
Ozarker. It is written of old time, and handed down to us
by the Grannys, that we are expected to be *perfect*.
Not just good, Mister Jones. Perfect. That likely *needs*
an eternity, for the doing. And each time we die, we
begin again, and we do it over until we get it right."

Coyote thought of some ancient religions he'd read about,
and of boddhisatvas, and of a ragbag of doctrines he knew
little of and cared for even less; and he thought of the
obvious questions.

"On Old Earth," he said carefully, "there were times
when little children died of starvation by the tens of

thousands . . . Are you saying that they must do that over
and over again, for all of eternity?"

She raised one index finger beside her face, in the
gesture of all Teachers.

"I speak for *this* world, and for no other," she told
him. "But I will answer your question, since there are
tadlings that die in dreadful ways on this world, too,
though nothing like what you describe for Earth. Think,
please . . . such a life, only a year or two of awfulness,
undeserved . . . Very swiftly, Mister Jones, a human being
would get that life right. Would do it perfectly. It would
not take very many times round the circle, for such
a life."

"And then what happens? When it has been done perfectly, I mean."

"There are choices, then," she said. "But I'm not a
theologian—you might want to talk about this with one of
the Reverends."

Coyote thought about discussing it with the Reverend at
Brightwater, with his ample belly and his ampler self-
regard and his pompous interminable droning sermons.

"No," he said. "I'll rely on you."

"For such a one, then," said Teacher Philomena, "there
are choices to be made. They may leave their timeline for
a manner of being we know nothing about, to become part
of the One. Or they may choose to stay, for the greater
good of all the rest. Or, they may choose to take the place
of some *other*—that maybe is not doing well and shows
little promise of doing well. To help eternity along, don't
you see. There are those that hold it back more than
somewhat."

Aha, thought Coyote. There it was. The good old
boddhisatva part.

"There is a place on this timeline," she said, touching
the outermost circle with the tip of her shoe, "a place . . .

a spacetime . . . where *everyone* has at last gotten it right and perfect. And then we shall all be free."

"But it will take a terribly long time?"

"It is all there," she answered. "All the time there is. And it's at our disposal."

She was watching him through narrowed eyes, he noticed, interested in his reaction as a teacher always is interested, and he wondered what she was not telling him. There was something else, he was sure, something she was not mentioning, something that was not what "every Ozark child knows." Something that *was* a secret.

He was curious, his greatest failing always there ready to get him into trouble. He wanted to hear the rest of it, while he was at it; without thinking, he pushed her, just a little.

HE IS A GOOD MAN . . . I SHOULD TELL HIM THE REST OF THE DOCTRINE.

Not with force, just gently. Tentatively. Thinking that she would not notice anything more than a sort of inclination to tell him more, seemingly coming from within her own self, toward this good and willing student.

She surprised him. Like a snake coiled to strike, the Teacher went tense, her hands spread wide before her face and her eyes flashing cold fire.

"How dare you!" she flung at him, and although it was a cliché it did not strike him as funny. Not this time.

"Teacher Philomena, I am so sorry," he began, but she was having none of it.

"We try very hard," she hissed at him, "to be patient with you. It is not your fault that you come out of a fouled culture, nor that you are ignorant as no Ozark child could be ignorant. But you go too far, Mister Jones! You abuse our courtesy!"

"I didn't—"

"You didn't think I would *know*? How arrogant you are!

Mister Jones, you are taller and bulkier and far stronger than I am physically—would you reach out with those hams you have for hands and shove me into the river? No? Then what makes you feel that it is permissible for you to use the strength of your mind to shove *my* mind? How is that different, less ugly, less barbarous, Mister Jones? *Explain* that to me!"

Coyote hung his head, like a boy of six caught putting something nasty down another child's tunic, and said not one word. It did not require telepathic receptivity to feel the waves of contempt washing over him from Teacher Philomena.

"You come from the great Tri-Galactic Federation, Mister Jones! With its twenty thousand worlds and its mighty spaceships and its intergalactic system of travel and communication and government. . . . and *spies*, Mister Jones! And weapons of coercion! And you look at us and think we are quaint, do you not? A lot of farmers and peasants stumbling around riding Mules. . . . Just *savages*! To do with as you will!"

"No," he mumbled miserably, shaking his head, wishing *he* could have the opportunity to do just this tiny little piece of time over again and try to get it right. He had been so sure that only Responsible and the Magicians of Rank had mindspeech. He had never thought to ask about the Teachers.

"Words! Words are *cheap*! It's what you do that speaks truth, Coyote Jones, not what you say with your lying mouth! And I will tell you nothing more, Mister Jones, not this day or any other, because what I tell you is *wasted*—you don't listen, you don't see, you don't hear, you don't *think*! *Shame* on you!"

He didn't look up as she turned and walked away, leaving him standing there with his arrogance hanging out, making small fumbling motions with his hands and feet. To get through the moment, he rubbed out the diagram of eternal circles with his toes. And then, when he was absolutely sure that she had had time to get far ahead of him so that he wouldn't have to face her, he walked back into Red Arches.

Here I come, he thought. Going along the road, trying to be as inconspicuous as possible. Here I come, The Ugly Alien.

It had only happened because he'd been so bloody frustrated, so bloody out of sorts. He'd started out acting like a child, and she'd amused him, politely, as she would have amused a child. And then he'd forgotten his mood, and his manners along with it. And it had looked like just exactly what it was. Fascination with the exotic customs of the primitives. He could hear Tzana Kai now, telling him what *she* thought. She, too, would say shame on him.

What a faith, though! If the woman had been telling him what in fact every Ozarker really and truly did believe, what a faith that must amount to! And he had no reason to think that she had told him anything other than the absolute truth. She hadn't spoke of doubters, of splinter groups that believed other things . . . Teacher Philomena had said "every Ozarker" knew and believed what she had just told him.

It might be true. It could be. The population was abnormally small, kept that way by the firm control of . . . something. The Grannys, he suspected. The process of change was held back by the educational system and by the irrational prejudice against technology. It could in fact be true that everyone, or almost everyone, on this planet had a shared faith that was as the Teacher had described it.

There was something there, he thought. Something important. Something that mattered, if he could just . . .

Suppose, just suppose, that what fueled the so-called

magic on this light-forsaken lump of a planet was in fact the energy generated by the absolute faith that the Ozarkers shared? It had to be a powerful force, no need to drag "magic" into it. That much faith, that much shared faith, had *always* worked seeming wonders! It could be. It could be. It was a fragment of a thread of a clue. He had nothing else; he didn't dare ignore it.

What if, just what if this faith, which was not only a faith in the idea that life must begin over and over until it was perfect, this faith which was also a faith in magic and a faith in the entire consensus reality of Ozark, what if this faith was just like a power supply? What if he could simply *tap* it, as he would have tapped an electrical reserve or a charged storage cell?

"I have to think about this," he said out loud, completely unaware that he was back in the town and drawing curious glances from the people he shared the streets with. "By the Light's blazoned and blasted Beard, I have to think about this . . . I have to figure it out!"

But how did he go about it?

CHAPTER TWELVE

It was a matter of honor. It was not a matter of logic, they were all agreed on that. Logic did not enter into it, nor did prudence or common sense or any of the lukewarm so-called virtues that dominated so many people for whom the Phonans had little more than contempt.

Honor! That came before all else. They were the Octaves; and they had been humiliated in a way that could not be forgotten, a way that led to a constant drone of discord, jangled noise, cacophony, in the chfla pools. A way that tainted every attempt at harmony. The instrument of that dishonor was the people who—on the basis of a paltry thousand years in residence!—called themselves Ozarkers. Never mind the ancient peoples of that planet. The Ozarkers presumed to call them by Ozark names. Called the great leviathans of their oceans "Wise Ones," called the peoples of their desert "Skerrys," called the small furred folk they had driven into the caves beneath the earth "Gentles." Foolish, puerile names, such as children would devise. And the "Mules!" The Mule, who had been first on that planet and had long since evolved beyond the age of technology and dispensed with such childishness, who had done so while the others were little more than dumb creatures—the Ozarkers had named the Mule for a Terran beast of burden, and had no more intelligence than to behave toward it as if its individual members *were* beasts of burden. The Ozarkers gave names as if they had a right to do so, when they could offer no more than brute noises of ignorance, from vocal tracts incapable of sophisticated sound. Poor savages, they could not even *pronounce* the true names of those whose homeworld they had taken it upon themselves to share.

And it was these creatures, these stumbling humanoids hardly out of the ooze, who had also taken it upon themselves to humble *them*, the Phonans! Oh, it could not be borne, could not be let pass. There was no discord about that.

BUT WHAT ARE WE TO DO?

What *could* they do, with the watchful eyes of the Federation on them, and the watchful minds of the Communipaths standing ready to monitor them like common criminals?

SOMETHING SOPHISTICATED IS CALLED FOR. SOMETHING WORTHY OF A PEOPLE SUCH AS WE ARE, AND HAVE BEEN THESE MANY THOUSAND YEARS, AND SHALL BE ALWAYS. SOMETHING AS FAR BEYOND THE PATHETIC EFFORTS OF THE TERRANS, AND THEIR SPAWN THE OZARKERS, AS A LASER IS BEYOND A STICK SET AFIRE FOR A TORCH. SOMETHING *SUBTLE!* SOMETHING THAT TEACHES THEM THEIR PUNY PLACE.

It was and it was not DO-323 who spoke; for this solemn congress the privacy constraints had been set aside, and the open mode chosen, so that the mindspeech came from DO-323, from DO-11, from DO-894, from every senior dominant male of every octave, as a single thought.

PERHAPS, a young male had interjected, he and many others like him, hot of blood and untested of mind, PERHAPS WE SHOULD WITHDRAW FROM THE FEDERATION. And the older males had vibrated indulgently with amusement; it was the sort of thing young males always thought of.

WHY, asked the dominants, WOULD WE DO SUCH A THING AS THAT? IT IS THE OZARKERS WE WANT TO PUNISH, NOT OURSELVES. AND IT IS WHOLLY FITTING AND PROPER THAT THE FEDERATION SHOULD SERVE US AND SEE TO OUR NEEDS PRECISELY AS IT DOES, AND FOR SO PALTRY A RETURN. IT IS THE PROPER ROLE OF INFERIOR CREATURES TO SEE TO THE WELFARE OF THEIR BETTERS IN ORDER THAT THEY MAY FULFILL THEIR DESTINY. WHY SHOULD WE EXCUSE THEM FROM THEIR DUTIES?

Rebuked, the young males dropped their ensemble efforts and joined the unison channel. No one was angry with them—they would learn with time, as the others had learned with time. But they were embarrassed, and they hurried to blend into the unison and be rid of the isolated attention they had brought on themselves.

WHAT, THEN? WHAT SHALL WE DO?

They set their minds to it, letting all that they knew about the Ozarkers flow through the pools and be shared by everyone, letting items of interest, items for consideration, bubble to the surface of their thoughtstreams and then drop again as new ones took their place. And the time came when they achieved the beginning of a consensus, and discussion could begin.

CONSIDER THE CURRENT STRUCTURE OF WHAT THE OZARKERS ARE PLEASED TO CALL THEIR "CULTURE." WE HAVE THEM AT A CRUCIAL TIME, A TIME WHEN THEY WALK A DELICATE LINE OF

BALANCE . . . A BALANCE THAT COULD BE DE-
STROYED BY ANY ONE OF THREE OF THEIR FE-
MALES.

RESPONSIBLE OF BRIGHTWATER, it went on.
SILVERWEB OF MCDANIELS, SHUT AWAY IN HER
TOWER IN TRAVELER KINGDOM. AND TROUBLE-
SOME OF BRIGHTWATER, ON HER MOUNTAIN.

THREE STRONG TETHERS, THOSE FEMALES!
BUT REMOVE ONE, AND THE FABRIC OF THEIR
SOCIETY, SUCH AS IT IS, IS WEAKENED. REMOVE
ONE, AND ONE DIMENSION IS LOST; THE BAL-
ANCE COLLAPSES. IT WOULD SET THEM BACK.

HOW FAR?

FAR! GENERATIONS! IT IS A SIMPLE MATTER OF
REMOVING *ONE* OF THEM.

There was a shocked resonance in the pools, hearing
that. Not that the Phonans had any absolute prohibition
against causing the death of another, but they did not
ordinarily speak of it openly. And the males, the tonic as
well as the dominant responsibility, that eternal philo-
sophical enigma, spoke hastily to correct the confusion in
the motif.

THERE ARE MANY WAYS TO UNBALANCE THAT
TRIANGLE OF FEMALE POWER! AND DEATH IS
NOT THE ONE THAT COMES TO MIND!

They were rewarded with a sigh of relief from the rest,
and took the opportunity to say a few well-chosen words
about leaping to conclusions. And when suitable apologies
had been made, they agreed to explain.

EACH OF THE WOMEN IS A DIFFERENT TERM
OF THE EQUATION THAT SPELLS OUT OZARK.
TWO OF THEM ARE PROBABLY NOT MOVABLE
EXCEPT BY VIOLENCE. RESPONSIBLE OF BRIGHT-
WATER IS THE MIDDLE TERM, AND SHE IS AS
SOUND AS A MAJOR TRIAD—WE HAVE TRIED

SHOVING *HER* BEFORE, AND HAVE YET TO SUC-
CEED IN EVEN DISTRESSING HER VERY MUCH.
AND SILVERWEB, SITTING AT THE EXTREME OF
GOOD, WEARS THE ARMOR OF HOLINESS . . . IT
WOULD BE HARD TO MOVE HER. GOODNESS
SUCH AS THAT HAS ITS OWN SAFEGUARDS, AND
THEY ARE MIGHTY. BUT THE OTHER ONE, NOW,
THAT TROUBLESOME! SHE IS CONSECRATED TO
EVIL—SHE WOULD BE THE WEAK ONE. THAT IS
OBVIOUS.

CAN WE BE SURE?

SURELY GOOD IS MORE POWERFUL THAN EVIL?
SURELY THE PENALTIES FOR CORRUPTING A
WOMAN OF EVIL—IF THAT IS NOT A CONTRADIC-
TION IN TERMS—ARE LESS THAN FOR CORRUPT-
ING A GOOD ONE? THE DANGER OF THE TRIAL,
FOR US, WOULD BE FAR LESS.

There was a period of thinking about this, and of letting
images play through their minds. There was a time of
forming a plan.

IT MAKES SENSE, they agreed finally, males and
females, elders and youngers, even the children. IT IS
WORTH TRYING. IT IS PERHAPS BRILLIANT.

The REs, senior females of the octaves, were obligated
to point out that it would be very expensive. Even if they
failed.

WHAT GOOD IS OUR WEALTH TO US IF WE ARE
DISHONORED? boomed the males.

THINK, pleaded the REs, HOW IT WILL DRAIN
THE PSIBILITIES OF OUR ADEPTS!

THAT IS ONLY ONE MORE KIND OF WEALTH,
AND EQUALLY WORTHLESS TO A DISHONORED
PEOPLE.

IT MAY ALL BE FOR NOTHING.

WE WILL HAVE *TRIED!*

There was a long silence, and then a giving way.
SO BE IT.
For the honor of Phona.
The adepts gathered together the resources of their
minds, while the others maintained the essential harmo-
nies of the background, and it began.

Troublesome wasn't especially concerned at being waked
by the sound of voices with nothing recognizably human
attached to them. Living with evil as she did, working at it
all her life long, it was not uncommon for her to dredge up
stuff that had something to say and chose to say it to her.
There'd been the time it had chosen to speak through a
feydeer, to very little purpose. A time when it had taken a
tall pine as its voice. A time when a boulder served. And
other times, stranger than those.

None of it bothered Troublesome. She had grown up
with magic all around her, had observed the Grannys
dealing with such ragtags of leftover life as the poor
Bridgewraiths with no more alarm than they showed dealing with any household annoyance, had strangled unspeakable weakedness in a sacred spring. It took more than a
disembodied voice to get her attention. And so she lay in
her bed that cloudy morning, with the wind whistling
round her cabin roof, and listened carefully to learn what
sort of thing it was she had to deal with this time.

"Come to the window, Troublesome of Brightwater," it
had been saying, and its voice was lovely, lovely. It was a
voice of deep scarlet velvet, a voice to call the birds down
out of the trees and the snakes up out of their holes. She
could have lain there in her bed and listened to it for a
good long time just for the pure pleasure of it; whatever it
was, it had the knack of melody and of timbre. But it
wasn't satisfied with just having her for admiring audience.

"Troublesome of Brightwater, *sweet* Troublesome," it

crooned at her, "get up now! Get up, and come to the window . . . *there's* a sweetheart, *there's* a dear love!"

Sweetheart. Dear love. Troublesome sat up in her narrow bed with her back against the wall and cocked her head, sharply aware now. She fancied more the ones that began with phrases such as "great whore" and "vile witch" and "mother of all murdering sons of whores" and such like; always, those were more easily managed than the soppy ones. And this looked to be one of the soppiest she'd come across yet. Did it just speak, she wondered, or could it listen, too? She'd best find out.

"Lovely Troublesome, sweet Ozark woman, beautiful Troublesome of the face like a splendid flower, do get up . . . there's a love . . . do get up and come to the window," it coaxed her.

"Believe I'll stay right here," declared Troublesome, chuckling low. "If I get up, I'll drown in sugar."

She waited, and there was a kind of thrum, as if a string had been plucked, and when it spoke again it had shifted its register a tad.

"Troublesome of Brightwater," it said, still scarlet velvet but without the maple syrup over it, "please come to the window, that we may show you something."

"Show me what?" she scoffed at it. "Toads and spiders? Trolls and goblins? Turds and whey?"

"Come to the window!" it insisted. "Come and see."

"Hmmmmph."

"Troublesome of Brightwater—"

"I know," she said back. "Come to the window! I know what's outside my window this day. Drifting fog and mist. The mountain, falling away down. Pines and vines and a dozen little springs hidden in ferns and cold cress. And critters, of course."

"There's something more, Troublesome of Brightwater! Something more."

"Worth my time, is it? Worth my trekking over there and leaving my comfortable bed?"

It almost snickered, which was a new wrinkle. And it made a few observations about the lack of comfort to a straw tick laid over ropes and tied to a plain wood frame. And it suggested to her again that she get up and go see.

"Well," said Troublesome finally, "I suppose you won't hush unless I do go look, will you?"

"We have all the time in the world," it crooned. "And we can wait forever."

"Saying over and over and over, 'come to the WINdow, Troublesome of Brightwater.'"

"If need be."

"Can't say as I'd care for that," Troublesome observed. "It's a mighty boring refrain, let that be noted. I'd rather go look."

She threw back the cotton sheet she had drawn up to her waist and went naked to a small window that looked down Mount Troublesome toward the rest of the world. Get this over with, she could move on to her breakfast.

"Look, Troublesome!" it said. "Behold! What do you see?"

She primmed her mouth and rubbed at her eyes and looked, and she gave it a couple of points for effort. As displays went, it was more than tolerable. The great necklace of rubies was splendid, and the ropes of pearls were a nice touch. The chests of gold coins were trite, but they had a nice shine to them, and no doubt somewhere in the universe there were peoples who still craved the glow of gold. It was all quite magnificent, and it stretched away as far as she could see, treasure piled upon treasure piled upon yet more treasure. Treasure of precious stones and precious metals and precious cloths and furs. It was certainly done with a lavish hand.

"It's a spectacle, I'll grant you that," she said, when she felt she'd enjoyed all of it she could tolerate.

"It can all be yours," said the voice(s).

"No doubt," said Troublesome.

"All this can be yours—"

"That'll do," she said. "I've heard that one a good deal. It's been done. All that can be mine if I'll what?"

"Troublesome of Brightwater, we are not entirely without knowledge of these things," it said, and she thought it sounded a bit pettish. "We are not so crude as to ask anything of you in return for this treasure! It is yours because you grace the world with your beauty."

"Do tell! Just my beauty, eh? My flat breasts and my flat hips and all six feet of me towering over the other ladies like I do? You're generous, and your tastes are unusual. You're sure you wouldn't rather have my soul?"

"Oh, no," it said. "You misunderstand. This is treasure freely given, sweet Troublesome. You have only to say that it pleases you."

"Well, it doesn't," said Troublesome briskly. "Clutter, *I* call it, and I wouldn't have it if you paid me to take it. I'll thank you to get all that truck off my mountain, and to be prompt about it."

She chuckled, still thinking of breakfast, and scratched one naked buttock where something small had bitten her during the night. Time to turn out that straw tick, she thought. In the window, the panorama of wealth-beyond-all-worldly-ken shimmered and wavered and blurred and was gone, and she was glad to see it go.

"We misjudged you," said the luxurious voice. "We apologize. We have been . . . crude."

"Well," said Troublesome, "don't worry about it. I've seen crude before, and no doubt I'll see it again many and many a time. You just go try that out someplace else, why don't you, and let me get on with my day."

"There's more," it said. "We have only begun."

"Oh, law," said Troublesome mournfully. "*Don't* begin with the mansions and the carriages, would you not? I have no interest *what*soever in mansions and carriages, nor in fine gowns either . . . spare me."

Whatever had been coming up in her window flickered again, a bit abruptly, and Troublesome congratulated herself. Two down, that much less to go. She knew quite well that it would do her no good to just turn her back; they'd only put the stuff in one of the other windows, or on the floor, or inside her eyelids if she forced them to that. It was a matter of letting it run its course, and she was prepared to.

What came up next, however, took her aback.

"Well, *look at* that!" she breathed. "I would not have thought the human body could even *get* into such positions as that!"

While the voice was going on and on about all this being hers, just for the accepting of it, and no price asked, Troublesome wondered what she'd do with it. There wasn't room in her cabin for a horde of copulating couples, and the racket they were making was an abomination.

"You're a virgin, sweet Troublesome," it said, "and that is a terrible waste! We will give you joy, we will give you ecstasy undreamed of by mortal women . . . we will give you bliss beside which all other treasures pale into nothingness."

"Not likely," Troublesome snorted. "Think I care to roll around on the floor with a hulk of manflesh troubled by all those attachments sticking out into the air, or worse yet, sticking into *me*? I do hope I have some sense of dignity, and it'll be a long cold sleety day in hell before any such noise as those females of yours are making comes out of *my* mouth! I've heard butchering done with less caterwauling!"

"Those are cries of ecstasy, sweet Troublesome!"

"Piffle."

"You dare not look fully," it suggested, "because it brings your blood boiling into your loins, and you are afraid."

Troublesome thought that over, considering the question. It was possible. Might could be she was just scared ignorant. And she turned her full and most scrupulous attention to the bacchanal that had replaced her decent mountainside and looked it up and down as thoroughly as she knew how.

"No," she said after a while, "I don't believe that's it. And I believe you'd have done better to give me just one honest couple in a plain bed, with wedding bands on their left hands. I don't believe I'm cut out for what you've served up there. Bliss you call it and bliss it well may be, but I don't fancy it. It sends *nothing* boiling into my loins, as you put it, though it's a marvel to see all those different ways of doing just one thing."

"Truly," said the voice(s), "truly it does not make you ache for the touch of a man? Thrusting there in your most secret parts? For a man who never tires, who never wearies unless you ask him to? Or perhaps a woman, sweet Troublesome, like those there at your right hand?"

"Dozens, no!" she said. "Nor for a turtle, nor for a bullfrog, nor for a nanny goat, either. You'd best take that away, thank you very much."

"You feel *no* hunger, then, sweet Troublesome?"

"Oh, I didn't say that! What I hunger for is my breakfast, that you're keeping me from with all this hooha—"

She stopped short, took one look, and excused herself for a moment. When she came back to the window she was carrying three pieces of cold fried cornbread in one hand and a mug of black coffee in the other, never mind that the coffee was cold too, and left over from last night's supper.

"*This*," she said, sitting down before the window to be more comfortable as she ate, "is what I had in mind. Though I wouldn't care if the coffee was hot instead of cold." And when they hotted it up for her, she thanked them; she wasn't too wicked to be mannerly when it suited her.

"Now," she said, "you go right ahead. I'll just eat while you're at it, and that way I can keep my mind on it better."

The image in the window wobbled, and the tables of opulent food and drink ran like wet paint into one another and went away.

"Thank you," she said again. "Enough to make a body queasy just looking at all that, let alone eating it. What's next?"

The window took on a soft silver color, and framed a single book of the old-fashioned kind, its cover burgundy leather and its paper something thick and white and handsome.

"Tasteful," said Troublesome. "You're sure you haven't got two or three million more of those to pile up there for me in a heap?"

"That book," said the voice, almost sternly, "is the only book that matters, for it has within its covers all the wisdom of the universe. The way to every science, Miss Troublesome. The foundation of principles upon which all science rests and from which every science past and present and future may be derived. All that we have shown you before is as dust beside this one book . . . and you may have it for your own. The wisdom of the universe, Miss Troublesome. For the asking."

Troublesome cocked her head, and they brightened up the image for her and even opened the volume and let her have a glimpse of its pages, although they kept the print too blurred for her to make out anything it said.

"That's more like it," she said seriously, and they ran a narrow gold border round her window frame. "But I don't want it."

The image wobbled; she'd surprised them.

"Think what you are saying!" it said. "Think what you are refusing!"

"Get ready," said Troublesome, taking a last bite of cornbread. "Here comes the wisdom of the universe all rolled up for you in one line. Are you ready? It goes like this: AS YE SOW, SO SHALL YE REAP. Now isn't that less hassle than a whole book of stuff, that's got to be dusted and put away and the mildew wiped off it every day or two, and the coffee wiped up when you spill it on the nice paper? Here, I'll do it again, so you'll have it right to hand: AS YE SOW, SO SHALL YE REAP."

The book disappeared and the window went blank, and the voice came back at her all cold and steely now and no scarlet velvet to it, and it said that she wasn't taking this seriously.

"Quite right," she acknowledged. "And don't you be coming at me telling me that all this wealth and bliss and wisdom and whatnot is mine for the asking, no strings to it, if there's a string that says I'm obliged to take it seriously. You can't have it both ways."

"*As ye sow so shall ye reap* is a platitude. It is *not* a science."

"It will not build a device that kills, you mean. It will not destroy planets, of itself. It will not raise buildings that hide the sky and the sun and the stars in all their glory. It will not let a man hurl himself toward destruction at the speed of light. It will not let monsters be born by the useful thousands, for the twiddling of a dial. All those things."

"Sweet Troublesome—"

"You're wasting your breath with all that honey," she snapped, "and you're only wearying me. I tell you there is *no* science that is based on anything more than the principle of equilibrium. And there is no principle of equilibrium that is more basic than as ye sow so shall ye reap, from which *all* things—the wicked ones included, if I *must* be serious with you—from which *all things whatsoever* may be derived. And will be, whether a body likes it or not. Now get on with it."

To Troublesome's great satisfaction, they gave her her mountainside back, instead of trotting out another inventory of alleged delights.

"Are you through, then?" she asked, brushing the crumbs off her thighs onto the plank floor.

"Not quite."

"Law," said Troublesome. "Why ever not?"

"Sweet Troublesome—and we do call you sweet, for sweet you are, and luscious and ripe for the picking, and beautiful beyond all other women of your kind—sweet Troublesome, what if you could have it *all*?"

"Have it all? You care to clarify that?"

"*All*," it said. "Wealth *and* power *and* the pleasures of the senses *and* wisdom *and* all the rest of it. The power and the glory, sweet Troublesome. What if you could have every last smallest bit of it, all for the asking?"

Troublesome leaned back a little, bracing herself with the palms of her hands flat on the floor, and smiled, waiting to be shown.

Her window clouded again, and she saw a scene begin to shape itself there. She saw a woman, sitting in a chair of unfamiliar style, but clearly a chair, and beside her a window like Troublesome's own window, but not roughly made like hers. And beyond that window, where the woman gazed, there were planets by the tens and hun-

dreds of thousands, stretching away across the spangled
black of the sky behind the sky. And on every one of them
Troublesome could see, as if her eyes were the lenses of
miracles, worlds full of beings going about their daily
business, all of it infinitely small but infinitely detailed, all
of it open to her gaze.

"We use symbols," said the voice, gone velvet again.
"You must realize . . . it is more wonderful than that, but
we would be here an eternity if we tried to show it in its
full and real shape. Look well, Troublesome of Brightwater
. . . you see that woman?"

"I see her. Does she have a name?"

"No, she has no name. She is called only The Lady of
the Spaceways, and that, too, is symbols. Everything that
is, she may have—to take, if she chooses, and to give, if
she chooses, except those things that are reserved to the
Almighty. She lives, sweet Troublesome, for nine hundred ninety-nine of your years."

"And?"

"And we are prepared to set you at her right hand," it
said, "where you will be beloved of her and live so long as
she shall live, taking as she takes—though she takes little,
sweet Troublesome—and giving as she gives, and she
gives with abundant grace. Beside her, Troublesome, you
would be only a child, but she would share all that she has
and all that she knows with you. And she would love you
like her own."

Troublesome swallowed hard, and she found that she
could not take her eyes from the Lady, or from the great
universe the Lady watched over. As for the being loved
part . . . Troublesome had had no mother, or as near as
none, for her mother had never been allowed to love her,
and would not let her love. No one had ever held her, no
one had ever touched her tenderly, no one had ever said,
"I love you, child." Not to Troublesome. There had been

the matter of needing her banished, and making her fit for that; there had been no place for love.

"Say the word, Troublesome of Brightwater," the voice said softly, "only say the word. And we will set you there among the stars beside the Lady."

Well, thought Troublesome, feeling the tears burn her eyes even though they would not fall, and then to her amazement feeling them wet and warm upon her breasts, she who *never* cried! Well, this has not all been wasted. I have learned something from this. I have learned what it feels like to be tempted, and no doubt it will do me good.

"Well, Troublesome of Brightwater? Will you say yes?"

Troublesome closed her eyes tightly, and wrapped her arms around her breasts, and rocked gently in her pain; as she had expected, it did no good, they merely used the inside of her eyes as their canvas and showed her the same wonders.

Troublesome fought, and she thought she would choke on the word, but she got it past her lips at last.

"No," she said.

"No!"

"No." Sure now, and firm.

"You *want* it, Troublesome!" the voice said, and she heard the desperation in it and was grateful, for it meant that this was the worst of it. If she could get past this, it would be over.

"I'll not deny that," she said quietly.

"Then take it! Why shouldn't you? What's to stop you? You want it with all your heart. . . . Say *yes*, sweet Troublesome!"

Troublesome said no.

And held her breath.

And they gave her back her mountainside again, none the worse for wear.

As for Troublesome, she was worn out. She went back to bed, pulled her sheet clear up to her neck, and slept until the moon woke her laying a bar of white across her floor.

CHAPTER THIRTEEN

When the Magician of Rank finally arrived for a showdown meeting, it seemed to Coyote that he'd been trapped in Smith Kingdom for months; he stared at the man dully, as does an abused and surly animal with a broken spirit, and he offered nothing by way of greeting but a mumbled growl.

And Joseph Everholt Purdy did not stand on ceremony, either. The only concession he made was to accost Coyote when he was sitting alone on a tombstone that read "Here lies our beloved sister Sharon Ann of Airy" in the city graveyard, instead of lambasting him before an audience. Coyote was properly grateful, to the extent that his state of numb frustration allowed him to feel any emotion at all.

"I suppose it has occurred to you," said the Magician of Rank, without preamble. "that Smith Kingdom will be canceling those treaties signed a week ago today."

"Only a week?" Coyote was amazed.

"A good long time, a week," said the Magician of Rank. "Under the circumstances." He coughed softly, and rubbed his hands together, watching Coyote for some volunteered communication; when none came, he repeated himself. "It *has* occurred to you, Mister Jones?"

"It has entered my mind."

"Well, then. The treaties being null and void by reason of fraud—"

"There was no fraud," Coyote interrupted, but the man ignored him.

"By reason of fraud," he said firmly. "Indeed there was fraud, and a *substantial* fraud! For Smith Kingdom elected to join something called the Tri-Galactic Federation, represented to us as being a powerful alliance of more than twenty thousand member worlds, with technology advanced beyond anything we on Ozark have so much as dreamed of."

"And so it is," said Coyote.

"Twenty thousand strong it may be, Mister Jones, and technology it may have—but powerful it is *not!* An alliance of that size that can be completely hamstrung by a couple of Magicians of Rank on one small planet? I call that *puny*, Mister Jones . . . I might say I call that pitiful. We of Smith were misled, and we are under no obligation to abide by any decisions made as a result of your fraudulent misrepresentation."

"I don't care," said Coyote, always the superb diplomat.

"Then perhaps you'll be good enough to hand me over the originals of the treaties, that you were intending to take back to your government—if you hadn't been trapped here like a bug in a jellyjar."

Coyote glared at him, for no reason except that that was what he felt like doing, and the Magician of Rank tightened his lips and folded his arms across his chest.

"I asked for them only for the sake of tidiness, Mister Jones," he said quietly. "It makes no real difference whether you give them to me or not. They being only blank pieces of paper now, you may confiscate them if that strikes your perverted fancy."

Coyote scowled as fiercely as he was able, but he reached into the pouch he'd been carrying all this interminable week and pulled the documents out for one quick look. They were blank, as advertised.

"Disappearing ink?" he sneered, shaking them in one fist.

"Deletion Transformation," said the Magician of Rank.

"Oh, BEMdung," said Coyote, and handed them over. "I don't care," he added.

The Magician of Rank smirked, absently settling the seven smooth pleats of his cape where they were fastened at his shoulder with a silver bar. Coyote had no finery to fool with; he settled for smirking back.

"Your behavior is childish beyond description, for a grown man," observed Joseph Everholt.

"I know that. I don't care."

"I see. Well, care or not, Mister Jones, you'd best grow up with minimum delay, because you have a new task before you, and it is wholly and completely your responsibility "

"Go away, Joseph Everholt," said Coyote. "You've got your papers, the whole thing is over and done with. It's *over.* . . . just go away and leave me to my misery."

"Mister Jones." The voice was grim, and it wasn't going to go away."

"What?"

"I said that you had an obligation to carry out a task. I was not joking, Mister Jones."

"BEMdung."

"*You*, Mister Coyote Jones, are going to have to find a way to leave Smith Kingdom, and that right promptly. Because *you* are the one obligated to pass along the message to the rest of Ozark that Smith Kingdom has withdrawn its secession and canceled its treaties with the Tri-Galactic Federation. So that that cursed wall will come down, and so that services may be restored. That is your duty, Mister Jones—*you* are the representative of the Federation. Considering what was promised, and what has not been done, it is the very least that you—as representative of the Federation—can do."

Coyote looked at him, without sarcasm or temper this time. He said, "Joseph Everholt Purdy, I don't know how to get out of here. If I did, I'd have been long gone."

"You will have to find a way."

"Why?" Coyote waved his arms toward the streets of Red Arches. "Nobody's suffering any pain, except me. Nobody's starving. You've got a whole district at your disposal, as big as a lot of countries on other planets. You've got farms and towns and rivers and forests . . . what's the big rush?"

The Magician of Rank's eyes widened, and he stood there shaking his head as if the sight of Coyote were a sad and sorry spectacle, and sighed a long exasperated sigh.

"Mister Jones," he noted, "apparently you find this trivial."

"Well, I can understand that it's very inconvenient, but I don't see it as serious."

"Very insightful of you."

"Thanks."

"Do you see any coffee plantations around you, Mister Jones? Do you see any salt mines? Any sugar fields? Do you—"

"What are you getting at?" Coyote interrupted crossly.

"Mister Jones . . . many of our most essential supplies, food and medicine and industrial materials and agricultural materials and goods of all kinds, come to us from outside Smith Kingdom. We have our own vegetable gardens—you've seen those, and have personally destroyed one—and we have crops and goods that we produce here. But we don't have everything we need, not by a long shot, and there are many things in short supply already—in a month, they will be completely gone, and that will not be amusing."

"Don't you have stockpiles?"

"Why? We've never had to consider any such thing as stockpiles. There is always—except right now, Mister Jones—a free and constant stream of commerce among the Kingdoms of Ozark."

"Oh," said Coyote. "I didn't realize there were going to be shortages."

"You didn't, eh?"

"No. I didn't."

"There is also the matter of physical barriers," the Magician went on, his voice growing colder with every sentence. "There were people here in Smith when that wall went up who don't live here, who were visiting here or here on business. They can't go home to their families, Mister Jones. They can't even get a *message* to their families, nor receive one. And it works both ways—there were people of this Kingdom who just didn't happen to be inside its borders when that wall went up. They can't come home, Mister Jones. They can't call home by comset, they can't send a letter; they are cut off. You find that trivial, do you?"

Through the numbness, Coyote felt the beginnings of shame. He should have thought of these things. He should have had the simple sense to realize that of *course* you couldn't just seal off an entire region without any warning, as had been done here, without inflicting serious harm. He drew a long breath, and rubbed fretfully at his mouth and chin, and tried to think what he could say.

"And then there are business matters," the Magician of Rank continued. "There are people whose livelihoods depend upon interaction with other Kingdoms, people with complicated dealings beyond our borders, people who had urgent appointments and duties elsewhere—they can't see to those things. They can't even let their associates know why they haven't appeared to fulfill their roles and obligations. And I assure you, we cannot count on Brightwater to have made any explanations for us."

"I'm sorry," said Coyote. "I'm so sorry."

"And then there's education. Our children are educated by comset after the age of seven, and our comsets aren't working. The children are falling each day more and more behind in their lessons, and we have no way of making up that deficiency. Our Teachers are doing what they can, but there are only a few of them, and the routine education of children is not what they were trained for."

"I'm sorry."

"You're sorry! You keep *saying* that!"

"Well," Coyote insisted, "I *am* sorry. I know that doesn't help any, but I am sorry. I should have realized. I should have known. I'm so stupid I can't stand myself. But I come from a place where nobody has the kind of routine needs that you're discussing, Joseph Everholt—I'm a city boy. I'm used to everything being available as a right and privilege, just because I'm a citizen. I'm spoiled. I forgot that everything isn't just automatically available here. I'm the worst kind of off-worlder, and I'm ashamed. And you don't have to go on with the list. I'm convinced. I understand."

"My congratulations on your so recent enlightenment," observed the Magician of Rank with practiced sarcasm. "I will spare you the rest, then, except for pointing out that it will be many a long year before the other Kingdoms allow us to forget what we have done . . . if they ever do. And I would like to point out to you how lucky, how very lucky, it is that when the wall went up, this Kingdom had its Magician of Rank and its Granny present inside the wall. That was just blind good fortune."

Coyote nodded, biting his lip. "You couldn't just use magic to take care of all this stuff?" It was petty, but he couldn't resist getting off a point or two.

"No magic that couldn't be counteracted instantly by the Magicians of Rank who are helping Brightwater in this," came the patient answer. "I am only *one* Magician of Rank, Mister Jones."

"Sure. I see what you mean."

"Well? Now that you understand the situation, what are you going to do about it?"

"I wish I knew."

"That's not encouraging, Mister Jones."

"It's not meant to be. I've been stupid. I'm ignorant. I am sorry and ashamed. But Joseph Everholt, if I had understood the situation from the very first minute I don't see what I could have done. And I don't see what I can do *now*, unless you'd like for me to request that the TGF invade Ozark with a military force and order that wall taken down at the point of a laser. Do you want me to do that?"

"Could you?"

"Yes. There's an arrangement for getting messages out to my government. I could do that."

"Wouldn't it have been more sensible to ask them to send a diplomatic team to try to *reason* with Brightwater and her allies first, before the lasers? Have you done that, at least?"

"No," said Coyote sadly. "I haven't. I told you . . . I didn't realize this situation was serious. I truly thought it was only inconvenient. And you remember that I was issued a set of *very* firm orders about no offworlders being allowed in Ozark's airspace ever again. Do you want me to call in a diplomatic team now, with the inevitable result that they will be tossed all over the sky by your telepaths—excuse me, your Magicians—and will go home to report that? Which will mean that the next group out will have the lasers . . . missiles, that can be fired from *off* the planet—and the troops? Is that what you want?"

"Dozens, man, of course I don't!"

"Well, then? What could I do, Joseph Everholt?"

Coyote wondered . . . should he tell the Magician of Rank about the Communipaths being able to contact the Ozarkers through Responsible of Brightwater? He wasn't at all sure what kind of trouble that might cause. So far as he could tell, people didn't know that Responsible had any unusual abilities. Even the Teacher had not said anything to indicate that she saw the function of the Responsible in each Ozark generation as anything more than symbolic. What sort of havoc he might wreak here if he spilled some ancient beans, he didn't know—he decided once again to keep that information to himself. For now, at least. Later he might have to reconsider his decision.

The Magician of Rank was growing impatient. "What *are* you going to do, Jones?" he demanded. "I think I understand fully what you *aren't* going to do!"

"I don't know."

"Now *see here*—"

Coyote had had all he could bear. Humiliated, degraded, shamed, agonizingly conscious of one ugly failure after another, he nevertheless had had all he could stand.

"Don't do that," he said sharply, cutting the man off. "Don't. And don't do anything fancy, either. Because if you turn me into a toad, or hang me from your church steeple, or in any way interfere with me as a way of demonstrating your very justifiable outrage at the mess I've made, you'll be on your own. I won't be able to help."

"We seem to be on our own *now*, Mister Jones!"

Coyote sighed, remembering yesterday, when he had

tried using a telepathically projected THERE IS NO WALL THERE, AND NO BARRIER . . . I THINK I WILL WALK RIGHT ON OVER TO THAT TREE, and had had the pleasure of seeing the projection work splendidly. People marching docilely into the wall and being knocked flat by the impact of the "illusion." Picking themselves up bruised and dusty and embarrassed, wondering what on earth could have made them do anything so stupid.

"Let me *think*, friend," he said slowly. "Give me room. Now that I know it's urgent, now that you've waked me up—get back and give me some room to think about this. Let me see if I can't figure out what to do next."

He must have looked as desperate as he felt, because the Magician of Rank gave him a long steady glance, and nodded his head.

"All right," he said. "All right, Jones. That's fair. And I will say—it never occurred to us that you weren't aware of the gravity of the situation, or I would have spoken to you sooner. It seems awfully obvious."

"It should have been obvious," agreed Coyote wearily.

"Can I do anything to help you?"

"Yes. You can go away and let me think."

"Very well. I'll do that."

"Thank you."

"We're counting on you, you know."

"I know." The Light help us all, Coyote thought, I know.

The Magician turned to leave, and Coyote watched him walk away, feeling battered all over, grateful that Joseph Everholt Purdy hadn't insisted on staying and watching The Secret Agent In Action. But then, almost at the edge of the graveyard, where an ironwood picket fence separated it from the sidewalk, he stopped as if he'd thought of something, and he came back.

Once he was within hailing distance, he called to Coyote. "Mister Jones! One minute!"

Coyote dropped his eyes quickly to the pink roses, as if he hadn't noticed.

"Mister Jones, you're being childish again."

True. Coyote raised his head and put on his most adult look.

"There *is* something I can do," said the man.

"Yeah? What's that?"

"I'm going to send the Granny along—you just stay put right there where you are!"

And he turned again and was gone before Coyote had a chance to put the question about what the blazes good a Granny could possibly do in this situation.

Coyote settled for asking the open air and the spirits of the dear departeds all around him. "What good," he demanded aloud, "could a Granny possibly do or be in this situation?"

Every Kingdom, he knew, had at least one official Granny, sometimes more than one. Her function was, as he understood it, to name the girl children—something the Ozarkers seemed to take with deadly seriousness, to run a sort of kindergarten for little girls called Granny School, either in person or by comset, and to deal with minor problems of house and garden. Grannys could tell you why your tomatoes weren't coming up right, and they could fix herbs that would take care of your head cold, and they knew how to get spots out of cloth and wasps out of attics . . . the kind of things that he would have expected ordinary grannies, as opposed to Grannys, to know how to do. They were exceedingly busy women, and spoke an amazing mixture of ancient Hill English and plain cantankerousness that the Ozarkers called "formspeech," and he had the greatest respect for them. But he was damned if he could see any function for a Granny in his present dilemma; this was something far beyond house and garden and birthing. Perhaps the Granny would see that herself and tell Joseph Everholt Purdy the 46th to go chase himself.

But no . . . Coyote was still sitting there, going over and over the ridiculous mess and longing for a way to disappear forever, not just from Planet Ozark but from the universe at large, before anybody could tell him what they thought of him. And barely ten minutes into his funk, here came the Granny, picking her way around the graves, her glasses down too far on her skinny nose, and moving with admirable speed in her black pointy-toed high-heeled shoes.

Coyote was not a total barbarian, whatever the Ozarkers might think; he stood up and greeted her politely.

"Hello, Granny Sherryjake," he said. "Ma'am."

"Jones," said the Granny. "Howdeedoo."

Howdeedoo. Oh sweet suffering stupendous saints and spirits, thought Coyote. Here I sit, whipped by a society that still goes around greeting people with "howdeedoo." It rankled. It *galled*.

"The Magician of Rank sent you," he said tentatively, for want of anything better to say.

"He did. And about time, to my mind. Out here prancing in the *grave*yard, shouting at each other and bad-mouthing each other . . . it's not even decent. Both of you with no more respect for the dead than you've got for an old broomhandle! *Dis*gusting, *I* say! Just plain *dis*gusting!"

"Granny," said Coyote, "we weren't prancing. Or shouting."

"Uhuh. Young man, I don't have time for your fairy tales. I should hope I know *men*, me as has spent sixty years and more abiding them—I know what youall were up to, and there'll be an end to it now."

"Yes, ma'am."

"You and I, we're going up to the Castle . . ."

She stopped and looked at him, and her tongue clicked like hail on a metal roof. "Never you mind telling me you can't or you won't," she said flatly. "Just you put that out of your mind. For you *will* go, however much it offends you to go among the decent people you've so sorely wronged, and you with nary an excuse to offer them. We're going to the Castle, and we'll sit decently in one of the parlors with a good strong ale to hearten us, and we'll talk this over."

"Granny," Coyote managed, hoping that forceful dignity was what he was conveying, "I really can't. And I think that Joseph Everholt was mistaken—kind, certainly, but mistaken—in bothering you with this. I appreciate your coming down here, but I don't need someone to soothe me or hearten me or whatever it was you had in mind. I just need some time—alone—to think this over."

The Granny sniffed. "You don't know any more about what you need," she told him, "than a babe knows it needs diapers. And without some help you'll make just that same sort of mess, too, not that it isn't mess enough right this instant to fill a sizable pail. You hush your sass, and you gather yourself up and you follow me, and we'll tackle this; and the only mistake that Joseph Everholt made was sending me after you instead of bringing you along hisself, *which* is just like a man! Mind those roses, now!"

Coyote considered not following her. And he even stood there for a few seconds thinking that he *wouldn't* follow her, because it was *dumb* to go up to the Castle and chat with an old lady when he had real problems to solve. But he found himself, resentful and bewildered, following docilely in the Granny's wake as if his feet had minds of their own. He was certain that he'd turn aside with some firm remark about not having time for this and thank you all the same, which was true, right up to the instant when he found himself sitting in a big wide rocker facing the Granny, with a mug of ale in his hand and her knitting away like sixty.

"Now," she said, "now, this is proper. Now we can get right to it, now we're out of the *grave*yard. You, Mister Jones . . . you describe the problem to me, as best you can. I'll listen."

Describe the problem?

Let's see. Granny, he could say, I am the most powerful projective telepath in the entire known universe. I am a man who is sent to *solve* problems, not to create them. I am a man immune to telepathic projections, a man who cannot be fooled by the psi shenanigans of lesser mortals, a man who can sort the real wheat from the illusory *chaff*, by the Light! I come from a government representing an empire more powerful than any the world has ever known, an empire that stretches across three galaxies. And I know, beyond any question, that there is *no such thing as magic*.

And I am stopped, stumped, cut off, whipped, destroyed, by a wall put up by magic, maintained by magic, and as impossible as a twelve-headed billy goat. Ma'am.

"Granny," he said, "I don't have anything to say."

"Oh? Nothing at all?"

"No, ma'am, Granny."

"Shy, aren't you?" she said, looking vaguely sympathetic, and to his horror Coyote felt himself blushing.

"No, I'm not shy!" he said, short and snappy.

"I see. And that's why you're the same color as my yarn here, as is going to be a party shawl in crimson wool."

"Shoot," said Coyote.

"And witty, too," observed the Granny. Her needles flew, and he stared fiercely into the mug he was holding.

"Mister Jones," she went on, "you drink your ale, why don't you, afore it gets all warm and nasty, and I'll just tell you how *I* perceive this matter! Go on, boy, drink it, it'll do you a world of good—and you listen sharp."

Coyote groaned, but it didn't slow her down.

"There's two ways of dealing with a truly difficult problem," said the Granny. "Suppose you've got power aplenty available, you can always use it to overcome the system you're up against. That's one way. And then suppose it's *not* like that; suppose you're hopelessly outclassed and outranked—then there's the other way. And that's to work *with* the system, and use it against itself. You follow me, Mister Jones?"

The question was rhetorical; she didn't wait for an answer. "Now you find *your*self up against something you've not come across before . . . if I recollect what you've told me, and had no more sense than to tell others, you're as ignorant of magic as a little child, and helpless besides because you're pretending there's no such thing. Never mind Mules as fly with no wings, of course; we don't believe in magic, *no*sir! Never mind getting on a Mule's back and being hundreds of miles away before we can draw a breath, with nary a thing in the middle—*we* don't believe in magic. Never mind something as can take your flying machines and fling 'em like toys till you puke your poor guts up, with nary a sign of anything to make *that* go—we don't *believe* in magic. Well . . . that's all right, if you fancy failing, Mister Jones."

He might have said something to that, but she didn't give him a chance; she went right on. "I do believe," she said, "that if I was you I'd look around me and I'd say here's something called magic that *works*, at least for here and at least for now, for all these many thousands of intelligent folks. And I believe I'd at least consider the possibility that it might could work for me, *too*, provided I was willing and respectful. And I believe I'd say to myself, now *let me* see . . . how can I sort of tap into that supply of stuff that everybody else is running on? And I believe I'd remember that in that system of magic there's only four things you can do."

The Granny leaned toward him and punctuated every one of the four by jabbing him in the chest with her knitting needle.

"There's insertion," she said. *Jab.* "That's putting something where there wasn't anything before. There's substitution." *Jab.* "That's putting something in *place* of something else. There's deletion . . . that's taking something away that was already there. And then there's movement; and that's moving something to a new and different location in this world. And that's all there is, Mister Jones."

Coyote had every intention of looking completely unimpressed by this tirade. Superior Offworld Secret Agent Courteously Tolerates Smartass Primitive. But the Granny was smiling at him with great satisfaction.

"There, you see?" she said, tapping him once more with the needles. "You *can* understand common sense, Mister Jones, provided you try!"

"But—"

"No buts," said the Granny. "You just go take a good long look at that fool wall one more time, that you need to get over or get under or get around or get through, and you ask yourself two questions. ONE! How can I tap into the flow of magic, that everybody else is running on, and use it to deal with that cursed thing? And TWO! Which of the four things that magic does do I *need*, to make that cursed thing go away? And I do believe you'll find that something will come to you, Mister Jones!"

He sat there, frozen to his rocker, until the Granny tipped her head back and glowered at him through her glasses.

"Well?" she demanded. "Why are you still sitting there like a lump, Mister Jones? You've had your ale, and you've had your rest, and you've had your little chat . . . any particular reason why you should still be sitting there like that gawking at me, while the world goes to hell all around you?"

"No, ma'am, Granny Sherryjake."

"Then I suggest you be *off!*" she declared, and he left her there with her shawl-in-progress and went bumbling out of the Castle falling over his own two feet and drunk with more than the effect of the ale on an empty stomach.

One, she'd said: how can I tap into this magic that everybody else is running on? That one he'd already thought out on his own, after a fashion; it had at least flitted through his sieve of a brain. And *two*: which of the four things that Ozark magic does is the one I need?

Coyote thought he could remember both of those long enough to get to the wall.

If he didn't get lost first.

CHAPTER FOURTEEN

There was no question in Coyote's mind about which of the four possible varieties of "magical" operation he was going to use. There was the basic and overriding principle: "magic" worked on Ozark because the Ozarkers believed in it. It wasn't going to work for him if he didn't believe in it, too. And there was only so much he could manage to believe.

There was no way he could believe in magic deletion, that made things disappear. Or magic insertion, that made things appear from out of nowhere. As for substitution, that was even worse; say you were going to substitute a goat for a sheep, even if you got a perfectly ordinary goat from a perfectly ordinary field, you still had to make the sheep disappear before you could substitute the goat, even if the "magic" made it look as if it all happened at once. Coyote couldn't muster up a scrap of faith in such alleged procedures. He knew better than to try.

But *movement* was a different matter. That, he could believe in. Not just because he had himself been "moved" instantaneously by a Magician of Rank on Muleback, but because this particular process was obviously only telekinesis. He had said so to Teacher Philomena, before he'd disgusted her so deeply that she refused to have anything more to do with him; and she had smiled and observed that different cultures have different magic words—he should have had brains enough to follow through on that at the time.

Telekinesis. The moving of objects and beings, through the power of the mind, by psibility. Even telepathy was no more than the telekinetic movement of information! He could believe in that; he had believed in it all his life, and had seen it demonstrated as a routine skill from the first day he could remember, when he had been a tiny child in the Communipath Crèche. He was perfectly comfortable with telekinesis.

And he had no difficulty believing that the absolute faith the Ozarkers had in their "magic" created a pool of energy available for the taking. He had incited too many groups to an emotion of his choice and then stood back and watched the mind of the mob raise that emotion to absurd heights to be ignorant about the power of consensus, or the awesome contagiousness of mass emotional states.

What he had to do, therefore, was simple enough. He had to move *himself* outside the damn wall, that was all. By telekinesis, redefined as a "Movement Transformation." Powered by Ozark faith. All he had to do was get beyond the wall, outside the boundaries of Smith Kingdom, and every house he came to would have a working comset on which he could transmit the message that Smith had changed its mind. Nothing fancy; just a quick telekinetic hop.

Okay. . . . when on Ozark, do as the Ozarkers do. That meant he had a rule to write. And he took a leaf from the Teacher's book and picked up a stick to do the writing with.

He knew how to begin, from his briefing session with Tzana Kai at the very beginning of this string of misadventures. He'd need a boundary symbol, #, to mark the beginning and the end of the rule. He'd need an X to be the first term and a Y to be the last one, to serve as the variables—pieces that didn't matter to the rule but allowed for the possibility of miscellaneousness. He sat down at the bottom of a flight of worn stone steps leading up to a small park that was deserted by decent hardworking Ozarkers at this hour of the day, and wrote that much in the dust at his feet:

X . . . . . . Y

And there was himself, the thing to be moved. That would be term two. Hmmmmm.

X   COYOTE   Y

  1   2   3

Goes to?
Goes to what? Or where? Outside the wall?
That wouldn't do it; that would be like saying "up" or "West." He could end up in the Extreme Moons that way, for all he knew; he had considerable respect for a telekinetic power that could pop Mules from one end of a world to the other in the twinkle of the proverbial eye. He had to make it more specific, so that he could write his destination into the rule as a *term*, somehow.

He looked around, scanning the distance for something that could serve him as landmark, and he found what he needed almost immediately. Straight ahead of him beyond the wall, on the side of a gently rising hill, was a substantial boulder, maybe twenty feet across and a good twelve feet high. Tentatively, he wrote in the dust again.

$$\underset{1}{\underline{\# X}} \quad \underset{2}{\text{COYOTE}} \quad \underset{3}{\text{BOULDER}} \quad \underset{4}{\underline{Y \#}} \longrightarrow 1, 0, 3+2, 4$$

He stared at it, squinting against the sunlight. It couldn't be that simple, of course. It just said, "Here's this set that contains Coyote and a boulder; move Coyote to the other side of the boulder and no farther . . . or move Coyote so he and the boulder are together. . . ." He could think of a dozen other ways to do it, and he wished he knew which was the *right* one. Obviously, he had to clarify that "boulder" bit; just "boulder" wouldn't be enough. He had to do something about identifying the specific boulder in question. He had to visualize that boulder in such detail, in such vivid completeness, that there could be no mistake about where it was that he was to go.

He studied the boulder, and in his mind he constructed a careful image. There was the boulder itself. White, streaked with pale brown and yellow. A deep hollow in it all around, where a man could sit comfortably and lean back against the stone. He imagined its texture, grainy against his skin; he conjured up in his mind the sharp dusty smell the stone would have if you pressed your face to it. He got that stone, the look and the texture and the size and the smell . . . even the taste, if you touched your tongue to it . . . as sharp in his mind's perceptions as the step on which he sat. And then, carefully, so carefully, he imagined himself sitting in that hollowed pocket. Saw himself, leaning back against the stone, saw his legs crossed and his left foot pressed to the rock, saw the glint of his red hair and beard against the stone.

He was just thinking, mournfully, that it wasn't good enough, because he didn't know how to write all that stuff into the damn *rule*, when the lights went out.

CHAPTER FIFTEEN

It was Teacher Letha of Lewis, making her way on the back of her Mule toward Castle Wommack through the Wilderness Lands of Kintucky, who found Coyote.

"Whoa, Snowbird!" she said sharply, and the Mule stopped to let her down. She slipped from its back with a soft noise of concern, gathered the skirt of her habit through the metal ring sewn into its seam for that purpose, and dropped to her knees beside the man sprawled there in the hollow of the hulking boulder. He was unconscious, she saw, and deeply so; her fingers, probing at the terrible damage the rock had done him, drew no response, no gasp of pain, not even a reflex withdrawal from the stimulus.

It was serious, then, and urgent; she wasted no time.

"Snowbird, this is bad," she said, turning her head to speak to the Mule. "You go back to the Castle, fast as you can." When they saw Snowbird without her, they'd send someone in a hurry, and hurry was surely indicated. The Mule whuffled at her and set off through the trees; she was intelligent and reliable and willing, an unusual combination in a creature whose brains could always be relied upon, but whose disposition tended to the spectacularly negative.

She gave the man her full attention, then, speaking clearly in the voice of reassurance, calling for *his* attention even in the depths of unconsciousness.

"You will be all right, sir," she said firmly. "There'll be help along in a few minutes, and we'll take care of you. You are going to be just fine; don't you fret. You just hold on, now, until the Magician of Rank gets here, and he'll see to you." And she went on like that, steady, holding him in the net of her skilled voice. She dared not move him enough to cradle him on her lap, though she hated to see him hurt like he was and lying on that bare harsh stone. The minutes crawled, because it was a considerable distance to the Castle from where he'd fallen, and his breathing seemed to her irregular; she adjusted the intonation of her words for that, and paced him carefully back to the measured full breaths that he needed. She added touch as well, her hands on those parts of his body that she could be sure were unhurt. In her heart she managed also a constant prayer . . . and at last Snowbird appeared between two great oaks, with the Magician of Rank on her back.

"Thanks be—you're here!" said Letha. "He's very bad."

Feebus Timothy Traveler the 6th, Magician of Rank to Castle Wommack, swung down from the Mule and went swiftly to examine the man, but to Letha's amazement he did no more than look at him and then draw back, instead of setting at once to the task of healing.

"Feebus Timothy!" protested the Teacher. "There's no time for you to dawdle about! Look at him . . . he has to have gone headfirst into that boulder, and at a considerable speed—it's done him dreadful damage. How could such a thing *happen*?"

It was an interesting question. It was as if some giant

hand had held the man directly over the hollow in the boulder and then slammed him forehead first into its surface. Thrown from an animal's back, perhaps? But no Mule would do such a thing, and Ozark had no other beast of burden. Thrown out of a tinlizzy? Impossible. Not in these deep woods!

"I don't know how it happened," said the Magician of Rank. "I wouldn't care to speculate."

"And you needn't speculate," she said urgently. "Only help him!"

"No," said Feebus Timothy. "No, I'll not help him. But I'll *get* help . . . I'll be right back, Teacher Letha. We'll need to bring a lizzy as far down the road as is possible, and then two strong men with a litter to come in here after him and carry him back."

The Teacher was shocked, and bewildered. That would have been needful if there'd been no Magician of Rank available to help, as was sure to happen now and then with only a handful of them to serve a whole planet, no matter how quickly they could SNAP through time and space. But Feebus Timothy was *here*—he had the skill and the knowledge to heal the man if healing was still possible.

"I don't understand," she said, as the Magician of Rank strode to the Mule, mounted and SNAPPED out of her sight. And he'd heard her; the first thing he said when he reappeared three minutes later was, "There's nothing to understand. The man is not an Ozarker; he's the off-worlder that tried to sell us that bill of goods a little while back. I know nothing of healing off-worlders."

The Teacher looked at him sharply, and then she looked at Coyote, examining each of them with a practiced eye.

"So he does. But I know better, Teacher Letha; I've heard him described often enough, and I'm not likely to forget that hair, or that beard, or for that matter, the ungodly *size* of him. He meets the descriptions, and some left over."

"As I said to you already," insisted the Teacher, "be he Ozarker or be he Terran or be he from the depths of hell, there appears to be *no* difference between him and you. We have men as large, and with hair as red. What are you fussing about?"

"That is the *out*side of him," Feebus Timothy told her. "Inside, it may be a different story. And it would take only a very small difference to make my magic a danger for him instead of a benison. I'll not touch him."

The Teacher stood up, brushing the dust from her hands, and looked at the Magician with narrowed eyes. "That's nonsense," she declared flatly. "You know that if he's not helped he will die! In such a case, a person does not worry over the hypothetical."

"The man is not our problem," snapped Feebus Timothy, "and I'll not have his tending—and its result—laid at our doorstep. It was Brightwater that made the mistake of letting him ever set foot on Ozark, and it is Brightwater that shall see to him now."

"For shame!" hissed the Teacher. An ordinary man would have flinched at the lash of her tongue. But Feebus Timothy was no ordinary man; he only raised his eyebrows at her and looked annoyed.

"There's the tinlizzy now," he said, nodding toward the soft humming sound of its tires on the distant road. "Any minute, the men will be here to take him back to the Castle."

"Why bother?" asked the Teacher coldly. "He won't live through the ride back. If you won't stoop to help him, let him die here, and spare him all that jostling; if you must murder, Feebus Timothy Traveler, have the grace to do it kindly."

The Magician of Rank's lips curled, and his eyebrows

met over his nose, and when he spoke the contempt in his voice was as ugly as his face.

"You see him, Teacher Letha," he sneered. "You see the way his head is crushed? You see that blood?"

"I saw it before *you* did, you and your black heart!"

"He lives, does he not? Surely you do not think that he manages that without help from me?"

"So!" The Teacher struck her hands together. "So it's not that you won't stoop to give aid, it's that you'll stoop only a grudging inch!"

"I have stabilized the man; he will not die in the next few hours. And that is quite enough for me to do, young woman, and all that I *will* do—furthermore, if you claim I did it I will say you lie."

At another time the Teacher would perhaps have challenged him, for if he was respected and his word silver, *she* was both loved and revered, and her word priceless. It was very unlikely that anyone would believe him if he accused her of lying. But this was not a time for quibbles over precedence and dominance, and it was her turn not to stoop. Instead, she went quickly to direct the Attendants bringing the litter, and to advise them to be very careful and gentle. Her concern now was to get him back to the Castle and into a bed, and a Granny there to nurse him with deft hands. A Granny was not a Magician of Rank, but she was not nothing at all, either. And Letha herself would send to Brightwater for *their* Magician of Rank, to come and do what Feebus Timothy in his meanness of spirit had refused to do.

It was a curious blind spot that the Magicians of Rank had about Brightwater, she thought. They were like male children in their teens, resentful of the parent that had fed them and clothed them and sustained them and to whom they were therefore beholden. And anything that they could do to score a small point against Brightwater—

provided it was at no risk to the services Brightwater provided—any such thing, however small, delighted them. She had seen it before, and it sorrowed her that she was certain to see it again. It seemed to her that with the powers they had, the Magicians of Rank ought to have been far beyond such pettiness.

The Attendants had brought a tinlizzy with a long open space at the back, and she rode there beside the offworlder, with her voice and her hands tending him through the ordeal of the ride and the ordeal of being carried up the Castle stairs.

"Be easy," she said to him, and laid a gentle-strong hand on his chest, since touching his head was out of the question. "Be easy, sir, and soon we will have you set to rights. And Feebus Timothy there, for all his selfishness, will not for one instant left you sink lower, if for no reason other than his pride. He would not want it said that you died in his care, and his concern for his reputation is greater than his joy in spiting Brightwater Kingdom. You be easy, and be strong, and be steady . . . we will look after you."

At Brightwater, Veritas Truebreed Motley took the comset message Teacher Letha sent, and made a face. The servingmaid who had called him looked at him inquiringly, and hoped the problem was nothing that could be turned into a complaint about *her*.

"Is there something wrong, Mister Veritas?" she asked cautiously. "Shall I do something, sir? Shall I get the Granny for you?"

"Don't fuss, girl," was all he said. He left her standing there without so much as a thank you, and off he went down the corridor toward the front room, his long cape swinging behind him and his sandals silent on the stone floor.

He was looking for Responsible, and he found her with her mother and her grandmother and the Grannys, all five of them comfortable in rocking chairs, as if they were ancient queens with slaves at their beck and call to do all the work.

"Well, ladies!" he said, stopping in the door to give them the benefit of his most icy sweeping glance. "I wasn't aware that it was holiday in Brightwater!"

Thorn of Guthrie made a soothing noise, and Ruth of Motley clucked her tongue sympathetically, and they both allowed as how it was dreadful the way the staff took advantage of Veritas Truebreed's good nature.

"It's not the staff I'm remarking on," he said. "It's the five of you! This hour of the day I should think you'd have something to do other than sit around rocking and gossiping."

"Veritas," Responsible observed, "you sound like a Granny."

"And I'll back him," said Granny Gableframe sturdily. "It does make you wonder what this world is coming to, not to mention all the other worlds that are no doubt in worse case than this one, and I've been saying this last hour that there were people as would be grateful to have the time we are wasting."

"Granny," Responsible objected, "I've been up since well before five, and busy the whole time, and I'm worn out. Grandmother was helping me by the time it was light, and my mother—though not precisely helpful—was encouraging us in our labors. We are *all* of us worn right down to the fuzz on the frazzles. And if that doesn't suit Veritas Truebreed, he no doubt knows what I would suggest he do about it."

Veritas ignored her. "Worn out or not," he said, "I need you, Responsible."

"No," she said. "No, you don't need me."

"I do. We're wanted at Castle Wommack."

Responsible went suddenly still, and Granny Hazelbide looked at her from the corner of her eye; she looked like a startled animal that goes dead quiet in the hope the hunter won't see it. But she spoke serenely enough.

"*You* may be wanted at Castle Wommack," she answered, "though I can't imagine why they need you when they've a Magician of Rank of their own, *and* three town Magicians, *and* two Grannys. But there's not one thing *I* could do there, and no reason for them to want me."

"I beg your pardon, Responsible of Brightwater," said Veritas sarcastically, "and it saddens me to see a woman so young and thought so promising that can't even work till noon without collapsing in a chair and declaring that she can't go on. But I assure you that you *are* wanted at Wommack. And that I will not go without you."

Responsible sighed a weary sigh, and leaned back in the rocker, and closed her eyes.

"What is it?" she asked him. "What's the fuss at Wommack as requires my dilapidated presence and your tender sympathies?"

"Mister *Jones* has somehow managed to turn up there," stated Veritas. "Mister *Coyote* Jones. How he did it is entirely beyond either my sense or my imagination, but they tell me it is so."

"Perhaps," said Responsible demurely, "he put his mind to it."

"Whatever he did," said Veritas crossly, "he did it badly, and he landed on his head on a rock and bashed in his skull. I gather he's in a very bad way. And Feebus Timothy Traveler is taking the position that Coyote Jones was *our* guest and remains *our* problem, curse his pompous eyes and his windy belly and his—"

"That's enough such talk!" Granny Gableframe cut in.

"There's ladies present, and most of us genteel, if you hadn't noticed that yet!"

Veritas Truebreed gave her a mocking bow, and begged her pardon. "Jones is alive, they tell me," he went on, "but just barely. And we're needed at once."

Responsible opened her eyes and looked at him.

"They've got no women at Wommack to change his linens or see to his oatmeal?" she asked him.

"What?"

"Well, I see why *you* are needed," she said. "That's clear enough. But I see no function for me, Veritas Truebreed. I have no more healing skills than your Mule. You go on, now, and we'll all cheer."

"I am a Magician of Rank," said Veritas, thin-lipped. "I am *not* a diplomat, nor yet an elected official. And once I have seen to this offworlder's injuries, we'll need someone who can specify what happens *next*. Does he stay at Wommack? Does he come here? Does he go to jail for violating the instructions to spend only one hour on Ozark and then be gone—praise be to the Almighty—forever? Do we send him back, do we keep him, do we throw him off a parapet? My role is to heal the man, not dispose of him!"

"Take the Master of the Castle with you, then," suggested Responsible.

"He's away, and his brother as well, and your grandfather with them; there's only you, Responsible. And while you're chatting about it, Mister Jones has probably died."

"Old Feebus wouldn't let that happen," Responsible scoffed.

"I don't know what the injuries are," said Veritas, "and I don't know how mean Feebus Timothy is feeling this day. Will you come along now, and stop this indecent delay? All those years Feebus spent at Castle Traveler did nothing to sweeten his disposition or fill his breast with tender charity, Responsible—there's no knowing what he's capable of."

Granny Hazelbide had been watching, and thinking; she spoke up then, surprising them both, and stated flatly that she didn't believe there was any reason atall for Responsible to go to Wommack.

"Veritas," she said, "you go fix the cursed man. And then you bring him on back here on the Mule, and Responsible can see to what comes next after you get here. Just fetch him on back, and leave the child alone!"

The Granny knew the minute her final sentence left her lips that she'd made an error. Responsible, as could have been predicted, drew herself up straight in the rocker, glowered at the Granny, and said, "That's all right, Granny Hazelbide. I'll go, since Veritas Truebreed is afraid to face the Wommacks without me."

"I am *not* afraid to face the Wommacks!"

"I'll go all the same," declared Responsible, and rose awkwardly.

Granny Hazelbide leaned forward and said something about being hanged for a sheep. "I don't think you ought to go, Responsible," she fretted. "I'm dead set against it. I feel a pain, child, right between my shoulder blades. . . . I believe I'm going to need you here to help me get up to my bed. It would be plain wicked for you to go off and leave me—oh, law, there it is again! And just as *sharp*, child! It's like a red-hot needle piercing my breast!"

"That's your conscience hurting you, Granny," Responsible said, "and if *it's* going to kill you there's no hope for you; you might just as well die of it down here and save us all the labor of carting you down to lie in state there in the corner. I wouldn't *presume* to set myself against your conscience!"

With that, she marched right out of the room and on to

the stables where the Mules were kept. Veritas Truebreed, two paces behind her, was curious.

"It's not like the Granny to try to spare you work, Responsible," he noted. "Why do you suppose. . . ." And then he stopped short and slapped his thigh like any common stableman. "Surely she doesn't think that Lewis Motley Wommack the 33rd would have another try at teaching you manners! It's been nine years since that episode, and never a word out of him all this time!"

"That's not what worries the Granny," said Responsible, climbing up behind him on the Mule. Responsible could lie as well as anybody, when she had good reason. "The Granny's worried I'll brain Lewis Motley with a rock and give you a matched set of idiots to practice your Formalisms and Transformations on. And she's a fool to have such notions."

"Oh, surely," said the Magician of Rank. "You're such a *nice* young woman, Responsible! So sweet. So kind. So charming. So—"

"Day I want to sit behind manure and fly through the air, Veritas, I'll let you know," said Responsible. "In the meantime, will you be so kind as to SNAP us out of here?"

The Magician of Rank grinned, delighted to have made her cross, not that that was difficult, and SNAPPED for Kintucky.

CHAPTER SIXTEEN

Responsible sat quietly in Castle Wommack's front room, in one of the straight and spartan chairs that the Wommacks preferred. No upholstery here, no curtains or rugs or ornaments; no rockers, except those reserved for the Grannys. On the other hand, there was none of the stark grim atmosphere that marked Castle Traveler, giving expression to an unhealthy religious zeal and an obsession with denying the flesh. There were times Responsible marveled that the Travelers allowed themselves to eat or drink; Wommack Kingdom was not like that. Here, there was no softness; but the result was neither stark nor grim; it was a kind of handsome simplicity, a use of honest wood and stone and metal and glass, of sufficient quality and beauty that it *required* no ornament.

It was beautiful, to Responsible's way of thinking, though vastly unlike Castle Brightwater, with its vases of massed flowers and its lavish use of quilting and embroidery and skilled weaving and all the color and texture and pattern of fine needlecraft lovingly assembled. Castle Wommack was beautiful in a different, but equally satisfying way; it rested her eyes and her spirit to look at it, to let it surround her.

She was waiting while the Magician of Rank did his work, mending the pitiful offworlder's grievous wounds. Veritas didn't need her for audience while he worked, and wouldn't have appreciated her presence; he would send for her when the man was alert and well enough to talk. All that he had done by way of preliminary discussion was ask Responsible how she thought Jones had managed to get out of Smith Kingdom and over that wall.

"He is what passes for a Magician, where he comes from," she had said. "I expect he used what passes there for magic."

"That's all you have to say?"

"Law, Veritas Truebreed, I wasn't there," Responsible objected. "How would *I* know what the man did or how he did it? Obviously, he wasn't aiming to do what he *did* do! It was you Magicians of Rank that put that wall up and tangled it to keep him—and all of Smith Kingdom—in. Seems to me you'd know how a body could get past your own tangle!"

The Magician of Rank could have remarked that the wall had after all been her idea in the first place, but he didn't care for the sound of that—he and the other Magicians of Rank would have thought of the same measure on their own, if she hadn't stuck her nose into their business. Instead, he tightened his lips to a narrow line and spoke to her severely.

"What I want to know, Responsible, is how in the name of all the diverse Dozens the man could have possibly acquired the injuries described to me. So far as I know, you can only get the top of your head smashed in by falling from a high place, or being flung out of some vehicle at a high speed, or being bashed over the head by somebody else armed with a blunt instrument. There was nothing tall enough where he was found for him to have fallen that far, or that hard; there wasn't space for a vehicle to move at anything more than a snail's pace. *How* did he get his fool head smashed in?"

"Perhaps it was somebody armed with a blunt instrument," she said.

"On Ozark?" The Magician of Rank was shocked. "Ozarkers don't bash people's heads in. Don't be absurd."

"It happened to him once before," Responsible noted, "after he tore up an innocent vegetable garden—an Ozarker bashed him right over the head. With a rock. Might could be that allowing him here at all has contaminated our society—perhaps physical violence is the result of that contamination. Maybe, Veritas Truebreed, it was Teacher Letha herself that hit him, armed with a great staff of ironwood . . . what do you think?"

"I think you are insufferable," said Veritas. And he had whirled on his heel and shown her his elegant back, while she smiled after him.

She had been deliberately teasing him, of course, but it had not all been a joke. Like the Magicians of Rank, she worried that contact with what Earth and its peoples had become was dangerous. When she'd called that comset vote on the question of joining the Tri-Galactic Federation, she'd been terrified that she'd be wrong and the Families would leap to accept the offer. When Smith Kingdom had sent notice of its secession to become a TGF memberworld, she had not been surprised; she had been grateful that it was the only Kingdom that had been tempted. And supposing she could now send Coyote Jones home with the final refusal and the ban on future contact—suppose that when Jones told her his government would actually abide by the agreement and leave Ozark alone, he spoke the truth—that didn't make her fully comfortable about the situation. Because now the people of Ozark knew the Federation existed, with all its bounty and power. Now they knew what they *might* have, if they only chose to ask. Down the road a ways, in a period when hard times plagued some one or more of the Kingdoms, Responsible could well imagine the younger Ozarkers bitter and resentful because the Federation's offer had been refused. They would talk of selfishness on the part of their elders, and hidebound rigid conversatism, and being set in your ways; and they might well clamor for a re-opening of the question, now that they knew it was always an option available to them. She didn't think she could set that right with a wall, not if it went clear round the planet.

It *was* a contamination. A poison. It was a horrible rebeginning of the vileness the Ozarkers had fled Earth to escape, and it turned her cold inside and out. That it had been her own carelessness of mind that had set it in motion made it even worse; if that stray thought of hers had not gone wandering into the Federation's communications networks, Ozark might still have been nothing more to it than one of countless unexplored strange areas in space. Ozark might have gotten away with a second thousand years of peace had she guarded her mind more scrupulously.

When Responsible had gone in numb misery to Granny Hazelbide to report what the woman who called herself "a Communipath" had told her, the Granny had not been comforting. "Responsible," she had said, "you brought misery on this world once before, this way! Just the same way, not watching what you thought and who you thought it at. Tormenting Lewis Motley Wommack with your shameless mindspeaking! Not enough that your carrying on brought us civil war and very nearly saw us fall to the Garnet Ring—that wasn't enough for you, eh, Missy? Not enough to cure you? Now you've got to go flaunting your mindgabble at the universe at *large*, jumping up and down and hollering 'Hello! Hello! Here we are! Come and get us!' You don't *learn*, Missy, *do* you?"

I guess I don't, thought Responsible, remembering the way the Granny's eyes had flashed sparks at her, and the cut of her tongue; shivering, she curled up as best she could in the chair and closed her eyes. And I don't know what to do now, either, she thought. I am supposed to know, but I don't. And she wished, as she so often wished, for her sister Troublesome. Who would have been tender with her and told her it was not, truly not, her fault.

"Responsible?"

She opened her eyes, startled, and nodded to the Magician of Rank.

"Hello there, Veritas. You finished with Mister Jones?"

"He'll need to rest a bit," said Veritas Truebreed. "But he's fit to travel, and he's fit to talk."

Responsible nodded again, and stood up, stretching. "I'll go speak to him now," she said.

The room was much larger than the sickroom where she'd put Coyote at Brightwater, but then everything here was enormous by Brightwater standards. Wommack Castle had four hundred rooms, as she recalled; it was an enormous place, built entirely from the abundant native stone of Kintucky. Except for its size, though, the room was much the same as Brightwater's sickroom. A bit barer, perhaps. Not so many pillows on the bed. And the man had noticed that; he greeted her with, "Hello there! I much preferred the pillows you had back on Brightwater, the last time you Ozarkers beat me up. These aren't nearly as comfortable."

"We didn't beat you up, Mister Jones," Responsible retorted. "You beat up your *own* self. Nobody pitched you headfirst into that boulder but you yourself, and do not tell me that you don't know it, for I won't believe you."

He stared at her, and made a face, and shrugged his shoulders.

"I suppose you're right," he said. "But a case could be made for my version."

"How so?" Responsible sat down on the chair beside him.

"Well," he said, "the Granny that gave me the clue about getting out of Smith Kingdom never mentioned the hazards of the method."

"I expect she thought you were all grown up," Responsible observed. "And in full possession of your faculties."

"I expect she did. Still, she could have told me. Just in case she was mistaken in her estimation."

"How in the blooming world was the Granny to know you were going to throw yourself into a big old rock, leading with your head? Who'd have thought such a thing as that, from a man of the powerful Tri-Galactic Federation, an agent of its mighty government, and him with a reputation for most elaborate magical effects provided the audience is two tadlings?"

"Ah, hell, Responsible of Brightwater," Coyote complained, "I don't feel well enough to play pattycake with you. I meant to land on a different rock, and I meant to land feet first—I just bungled it. Just don't bully me!"

"Tsk," went Responsible.

"You see before you a man who is probably the most total of all failures within the last century of recorded history!" Coyote insisted. "You see before you a man who will go home to contempt and degradation and—if he is very lucky—to permanent retirement. You see a man battered and beaten and at the end of his physical and emotional rope! Don't you view that man with any compassion at *all*?"

"I have been looking at sorry men all my life long," she

told him comfortably, "and listening to them moan. I may have gotten just a tad calloused."

"I am *different*," he insisted. "I'm not one of your Ozark men. This is not my home. Your ways are not my ways, the Light be praised for *that*. I'm a poor wayfaring stranger around here. Ripped out of my world and dumped, with fancy effects, into yours. Think how I've suffered!"

"You could've stayed home," she pointed out. "Safe in the bosom of your own kind."

"Miss Responsible," he said solemnly, "I have been traveling these three galaxies all of my adult life, and I have called at many worlds—and *never* have I met with the abuse that I met with on Ozark! Not once. Not even on worlds whose misery—before they had the good sense to join the Tri-Galactic Federation—would tear your heart. I had no reason to suspect I wouldn't be met with courtesy, at least."

Responsible chuckled. "Mister Jones," she said reprovingly, "the truth is not *in* you."

"Haven't you anything to say except abuse?" Coyote demanded. "Not even one kind word?"

"Don't provoke me, Mister Jones."

"Provoke her, she says! You've *won*, Responsible of effing Brightwater! You, and your people, you've *won*! You came out on top, every single time! You're supposed to show the generosity of the conqueror for the vanquished!"

"You look for such truck as that," said Responsible, "you'll be here a while."

Coyote stared at her, and she stared right back, and then he said, "You are an absolutely *revolting* woman, you know that?"

"I expect I do. I've been told often enough."

"Doesn't it bother you? How do you *stand* it?"

Responsible tugged at her braid, crossly, and said, "I wasn't put here on this world to be popular, Mister Jones."

"That's a good thing, isn't it?"

"I expect so. And if we've settled all your questions about my personal unsatisfactoriness, do you suppose we could get down to business? If you're feeling strong enough, that is."

Coyote cleared his throat. "I felt stronger *before* you came in here and treated me with a total lack of consideration for my condition or the common decencies," he said.

"Do you think you can handle a little business all the same? Or shall I call the Magician of Rank to see what he can do for you?"

"I can handle it," Coyote told her. "I'll get by on the rage alone."

"Rage is powerful stuff, properly applied," Responsible advised him. "Mind you don't smash the *in*side of your head."

"Could your M of R fix it if I did?"

"I can't say," she said. "Ozarkers don't go in for that kind of thing—not much call for head-doctoring around here."

"Okay," said Coyote. "Okay. I guess you've earned the right to brag, after my recent performance. But it's not attractive."

"Mister *Jones*! I am here to talk business." It was as flat as her chest, and no more appealing.

"Talk it, then."

"I want to know what you plan to do now. And what we can expect from your cursed Federation. What's the next surprise you've got tucked away in your dittybag for us?"

He blinked, and settled back on the pillows, and she saw him decide to be serious for a change.

"Are you worried about that?" he asked her. "That's very hard for me to believe, under the circumstances."

"Well," said Responsible, "we may have whipped you personally to a faretheewell, Mister Jones. But you are just one poor sorry man. No doubt there's a lot more where you came from, not all of them quite so sorry. I don't deceive myself that managing to discombobulate one lone male means things between us and your government are settled. And I would appreciate knowing what I can look forward to, down the road."

"Responsible," Coyote announced, "What you can look forward to is the absolute certainty that we won't bother you again."

"Why? Or why not, as the case may be?"

Coyote shrugged. "There are a multitude of other planets in the Three Galaxies for us to occupy ourselves with," he said. "Ozark is a teeny curl on a tiny whisker on a minute flea on a very small frog indeed, for us."

Responsible was silent, but she was biting her lip, and Coyote knew she did it to keep from grinning at him, or worse; and he thought with longing of the arms of Tzana Kai. And the *words* of Tzana Kai.

"Lady," he said with feeling, "I want to go home. Do you suppose I could go home?"

"I suppose you could," she said reasonably. "But I also suppose you ought to settle the matter you were sent here to settle, first."

"I've settled it! I've explained it to you! The Federation will not bother you anymore. Nobody's going to come calling. We'll put it in the rules and regulations—*stay away from Planet Ozark, they don't take to strangers.* I *swear* it!"

"There's the other matter," she said.

"*What* other matter? There's no other matter."

"Mister Jones, you are a wonder."

"Well? What other matter?"

"The matter of my wayward mind," she said sadly. "You go home without seeing to that, you'll be back, and we'll all suffer for it. Let's settle it, while you're here. And let me tell you, from the bottom of my heart, Mister Jones, how grateful I am that you've not told on me. If I believe you about the rest of it, it's because you've held your tongue about what brought you here. I thank you, Mister Jones, for you could have made great trouble for me and for Ozark if you'd had a mind to."

Coyote inclined his head graciously.

"You're very welcome," he said. "Glad to be of service."

"Now. To that matter."

"All right," he agreed. "To it."

"I didn't mean to do it," she said. "I don't even know how it happened. If it was happening all the time—I mean, if every time I used mindspeech it went roaring out through space like that—I expect you'd've been here long long go."

Coyote nodded. "It's been thoroughly discussed," he told her. "By experts. And we are convinced now that it was just a freak. An accident. Some freakish combination of the weather. . . . I don't know, but I think it was a lot like a stray radio wave. I doubt it ever happens again."

"You truly do believe that?"

"I truly do. And so does my agency, which is what matters."

"Well!" said Responsible. "Now that's a refreshing change!"

"You have this kind of trouble often?"

"No. But when I have *any* kind of trouble, the tendency on Ozark is to take it for granted that whatever I've done I've done on purpose. Without always bothering even to ask me first. Even when, like this time, I don't even know I've done it."

"I see."

"Mister Jones, I give you my solemn word," she said, leaning toward him. "I will not ever—and would not ever— send a thought of mine, or a deed of mine, or a *breath* of mine, beyond the limits of this one world. If it should by mischance happen another time, Coyote Jones, let it be recorded by your government that it is yet another accident, and no threat to you."

"It's not so much that it might be a threat," Coyote said, seeing his chance and grabbing it. "At first it was; but once we'd talked to you, we knew it wasn't a threat. We knew the chances of a repetition were infinitesimal. Threat wasn't the problem. It was the terrible *loss*."

"I don't understand," Responsible said. "You care to explain?"

"The Tri-Galactic Federation," Coyote said gravely, "is a vast empire—you must not make the mistake of judging it by *my* incompetence. It is truly and awesomely a great Federation. It was claimed, once, that no such thing could ever exist, no matter how sophisticated the space travel—we have proved that to be wrong. But that doesn't mean we have solved all our problems. We have a great deal of magnificent technology to help us manage, but there are many tasks that we can't *do* with technology."

"Such as?"

"Such as communication across space. Without the Communipaths, we couldn't do that. The reason we call the Communipath Network 'the Bucket' is that it works the way a bucket brigade used to deal with fires on Old Earth . . . the Communipaths pass the messages along from one to another, like people used to pass buckets of water along a line. They have a great range, Miss Responsible, and they can do that very fast. They're essential to our survival. They make the Federation possible. And there are many things like that, many things that depend upon psibilities."

"Your magic," she said immediately.

"Not magic! Psibilities! Part of psience, with a *p*! Not magic *at all*. And it just happens, friend, that the power of the psibilities demonstrated by your Ozarkers—whoever it is, whether it's all of you or just your Magicians of Rank or whatever—is enormously greater than anything we have in the Federation! Do you understand how that looks to us, what it *means*? None of our telepaths, or all of them together, could set up an illusion of empty space as big as a planet and maintain it over time." He snorted. "None of our telepaths could set up an illusion as big as an *egg* and maintain it over time! And that does appear to be what's done here, Responsible. I didn't believe it at first, but I do now."

"Aw shucks," she said, looking him right in the eye. "It's no big thing. It's a little old Spell of Invisibility."

Coyote refused to be drawn into that game. He went right ahead with his explanation. "We would have been so very glad to have access to the information you people have, and to your talent, for the benefit of all our member worlds. For all of us, and for Ozark as well, it would have meant a kind of leap forward that I don't even know how to describe. But wonderful, you see. And now that won't happen. Can't happen. Now you will be shut off from us, and we can't learn from you. That is a tragic loss, Responsible, and I won't pretend it isn't."

He waited, watching her, but she said nothing. And finally he asked her a careful question.

"Is it possible," he asked, "that you people of Ozark would consider *sharing* some of what you know about the power of the mind? For the sake of many billions who need that information, and whose lives would be bettered by it? If we didn't bother you, Responsible, if we left you strictly alone as promised, but I just took some information home with me and passed it along to the people who train our telepaths?"

When she still didn't answer him, he groaned, and thumped his pillows with one frustrated fist.

"Don't you even *care,* Responsible of Brightwater," he pleaded, "if there are billions of innocent people who could be helped to a better life if it weren't for the selfishness of Ozark? Doesn't that move you at all?"

"No," said Responsible promptly, without any hesitation, and he jerked as if she'd struck him. And before he could elaborate on it, she said, "If you'd like to hear some details about how little we care, you might stop on your way home and see my sister Troublesome. Assuming your magic's good enough to get you up her mountain, Mister Jones. She'd be most happy to oblige."

He looked at her as if she were worse than repulsive, but she didn't mind. She was thoroughly accustomed to being found loathsome, and to having all her perceptions and all her behavior despised. Here in this Castle, so close to the man who had no doubt despised and loathed her more than anyone else, she was more than ordinarily aware of her unsavoriness. And she hoped, should she find herself face to face with Lewis Motley Wommack the 33rd after all these years, she'd be able to offer him loathing for loathing, in equal measure. Surely he would not dare to presume on having taken her maidenhead, on having shared her bed those few times; he had no way of knowing he was the only man ever to have shared her bed. But if he *did* presume, she would be ready for him. She hoped. If she could just manage never to look into his eyes.

The chilly voice of the off-worlder brought her out of it.

"Then if you've no objections," he was saying, "I'll get up now and go on home and report all this. I'm sure somebody here at Wommack will get me back to my flyer."

"Their Magician of Rank will," she answered. "The one that wouldn't do you the favor of healing you. Just tell him you'd like to SNAP back to Brightwater Castle; you know the way from there."

"Fine," he said, stiff as a wire. "*Good-bye.*"

"Good-bye, Mister Jones. Have a good journey home."

"And don't come back."

"And don't come back," she agreed.

"You needn't concern yourself. I've seen all of you people I care to see. And the peoples of the Federation would agree with me. You Ozarkers don't *deserve* the company of others."

Responsible didn't answer him, that being a total waste of her time. She just left, closing the door quietly behind her.

CHAPTER SEVENTEEN

Jason Trueharper Purdy the 6th knocked at the Magician's door in the town of Fraction, in Purdy Kingdom. When the Magician opened the door himself and looked out inquiringly, Jason Trueharper wasted no time on preambles.

"You'd best come," he said. "My Deborah's killed herself."

The Magician was a Purdy, too; Jason was his kin, and Deborah as well. He might have been more gentle with someone outfamily, but as it was he was brutal. He said, "That's a filthy damn thing to say, Jason! Have you gone crazy?"

The other man just stared at him, unmoving except for his hands, which were clasping and unclasping, and he said again, "Thomas Guthrie Purdy, you'd best come."

"What do you *mean*, saying Debbie's killed herself?"

"Thomas," said the father, in a voice that made the Magician's flesh creep, "will you please just come?"

They found the girl already laid out in a white dress she'd worn for Sunday best in the hot summers, with her

hair plaited in two long braids and her hands folded over
her breasts. Her mother and grandmother had seen to
her, and had laid a garland of white roses and sweetfern at
her feet.

"Morning, Thomas Guthrie," said the tearful women,
and he nodded at them, the barest minimum of manners.

"What is all this?" he asked sternly. "What's happened
to Debbie?"

"I told you on the way over here," said the father. "I
told you. She hanged herself from a rafter in our barn.
And I cut her down myself and brought her in the house
to be made ready and decent; and I came for you. I *told*
you."

Thomas Guthrie Purdy the 7th stepped forward and
leaned over the dead girl, studying her; he bit his lip
hard, frowning, and laid his skillful fingers on her throat
under the wide collar of the dress.

"What are you doing there?" Jason Trueharper's voice
shook. "Let her alone now, she's been hurt enough!"

"She can't be hurt any more, Jason," said the Magician
steadily. "You just let me do my work."

"There's nothing to do," said Viola of Smith, Deborah's
mother. "It's all been done, and done right and proper,
and—" Her words caught in her throat, and she turned
her back on them suddenly; Jason went swiftly to steady
her. But the Magician's hands were still busy. He seemed
fascinated with the body, turning it from side to side to
look at it more closely, even unbuttoning the top two
buttons of the dress to look underneath the cotton piqué
bodice, ignoring the grandmother's sharp shocked protest.
And when they would have stopped him he gave them a
look so fierce that they moved sullenly back again and
stood three in a row watching him, the women weeping
silently and the father still wringing his big hands.

Finally, the time came when Thomas Guthrie had finished with the examination of the corpse. His face was as white as theirs, and his mouth pinched. "Where's your comset?" he asked them, avoiding their eyes.

"There, in the front room," said Viola of Smith. "What do you want the comset for, at a time like this?"

The Magician paid no attention to her. He went straight to the small set, punched the studs that he needed, and spoke to the Attendant who answered at Castle Purdy. "Young man," he said, "I want you to take a message to your Magician of Rank—is he at home?"

"Yes, sir," was the answer, "but he's just getting ready to leave."

"Well, you look sharp and stop him! You tell him that Thomas Guthrie Purdy the 7th, Magician of Fraction, called him, and that there's an emergency here. You tell him to come to the house of Jason Trueharper Purdy the 6th, three miles out of Fraction on the old bridge road. You tell him he'll know it by the row of blue snowball bushes that border the front yard, and my Mule standing at the door. And you tell him this is the worst I've ever seen. He's to *hurry*."

"I don't know if he'll come," said the Attendant dubiously. "He has a terrible long list of people as are waiting for him, and he said he'd be gone the whole morning long."

"Young man," said the Magician of Fraction, "you go tell him what I said, word for word. You tell him there's nothing he's got to do this day that is as important as what I need him for. You make him to understand . . . or you go bring him to the comset and I'll explain it myself, if you don't think you can manage. This is an emergency!"

"Yes, sir," said the Attendant. "I'll go right now. I'll see that he understands, sir, and I'll send him."

"I'll be waiting right here," the Magician told him. "If he seems doubtful, you bring him right back and have him call me."

"Yes, sir!"

The image on the screen faded, and Thomas Guthrie turned to face the family. "All right," he said tensely, "that's done. Now we must just wait till he gets here."

"Thomas Guthrie," pleaded Viola of Smith. "I know that suicide is a terrible thing . . . it holds us all back. I know. I know it's the most selfish of all things that are in this world. I do know that—I know it's a sick act, of a sick mind. But Deborah, she'll pay in full. And her father and I, and all our family—we'll be disgraced, and there's our grief to mix with that. We'll pay. Her brother'll be hard put to it to find a wife now, for they'll be talking of a tainted line, all over this county. With all that, in the Creator's blessed name, Thomas Guthrie Purdy, must you also shame us in front of the Magician of Rank?"

Thomas shook his head, strangely, as if there were something in his ear worrying him, too deep to reach; and he wouldn't look at her. "Please, Viola," he said softly. "It will be all right."

"It *won't* be all right! How can you say so careless and cruel a thing? Nothing will ever be all right again! *Suicide*, Thomas Guthrie, think! Suicide. . . . oh, I wish I'd never ever been born, never seen this dreadful world . . . I can't bear it!"

"Wait," said the Magician. "Please. It won't take Titus Brandywine five minutes to get his things and SNAP here. Just wait."

"But I don't under*stand*, Thomas Guthrie!" wailed the mother, and her own mother stepped in then.

"Hush, Viola," she said. "That carryon'll only make things worse. Thomas Guthrie's got a good reason for what he's doing or he wouldn't be doing it."

There was a knock at the door, making them all jump, and Jason Trueharper called "Come in!" to the Magician of Rank from Castle Purdy.

"Send the women away," said the Magician harshly. "Viola of Smith . . . Maryann of McDaniels . . . You go on, now. We have business here, now he's come, that you're better off not hearing."

The mother would have objected, but the grandmother was a strong and forceful woman; she took Viola by the shoulders and half-carried her from the room, closing the door behind her and leaving the three men alone with the dead girl.

"Well," said Titus Brandywine McDaniels the 53rd, in the sudden silence. "You say there's an emergency here— where is it?"

"It's my Deborah," blurted Jason Trueharper. "She's killed herself. Hanged herself. Cut her down myself, from a rafter in the barn, not an hour ago."

"She's *dead*?"

"Long dead," said Jason. "And laid out."

The Magician of Rank looked puzzled, and turned to speak to his junior colleague.

"Thomas Guthrie," he asked, "why did you send for me? If the girl's dead, there's nothing I can do here. Granted it's an awful thing, but I can't change it." And when the younger man said nothing, he spoke again, impatiently. "Will you speak up, man? Or shall I go on back to the work I had before me this morning?"

"Titus Brandywine," said the Magician, slowly, "this is more than an awful thing. It's worse than you think."

"How can it be worse?" demanded Titus. "What can be worse than suicide?"

The Magician cleared his throat, and his words, when they finally came, were strained and laboring. "Titus Brandywine," he said, "something's wrong here."

"Well, of *course*—"

"No. Wait. It's more than that. Jason Trueharper Purdy here, he claims his daughter hanged herself. Claims he

cut her down from the rafter in his barn. Well, I'm happy
to say that I've never seen anyone as was hanged, by their
own hand or another's. But I do know the human body,
and I do know death and its works. And Titus Brandywine, that girl never hanged herself! There's not a *sign* of
her hanging herself!"

The father broke in, protesting fiercely. "That's not so!
Why, you can see the mark of the rope on her poor neck!"

The Magician gave him a sorrowing look, and said,
"Jason, you're ignorant. That's not the kind of mark you'd
find if you hanged a living person."

"What are you saying?" cautioned the Magician of Rank.
"You take care now, what you say."

"What I am saying," said the Magician doggedly, "is
that Deborah was already gone from this world when that
rope went around her neck. What really did happen, I
can't say—but she did *not* hang herself. Somebody hanged
her—after she was dead." And he shuddered, and stared
at the floor.

Jason Trueharper Purdy made not a sound; he was like
stone, only a muscle twitching up near one eye to show
that he'd heard. He stood there without moving, waiting
with the Magician, while Titus Brandywine went quickly
to look at Deborah of Purdy for himself.

When he came back, the Magician of Rank was pale and
solemn.

"Jason Trueharper Purdy," he said. "I will ask you now
for the truth."

"You have it!" The words were short, bitten off as they
were spoken.

"I do not, and well you know it. You'd best tell us,
man."

"She hanged herself. From a rafter. In my barn. I cut
her down." Chopping the words. A little gasp of breath
between each few of them.

"Jason Trueharper Purdy the 6th," rapped out the Magician of Rank, "you *lie!*"

"I do no such thing!"

"You do! You *lie*. And what manner of death could that child have chosen for herself that would make you hang her from a rafter because you thought that would cover it *up*? I have pondered long and hard, standing there beside her, and I cannot think of any reason why you would do any such mad thing. Unless. . . ." He scowled suddenly, a thought taking him. "See here, Jason Trueharper, is it that there's more to this? Is there a young man dead somewhere, and the two of them dying together? Did you find Deborah of Purdy in the arms of a lover, maybe a lover with a wife already his own, and the two of them dead?"

"No!" shouted the father, raising his clenched fists. "*No!* I swear it! Oh, no, you are not going to tarnish her name for the sins of lust, now she's dead! I'll not stand by and let you do that! I'll—"

"Easy!"

"I can't be easy, when you say such a foul thing!"

The Magician and the Magician of Rank looked at each other, and then at the panting man with his wild face and his eyes berserk. And the Magician spoke first.

"Jason," he said. "It had to be asked. If there was another dead, surely you understand that we had to know that. But I think you're telling the truth, and so does Titus Brandywine; the only question is, then, what kind of death did Deborah die that you felt you were obliged to lie about it and hang her dead body? What could she possibly have done to herself that would call for such measures?"

For the first time, Jason Trueharper showed signs that his resolve was shaken. He shuddered where he stood, as the Magician had shuddered, but it didn't stop. The Magician of Rank nodded, and said, "Thomas Guthrie, that's shock. You'd better look after him."

"I will. And then what are we going to do?"

"I wish I knew. Take him—somewhere. Take him to the Castle, I suppose, and let him rest. Take Deborah, too, poor child. I'll help you with them. And then we'll have to talk to him some more."

"Sweet Almighty, but this is a nasty business!" said the Magician of Fraction.

"That it is. And we have it to deal with."

There was some question, later that day, when a meticulous examination of the body had made it absolutely clear that Deborah of Purdy had died not of hanging but of a swift poison, as to whether it was necessary to go any farther. After all, the girl was dead. The deed was done. If her father had gone a little crazy with his grief, and if his madness had manifested itself in a bungled attempt at calling the poisoning a hanging, what of it?

"Perhaps," proposed the Master of Castle Purdy, "that wasn't all he did. He might could of put her into the creek awhile, and then a pillow over her head, and then the hanging . . . The man was deranged there for a little while, not himself. It makes no sense, but when did madness ever make sense?"

The Magician of Rank tapped the table edge impatiently.

"There speaks the public," he said crossly.

"Why do you say that?"

"People think that madness makes no sense," said Titus Brandywine. "They are wrong. Madness, most of the time, is absolutely logical, according to the very strange ideas that the one who is mad bases his actions upon. There is often a rigorous logic to the doings of a madman that makes science look sloppy. And that's what we need to find here." Ozark had little madness, and what it had was mild stuff, but Titus Brandywine fancied himself something of an expert on it nonetheless. It was a kind of hobby of his.

"I don't understand what you're getting at."

"We need to find out what sort of fool idea Jason Trueharper Purdy got into his head that made him think suicide by poison was so horrible and shameful that he had to try to make it look like some other kind of death. Poor ignorant man . . . he didn't know much about it, did he?"

"Thank the Creator he didn't," said the Magician steadily. "I can't say as I'd relish being able to brag that the people in my district were experts in the manners and mechanisms of violent death, Titus Brandywine! I'm *glad* he was ignorant. But I am sorry that he was deranged by his grief and made this dreadful matter worse."

"*What* could he have been thinking?" It was the Master of the Castle, looking sorely bewildered. "I'm ignorant, too—I'd of thought that if you were mad there'd be no sense atall to the things you did. I stand corrected. But what could it be about the poison? I don't see any more dishonor to poison than to hanging, myself. No. I don't see it."

"No more do any of us," observed the Magician of Rank. "And that is the problem. We need to see it, so that we can understand."

They sat there thinking, three troubled men, in the light from the window, until finally the Magician of Rank began to speak, in a voice heavy and reluctant.

"There is a less distorted way of looking at this," he told them.

"What is it?"

"Perhaps it wasn't the *manner* of the death that he was trying to conceal. Perhaps it was the cause. The *agent* of the death."

"Titus Brandywine—"

"What if she didn't kill herself at all? What if someone else killed her?"

"An accident, you mean."

"No! If Viola of Purdy had given the girl poison in place of a potion for some sickness, if there'd been a tragic accident, the family would have been torn up by that—but they wouldn't have claimed it was *suicide*. An accident is a terrible thing, but it's not wicked, it's not dishonor. That would *truly* make no sense. No. I mean, what if Deborah of Purdy was murdered? Then it would make sense—maybe. Except . . . if someone murdered her with poison, why not leave it at that? Why try to change it to hanging? Why not *say* she poisoned herself?"

The Magician made a soft, sick noise, and the other two men looked at him.

"What is it, Thomas Guthrie?" asked Titus. "If you have an idea, speak up—we *need* ideas."

"That tiny spot on Deborah's arm. High up, near her armpit. Remember . . . we were saying she must have been jolted against a nail or a splinter of wood, when she was being lifted to the rafter."

The Magician of Rank said a broad word, and the Master of Castle Purdy frowned and objected that he'd like to be let in on this.

"It was such a tiny mark, we didn't think," the Magician of Rank explained. "But now it's brought to mind . . . I don't think it was like the mark of a nail. I'll have to go look more carefully, much as I hate to disturb the body again. But I very much fear Thomas Guthrie has hit on it—gentlemen, now I've had a moment to consider it, I do believe that's the mark of an old-fashioned hypodermic needle. Jason Trueharper knows all about such needles, from giving medicines to his livestock; he'd have had no trouble putting the poison into her arm. It would make sense. Because if she'd drunk the stuff she'd have suffered so—if she got it by injection, it would have been very very quick. Easier for her. And he is tender of heart, that man."

"And Viola of Purdy! She's used to giving him a hand with the stock! It could have been *her*, Titus Brandywine!"

"Or the brother. Any one of them would have known how to do it. Even the grandmother, so far as that goes."

"And that would make it all logical enough," summed up the Magician of Rank. "If one of the family *killed* her—it would be entirely logical for Jason Trueharper, poor fool, to try to make it out to be a suicide."

"Gentlemen," hazarded Thomas Guthrie, "we are sitting here talking of *murder*. Murder, on Ozark!"

And so they were. If you did not count the deaths in the civil war as murder, and no one did, it having been as just a war as any war, this would be the first murder on Ozark in seven hundred years. If murder it truly was.

"*We don't murder*," protested Donovan Elihu Purdy the 40th. "It doesn't happen on this world."

"Think, friend! Think how Jason Trueharper has behaved."

"There could be some other explanation!"

"Tell us what it is, then."

"You're mighty quick to believe the worst. And of your own kin!"

"Donovan Elihu!" said the Magician of Rank. "I said, *think*! What, in all this world, is *worse* than suicide?"

The Master of Castle Purdy put his head in his hands and groaned. "Murder," he said dully, muffled by his position. "Murder is worse than suicide. You're right. Only murder would cause a man to try to let on as there'd been a suicide, when there hadn't. But how do you know . . ." He looked up at them, his hair rumpled and his eyes frantic, as eager now to make it suicide as Jason Trueharper had been. "How can you know the girl didn't inject *herself* with the poison? She'd have known how, a grown girl like her, she'd have helped many a time with the medicines! It could have been her! And then when her father found her, he lost his mind for a while, just like we've been saying! You can't know it wasn't like that!"

"No." The Magician of Rank shook his head. "That needle mark is high on her left arm, Donovan Elihu, clear around at the back, almost into the armpit—a spot where somebody might reasonably hope that it might not be noticed, especially if they weren't questioning the manner of the death. You try; you couldn't give yourself an injection in that spot. It can't be done."

"Then it *is* murder?"

"I think probably it is." The Magician paused for a moment, and the others saw him swallow hard. "You know, whoever did it was such a plain fool that they didn't even realize it mattered that Deborah was left-handed."

"She was? Are you sure?"

"I asked her father, and he told me himself. Like a babe, all trust and no motherwit whatsoever."

"Oh, the Almighty have mercy on us," breathed Thomas Guthrie.

"Which one of them?" Donovan Elihu's voice was hoarse. This was a terrible thing. More trouble for the Purdys, that were always in the very middle of trouble. The first murder in seven hundred years, and it had to be a Purdy. And not even done *right*! He could hear it now. "Which *one*?"

"We'll have to find out."

"What if we're wrong?"

"Then we'll find that out, too, and we'll rejoice in our error. But I'm afraid we aren't wrong. I wish I *could* think we were wrong."

"Well, how are we going to *do* this?"

That was a very good question. Ozark had no homicide labs, no police departments with staffs of experts at fingerprints and hair clipping analysis and all the apparatus of forensic investigations, not even at twentieth-century levels of expertise. They knew of such things from the records brought from Old Earth, carefully copied as each microfiche or tape or film or program grew old, to preserve the history. But there'd been no need to set them up on Ozark. Crime they had, as does any peopled world. They had thieves, and they had minor assaults, and they had those who would try to cheat others, and they had liars. They had gamblers; they had, to their great disgust, the occasional harlot. But they had no murderers.

"Well," said the Magician, taking a long breath, "I think it's easy enough. We'll just have to use magic."

"Is that ethical?" asked Donovan Elihu Purdy, surprised.

"Ethical? We're talking of *murder*! Of course it's ethical."

"Can you do it?"

The Magician of Rank smiled. "He can't, unfortunately; but *I* can. I'll have to call in some help—but I can do it."

"Then go do it. Go do it, and be done with it. Let's know who has fouled Purdy Kingdom in this especially nasty way!"

The Magician of Rank nodded, and pushed his chair back from the table, moving as does a man who has worked too long and too hard. "You two go wait in the front room if you want," he told them. "Or here, if you'd rather . . . it makes no difference. It will take awhile."

"How long?" asked the Magician.

"Two hours. Three. Maybe a little more."

The Magician of Rank left the room, and Donovan Elihu said, "We can't just sit here three hours, like this."

"I know," said the Magician.

But they went on. Just sitting there.

CHAPTER EIGHTEEN

That evening, they confronted Jason Trueharper Purdy
with what they knew, thinking they could move on to the
question of a proper punishment for the crime—not that
any of them had much of an idea what that punishment
should be. They went to the small bedroom where he was
waiting, kept there by a simple Binding Spell, and they
told him without fuss that they knew he had murdered his
child.

But he faced them down boldly, instead of collapsing as
they had been certain he would, and he looked straight at
them, and he said, bitter and thick, "You have all gone
raving stark crazy!"

"No! No, Jason, we haven't gone crazy at all—it is you
that has suffered some ailment of the mind."

"I am no murderer!"

"That is so," said Thomas Guthrie Purdy, "you are *not*.
But you *are* a man who has committed murder one time.
This one time."

"No! Never!" he shouted at them.

"Jason," they said, "give it up now. It's no use—we *know*."

He turned his back on them and stood facing the stone wall, his arms folded over his chest. And Thomas Guthrie tried again; the man was, after all, a cousin of his. "Jason," he said, "it's time now to give it up and let us get on with this matter."

"I did not kill Deborah."

The Magician from Fraction, and the Magicians of Rank who had come to help Titus Brandywine, and Titus Brandywine himself, looked at one another glumly, weary of it even before it really began. One of them said, "You, Titus Brandywine—he knows you. He's used to dealing with you. *You* speak to him."

"No good him speakin' to me either," said Jason sullenly, still with his back to them, "because nobody—*nobody*—is going to make me say that I killed my own daughter. Even if it was true, there'd be no way you could know it, and it happens it *isn't* true! And I think you're foul, all of you, foul carrion, to go accusing me of such a thing at such a time . . . as if it wasn't burden heavy enough to have lost my child and lost her to her own hand! Stop torturing me now, and let me go on home to my poor wife."

"Jason," said Titus Brandywine McDaniels, "turn around and look at me."

"Got no desire to look at you, Titus."

"Then I'll come around there and look at *you*, and you can turn your back and stare at the Magicians of Rank assembled or you can look at me, whichever you choose."

The accused man shrugged his broad shoulders, and turned to stare over their heads, his fists clenched at his sides and his jaw set hard.

"Won't do you no good," he declared. "You can't bully me."

"Jason Trueharper Purdy the 6th," said Titus Brandy-wine, formally, "be advised that we, Magicians of Rank of Planet Ozark, have—by means of a valid Transformation—duly determined that you did cruelly murder your daughter Deborah Alice of Purdy by injecting a poison into her left arm. We accuse you hereby, and we ask that you confess for the sake of your own soul."

Jason's mouth had twitched when they mentioned the poison, there had been the smallest flicker of surprise in his eyes, but he made no sign, only shook his head and went on staring past them.

"Your magic can be mistaken," he said. "I mind the time you thought it would do this world no harm for you to put Responsible of Brightwater into a state as near death as made no difference. And I mind that you came close to destroying us all by that piece of ignorant foolishness. And I mind many a time a Magician has said that something would come of a Tuesdy and it's been Wednesdy before it ever happened. Times a Magician has said to look for somethin' under a certain tree, and it's been a yard away and under a berry bramble. Times a Magician's been asked—"

"Jason," Titus Brandywine broke in, "stop it! You're speaking of Magicians, and often no more than apprentices, or the ones getting on into their doddering years! I tell you it was three *Magicians of Rank* that worked the magic to find Deborah's killer! How many examples can you give me of an error in magic from a Magician of Rank? And don't bring up that matter with Responsible of Brightwater again, for it's not the same thing at all."

"It was an error," spat Jason Trueharper. "An error! A serious and awful error, that near caused the death of us all! And it was you high and mighty muckamuck Magicians of Rank as made that error! Don't tell me to stop speaking what is the Almighty's *truth*!"

The Magicians of Rank, and the Magician of Fraction, looked at one another again in consternation, not sure how to proceed. They could have explained to their prisoner that the matter of Responsible of Brightwater had been something hidden from them and hidden from all their magic by a Timecorner, a kind of jog in spacetime around which it was not possible to see. Their error had been in going ahead, putting Responsible into pseudocoma from which they were not able to rouse her, even when they knew they didn't have enough information—it had not been an error in their magic, but an error of arrogance. But there was no reason to think that all that would do anything more than cause the man to switch to some other line of argument, perhaps based on their arrogance.

"Jason," said Michael Desirard McDaniels the 17th, of Castle Farson, finally, "what would you have us do? We cannot set you free, for we know you to be a killer. We cannot stand here and argue with you forever, for we are needed back in our own Kingdoms. There must be some other way to go on."

Jason gave all of them a defiant look, the look of a cornered animal. "Why don't you use your magic to *force* me to agree to your lies?" he sneered. "You could do that. I know you could. What's stopping you? Seems to me that would warm your black hearts!"

"That would be very wrong," answered Michael Desirard. "We could go out on the street and bring in anyone at all, and force *him* to say he'd killed Deborah. You must confess of your own free will, or it is no true confession."

"Well, I never *will* confess, without you force me by your black art," cried Jason. "Never!"

"Jason . . . what do you want of us?"

"My Deborah back, and her whole again and in her right mind."

"We can't give you that."

"Can't you? Can't you raise the dead, then?"

"You know we can't."

The man narrowed his eyes, and they drew back from the passion they saw flare in them, and waited for him to speak again.

"I want a trial," he told them. "A full trial. I want lawyers and judges and witnesses and a jury. I want the whole thing! And come the day you find a *jury* as says I'm guilty of the deed, *then* you might could call me murderer! Not before . . . not ever before."

"Jason—"

"No! No more talk! You asked what I wanted, and I have told you! And I am entitled to every last bit of it, by Ozark law!"

Titus Brandywine McDaniels raised his arms, his hands in front of him, palms forward, and the spate of murmuring stopped at once; in Castle Purdy he was by convention the one who gave orders if orders must be given.

"You're a damn fool, Jason Trueharper," he said disgustedly. "First you turn on your own like a mad dog. Then you destroy all thought of mercy in those that would help you, by your hard heart and your wicked spirit. And never a thought of the terrible waste of time and energy and funds best used in other ways. Never a thought for the misery of your family, dragged into open court and their trouble to be paraded for all the world to see. No. . . . you must demand a full trial, like any common murderer of Old Earth, too cowardly to own up to his deed and take his just punishment! There's nothing in you but your bitter selfishness!"

He paused, and waited, but Jason said nothing, and he lowered his arms. "So be it, then," he said. "When all is ready for your trial, someone will come for you. Till then you'll stay here, and you'll be fed and looked after."

"And my lawyer?"

"And we'll send you a lawyer. This very day. And now we'll leave you—we advise you to pray."

Deliberately, Jason Trueharper Purdy spat on the floor at their feet.

"Then we'll have you prayed *for*," said Titus Brandywine; and he turned and led the Magicians of Rank, and the Magician of Fraction, out of the room.

If it had been an ordinary crime, and the criminal fool enough to demand full trial, he might have languished three months or more while the Ozark system of justice was cranked up and oiled and made ready to function on his behalf. It happened rarely; the penalties from crimes were well-known, and most criminals were willing to let the matter be settled by the nearest Magician, with an ordinary citizen or two present to witness the proceedings and see that there was no abuse. But this was not an ordinary crime, and the Magicians of Rank were in full agreement that it must be handled swiftly, no matter what extraordinary measures that required.

In less than a week they had a trial set for a Friday morning and the town hall meetingroom in Hightower cleaned and polished for the occasion. They had Clarence Stepforth Purdy the 24th, a Magician only one step away from promotion to Magician of Rank, and a lawyer of considerable reputation, empowered to serve as judge. Two lawyers had been assigned to the unfortunate defendant; two more had been given the charge of prosecution. And if the lawyers for the defense were utterly ignorant of the law as it pertained to murder, well, so were the lawyers for the prosecution—it was a fair arrangement, with the ignorance equal on both sides of the case. Everything that the defendant asked for was provided, if it *could* be provided.

His only really outrageous demand had come when he

asked for comset coverage of the trial to go all over Ozark;
and that had obviously been no more than a foolish speech
meant to shock them, no more than his defiance and
misery talking. When they protested that he would be
crucifying his family if he paraded his shame in that fashion, he withdrew the demand as hastily as he had made
it. It was bad enough that they had no pretext that would
allow them to keep out the fifty spectators for whom there
were seats in the meetingroom, without adding the entire
population as potential audience.

The trial moved swiftly enough once it began. The
judge and jury, and the fifty Ozarkers lucky enough to find
places, paid careful attention as Titus Brandywine McDaniels presented the claims of the Magicians of Rank, paid
careful attention as the defense brought in a parade of
witnesses who spoke firmly of Jason Trueharper Purdy the
6th as a good man 'and a good farmer and a good husband
and a good father. All the Magicians of Rank were there,
three at a time in rotations of one hour, and it seemed to
them that the thing went by in a blur of speed. Noon
came, and there was nothing much left to do but the
cross-examination, and nobody very sure how to do that;
certainly the essential goodness of the defendant as a
person was not in question, not even in the minds of the
prosecution. The judge called a long noon recess, by way
of gaining a little time to think, and the Magicians of Rank
then present were grateful; they called a hasty meeting in
his chambers to discuss the situation.

Clarence Stepforth told them nothing new when he
observed that it wasn't going well.

"We know that," said Titus Brandywine. "We do know
that."

"Is this what you expected, exactly?"

Titus sighed. "I don't *know* what we expected," he said.
"We've never done this before, any of us. I suppose we

expected that when the time came to step up in that
witness chair and swear on the name of the Almighty,
Jason Trueharper would discover that he couldn't go on
lying. Not in front of everybody, under oath."

"It appears that you were wrong," stated the judge.
"He's as solid as this desk." And he thumped the desk a
resounding whack to demonstrate.

"Yes, he is."

"You're still sure he's guilty?"

"We're sure."

"Then why," asked the judge patiently, "doesn't he *act*
guilty? It's not as if he was a hardened criminal in the
ancient sense—or even the modern sense—of the word.
The defense has shown us what we already knew: this is a
good and decent man, devoted to his family, who's never
done anything wrong in his whole life beyond the ordinary
pranks that go with being a *child*."

"They used to have what was called an insanity defense," put in Shawn Merryweather Lewis the 7th, Magician of Rank to Castle Motley, who had done a little
research before he arrived. "It was used in all three of the
other murder trials held on Ozark, long ago."

"Well, yes," the judge agreed. "But it was used by the
defense! It can't come from the prosecution, Shawn
Merryweather. And furthermore, that man is as sane as
any of us—it would be ridiculous to call him mad. Overwrought, for sure. Terribly upset, under a great strain,
emotional, maybe hysterical. But he's not insane, not the
way the *law* defines the term."

"And he's going to get off," concluded Titus Brandywine
McDaniels.

"Oh, I think so, yes," said the judge. "His judgment
and so on are completely gone, right now, but so would
yours be—that's not going to hurt him with the jury.

There's nothing to convict him on atall. It's his word against yours."

"But we're Magicians of Rank!"

"So?" demanded Clarence Stepforth. "That's not evidence. Where would we be, O Magicians of Rank, if all it took to convict a person on this world was your word that he was guilty? There were places like that on Old Earth, but we don't *do* that on Ozark."

He was right. There was no argument about that.

"But you do believe us?" asked Michael Desirard McDaniels.

"Does it matter?"

"I wouldn't ask if it didn't matter."

"Well, then, yes—I do believe you. But it makes no least difference. No difference whatsoever. It wouldn't be evidence if every single man, woman and child on Ozark believed you. It would still be yourall's word against that man's, and no way to choose between them."

"What would we have to have to convict him?" asked Shawn Merryweather. "What would it take?"

"Evidence. Fingerprints, chemical stuff . . . that kind of thing. Which I happen to know you haven't got, and you've no way of getting. Or else an eyewitness. *Which* I know you haven't got, etc. I'd say it's hopeless."

"And that man will have killed his own daughter, in cold blood, and he will still go free to live out his life in peace?"

"I don't know about the peace," said the judge grimly. "I doubt he'll know much peace in himself. But that he will go free—yes. There's no way a jury could convict him; and if they were willing to do that on your word alone it would be a day of shame on Ozark."

There was silence in the small room, such a silence that you could hear the breathing of the four men gathered there; you could almost hear their thinking. At last, Titus

Brandywine spoke, slowly and cautiously, measuring the words.

"If we can get you eyewitnesses," he asked, "will that suffice? Would you then instruct the jury to convict?"

"Eyewitnesses to the murder?"

"Yes."

"I thought you didn't have any!"

"We can get them—if that would do it."

"Well, *yes*, that would do it. Of course. But I don't follow you—if you had witnesses, why haven't you brought them out long before now?"

The Magicians of Rank stood up courteously, their fingers flashing in the hand alphabet they used for communication at such times.

"It will be made clear," said Titus Brandywine McDaniels the 53rd. "When court begins again."

Outside on the lawn the other Magicians of Rank were appearing on their Mules, responding to the mindspeech summons of their colleagues. They spent a hasty half dozen minutes in the shade of a tall blue oak in the farthest corner, disputing among themselves. There were those who felt that what was proposed was not ethical. They felt it was no better than using magic to force Jason Trueharper to confess, and they said so.

"And besides, he can still deny it," insisted the Magician of Rank from Castle Smith. "What's to keep him from claiming it's all an illusion?"

"Nothing," agreed Titus Brandywine flatly. "And that's precisely what makes it different. If we force him to confess, he's helpless. But if we do *this*, he can still claim that he's innocent, and we can't stop him."

"I still don't like it."

"Do you like murderers walking free on Ozark?"

That was a question that had no simple answer; the Magician addressed made no attempt to answer it.

They all went into the courtroom when they heard the bell, waited while the judge called everyone to order, and proceeded to make their case. The defense waived the right to cross-examination, first, agreeing that everyone who had sworn to the essential goodness of the defendant had been telling the truth, admitting that they had no one prepared to come forward and swear to his essential wickedness. And then, with a fine flourish: "If we may have the court's attention, Your Honor, we have some new evidence to present. We call the Magicians of Rank of Planet Ozark as witnesses for the defense."

The judge's eyebrows went up, and there was a rustle of curiosity, and then uneasiness, as the thirteen Ozark Magicians of Rank filed down the center aisle and assembled at the front of the room in a small circle. They made an impressive group in their fine costumes, in marked contrast to the simple cottons and denims that were the daily garb of the Ozark citizen. No one present could recall ever having seen all thirteen together in one place before; it was overpowering, somehow, and they weren't sure they liked it. The judge half rose from his chair, thought again, and sat back down distractedly. He didn't think he liked it much either, but he had agreed to let them proceed with . . . what? He was no longer sure.

The Magicians of Rank raised their arms in the long full sleeves caught tight at their wrists, all of them together. They spread their fingers wide, all of them together. There was a flurry of hands and fingers, tracing shapes in the air, far too swiftly for anyone to perceive what those shapes were intended to be, all of it done perfectly and exactly together, all of it done in total silence. And then there was a gasp from the audience, and a scream from someone more nervous than the others, as the double-shafted golden arrows flew from each pair of hands to join, arrowhead to arrowhead, in the center of the circle of magicians. It would have been less alarming if it had been accompanied by thunder and lightning, or clouds of smoke, or eerie cries; the silence, and the ring of golden arrows, were far worse.

And then the arrows disappeared, and the Magicians of Rank drew back a few steps—but their arms were still raised and their fingers still spread wide. Whatever it was they were doing, it was not yet over.

The judge made no protest; like everyone else in the room, including Jason Trueharper, he was stunned into paralysis. There before them, before their amazed eyes, stood another Jason Trueharper. He stood beside his daughter Deborah, both of them laughing, and the girl alive and well. They saw the man lean to put one arm around his daughter's shoulders . . . saw him set the deadly hypodermic to her arm all the while that he smiled to her face, saw him shove the plunger home and draw the needle out, saw him gather her puzzled and protesting into his arms. Saw him hold her while she shuddered, and whimpered once, and struggled briefly, and then went limp against him. Saw him carry her—it seemed that the ground moved under his feet, that he held still and it was the scene that changed—saw him carry her to the barn, saw him throw the bar on the barn door, saw him sink to the floor and rock Deborah in his lap, weeping. Saw him put the rope around her neck and throw it over the rafter, settle the ugly noose, and let her body drop. Saw him step back and look at the scene, as if to check it for correctness. Saw him adjust the girl slightly, to change an arm that seemed awkward in its placing, perhaps. Saw him kick over the milking stool under her feet, that he'd stood on to do the awful deed, and scuff the straw on the floor as if someone had stood there hesitating awhile. Saw the man put his hands over his face and shake as if with fever, saying over and over, "Oh, my Debbie! My Debbie!" Saw him turn, and leave her. Saw her hanging there, dead and alone.

Where he watched in the front row, Jason Trueharper Purdy stood up and shrieked, and now he did indeed sound like a man insane.

"All right! All right!" he screamed. "All right, I did it! The Almighty have mercy on my soul, I killed her, and I would do it again! I did it! Only take it away, take it away! I cannot stand the sight of it!"

No one could. The Magicians of Rank moved their hands again, for the sake of common decency. Golden arrows came and went. And the hanging girl, the terrible hanging girl, was gone. Nothing there, except the court-room, and the spectators as pale as the girl had been.

"Your Honor," said one of the defense lawyers, stepping unsteadily forward and making useless gestures with his hands, "we rest our case."

When they could breathe again, and it was quiet again, the judge spoke gently to Jason Trueharper.

"Mister Purdy," he said, "we have all heard your con-fession. The matter is settled. But it may be you would like to explain. It would be best, Mister Purdy, if you explained."

Jason drew a long breath himself, and nodded.

"I'd like to do that," he said. "Since things are as they are."

"Please. Go ahead. Why did you do this terrible thing?"

All the time that he talked he stared down at the table in front of him, as if he were reading words written there.

"It was the day before, when she started it," he said. "She came to me, my Deborah, that was all my hope and my pride. And she was complaining, and whinin' and carryin' on. Wasn't fair, she said. Wasn't *right*. She'd been cheated, she said. All those good and fine things as had been offered to us, she said . . . the free houses—she wanted a house of her own, she always did—and the free clothes and the money and the work that paid such a good wage and was guaranteed. . . . She worked hard, did my Deborah. We *all* worked hard. Might could be it seemed to her we worked *too* hard, many and many a time. And she said it wasn't fair that there was a way to end all that and everybody have enough of everything, and plenty of time and comfort to enjoy it, and she couldn't have it just because there were *some* as didn't want it.

"She said she wasn't going to stand for it, she knew her rights. She said nobody had the right to turn it all down for her, or for the other young people. Just because we were all too old and set in our ways to enjoy anything, we thought everybody ought to live like animals, she said. She was so young, you know? She was so pretty? She was too young to do more than hanker after all the baubles and the trinkets—you mustn't hate her. I know I didn't hate her . . . I loved her with my whole heart.

"She had a plan. She was going to petition, you see. Not just for herself, either, she planned to stir up as many of the other youngsters as she could. And all of them would demand the right to emigrate, you see, to go to the nearest planet as was a member of that cursed Tri-Galactic Federation, and be *its* citizen, and live its life of ease. And nobody could stop her, she said, or stop any of them, because it would be hundreds of our young people, all demanding their rights. She said they were tired of living in the past . . . wanted to be part of the universe of *today*, not live forever in history. She said we couldn't keep them slaves to our stupid ideas, because now they knew what it would be like to be free. She was calling a meeting . . . she had it all planned.

"And there would of been plenty of others to join her, you know. There's foolish youngsters, too foolish to know what's best for 'em but too near grown to spank, all over Purdy Kingdom. And I know there's plenty such in all the other kingdoms. And she was bound and determined, was my Debbie.

"I had to *stop* it, you see! It was like she was a cancer. Like she was a dread disease, or a plague, or a blight on the pastures . . . it would have spread everywhere, we never never would have been able to stop it once it got started! I. . . ."

He stopped, and sobbed deep in his throat, and then went on, to get it over with.

"It had to be done. Same as if she'd carried a plague. Same as any kind of evil as threatened Ozark, no matter if she was my own dear child. I reckon we never came all this terrible way out here, and worked all these long years, and Tinaseeh and Kintucky still no more than wilderness and as much work left to do as done already, only to see our younguns turn around and go back to the wicked ways we left behind! I think on it now—might could be I ought to of shut Debbie up in the attic, kept her hidden away and prayed she'd learn sense and not killed her . . . but where would I have said that she'd gone? Do you think—might could be there was some other way I could of kept her from doing it? But I couldn't think, then, don't youall understand? All I could see was Ozark part of Old Earth again, part of that empire, and it *all for nothing*, all we've done! And the guilt for it, staining my Debbie's hands, going in all the history records. . . . oh, I did the only thing I knew to do, for all of us and for my child. And I am not ashamed that I did it. You hear me?"

He looked at them then, looked all around to be sure everyone looked back, with his shoulders straight and proud, and they understood why he had not acted like a guilty man. He had been sure he was right, and nothing that had happened yet had shaken him in that certainty.

"I killed her, because it had to be done and it was my place to do it. And then, for the sake of my son—so as he'd not grow up the son of a murderer, and a child-murderer at that—I called it suicide. She was so young; I figured people would think of that, and they'd forgive her. And I tried, I *tried* to make it look as how she'd killed her own self, but I didn't know how to do it right, don't you see. I never grew up with wickedness, I never knew how things like that were done, I didn't understand . . . I just thought, well, I'll hang her from that rafter, and then they'll believe she did it herself. And I was wrong, of course. And I've made a foul thing worse. But I am not ashamed, because it would have spread among the young ones like wildfire spreads on the dry grass, and I had to do what I could do to stop it."

At the front table, the judge leaned toward the Magicians of Rank and asked them, whispering, "*Is* he insane, after all?"

"No," whispered the nearest one. "Just a good and foolish and very stupid man. Not insane."

Jason Trueharper didn't hear them; he wasn't even interested in them. He looked better, stronger, the tension gone out of him. He said one last thing.

"And may the Almighty curse Brightwater, and the daughter of Brightwater, as let that off-world filth set foot on Ozark and brought down this hell upon us all!"

Responsible hadn't known about Jason Trueharper Purdy and his daughter when she spoke to the Magician of Rank about contamination, but the report of it was sitting on her desk waiting for her when she got home. First the death; then the arrest; then the trial, and the poor foolish man's

explanation. And all the jury walking out, refusing to serve
any longer, saying they could not judge this man who had
only done what they might very well have done themselves, had they been in his place. Saying they weren't
even sure it *was* murder, or, for that matter, *what* it was.
And every last one of them adding another curse for
Brightwater. The Magician of Rank who had forwarded
the report had no doubt found it satisfying to include that
sentence: "Each member of the jury in turn, as they filed
from the room, said 'And may the Almighty curse Brightwater, and the daughter of Brightwater, as Jason Trueharper
Purdy the 6th has shaped the curse!' "

Placed the blame that squarely and that easily, did
they? As if there'd been any way that Brightwater could
have kept the off-worlder from landing. Or any way they
could have kept him from coming back again, and bringing
with him his seductive offers of wealth and luxury and
ease! What would they have had Brightwater do?

"The judge, and the Magicians of Rank assembled," the
report concluded, "gave Jason Trueharper Purdy the 6th a
full pardon, and sent him on his way. Not for lack of
horror at his deed, let the record clearly show, but in
recognition of the principle that no man may be tried
twice for the same crime."

So. The man had gone home. And all the people present, and all the Magicians, of whatever rank, had gone
home. Home to talk about these extraordinary events.
And by this time next week there would be another two
dozen young Deborahs, and their male counterparts, all
clamoring for precisely the same things Deborah had clam-
ored for. What would they do, the fools, helpless as they
were to reason from A to B without assistance? Kill every
child that mentioned its longing for a lifetime of pretty
toys from the Tri-Galactic Federation?

Responsible of Brightwater laid the report back where

she'd found it, and walked over to her window to look out on Brightwater, fair and lovely under the light of Ozark's sun. It looked like a paradise, still.

"But the snake's here now," she said aloud, the Teaching Story bright in her mind's eye as if that sun shone on it, too. "And the Apple of Forbidden Knowledge—that's here. The Almighty help us all."

CHAPTER NINETEEN

Coyote lay there in the bed, brooding. He felt cross. He felt abused. He felt suspicious, glumly certain that things were not as they properly should have been. His head wounds and broken bones had been healed, and he was grateful for that; he hadn't seen the boulder he'd teleported into in place of the one he'd been aiming at, but from the descriptions of his condition he knew it had been no featherbed. But nothing had been done for those injuries that were not actually a danger to his life. He ached all over . . . as if he'd been flung head first into a boulder, to be exact . . . and that did *not* add up to the total advertised. Anybody sufficiently skillful to repair the kind of damage he'd done to himself, without so much as a scar or a mark left behind, was capable of eliminating the unpleasant side effects of such damage. That he hurt as he did now could only mean that the Magician of Rank had given him an abbreviated version of the usual treatment.

He lay thinking, trying to decide. Should he admit that he hurt, and ask the Wommack Magician of Rank for a touch-up before takeoff? Or should he grit his teeth and preserve the last tattered fragments of his image as The Sophisticated Man From Outer Space? He was considering the limited merits of each alternative, and searching for something better, when there was a knock at the sickroom door.

Maybe Responsible and Veritas Truebreed had been sufficiently moved by charity to send someone along to console him in his misery? That would be nice, because he could use consolation, and getting up to look for some had no appeal at all at that moment. He eased himself up gingerly on the pillows, gave his beard a couple of tidying flicks with his hands, and shouted, "Come on in, and bring your magic with you!"

The man who came charging through the door was not a Magician of Rank; he wasn't wearing the costume, and they never appeared in any other garb. Coyote had no idea who he might be. He came in like a wind rising, with both hands outstretched to greet the stranger, everything about him humming along at peak efficiency, and Coyote decided he had never before seen anybody who looked as alive as this man did—he fairly crackled as he moved.

"Well, divvy the Dozens!" he cried, grabbing Coyote's hands in his. "You're still here—I'm in luck!" He stood there holding on, grinning as if he were thoroughly delighted, and Coyote found himself grinning back in spite of his battered condition and his misery.

"Good morning?" said Coyote tentatively, wondering if his dignity demanded that he take his hands away. He wasn't used to having his hands held, even by Tzana Kai.

"*Isn't* it?"

The man let go of Coyote's hands, saving him the trouble of deciding how to handle that. And then he sat down in the chair beside the bed, tipped the chair back on its rear legs at what looked to Coyote like a very risky angle, clasped his hands behind his head, stretched his feet in their green leather boots out in front of him, and smiled the glorious golden smile of an angel.

"Do I know you?" Coyote asked him.

"No reason why you should, but I can fix that," said the man. "I'm Lewis Motley Wommack the 33rd, uncle to the Master of this Castle, and better him than me. And you are the off-worlder, Coyote Jones, no middle name, citizen of the dazzling Tri-Galactic Federation. And you don't know how glad I am to see you."

Feeling absurdly pleased, Coyote demanded to know why, precisely, this splendid person should be so glad to see him.

"Because I rather expect that this is not only my first but also my last opportunity *to* see an off-worlder, and I was afraid I was going to miss you. I had visions of old Veritas and that harpy hauling you away with them to Brightwater before I could even get in here to say hello. I've been hiding down the hall, waiting."

"Hiding . . . and waiting," Coyote repeated after him. "Why?"

"Hiding from Responsible of Brightwater and her performing potentate," Wommack explained. "And waiting for them to leave. I thought they were never going to."

Coyote frowned. Something was nagging at him, some vague memory from the endless gabble of the Brightwater Grannys during his week of house arrest.

"There's something . . ." he said slowly, "something I can't quite put my finger on . . ." And then, belatedly, a neuron fired in his head, and he remembered who this man would have to be.

"By the beards and the private whiskers of all the sainted and sanctified ancient apostles," said Coyote then, with genuine feeling, "you're Lewis Motley Wommack the thirty-effing third! Which means that you are the man who started the Teaching Order on Ozark, as I recall, and *that* must have been some project! And more to the point, unless somebody's lied to me you are the person who had the Magicians of Rank put Responsible of Brightwater into a coma! And damn near destroyed the whole planet in the process!"

"That was a long time ago," observed Lewis Motley. "I was much younger then."

"I *do* have the right Lewis Motley Wommack the 33rd?" Coyote asked.

"The very one. The one and the infamous only. That's the point of numbering us."

Coyote let a long slow breath out through lips too bruised to whistle with, and he stared at the man beside him with undisguised fascination. "Lewis Motley Wommack the 33rd! In the flesh!" he marveled. "Now I can die happy!"

Wommack gave him a long look, and grinned a little; his face was undergoing a considerable struggle between pretending to be solemn and cracking up completely.

"The Grannys," he said, "talk too much."

"They weren't talking about you specifically," Coyote told him. "You were a kind of incidental datum. They were telling me about that Out-Cabal nonsense and the Garnet Ring trying to take over Ozark with giant energy crystals, and the civil war, and how Responsible was in a coma—you got tucked into all that as a kind of sidelight."

"It wasn't a coma," said Wommack. "It was only a pseudo-coma."

"Uhuh. Suspended animation, apparently, the kind of thing we do for long spacetrips. But maintained, so help me Helga Dik, by magic alone. Or so Granny Hazelbide told me."

Wommack said nothing at all, and Coyote went right on staring at him. The man was a wonder. Not handsome, just beautiful. He had thick curly hair, and eyes of a deep

Suzette Haden Elgin

violet blue, and a magnificent powerful body. And that vital whatever-it-was that made you feel that not only would you follow him anywhere, you'd be happy to pay for the privilege. Charisma. There sat charisma, personified.

"If I'd done what *you* did," said Coyote after a while, "I'd have been hiding from Responsible of Brightwater too. I'm not sure I'd have been willing to stay as close as down the hall."

"I'm not afraid of her," said Lewis Motley Wommack. "I just don't want anything to do with her."

"More fool you, then, Wommack," snorted Coyote. "I'm scared blind of that woman. I'd rather deal with a betentacled alien."

Lewis Motley chuckled.

"Since you brought it up," he said, "in this case *you* are the alien, and you are a powerful disappointment to me. I'd take you for one of our own red-headed Lewises if I hadn't been set straight in advance, and that's not what one fancies in aliens. I was more of a mind to see little eyes on stalks, and horns sprouting out of your elbows, and purple slime dripping from your nostrils. Maybe a forest of rainbow tentacles gently waving when you opened your mouth. That kind of thing."

Coyote liked this man. There was a kind of radiance to him that made you want to keep him near you. He found himself very strongly inclined to oblige the fellow, and since there was no particular reason not to do so, he *did* oblige him. Providing everything Lewis Motley Wommack had specified except the purple slime from the nostrils, which had struck him as excessively revolting.

Wommack jumped, and the chair teetered for a perilous second, but it did not tip over as it would have done with Coyote sitting in it. It only balanced delicately on its wooden legs and fulfilled its unaccustomed function nobly until the man recovered his composure.

"Ah, now," he said, "*that* is splendid! That's terrific! That's more what I was yearning for, Jones! Open your mouth and let me see the tentacles again, will you?"

Coyote obliged, opening wide, and got a satisfyingly enthusiastic reaction.

"Now *that* is fandangous magic!" Wommack declared.

"Not magic." Coyote shook his head. "A projected telepathic illusion. Sorry."

"Don't be sorry—just waggle stuff. Like that . . . perfect!"

"Do you want me to stay like this?" Coyote asked.

"Is it easy to do?"

"Nope. I hurt like the bloody blue billowing blazes."

"Let it go, then, Mister Jones. I've had my treat, and I shouldn't be greedy. My sister Jewel is always telling me that. And *you*, tell me what I can do for you in exchange for the fireworks."

Coyote relaxed, sighing, and said, "Are you serious?"

"Of course I'm serious."

"Then you can tell me *why* you had Responsible of Brightwater put into a coma. Pseudo-coma, I mean."

Coyote watched his companion carefully, ready to make quick adjustments and trims, not sure what to expect. Along with the information about the founding of the Teaching Order, and the Responsible Caper, the Grannys had mentioned Lewis Motley Wommack's famous bad temper. "As likely to throw you through a window as look at you," was how they'd put it. Coyote suspected that the episode he was asking about might not be Lewis Motley's favorite subject of conversation.

He was right. The light and the warmth all went away, and a cold front came through the room bearing frost, and Wommack said, "That's too high a price." Grimly. Ice and steel, sliced thin and honed to splinters.

"Why?" Coyote insisted. He was nowhere near ready to give up yet. He had the famous Ozark aversion to violence to protect him, for one thing, and then there was the way it would look if Wommack were to beat up on a guest lying there invalid before him. "What's too high about it? What you did wasn't against the law; and Responsible doesn't seem to have suffered any permanent damage. Unless she was a nice person before you got to her. Which I doubt."

"It's old news, Jones. *Moldy* old news."

"Ah, but I want to know."

"Why?"

"Because I am curious," said Coyote with complete honesty. "It fascinates me. Not knowing torments me. Why would you *do* an incredible thing like that?"

"Mister Jones—there is a question of honor here."

Coyote scowled at him. "It's obviously no secret, Wommack," he said. "Your whole damn *world* knew about it."

"That's true. They did. But they did not know why."

"The Grannys know why, Lewis Motley. And the Magicians of Rank know why."

"And you are neither one of those!" Lewis Motley's face was stern and grave, and his eyes held Coyote in a steady grip. It was not getting any friendlier in the room.

Coyote gave it a little thought, and decided it was worth the effort, and very deliberately provided all the previous effects *plus* the purple slime from the nostrils. And a few oddments extra that he'd seen in his years of tootling about the Three Galaxies, to offset the clichés.

Lewis Motley Wommack's mouth twitched at the corners.

"Cut it out," he said.

Coyote laid it on thicker. With sound effects and an assortment of exotic smells.

"Pheeeeeyeeew!" protested the other man. "How long can you keep that up?"

"Forever," Coyote lied. "How about this one?"

Lewis Motley Wommack burst out laughing, and rocked with glee on the back legs of the chair in a terrifying display of contempt for the laws of physics. "All *right*!" he said, when he had managed to bring the roaring down to a controllable thunder. "All right, I'll tell you. You've earned it, and I don't suppose there's any reason you shouldn't know. I certainly don't owe the daughter of Brightwater any favors. But *listen*, Jones—it's *damn* bad manners to poke into another person's affairs like this. It isn't *done*."

"Oh, I know that," agreed Coyote. "It's probably my worst bad habit. Maybe what you're about to tell me will cure me of it, with great benefit to all my friends and victims." He waggled one of his more spectacular appendages.

"Mister Jones, you have to stop that," said Lewis Motley. "I mean it. Because it's not a funny story."

Instantly, Coyote canceled the illusion and lay there as sedate as any middle-aged intergalactic businessman.

"Tell me," he said. "I'm not going to spread it any farther, Wommack, I promise you. I may be rude, but I'm not *that* rude."

"So you spread it farther," said Wommack, shrugging. "It doesn't matter."

"But I won't," said Coyote firmly, because obviously it *did* matter, very much. "Now tell. Be kind. Indulge a battered stranger just passing through."

"I was very young," said Lewis Motley Wommack, staring up at some undefined point above his head, "and very headstrong and very wild. And I lived in a state of perpetual curiosity—like you—except that mine was about women. It did me no good to have one, you see; it never helped. I just wondered, each and every time, what the *next* one would be like."

Coyote thought about the brisk and bracing morality that was all his experience on Ozark to date. He thought about how Grannys Hazelbide and Gableframe would react to what he'd just heard, and shuddered. And he noted aloud that that probably hadn't made Lewis Motley popular with the neighbors.

"No, it didn't. And they were right. It's a very good thing we Ozarkers have reliable methods of birth control and a tight lid on the population—thanks to the Grannys—or I'd have little offshoots scattered all over Wommack Kingdom. I'm old enough now that I wouldn't find that amusing. But *then*, ah, then, I didn't care. It was the challenge of the hunt. What would she be like? How would she react? What would I have to do or say to get her? I was infinitely . . . and disgustingly, I'm afraid . . . curious about the ladies."

"And you went after Responsible of Brightwater?" asked Coyote, bemused at the idea. "Just as you would have gone after any other woman?"

"Went after her, yes," answered Wommack. "And *got* her. In a way."

"What does that mean—in a way?"

The man's mouth tightened, and he looked at Coyote again.

"It's hard to explain," he said. "It's not something I'm *willing* to explain, no matter what kind of fancy tricks you do—don't waste your strength. Suffice it to say that I shared her bed a time or two, and that I found out a great deal more about her than I wanted to know."

"I see. So you had the Magicians of Rank put her into a coma because you didn't like her style in bed." Coyote's voice was as flat and as free of sarcasm as he could manage, considering the repulsiveness of the concept.

"*No!*" Lewis Motley protested. "Dozens . . . no, it wasn't that, Mister Jones. I was young, but I wasn't *pervert*ed. It was that I couldn't get rid of the creature. Now I'd had that that sort of problem before, of course. I'd bed some young lady, and tell her pretty lies, and then she'd

want to follow me around everywhere I went. T[...]
thing. I had a *lot* of trouble with that before I outgrew my
foolishness, and there are Kintucky women I am still
hiding from to this day. But Responsible was not your
usual hanger-on." He got up from the chair and went to
look out of the window, his back to the room. "What
she did," he said slowly, "was crawl into my *mind*. I
could have handled anything else. I could not handle
that. I could not endure that, Jones. It was unspeakable.
Foul. Grotesque. From the very blackest of your nightmares. She was *always* there! It was exactly as if she
were a great white worm, coiled inside my head, back of
my eyes."

Lewis Motley Wommack shuddered, now, in earnest;
he gripped the frame of the window in his hands, and
Coyote saw his muscles tense with strain.

"Everywhere I went," he said, "everything I did—Responsible of Brightwater went with me. She was a
parasite I carried, and I could not be free of her, not ever,
not even when I lay with some other *woman*."

He turned to face Coyote, and the look of revulsion on
his face was totally convincing.

"I am my own person," he said fiercely. "I will never
marry . . . I can't imagine sharing my life with some other
person. I was always like that; they say that when my
mother tried to nurse me I fought like a fish on a line, and
she had to give it up. I have always had to be *separate*.
And there was Responsible of Brightwater. *Inside* of me.
A part of me, uninvited. I never knew when I would feel
her there. . . ." He shuddered again, violently, and leaned
back against the wall. "You cannot possibly know what
that was like, for me."

Coyote nodded slowly, not daring to say anything yet. The
man must have needed to talk about this for a very long time.

"And so I called on the Magicians of Rank."

With that sentence, the tension left Lewis Motley, and he came back to lean over ⁄the footrail of Coyote's bed.

"They hated her, everybody knew that. I told them I wanted her *stopped*. I didn't tell them I'd taken her to bed; that was none of their business, as it is none of yours. But I told them she'd invaded my mind and taken up permanent residence there. Any sort of mindspeech is forbidden to Ozark women, Jones, and the sort I described to them was far on beyond forbidden. They saw to it. With *glee*, I might add, they saw to it. With the consequences you were told of—which I give you my solemn word, man to man, I had not for an instant anticipated."

"No," said Coyote cautiously. "I don't suppose you had."

"I was a young fool," said Wommack with contempt. "I was half in love with my wonderful clever young self. I thought it would all stay a secret—that no one would ever know. I never imagined that the Magicians of Rank would tattle—I had no idea they were such sniveling pitiful excuses for men. When things began to go wrong on Ozark, they fell all over themselves putting the blame on me. Jones, I never suggested pseudo-coma. I didn't know there was any such thing as pseudo-coma. That was their idea, and theirs alone. I meant Responsible no harm—I just wanted her out of my head. And I didn't specify how it was to be done."

Coyote sighed, and thumped a pillow with satisfaction.

"It's a wonderful story," he declared. "The kind of story that gets made into a song, and lives forever."

"Huh." Lewis Motley went back and took up his precarious position in the chair again. "It's more the kind of story you snicker about behind your hand."

"No," Coyote objected, "it's not like that. But that's not quite all of it, my friend. There's got to be a little more. What did Responsible *say* to you when you asked her to stop bothering you? What excuse did she give you? Did she just drivel on about not being able to live without you? Had to be near you every minute or she'd die? That kind of twentieth-century garbage? I can't imagine Responsible of Brightwater being like that—but she was younger then, too. And probably not very experienced."

"She was fifteen. And a virgin."

"Aha! That makes an even better story! And when you confronted her, what did she *say*?"

Lewis Motley cleared his throat. He cleared it again. "This is the difficult part," he said in a strange rough voice. "This is the part nobody ever understands. Nor will you."

"Go on. Try me."

"I never asked her to stop."

"*What?*" Coyote was stunned. "You *what?*"

"You *see*," said the man dryly. "I told you so. That's how my sister—and Responsible's sister—reacted. Just could not believe their ears."

"Me either," admitted Coyote without hesitation. "Up to now it's been a glorious tale in the old tradition—it's even made sense. But no more. The young lady—"

"She was no lady."

"Excuse me. Responsible of Brightwater, I should say, was doing a nasty psi-caper in your head, and you hated it. Considering how it made you feel, I understand that. And if you'd tried to deal with her and failed, I guess I could understand your bringing in the Magicians of Rank—probably. But asking them first? Before you even talked to her? That's crazy. For that matter, I don't even understand why they were willing to meet with you, let alone do what you asked them, on your word alone!"

"I was," said Wommack gravely, "at that time, serving as Master of this Castle. My uncle was dead—a suicide, Jones, and by this time I expect you know how rare that is on this world—and the current Master was too young to assume his duties. I took the job, though I would not take the title, while he grew. And although the Magicians of Rank would never have come to meet with Lewis Motley Wommack the 33rd, they were *delighted* to answer a call from the Guardian at Castle Wommack for assistance in his grievance against Responsible of Brightwater. That was a very different matter."

Coyote gave him a dubious look, and shrugged his shoulders. "Okay," he said. "I don't pretend to follow all that, but it's not my planet and it's not my culture. There's no special reason why I should understand it. But *why*, for the Light's sake, did you ask the M's of R for help without asking Responsible first? I don't care if you were the blinking Emperor of Emperors, Wommack—that makes no sense."

"Because. . . ." The man paused, and Coyote saw pain in his eyes, and was surprised. "Partly because of stupid pride, of course. I don't deny it. The women charged me with that, and there was a certain rightness to what they said. I was accustomed to always having everything my own way with women; I was accustomed to having them beg *me* for things. The idea that I should have to do the asking galled me. But that was only a trivial part of it. Tell me, Jones, have you ever had anyone share your mind as Responsible shared mine? Ever been invaded, taken over, like that? Even briefly?"

Coyote shook his head. "No," he said. "On Mars Central, I'm considered handicapped, because I'm deaf to telepathic communication. It's not like Ozark, where you think such things are reserved for your Magicians. In the Three Galaxies, we consider telepathy an ordinary part of everyone's normal behavior. But I can't do it. I can *send* telepathic information—you've seen me do that—but I can't receive much of anything. I can't know what that would be like."

"Well . . . it's a way of knowing someone far far better than you need or want to know them! But you see, I did not for one second suspect that she didn't *know* how I hated what she was doing. She was inside my mind—I took it for granted that she knew, that she was deliberately ignoring the way I felt about it, that she was enjoying her power to sicken me and turn my life foul. I know now that I was mistaken, but I didn't know then. Nobody understands that here; they blame it all on my headstrong pride and my arrogance. But I swear to you, if the idea that she didn't know what was happening had ever entered my head, I would have gone to her first. I don't know that it would have helped—she's not an ordinary woman. She might have laughed at me, and it all would have ended the same anyway. But I would have tried."

He leaned toward Coyote, the hurt glowing dark in his eyes, and he said, "Coyote Jones, I swear to you I did not know. I did not even guess." And Coyote believed him.

"Light's Beard, Wommack," he said softly. "You've fixed it, man. You've fixed it! That is one galloping whale of a wonderful story."

"I'm too close to it to see it that way."

"I believe you, you know."

Lewis Motley smiled. A wry, bitter smile. "My sister would tell you that you just don't know me well enough," he said. "Jewel has never forgiven me, and that's a hard thing. I've always loved her dearly."

"What about Responsible of Brightwater? Has she forgiven you?"

"How would I know?" He smiled again, but this time it

was one of those smiles you could have gotten warm by. "I've never asked her."

That was the last straw; Coyote was so astonished that he sat bolt upright in the bed, and immediately he regretted it. From the center of a haze of pain, he told Lewis Motley Wommack that that was the most ridiculous thing he'd heard yet.

"I've had no contact with her since that whole messy episode took place," came the answer. "Kintucky's a big continent, and still almost wilderness. There's enough to do here to last many men for many lifetimes. I've had no interest in traveling. And if business brought Responsible here I did what I did today—I stayed well out of her path. I would have gone out hunting, ordinarily, but I wanted to talk to you."

And then he grinned, suddenly, and said, "And I'm glad I *did* talk to you, my friend off-worlder! Despite my unsavory past and all this slop and slobber. Why don't you get out of that bed and give me a chance to show you around the town? Let me show you the kind of treatment Wommack Kingdom can give a man who has a taste for life."

Coyote eased himself back down in the bed, with a groan he could not stifle. "I don't have much taste for life right now," he said through gritted teeth. "Sorry about that."

Lewis Motley set the front legs of the chair down with a thud and peered at him closely, his eyes narrowed.

"What the devil?" he demanded. "Wasn't Veritas Truebreed Muckymuck here to set you to rights?"

"He was. But he gave me the cheap economy cure. To teach me a lesson, I suppose."

"Why would he want to do that?"

"I was monkeying around with his magic," said Coyote. "I don't think he liked that."

"*Uhuh*," said Wommack. "You just wait right there a minute."

He was back almost immediately with the Wommack Magician of Rank in tow; and he marched Feebus Timothy over to Coyote's bed, pointed one finger, and said uncompromisingly, "Feebus, you fix him."

"Fix him?" Feebus looked scornful. "Veritas has already 'fixed' him."

"You know better! First you were too lahdidah to soil your dainty fingers on him. Then your colleague from Brightwater comes along and does just half the job, to make a moral point. There's no reason why the man should be in that condition, Feebus. Fix him."

"I am not in the habit of tampering with the work of another Magician of Rank," said Feebus Timothy stiffly.

"And I am not in the habit of kicking any Magician of Rank in the butt," Lewis Motley retorted. "But I could bring myself to do it if I had to."

It was clear from Feebus Timothy's look of contempt that he was not one of the people impressed by Wommack's temper. But the matter apparently didn't strike him as worth arguing about. He gave one snort of disgust, raised his hands, and went through the finger-flashing procedure that Coyote had learned always produced one of the golden arrows with the double shaft.

There it was now. Flicker, flicker, whizz, it's gone.

"I didn't get one of those," Coyote noted.

"Didn't get one of what?" Feebus Timothy asked him.

"When I . . . uh, brought myself here. I didn't try for one of those fancy arrows of yours."

"Just as well you didn't," snapped the Magician of Rank.

"But why did it work? How come, with no arrow, I didn't just go on sitting there on a step in Red Arches?"

Feebus Timothy did a stone-face routine. "There are many tasks," he said, intoning all the way, "that can be accomplished either elegantly or primitively. The primitive methods tend to have less satisfactory—and less predictable—results, Mister Jones. As you found out. Little boys shouldn't play about with grownup toys; it makes nasty messes that other people have to waste their time cleaning up."

"Well, I guess that explains it," said Coyote jovially.

"Mister Jones—please. Are you more comfortable now?"

Coyote checked. He was. He felt absolutely wonderful.

"Now this is more like it," he said with satisfaction. "This time, I am properly repaired. I'd say you're a better Magician of Rank than old Veritas."

"I should hope *so*," Feebus Timothy sniffed. "You're all right, then?"

"I feel fine."

"See that you stay that way," said the Magician of Rank, and he went sailing out of the room without so much as looking back.

"Hey," said Coyote. "Look at your grateful alien! I can't thank him, so I'll thank you. Thanks, Lewis Motley—this is much better."

"Standard service, my friend. We heal *all* guests who arrive at the Castle with their heads smashed in and afloat in gore. No charge."

"But *damn* it all," Coyote complained, remembering, "I shouldn't have let him go like that! I need him to do his vanishing mule act and get me back to Brightwater, where my flyer is. I'm about ten days late for supper, Wommack."

"Then another couple of days won't matter. Stay overnight. We'll have a look at what Wommack Kingdom can offer tonight, and tomorrow we'll do something even more interesting."

"You really mean that?"

"Do I sound as if I were joking?"

"How come," Coyote demanded, because it had been

bothering him for the past twenty minutes, "how come you talk like a Magician of Rank? *Are* you a Magician of Rank? Unfrocked, or something?"

"No, nor yet a Magician."

"Then how come? You've been doing it all this time. 'One fancies . .' 'As if I were . . .' How come?"

"Because I choose to. Which suffices. And I choose to ask you, quite seriously, to stay, if you'll quit changing the subject. You'd be surprised what we could accomplish, you and I, in twenty-four hours."

"Responsible of Brightwater will have my head if I do that."

"I'll protect you," laughed Lewis Motley. "I promise—I will not let her get you."

Coyote told him about the fancy turbulence, and what that meant to the stomach of the unwary secret agent.

"You think she did that?"

"Either did it or ordered it up," Coyote said. "Sorry . . . much as I'd like to go cavorting with you, it's not worth the penalties once I get beyond the reach of whatever protection your hospitality offers me."

Lewis Motley's eyes went cold, and Coyote stopped, startled.

"What's the matter?" he asked. "Did I say something wrong?"

"No. I was just thinking how weary I am of having Responsible of Brightwater spoil my pleasures."

"Can't be helped. I still have to go home. Straight home."

"You won't change your mind?"

"Sorry."

"If you ever find that you can face the terrifying Brightwater female, I'd welcome you back."

"Sorry," said Coyote again. "It won't happen."

"She's only a woman!"

"You Ozark men may think so," Coyote said. "But I am *not* an Ozark male, and I don't tamper with her again. For one thing, I gave her my word. I promised I'd go without causing further trouble, and I promised I'd stay away. Me and all my ugly compatriots—we'd *all* stay away. For another thing, there are a lot of people back at Mars Central who will be wondering what's keeping me—some of them will want to slay me slowly, and some of them will just be concerned."

He was halfway to the door, waving absently to Lewis Motley Wommack and wondering where he'd find Feebus Timothy, when he remembered, and stopped short.

"Just a minute," he said. "I forgot something."

He paused, with his hand on the ironwood doorknob.

"You know those little flat green things you call Pickles?"

"Sure. They're taking over the place—I saw one lying out in the hall when I came in, and damned if I know how it got up all those stairs. Why?"

"It may be," said Coyote gravely, "that the phrase 'taking over' is more appropriate than you think."

"What do you mean?"

"Those things are not natural creatures, Lewis Motley. They're made out of fancy plastics and resins and similar stuff. And they're not nice to have around. They are a very sophisticated snooping device. They're spy-sensors, Wommack."

Lewis Motley's face wore an anger that made Coyote glad he wasn't on the receiving end of it. "Are you telling me," he asked, "that somebody is spying on Wommack Kingdom? That those things are planted here to spy on us?"

"Not just Wommack Kingdom," Coyote corrected him. "They're everywhere. And they're a direct remote line to an information-gathering agency located in the Garnet

Ring. If I were you, I'd smash the nasty little bastards."
He did not mention that the Federation had already taken
care of deactivating the devices, by pulling all the relevant
plugs at their source, on Phona. There was no reason for
the Ozarkers to know about that.

"By the Almighty and the Twelve Golden Gates!" roared
Lewis Motley, and his fist smashed into the arm of his
chair. "Are you sure of that?"

"I'm positive. The Garnet Ring sells their spy devices
all over the Three Galaxies, for legitimate use in law
enforcement, for household intercom devices, that kind of
thing. I've seen them all my life. And you Ozarkers must
have ten thousand of them lying around."

"All sending information back to the Garnet Ring!"

"That's right. And making it possible to convince you
people that there is a terrible mysterious group called
'The Out-Cabal.' There's no such thing. It's just nonsense, meant to intimidate you."

Lewis Motley stood up, and Coyote stepped farther out
the door; he had no desire to get in the way of what he
saw coming.

"I'll take care of it," said his would-be host through
clenched teeth. "By tomorrow there won't be one of those
hellish gadgets left on Kintucky . . . and I'll send the word
out. I wish you'd told us sooner!"

"Sorry," said Coyote. "It's been a little hectic—I kept
forgetting."

Wommack nodded, and headed for the door the way a
tornado heads for a barn. Prudently, Coyote got out of his
way and let him charge through the door first.

CHAPTER TWENTY

"You know, Mister Jones," mused the Fish, "I'm ready to concede that with this report you have at last reached your *peak*." He waved the microfiche under Coyote's nose, holding it between the tips of two of his fingers as if it were a spoiled pork chop. "I cannot conceive of any situation in which you could ever hope to surpass it. Not in lack of plausibility; not in number of total foulups achieved; not in accounts of behavior entirely unbecoming not just to a TGIS man but to a human *being;* not in outrageous gaps, and distortions, and excuses, and rambling nonsense; not in—"

"Fish," said Coyote. "Pescadoro. *Sir*, even. I can tell you aren't pleased with me. That message has reached my brain. You don't have to go on with the list. Furthermore, you know I'm not any happier about this than you are. But I have one more recommendation to present."

"You couldn't have! After *this*?"

"I do."

"What is it, Coyote? *What*?"

"Fire me," said his agent. "That way you'll get no more

of these ruined missions. *Release* me. I don't want to be a TGIS man. I have *never* wanted to be a TGIS man. When they told me at the Crèche that I'd been assigned to TGIS, I sat down on the floor and I cried. My work is unsatisfactory—I agree. Tear up my contract, Fish, please? I'll kiss you if you do."

"May the Light preserve me," said the Fish, in a devout tone that Coyote did not remember having heard from him ever before. "May the Light protect and deliver me, Its humble servant, from those lips with which you threaten me now." He looked as if he might very well spit.

"Fish," said Coyote, "you wound me."

"I do hope so."

"Well? Are you going to fire me? I'll go be a forest ranger someplace in the Third Galaxy, and never trouble you again, so help me Helga Dik."

The Fish ignored him. He went on scowling at the report and making little fretful noises of distress.

"Let me see if I've got all this straight," he said at last. "You want nothing but the moon and the stars and a couple of comets. Let me see. . . . You want us to put all the information about this mission, and all the genuine information about Ozark and the Ozarkers, on status CLASSIFIED TOP SECRET."

"At least. If there's something beyond that, put it there instead."

"That one's probably easy. The government isn't any more anxious for all this to get out than you are. If it got out, we'd have to explain it . . . horrible thought. You get your top secret."

"Good. That's a start."

"Then you want a guidebook insert—all of Planet Ozark, and its atmosphere, and a zone of twenty miles beyond that in all directions for safety—marked DANGEROUS UNPREDICTABLE VIOLENT WEATHER; KEEP

CLEAR; DO NOT APPROACH UNDER ANY CIRCUM-
STANCES. Is that right? Are you sure you don't want
PLAGUE ZONE put in there, too?"

"If you think you could get away with it, I think that
would be a good idea. But the weather notation ought to
do it. There's nothing out there but official traffic. And
nobody can see anything there. Flying through an empty
nothing with a violent turbulence warning isn't likely to
attract anybody."

"Mister Jones, you're dithering," observed the Fish. "I
am able to grasp the facts without your emendations."

"Sorry. This whole thing upsets me."

"It *should* upset you. Your failure to obtain even a
tentative agreement for exchange of information from the
Ozark psi-adepts is a major loss for the Federation. We
don't even know the magnitude of that loss. We don't
have any information except *anecdotes*. But clearly, it is a
substantial loss. . . . Mister Jones. Mister Jones, how could
you possibly have offended those people that *much*?"

"I don't think I did offend them," said Coyote stubbornly. "I think the *Earth* offended them. A thousand
years ago. Offended them so badly that they're not going
to get over it for another thousand years. They just don't
want anything to do with any of us, Fish. *Ever*."

"Surely you could have gotten permission for a scientific
exchange team to go to Ozark," objected the Fish. "Or a
diplomatic team to *negotiate* for the sending of a scientific
team? I am talking scholars, Mister Jones. *Scholars!*"

Coyote thought about the way Responsible of Brightwater,
or your average Ozarker-in-the-street, would feel about
"scholars." It was not pleasant, even as a minor meditation
on a completely hypothetical theme. "No," he stated, "I
couldn't have done that. And I don't think anybody else
could have either."

The Fish cleared his throat elaborately, and his nostrils flared. "Really," he said. "You're too modest."

"I'm serious! I'll grant you, somebody else could have bumbled through the mission with more *elegance* than I managed. I don't doubt that. I'm not known for elegance. And I will back you all the way in any claim that you should have sent someone else in the first place. I even suggested that to you, in the first place, and you wouldn't listen to me. Fine. I agree. But no matter who you might have sent out there, Fish, the end result would have been the same: *Planet Ozark in magnificent isolation*."

"With magnificent psibilities that the Federation *needs*," mourned the chief.

"Responsible of Brightwater didn't seem to think so."

"Well, who the blazes is Responsible of Brightwater to think anything of the kind?" shouted the Fish. "What does *she* know about it, anyway?"

"I don't know," said Coyote. "I don't know at all. But she is the only entity in all the universe, so far as I am aware, who is in contact with a whole circle of others like herself from both the past and the future. I find that, while anything but clear, *most* impressive—I don't have much desire to tangle with that, myself. And she told me in no uncertain terms that she did not give the skinniest little *hoot* how badly we might want to learn about what she is pleased to refer to as their 'magic.' I got the distinct impression that we could all die here and rot and sink back into the primordial *ooze*, for all she cared. She didn't so much as bother to ask me why we might want to learn from the Ozarkers, or what we might do with the knowledge, or what we might offer in exchange—nothing. It was just like the Ozark answer to our invitation to join the Federation—just *no*. Like that. *No*. And good-bye and good riddance. Fish, I tried. I really tried. But Responsi-

ble of Brightwater, whatever else she may have or be, has
no heart in her body. A rock maybe, but no heart."

The Fish studied his glum and obstreperous agent, and
he licked his upper lip with the tip of his tongue, considering. And then he said, "Maybe it's not a total loss."

"Right. I got away alive. That's a plus."

"That's not what I meant. I meant that perhaps we did
learn something useful."

"How so?"

"Well, if your report is not a total fabrication, you
somehow teleported yourself over hundreds of miles, instantaneously. Not with great skill, mind you, but you did
do that. Presumably you learned something from the experience that you could share with us here. We could
make good use of that little trick."

Coyote shook his head firmly.

"Nope," he said. "I didn't learn one thing. First thing I
did after I got back . . . well, second or third thing I did
. . . I tried to repeat that business. I sat in one corner of
an empty room, picked a target at the other end—said
target spread liberally with airbags so I wouldn't smash my
idiot head again—and I went through *exactly* the same
steps I went through on Ozark."

"And?"

"Nothing. Not so much as a flicker. And I wasn't really
surprised, Fish. I was just double-checking. Because, as it
says in my report—about which you should not be complaining, under the circumstances—what I did on Ozark
involved first and foremost tapping into the Ozarkers' *faith*
in their system of magic. That faith isn't available here on
Mars Central. No power supply. It doesn't work here."

"Hmmmmph," said the Fish. "A very negative attitude, Mister Jones. We of the TGIS do not encourage
negative attitudes. You were probably just tired; you could

try again. We will bring in a good medical hypnotist to help you remember."

"Look here," said Coyote. "Suppose that the only thing keeping a Greyhound spacebus up is the passengers' faith that it will not fall. One passenger scared it will fall isn't enough to shut off that faith and cause a crash, maybe five or six aren't enough; not compared to the millions sublimely convinced it will go right on flying. And it's the same thing here, Fish. The entire population of Mars Central is people who don't *believe* in magic, don't believe you can rocket yourself through space using ancient generative grammar rules extrapolated to serve as a grammar of the universe. Can't you just imagine how the linguists would react to that? And one person who does believe it—sort of—isn't going to be enough to cancel that mass faith. Which makes *it* a power supply—the local population, I mean."

"A power supply that keeps us from being able to use telekinesis for travel? Is that what you're saying?"

"Yeah, it's what I'm saying."

"Nonsense," said the Fish. "Mumbojumbo."

"Fish, think how long it was before people would believe in the psibilities at all. Think how people who *had* psibilities used to fail, centuries back. They'd put them on comset shows and they wouldn't be able to do even the simplest little baby tricks. Couldn't guess those silly Rhine cards. Couldn't make a compass needle move. Fish, what if the problem was just all that negative power, all that mass of belief in the impossibility of psi, that was holding the compass needle still?"

"I am not convinced," said the Fish. "Human beings *evolve*, Mister Jones. They change over time. Look what the *Phonans*, to choose an appropriate example, have come to be able to do. The Ozarkers, isolated and inbred, have just evolved to a new stage—"

"*Nah,* Fish. Listen. It took hundreds of years of little tiny piddly accomplishments on the part of some extremely powerful telepaths to create enough popular belief to even dent that negative force. You're not going to get past what's out there now—not even with a medical hypnotist."

The Fish puckered his mouth toward the base of his nose, and sniffed a long aristocratic sniff, and exhaled a long aristocratic breath.

"Wait," he said.

"Wait for what?"

"Let's carry what you're saying to its logical conclusion. It should then be the case that all we have to do to achieve the powers that are routine on Planet Ozark is convince *our* peoples that those powers are possible. That's what you're saying, isn't it, Mister Jones?"

Coyote leaned back in his chair and stared at his boss.

"Well, hell's hinges, Fish," he said, "that's hardly anything *new*. Yogis floating in the air. Wandering around naked in the snow. Walking coals without a blister. Saints with bodies that don't decay after death. Mountains that will throw themselves into the sea, provided you've got as much faith as a grain of mustard seed, whatever that means. Look at any of the ancient sacred books, they *all* say what you just said. Every single one of them."

The Fish began muttering about gross oversimplification, and drastic overstatement and understatement, and inadequate logic, and similar semantic pebbles, and Coyote closed his eyes.

"Whatever you say," he said. "I'm too tired to argue with you. We can come back to it some other time. What else have you got on the list?" He was weary clear to the tips of his clingsoles.

"Let me see. . . . Information goes to CLASSIFIED. Planet Ozark gets the KEEP OUT notice. Oh, yes, here we are. We cancel the application from Smith Kingdom for TGF membership, file it away, and swear on *any* handy sacred book that we'll abide by the new legislation and never ever do such a naughty thing again. I'll take care of that. And then we nudge the Phonans once again about letting Ozark alone, and put somebody on a regular surveillance schedule to make sure they *do* let Ozark alone."

He stopped, and looked at Coyote.

"Do you really think that's necessary?" he asked. "It's going to be an expensive nuisance if we do that, and it would have to come out of my private funds."

"You just bet your sweet little be*hind* it's necessary," Coyote told him. "Those animated licorice whips had every other inch of Ozark littered with their lightforsaken spy-sensor gadgets! And they're just champing at the bit to grab the place. I don't trust them."

"All right. If you feel that strongly about it, I'll authorize it for the time being. And I think I'll have somebody gently suggest to the Phonans that they apply for a Federation grant to build themselves one more asteroid."

"It's not the *same*. They want Ozark. They want forests and mountains and fruited plains and stuff."

"Don't we all? The Phonans are not especially different."

"They *are* different. They're way out there where they can do all kinds of things without getting caught. They're greedy, and spoiled. They're not about to move out to a frontier planet and get their goodies that way, the way any other people would in the same situation. And they are absolutely dedicated to the idea that they are the very latest thing in superbeings. They cannot believe they aren't entitled by divine right to anything their stringy little hearts desire."

"All the more reason for the asteroid, then. It may not be what they want, but it will take a little of the pressure off. I'll make a note that the grant application is to be approved, and we'll put another little bauble in the Garnet Ring."

"Okay. But watch them all the same."

"If you insist."

"I do. Is that it?"

"Well, we seem to be through," said the Fish, frowning. "I'm not happy about it. This is not what I had in mind. I don't even understand most of it, and your fairy stories haven't shed much light on the puzzles. But it seems to be all there is to do."

"Then it's time," said Coyote.

"Time for what?"

"Time for me to explain why you are *not* going to have Responsible of Brightwater kidnapped, Fish."

The Fish looked shocked. Stunned. *Hurt.* He went through a whole sequence of body motions to make that clear.

"I know, Fish," said Coyote, not the least bit impressed. "You're not going to involve me in it directly, because I have this warped set of strange principles and I'd find a way to sabotage the mission. But you've got *some*body lined up to do it, and you've got anti-turbulence gadgets being designed for their flyers this very minute. And they'll be off on the next shift to bring the lady here to *discuss* matters with you—so to speak. And make a liar out of me along the way, of course, but that's irrelevant."

"Now, Mister Jones," drawled the chief. "You have been under a strain. This has been a dreadful experience for you. You are overwrought. You are imagining things, and that's perfectly understandable. I assure you, the TGIS would *never*—"

Coyote stood up and gave his snappiest imitation of the military salutes from the antique threedies. He clicked his heels, very quietly, because clingsoles don't click—it was more like a soft whisper. And he rattled off, rapid fire, a list of similarly unimaginable and illegal TGIS capers carried out over the past ten years. At the same time, he projected at full strength a briskly waving flag, a skirl of pipes, and a stupendous reek of manure.

"Dear me," said the Fish. "Such a flair for the dramatic." His nose twitched as Coyote turned up the stench another notch.

"Fish," he said, "it would be a waste of your time. *If* you could do it. Personally, I'm not sure you could."

The Fish snickered, without breathing.

"Suppose you could—there's no way you could make Responsible of Brightwater tell you how Ozark's 'magic' is done. There's *nothing* you could do that she couldn't handle. You try dosing *her* by babbledart, she'll bring the drugs to a boil inside the darts and cauterize your fingers to the second knuckle."

"I thought you said the 'magic' wouldn't work off-planet," said the Fish. "Sit *down*, Mister Jones."

Coyote remained standing, and leaned on the desk. "It won't work off-planet for me," he said. "Or for you. But for Responsible? I bet it would, in which case she'd have you. And if it didn't, she'd still have you—you'd have kidnapped her for nothing, Fish. And boy, would you be sorry! She'd wear out every pair of ears on Mars Central in about two hours."

"My dear Mister Jones—"

"Don't try it, Fish! I *know* you. You are not about to give up on this. Not when there's the real possibility that such things as instantaneous telekinetic transportation and total weather control—and many other highly profitable gadgets—exist, right on the edge of this very galaxy. You're just sparing my delicate sensibilities. But I'm not fooled, Fish. And I'm warning you that it won't work. You try it, you'll repent it till you die."

Chuckle. Flash of white teeth. Coyote had to give him

credit; he was doing an impressive job of ignoring the screeching of the pipes and the stinking of the manure.

"You would stop me?" More chuckles.

"I wouldn't even try," Coyote said, and let it all go. He was exhausted. He sat down and slouched in the chair and muttered. "No need. The Ozarkers' favorite saying is 'As ye sow so shall ye reap,' and I am here to tell you most fervently that if you reap Responsible of Brightwater you'll wish you were dead. You give it some careful thought, my friend. You run it through your computers one more time. And if you had in mind picking up some less conspicuous Ozarker for your mindprobing—I suggest you remember that when Responsible of Brightwater was in pseudo-coma on Ozark and not available to the Ozarkers even the Magicians of *Rank* could not do magic! You think it over, Fish. You put *all* the data in the computers. And then you let it go. This is a time when we have *failed. Accept it.*"

"Mister Jones," crooned the old Fish, "I assure you— the case is closed. I would never for an instant consider any of the outrageous and illegal actions you are suggesting."

"Sure. And apple trees grow corn on the cob."

"Well, well . . . you're tired. It's time you had a break. You go on home now, Mister Jones."

"Everybody keeps telling me to go home," said Coyote sadly.

"It's been dreadful, hasn't it? *Such* a shame!" The Fish smiled, and rang up the Amanuensis to tell it that Mister Jones was just leaving.

Coyote sighed, and rubbed his eyes.

"I'm sorry it went so badly," he said, and he meant it. He stood up and stretched, trying to get some of the kinks out. "I really am sorry. But you know, if you look at the history of Earth, Ozarkers were *always* impossible to deal with. There's no reason why a thousand years of isolation should have changed that."

* * *

Tzana Kai didn't see it quite that way.

She lay in his arms and she listened, asking a question now and then, making an observation now and then, marveling at Coyote's ability to do everything as badly as it could possibly be done. And then she told him he was mistaken.

Coyote was already frustrated, positively pregnant with the wondrous baroque saga of Responsible of Brightwater and Lewis Motley Wommack the 33rd, which he had sworn he would not tell; he *ached* to tell it. He had been through abuse, both physical and verbal, without end. He had been to hell and back, over and over and over. He had *suffered*. And now he had to listen to Tzana tell him he was mistaken?

"*I am not*," he announced.

"You are. You are mistaken about Ozark and its unshakable isolation, Coyote."

He leaned up on one elbow, being careful not to jostle her, and objected strenuously.

"Hey," he said. "You don't know those people. They don't *care*. They don't care if they have to spend their lives slaving away doing things nobody else even remembers how to do. They don't care how long their lives go on being what they refer to as 'hard-scrabble.' They don't care what happens to the member worlds of the TGF. They don't care, *period*. They just want to be let alone. To lead, as they put it, 'decent boonely lives.' Believe me, I have been there, and I *know*."

"Nonsense!" said Tzana Kai, and Coyote regretted that he had not jostled her. In a minute he would dump her onto the pillows, that were so much less satisfactory than the Brightwater pillows, if she didn't stop arguing with him when she knew nothing at all of what she was talking about.

"Nonsense," she said again. "You just wait. Give them a
little while. Give them *time*, Coyote, to think about what
they've refused. Coyote, you blew in there and said 'Hello!
Here I am from the Wonderful World of Goodies, come to
brighten your primitive squalid little lives! Sign here!'
Ozark is a conservative society, that makes haste slowly—
naturally that didn't work. But you wait. They'll come
knocking at *our* door, now they know we're here, and it
won't be long either. You'll see."

He did dump her, then, and watched with satisfaction
as she landed.

"I hope you're wrong," he said. "I do hope you're
wrong."

"I should think you'd be all *for* it!"

Coyote forgave her; he had no capacity at all for staying
angry with Tzana Kai, who was the most satisfactory woman
in the universe and very possibly the most satisfactory
person in the universe. Ten seconds was all he could ever
manage. He lay back down and gathered her close again.

"Nope," he murmured into her hair. "I am not all for it.
If I thought there was any chance I'd be having to deal
with Responsible of Brightwater on some routine basis,
my sweet lady, you'd be seeing my tail as I fled for the
Extreme Moons. I want nothing to do with her. *No*, thank
you!"

"Poor little thing," said Tzana Kai gently; and that brought
Coyote up on an infuriated elbow again.

"Poorlittlething!" he bellowed. "Tzana, that woman is
mean. She is *tough*. She is *vicious*. She's thoroughly and
completely *horrible*. And she's only just getting started
. . . she's got about a hundred years left to get *worse* in.
What the unspeakable do you mean, calling her 'a poor
little thing'?"

"Well," said Tzana. "She's all alone out there. Everybody hates her."

"With good reason!"

"And she's got some kind of crazy role to play that keeps her forever with her hand to the plow."

"It seems that way," he agreed cautiously. Remembering his own insistence on CONFIDENTIAL TOP SECRET, he had said nothing about all the *other* Responsibles. Tzana was a good agent, and she was dear to his heart, but she had no need to know about that.

"And," Tzana went on, "she's got nobody at all to love her."

"Why would anybody *love* her? It's not possible to love her!"

"Exactly," said Tzana. "And I will lay you a wager, Coyote, that she thinks of that disgusting Lewis Motley Wommack every day of her life—that man who had her put into suspended animation, for whatever perverted reasons he thought he had. I'll bet you she wakes up every morning thinking of him and goes to bed every night the same way . . . and I'll bet you that when she wakes in the night, his name is the first thing in her mind."

"Tzana Kai!" Coyote was thunderstruck. "That's ridiculous! You don't have one scrap of facts to make a wild tale like that out of. Where do you *get* such stuff?"

"Think of it," she insisted. "In all her life, no other man's ever so much as looked at her—isn't that right? Only one man ever took the time to so much as notice that she existed—never mind that she only saw him once or twice. And then, for some unknown reason, he tries to put her to sleep permanently! Coyote, she's young, and she is all *alone*. Of *course* she dreams of Lewis Motley Wommack! And if there's more to that story—"

She turned her head and looked at him shrewdly, and he looked determinedly ignorant, and kissed her busily on her forehead.

"If there's more to that story," Tzana went on, "and I

would wager my life that there is, then she spends *her* life thinking about that pompous arrogant sonofabitch. Missing him."

"Tzana, he was a nice guy. I liked him. We got along, he and I."

"He sounds despicable," she said firmly. "I can't stand him."

"You can't stand him. And you feel sorry for Horrible Responsible. You don't know anything about either *one* of them."

"Poor little thing," Tzana said, one more time. "I hope she shows up on my doorstep, one of these days."

"Why? Why on *earth*?"

Coyote wanted to tear his hair out, or perhaps his beard.

"What," he demanded feverishly, "would you *do* with Responsible of Brightwater, should she show up on your doorstep, may such a catastrophe never come to pass?"

Tzana stroked his cheek gently, and she smiled at him.

"When she comes," she said tenderly, "I am going to spoil her absolutely rotten."

DAW

DAW Books now in select format

Hardcover:

☐ **ANGEL WITH THE SWORD**
by C.J. Cherryh
0-8099-0001-7 $15.50/$20.50 in Canada

A swashbuckling adventure tale filled with breathtaking action, romance, and mystery, by the winner of two Hugo awards.

☐ **TAILCHASER'S SONG**
by Tad Williams
0-8099-0002-5 $15.50/$20.50 in Canada

A charming feline epic, this is a magical picaresque story sure to appeal to devotees of quality fantasy.

Trade Paperback

☐ **THE SILVER METAL LOVER**
by Tanith Lee
0-8099-5000-6 $6.95/$9.25 in Canada

THE SILVER METAL LOVER is a captivating science fiction story— a uniquely poignant rite of passage. "This is quite simply the best sci-fi romance I've read in ages."—*New York Daily News*.

DAW

DAW BRINGS YOU THESE BESTSELLERS BY
MARION ZIMMER BRADLEY